Michael Jecks gave up a career in the computer industry to concentrate on writing and the study of medieval history. He divides his time between his cottage in Surrey and a house in Devon.

Michael Jecks' previous novels also featuring Sir Baldwin Furnshill and Simon Puttock, THE LAST TEMPLAR, THE MERCHANT'S PARTNER, THE CREDITON KILLINGS and A MOORLAND HANGING, are also available from Headline, and have been highly praised:

'A gem of historical storytelling . . . authentic recreation of the modes and manners, superstitions and primitive fears that made up the colourful but brutal tableau of the Middle Ages'   *Northern Echo*

'Jecks' knowledge of medieval history is impressive, and is used here to good effect'   *Crime Time*

Also by Michael Jecks

The Last Templar
The Merchant's Partner
A Moorland Hanging
The Crediton Killings
The Leper's Return

The Abbot's Gibbet

Michael Jecks

HEADLINE

First published in 1998
by HEADLINE BOOK PUBLISHING

First published in paperback in 1998
by HEADLINE BOOK PUBLISHING

10 9 8 7 6 5 4

ISBN 0 7472 5598 9

Printed and bound in France
by Brodard & Taupin.
Reproduced from a previously printed copy.

HEADLINE BOOK PUBLISHING
A division of Hodder Headline
338 Euston Road
London NW1 3BH

For Andy and Mandy,
the best friends anyone could hope for.
Thanks

Author's Note

Most readers will be surprised to hear the town of Tavistock described as a *port*. It lies many miles from the north and south coasts of Devon, and the River Tavy is not deep enough to allow large ships to navigate so far – nor was it in 1319.

However in those days a port was not a coastal town, but any place where merchants could bring their goods to trade, and living in a port conferred attractive rights upon the town-dweller. He was invariably free, in an age when men commonly owed feudal service to their lord, and could often make good money from sidelines: renting out rooms to visitors or selling food and drink. At the same time, citizens were free of tolls, so they could participate in the profits of the market or fair without having to pay for the privilege.

Certainly in Tavistock the citizens grew wealthy at the expense of older towns such as Lydford and Chagford, and their duties as townsfolk were minimal. The portmen could be called on to serve as port-reeve (a sort of cross between a mayor and a magistrate) or some other position; had to go to the Borough Court when called; had to use the Abbey's mill; had to pay rent to the Abbey – but that was about it. In exchange they no longer had to go to the Abbey's fields to work, which must have been a huge relief, because all too often people had to leave their own crops to wilt on the best harvesting days because their lord expected *his* to be brought in first.

For all the positive aspects there were few negatives. The citizens of Tavistock liked being free portmen.

* * *

The modern reader may also find the medieval legal system a little confusing compared with our contemporary juridical process.

There has always been a problem collecting enough information to be certain of convicting someone, whether or not it's the right 'someone'. Nowadays we have the Crown Prosecution Service, which sifts all the available evidence and tries to establish whether there is enough for a conviction before incurring the expense of going to court. If the solicitors in the CPS think there isn't, the case isn't brought, which is why you can find police officers in pubs muttering darkly into their whiskies about having to try each case before it ever comes before a jury, and if prompted with another whisky, they will usually continue by demanding how much the CPS itself costs, how much it costs to have the police preparing cases for the CPS, and how many extra policemen could be paid for by that sum.

In the fourteenth century, this would be incomprehensible. The concept of justice then was that the men of the jury were the *only* people who could determine a man's guilt or innocence. It was the ancient, accepted, understood, and fair approach. In those days, people had faith in the judgement of their peers. The process of justice was not complex. Although it wasn't consistent across the country, it was at least understandable to the average person, be they freeman or peasant, which is more than can be said for our present system.

For example, if a sudden death occurred, the man who found the body was expected to raise the *hue and cry*. This often meant little more than bellowing for help. Normally, the man who discovered the corpse, the *first finder*, would then be *attached*, or held until he had paid a surety to guarantee he would appear at the court. The four nearest neighbours would also be attached, as would any relatives who could be found; they would have to swear to the dead man's *Englishry* – the fact that he was English – in court. Meanwhile the hue and cry would chase over the country.

In theory the man accused of a crime would be arrested, and

the local court would try him before a jury of ten to twenty men
(the number varied in different areas) formed of local freemen
and others, and the matter would be closed. Sadly, real life is
rarely so straightforward.

For example, if the suspect managed to get to a known place of
sanctuary, he could stay there for a while. The local coroner could
demand that he should surrender, and some did. Most who did
so were not found guilty of murder, but of killing in self-defence
or by accident – which leads one to suppose that the posse must
have set off in hot blood, and once calmer counsel was taken,
even angry locals could accept the suspect's evidence.

The second course offered by the coroner was that of *abjuring
the realm*. Justice then, as now, was expensive. Far preferable that
a criminal should compensate the kingdom for breaking the
King's peace by paying, and then leaving for ever. A felon could
be granted his life, but lost everything else: home, money,
property – everything.

An abjurer had to leave the kingdom by the shortest road. He
would be taken to a stile or church gate away from the town
centre, and made to swear an oath on the Gospels before the
coroner that he would leave everything behind (most of which
would be taken by the local lord or the King), and make his
journey clothed in white and carrying a wooden cross to
demonstrate his penitence. The official would tell him which
roads he might take, where he could stay overnight, and which
port he must go to, and if he failed, he could be executed instantly.
If he left the road, if he remained for too long on his way, if he
ever returned to the kingdom, he could be beheaded, and the
men who visited punishment on him would be immune from
prosecution.

Lastly, it was often hard to get enough reliable witnesses to any
crime, and just as today we need *supergrasses*, the prosecution
sometimes depended on criminals ratting on their colleagues.
Now it is termed *turning Queen's evidence*; then it was called
approving. An approver was a man who agreed to confess and
give away his partners in exchange for his life. Afterwards he

would have to abjure the realm: not necessarily only because the law demanded it – such a man was not universally popular in the area.

I have been asked whether any of the characters in my books really existed. In the main, the answer has to be 'No', for the simple reason that chroniclers didn't take any interest in the lower classes. Peasants didn't merit comment in most records.

With the more important characters, I have tried to include any whose times were documented. Thus Walter Stapledon *was* the Bishop of Exeter; he was a powerful man who contributed to Exeter Cathedral, who was involved with the Ordainers and later helped create the Middle Party, who founded Stapledon Hall in Oxford (now called Exeter College), and who began a grammar school in Exeter. Later he was to become Lord High Treasurer to the King, until murdered by the London mob in 1326.

Likewise Abbot Champeaux was a real man, notable for his achievements in promoting his Abbey. He is described as an amiable and benevolent man, known for his piety, and from the records appears to have been fond of hunting (he kept getting told off for poaching on the moors), kindly with his more wayward monks, and generous.

That he was shrewd can be seen from his ability to increase the wealth of the Abbey. When he was elected Abbot in 1285, he inherited debts and had to borrow £200, a vast sum; by the time he died in 1324, the Abbey's treasury had acquired £1,200. This was based on his success in divesting himself of unprofitable lands and expensive responsibilities, in making astute loans to the Crown to finance wars, and in purchasing offices, such as warden of the stannaries and controller of the silver mines. The profits of these were huge, as can be guessed from the fact that Champeaux paid £100 per annum for the profits of the wardenship alone.

But these men, as they appear in my books, are fictitious. Chronicles give only bald facts – there aren't even pictures of these two men so far as I know – so I have had to invent them as

I think they would have been. Much the same is true of the Abbey and its fair.

Tavistock Abbey never regained its prominence after Champeaux's death. It had a period without an Abbot, and then Robert Bonus was forced on the unwilling monks, a man who had to be deposed for 'contumacy and intemperate behaviour' in 1333. John de Courtenay took over, but he was vain, addicted to hunting and field sports, and a spendthrift. The Abbey sank into decline as the plague laid waste to the nation, and never recovered. It, like so many others, was swept away in the Reformation. Now there is little to see of this once-great institution.

Michael Jecks
Godstone, August 1997.

N.B. For those who wish to find out more about Tavistock, Abbot Champeaux, and the history of the fair and town, I recommend H.P.R. Finberg's *Tavistock Abbey* (Cambridge University Press, 1951).

Chapter One

The sun was almost unbearably hot, the journey distinctly uncomfortable. Arthur Pole wiped his face with the hem of his cloak to clear the fine dust that rose from the road in thin clouds as hooves and cart-wheels stirred it.

'Is it far now, Arthur?'

Marion, his wife, was a few yards behind him on her new mare. An *amblere*, it was trained to give a lady a smooth ride, swinging first the legs of one side of its body, then the other, always moving left together, then right. It had been ruinously expensive, for training a horse in such a gait was difficult, but the gift was necessary to compensate her for having to make this journey at the height of the humid summer heat.

'Not far, dear,' he said. 'Would you like to halt and refresh yourself? We have wine, if . . .'

'Father, if you give her any more of your wine, Mother won't be able to stay on her horse,' his daughter called cheerfully.

Arthur stifled a smile as his wife snapped back waspishly. After two days travelling from Exeter, where he had been engaged on business, his backside ached, but his excitement made him want to get on. It was two months since he and his family had left their home on the coast and made the journey to Exeter to meet a steward of the King, and in his purse he had a written authority to buy wine on behalf of the royal household for when King Edward II visited later in the year. Now he was on the way to Tavistock

Fair to acquire the best available, and his profit should be enough to stock another ship with fleece to be sold in Flanders. With any luck he wouldn't have to visit any more fairs for two or three years, but could rest at his home living on the proceeds.

His daughter interrupted his musings as she came alongside him with her maid, and he could see her gaze fixed firmly ahead. 'Looking forward to it, my dear?'

'Of course I am. It's the first fair I've been to for five years, Father.'

'I only hope it justifies your enthusiasm.'

'Oh, it will! You've always told me that Tavistock has the best fair in the land.'

'Your mother will insist that I buy you the best, too.'

'Don't sound so sour!' she laughed. 'You wouldn't want me to dress like a beggar, would you?'

'Certainly not, especially for your wedding.'

His feelings for his daughter ran very deep. Partly it led from comparison with his wife. Where Marion could snap, Avice was gentle; where his wife was careful with money, Avice was generous; where his wife sought his errors and corrected them, Avice always congratulated him on his successes. In short, for Arthur Pole, the most important woman in his life was his daughter, and he would move heaven and earth to please her, no matter what the cost – and yet he wanted to make sure that his wife was not discountenanced. If she was upset, he would be the first to hear, every time, and he had no wish to see her with her nose out of joint over the matter of his daughter's marriage. She had set her heart on having her daughter, her only daughter, marry a squire, and join herself to a decent, noble family. It was her only desire, and he did love his wife and respect her wishes.

His words made Avice quiet a moment. She had always been a dutiful daughter, but the thought of marrying John of Hatherleigh was not thrilling. John was the son of a knight, but the purpose of the match was advancement, not love: John was related to the de Courtenays.

The family was the most powerful in Devon, and any attachment to them could only reflect well on Arthur, and as Marion had pointed out, with the dowry Arthur would grant, Avice need not worry about John's income. Yet she did worry, increasingly, as she thought of his thick lips and heavy brows, powerful shoulders and strutting arrogance. John looked the kind of man who might take pleasure in beating his wife.

Avice thrust the idea from her. The sun was shining, she was on her way to a fair, and the wedding was some way in the future. It was not worth worrying about. As Marion had said, he would probably listen to her, just as Arthur took advice from her mother. It was the way of marriage, in which the wife ordered all things in the household while the man saw to his duties outside. In any case, as she knew, it was the part of a daughter to accept the groom selected for her.

'Father, this house where we are to stay, is it close to the fair itself?'

'Yes, it's in the town, but it's only a short walk to the ground. I have stayed there before, in previous years, and there is plenty of space.'

'It was lucky you could find a place,' she said. Avice knew how quickly properties would be rented. One of the best opportunities the townspeople had for making money came from selling sleeping space to visitors for the duration of the fair.

'There was no luck. The owner was pleased enough to agree,' Arthur said. The amount he had offered had guaranteed it, but he didn't grudge the expense. His margin would more than justify the costs. 'Anyway, I didn't want to arrive with you and your mother and then have to hunt high and low for a miserable hovel.'

'Mother wouldn't like it!'

'Um, no.'

Avice glanced over her shoulder. Her mother was riding along comfortably enough with her maid beside her. Behind was Henry, her father's groom, while Arthur's steward rode in the wagon at the rear. It was the first time Avice had gone away with her parents on such an extended journey, and she was surprised at the military efficiency of the operation. The wagon held Arthur's strongbox, filled with money and important documents. In case of emergencies, Arthur had brought several pewter plates as well, which could be used either for entertaining or pawned for cash. The entourage, with the three of them, two maids, the steward and a groom, was the largest Avice had been a part of, and she was filled with pride that her father could make such a brave show.

She caught a glimpse of dust far beyond the wagon. 'Father, it looks as if someone else is making for the fair.'

'Eh?' Arthur turned and peered back. His first thought was that they were about to be waylaid, but his suspicion was groundless. There were only three riders galloping up behind them.

Outlaws were still all too common, especially on busy roads like this from Exeter. The famines of 1315 and 1316, still referred to with awed horror, had forced many to leave their land when the rain destroyed crops and left whole communities starving, and wandering bands of homeless and hopeless men robbed at will on all the main roads in the kingdom, but few of them could afford horses. The men approaching must be merchants.

'Good day, sirs,' he called as they came closer.

The first was a solid man in his late forties, paunchy, and with a florid face. His eyes were light grey, and creased with pleasure as he returned the merchant's greeting courteously enough. Arthur thought he must come from one of the cities in the Papal States, or perhaps Florence or Venice; his accent was strange as he returned the greeting, 'Good day. Are you travelling to the fair as well?'

'Yes. I have to buy wine. And you?'

'My son Pietro and I are to visit the Abbot of Tavistock.'

It was said with a calm hauteur, and Arthur accepted his subservient position. If the Italian could call on an Abbot, a man who ranked with a lord, he must be important. Once Avice was married to John, a little of that great family's importance would reflect on him, but until then Arthur knew he was only a merchant, someone who might be rich, but who was insignificant compared with a man of God or even the poorest member of the nobility. Caste was important, and Arthur knew his place in society. He might well be one of the most affluent men in southern Devon, yet to a knight or baron he was simply a commoner, and as such unimportant.

Arthur passed a measuring eye over the man. There was no doubt in his mind that the stranger was very prosperous. His tunic was expensive, of softly woven wool, and his shoes were of supple red leather. At his belt was a sword, and Arthur wondered a moment whether he might be a knight, but although he carried the trappings, something struck a wrong note. Neither he nor his son displayed a shield; neither had heraldic arms woven into their clothing. Their servant, who led two packhorses laden with goods and a large box, was dressed only poorly in a coarse tunic with a linen shirt beneath and ordinary hose whereas a knight's man-at-arms would have demonstrated how well-heeled his master was by wearing a costly uniform to display his rank and position. This servant was no better clad than Arthur's groom.

The quality of their horseflesh jarred too. Though the animals were caparisoned in the latest style, with bells hanging from the harnesses and expensive tooling on the saddles and bridles, the beasts themselves were of low standard, not good palfreys but broken-looking ponies. It made Arthur blink in surprise as he glanced from one to another.

The son, Pietro, was well-formed – tall, with raven-black hair and the flashing dark eyes of the Mediterranean. He was dressed extravagantly: his hose were tight-fitting, and he wore a parti-coloured tunic of red and green velvet. Arthur shot his daughter a glance. To his pleasure, he saw that Avice was maintaining a dignified lack of interest, staring ahead in her eagerness to catch sight of the town.

Arthur engaged the older man in desultory conversation as they rode, and found that his name was Antonio da Cammino; he was a merchant from Venice. From his speech, Cammino was wealthier than Arthur would have guessed. He spoke of a fleet of galleys trading between the cities of Italy, going as far as Palestine and Byzantium.

'You speak English very well,' Arthur complimented him respectfully.

'I have been dealing here for many years – I have an interest in some banking ventures. And now I am here to talk to the Abbot.'

'For business?'

The Venetian nodded. 'While there is enmity between your King and the King of France, there are opportunities to make money.'

Arthur nodded. King Edward II was involved in a lengthy dispute with the French once more. The French King insisted on his right to hear appeals from the English King's vassals in Gascony, but for the English to accept this, they must accept that the French crown was suzerain, and that was impossible while the Gascon territories yielded greater revenue than England. Edward II could not afford to see his lands diminished, they were crucial to him; he wanted to establish that he held Gascony as an alod, in full sovereignty, but the French wanted him to submit to the treaty of 1259 that conferred upon the French Crown rights of vassalage over the English King.

If the King was strong, there might be a way of negotiating a respectable settlement, but Arthur knew as well as any that Edward II was weak. He had no interest in politics. It was rumoured that he was more interested in certain male court favourites than in matters of state, and his reputation as a warlord had been crushed with his soldiers at the disaster of Bannockburn. It was hardly likely that he would consider war against France. How could tiny England ever hope to win a war against so massive and powerful an enemy?

But Cammino was right: there was always a way to make money, even in a war. A merchant like him, with his own fleet, could import wines from Gascony, or help provision an army, or simply lend cash to a baron or king in need. And while hostilities remained verbal, a skilful man could build up his stores against the time when they would be needed, and earn a good profit.

Cammino's son Pietro listened idly to the two men talking about their business, but he found his attention wandering to Arthur's daughter.

Avice Pole was elegant for her fifteen years. Her skin was pale, her features finely moulded, with soft doe-eyes and a slightly tip-tilted nose. Her brow was high, giving her a mature and intelligent look, and her hair, from what he could see under her fashionable little wimple, was chestnut. She looked serene and confident in her green tunic with the embroidery at hem and throat.

He was desperate to engage her in conversation, but Pietro had little experience of talking to women. His life had been one of constant travel, with few opportunities for dalliance, and he had no idea what topic would attract her. It was essential that he should see her again, intolerable that once they arrived in Tavistock he might not – ever. As their little company began to descend a hill he racked his brains to devise a scheme to meet her, but the solution was offered by Arthur himself.

'It has been pleasant to pass the journey in your company, sir. Would you be kind enough to accept a pot of wine with me? It will take time for my cart to be unloaded tonight, but there is a tavern at Tavistock. Perhaps I could entertain you there at compline?'

'I would be glad to, and you must bring your delightful wife and daughter,' he said, bowing graciously, and Pietro relaxed, shooting a quick glance at Avice. To his surprise, she was giving him a covert look from the corner of her wimple, and when he grinned, he was sure she returned it.

It was at the edge of a wood bordering the town's plain that they first heard the friar.

'Do you know what you're doing, eh? Do you realise your mortal danger? Everything you do is against Christ's teachings!'

To Luke, Cammino's servant, he looked like any wandering mendicant: thin, bowed as if from a great burden, with glittering, almost fanatical blue eyes. His hair, what was left below his tonsure, was grey with age, and his skin as brown as a peasant's, as if he lived all his life in the open air. He wasn't shouting or haranguing, but speaking sadly, as though convinced his message was essential if only people would listen.

At his side was a small gathering, most making merry at the cleric's expense, and children played behind. One man appeared to be listening with interest, however – a rough-looking, barrel-chested, middle-aged man with grizzled hair and the heavy build of a farmer.

'My friends, haven't you heard the words of St Augustine? He told us business itself is evil. *Money* is evil: it taints your immortal soul. Do not go to the fair to make profit; *profit* is evil! Do you go to buy new cloths and fabrics? They are the traps of the devil, leading to the sin of pride. Why do you want to flaunt expensive clothing and dress your women in gold and jewels? If you buy up things you don't need, you are guilty of the sin of avarice. The land is plentiful, there is food enough for all. . .'

Friars often selected individuals to harangue in order to

emphasise their points, and with relief Luke saw the man's eyes fall on Antonio and not him. 'Master, are you here to sell goods?'

Antonio glanced down at the friar with distaste. 'No, I am here to see the good Abbot.'

'You are a merchant, though. Friend, give up your life of evil! St Jerome told us a merchant can seldom ever please God. It's wrong to make money when you do nothing for it.'

'I work hard enough for my money,' said Antonio, flushing at the insult to his dignity.

'Buying goods wholesale and selling them for a higher price without doing anything to improve them is immoral, my son. It is condemned by canon law. My son, stop living your life of sin!' He had grabbed Antonio's bridle, and stood beseechingly, his eyes holding the Venetian's.

Antonio tugged his horse's head free and swore under his breath. 'My life is not sinful. I earn my money, and it's people like me who give alms to you and your brothers so that you can preach at us. Here ...' he pulled a few coins from his purse and threw them down '... take the money, if you don't think it will taint your flesh! Now, leave me in peace!'

Spurring his horse, he rode on, and the others followed. Luke heard Arthur say consolingly, 'These friars are a nuisance, but don't let him upset you. He can't understand business.'

'I'm just glad he didn't know I issue loans as well,' Antonio chuckled. 'Can you imagine what he would have said if he had heard I was a ... a *damned usurer*!'

Friar Hugo stared after the little group riding down the slope. There were times when he felt that the struggle to save souls was too much for him. People were uninterested in the life to come; they were too tightly bound to their narrow, secular lives and couldn't, or wouldn't, raise their eyes to heaven.

Much of it, he knew, was the fault of corrupt churchmen. Since the Pope had moved to Avignon his sole interest was finance. Appointments were sold, no matter where in the church. Simony was rife, with bishops paying a year's income for their benefices and then passing the cost down through the hierarchy, affecting – or infecting – all, from abbots to priests and friars.

And that was not the worst of it. Friars themselves were not living as St Francis wanted. He, Hugo knew, had forseen the problems; when a novice had asked him for a psalter, St Francis had refused him, saying that first he would want a psalter, and then he would want a breviary, and then he would sit in a chair like a great prelate and ask another brother to fetch it for him. To St Francis, the possession of a single item could lead to avarice and the desire for authority over others.

Now friars were living in halls, their food and shelter guaranteed. They had immense buildings, and some didn't even wear their habits but dressed as burgesses, ignoring the tonsure, letting their hair grow long and sporting beards. Many were known to father children. They would take small dogs with them when they went abroad, in order to tempt women into conversation, and then ravish them.

But Hugo took his vocation seriously. He rejected the world of money, of influence, of worldly goods. It was his duty – a solemn, holy duty – to save the souls of the sinners he saw each day.

'Brother?'

Hugo turned. It was the man who had stood by him as he preached. The friar gave a faint smile. If only one was prepared to listen, that was at least something. 'Yes?'

'Is it right that a man should take money from another when he doesn't need it?'

'Christ taught us that money is evil. It's right that a man who creates a barrel should be rewarded for his labour, the same as a man who makes a tapestry, or a millwheel, but making money from money is a sin. If a man takes money he has not himself earned from his own labour, he is guilty of avarice, and that is a sin.'

Some of the crowd had returned, hoping that the friar was to be the target of ridicule. A little boy with a stick poked Hugo's side, and he gently ruffled the lad's head. 'There's too much hankering after riches in this world. Look at this boy – he doesn't care for money. He doesn't need bells or jewels or gold. He is content. If there was no greed for money, the world would be freed of much of its discord.'

At the sound of steps he faced the road through the woods again. 'My friends, repent of your sins. Do you realise your peril? St Jerome said . . .'

'Shut up, priest. We don't need your sort to preach at us.' The speaker was a tall, swarthy character, with skin burned from wind and sun. He traipsed along at the head of a group of four, all dressed in cheap tunics and hose, and all armed with clubs and swords like men-at-arms. 'We know how religious you and your brethren are, eating meat every day and taking whichever woman takes your fancy.'

'My son, I eat little meat, only some fish. Does my belly look as if I live on meat and wine? But your soul, if you come to the fair to fill your pockets, will be eating the devil's food. If you come to make profits from other men's labour, it will . . .'

'Shut up, old fool.' The man shoved Hugo out of the way. 'We haven't time to listen to your prating.'

'Come on, leave him alone, he's doing no harm.' Hugo was gripped by the elbows and lifted from the roadway. The man who had questioned him now stood between him and the four. 'He's only trying to help people.'

'We don't need his kind of help,' said the spokesman. 'We're watchmen – from Denbury – here to keep the peace, and if you get in our way you'll not see the fair except through the clink's bars.'

'Well, in case you don't find me, my name is Roger Torre.

I'd be happy for you to try to take me to the gaol now, but
. . .' he jerked a thumb towards the town '. . . you might find
it hard to carry me so far. I'm heavy.'

Hugo could hear the light tone of Torre's voice, but his
stance betrayed his readiness. The watchman curled his lip,
but was in no mood for a fight after walking over ten miles
already that day. He shouldered his club. 'I'm Long Jack. If
you cross me, I'll make sure you regret it.'

'I doubt it,' Torre said cheerily, and stood back to let them
pass.

On they trudged, and Hugo watched them disappear
down the slope. 'Thank you, my friend, for speaking for me,
but don't put yourself in danger to protect me.'

'I reckon you need someone to look after you, brother.
But enough! Come with me, and I'll buy you some beer. I
want to talk to you about money.'

Chapter Two

Of all the roads he'd travelled since the murders, this one, with the unwanted memories insinuating themselves into his mind, felt the most ominous.

The trees met overhead, their branches intermingling to shut out the light and creating a cavern of twilight beneath. Here in the gloom lay the road. In the oppressive, muggy heat of late August, the horses' hooves and harnesses sounded dull. Soft grass underfoot deadened the tramping feet. The rumble of the wagon wheels, the squeaking of the axles and chains, the hollow rattle of pans knocking together, all sounded dead to him, as if he was riding on in a dream in which the pictures were distinct but all noise had been killed. Many years ago this environment had given him peace. Now it represented only danger.

As the track began to rise, he could remember that last journey as distinctly as if it had been last week, not years ago. It felt as if the road was taking him back to his past, and it was with a mixture of fear and hope that he jolted along. Both struggled to overcome him, but he kept his face expressionless. His fellow travellers could not guess at his emotions.

It was nearly twenty years ago, he recalled. Yet after so long, the smells and sounds were still familiar. This was the place of his birth. These were the smells of his childhood: herbs, peat fires, the tang of cattle in their yards, the musky stench of humans. Even the reek from the midden was oddly poignant.

Now, over the creaking and thundering of the wagons, he could hear other noises. There was hammering and shouting, the rasp of saws through wood, and echoing thuds as axes sliced into boughs. They were the noises of his youth, the cacophony of business as could be heard in any thriving borough, but in these surroundings they gave him a feeling of release, as if he was at last being freed from his isolation.

He came into the sun and stared down along the valley. The view was one he had held fixed in his mind over all the hundreds of miles since he had managed to escape. His nose caught a faint peatiness in the air, and he snuffed the breeze with a quick pleasure, like a spaniel scenting game, before the other memories flashed back into his mind and his face took on its customary blank hardness.

The wind was welcome. It was almost the feast of St Rumon, at the end of a hot summer, and the soft gusts were pleasant, cooling the sweat on the traveller's body as he glanced at his companions. Few among them could know how vicious and deadly those same winds would be in the dead of winter. He did; he had seen how the chill winter blast could kill men out on the moors.

But his thoughts were not bent towards the weather. With every foot and yard he covered, he could feel the memories rushing back to engulf him: her face, screaming; the bloody axe; the taunting cries and jeers as he ran from them – and later the disbelief that he should be the one accused, the one arrested for the inevitable trial, the one to be hanged.

He could see the gibbet in his mind's eye: a stark shape among the softly moving trees at either side. It had been dusk when he first saw it, and as he had passed it with his father, it had squeaked in protest to the wind, and made him shiver. It sounded eerie and evil. In later years he had rarely glanced at it – there were so many up and down the country – yet once riding back from Oakhampton, he heard it creaking and moaning in the gusts, and when he looked, the trees were waving their branches in a sinuous dance as if beckoning him. He had been fixed with a sudden horror, as if the gallows were calling to him alone.

At the time he must have been Hankin's age. He glanced at the boy. Hankin sat on the cart, reins slack in his hands, nodding somnolently under the effects of the warm sun and the quart of good ale he had drunk for his lunch. Hankin was the orphan of an English merchant in Bayonne, and when no one else would look after the lad, he had taken him on as apprentice. Hankin in some way filled the gap left by his wife, who had died from a haemorrhage while pregnant with their first-born, and he liked to think his own son would have been much the same, quick to learn and self-confident.

They were coming out of the woods now, and he slowed, to the loud disgust of the men and women behind, as he stared down at the town.

In the late afternoon of a summer's day, it was a scene of perfect tranquillity. From this direction, the valley looked like a wide saucer of land. The river was a glittering band cutting through the countryside like a curving steel ribbon. Smoke rose from the houses and hamlets dotted around the small plain, and the grey moorstone blocks of the church and Abbey stood somehow indistinct in the haze. The towers rose spectacularly, gaunt and bold in their grey simplicity. Little could compare with their stark squareness; their very regularity was a testament to their holy design. Nearby buildings were dwarfed.

Trees bordered the pasture, and rose up the slopes of the little hillocks. It looked as if the meadows and strip fields were isolated and surrounded by encroaching woods, whereas in reality the trees were being forced ever backwards as the Abbey's lands expanded. Every year the monks, farmers and burgesses had more of the massive trunks cut down for firewood or furniture, leaving space for sheep and cattle to colonise. The process was more or less complete, with the fringe of trees pushed so far back that only their topmost branches could be discerned over the rolling hills. His horse moved skittishly beneath him as the heavily-laden wagons passed by, and he dismounted and walked a short way from the track, sitting and staring down the valley.

It felt odd to be able to see once again the place where he had lived. It was his home, and the view brought a constriction to his throat, as if a ball of food had stuck. He swallowed but it wouldn't go away: he had an urge to hurry forward, as though the intervening years would dissipate and he would be renewed to youth when he arrived at the town. To eyes used to strange foreign cities, it was a curiously unexceptional scene, a commonplace outlook he knew well; yet it was also charged with danger, and he was aware of the latent menace represented by the huddles of cottages.

Staring at it, the muscles of his face set once more into their familiar mask. The loathing stirred again in his breast for the people who had forced him from his land and destroyed his life.

With a decisiveness he did not feel, he climbed back onto his horse and cantered to Hankin's wagon. There was a relief at rejoining the travellers. Among them he felt screened, obscured by their numbers – just one more merchant on his way to a fair. There was no point in delaying; he had waited too long already. Now all he wanted was to hurry to get there, to see the man he had come so far, and at such risk, to see. With that thought he smiled and continued down the plain towards the Abbey.

Jordan Lybbe had returned.

The roof was ripped apart piece by piece while David Holcroft stood and watched, distaste twisting his features as the squares of rotten wood were tossed, spinning, to join the pile before him. Each time he heard one crack, he winced.

The little shed was essential for the fair. It was here that the merchants would pay their tolls for the privilege of selling their goods. Tavistock Fair would attract people from as far away as Castile, and it was his responsibility, as portreeve, to make sure it was ready.

There was no need to have so many men, he knew, but if he let one go, the others would plead their own cases, and soon he'd have nobody. They scrambled all over, getting in each other's way and snapping shingles not already ruined. Each was fitted with a pair of dowels which hooked onto the lathes running along the rafters, and as the men worked along the pitch, he could see the wood splintering where the pegs fitted. They'd be lucky to rescue any, the way these cretins were working.

'Sir? The Abbot wondered . . .'

David Holcroft turned suspiciously. A youth stood by him, grinning. The Abbot's official kept his voice low and calm, but it was evident enough to the lad that Holcroft was controlling his frustration with an effort. 'Yes, yes. The Abbot wants to know when we'll have this job finished so he can be sure to earn as much as possible, and he's told you to come and see that I'm getting everything sorted out. Well, you can tell him from me that I'm standing here making sure these idle whelps get on with things, and the more interruptions there are, the slower the job will be!'

'I'm sorry, sir, I was only asked to—'

'To come over here and make my life a misery. Look, it's hard enough keeping the lazy buggers from the alehouses without having Abbot Robert sending his messengers across every few moments. What does he think I'm doing, eh? Sitting in a tavern and supping ale? He asked me to ensure that the booth was ready, and that's exactly what I'm doing. But when you report back, you can tell him that there are other things for me to see to, like making sure the shambles are laid out, and seeing to the weights and measures. Even the tron hasn't been checked yet.'

He shot a glance at the men, keen to be away. The tron

was the huge beam used to weigh goods. It had to be tested to make sure it was accurate, and that was just one more chore he must do when this nonsense was completed. With relief he saw that the shingles were all piled on the ground, and that most of the men had come down from the roof. Only two remained sitting on the walls, beating the panelling away from the frames with their hammers. 'Why didn't I get this done before?' he asked himself aloud now.

'There's so much to be done through the year, sir. Things like this are always forgotten till the last minute,' the messenger said encouragingly.

'It should have been done by Andrew last year,' David muttered, but he knew the work should have been done by *him*. *He* was the port-reeve.

Many looked on the job as a sinecure. It only lasted twelve months, being an annual appointment by the Abbot's steward, the port-reeve being selected from two or three names put forward by the town's jury, and as well as the allowance of a couple of shillings, there was freedom from the year's taxes. But after almost twelve months, David was worn out by his duties.

The port-reeve was the man who arranged the conduct of the fairs and markets. He had to tie together all the little details and make sure they went smoothly, to the Abbey's profit. The port-reeve must witness any large trades, ensure that the watchmen behaved, tally up any sums owed, tell the beadle of any amercements that must be collected . . . in short, he was responsible for any problem, no matter when it might occur.

There was no blaming Andrew, last year's incumbent, for not rebuilding the booth. It had been leaning when David was elected at Michaelmas last year, and now it was almost St Rumon's Day. From the end of September until now, the end of August, he had never found time to see to its refurbishment.

In fact, it had slipped his mind completely until the Abbot

reminded him the night before. He'd been with the Abbey's steward finalising plans for the layout of the livestock pens when the Abbot had entered. 'David, there was just one thing I wanted to ask,' he'd said, walking in quietly as David was about to leave, and the port-reeve had felt his heart fall to his boots.

'Er, yes, my lord?'

It wasn't that the Abbot was a harsh master – he wasn't – but he had a way of making a man feel as if he hadn't quite matched up to the high standard expected of him. Abbot Robert Champeaux was a difficult person to deal with: he was truly honourable and fair. His eyes twinkled at the tone of his port-reeve's voice. 'Have more wine, my friend. It is only a little matter, concerning the toll-booth on the Brentor road. It looks a bit derelict.'

'Oh, er . . . Yes, I suppose it does.'

'It is quite ramshackle. The roof has rotted, and the walls are sodden. I fear it could collapse.'

The last of the panels fell with a slap like a wet cloth thrown against a rock, and David shook his head good-humouredly. The Abbot had been right as usual: the wood was so wet as to be useless. Still, everything was worth money during the three-day fair. The shingles would be taken by someone needing cheap replacements for a shed or outbuilding – Roger Torre had already expressed interest – and enough solid timber could be rescued from the panels to make a trestle or box. Poor farming folk would be willing to pay for odds and ends.

The workmen had fresh panels stacked near the booth, and now they nailed the boards in place while others scampered back to the roof and began hanging new chestnut slats.

Turning from the little building, the port-reeve was faintly surprised to note that the messenger had left. He stared toward the fairground. The ditch had been cleared, and now formed the boundary. The grassed area was filled with stalls. Seeing the men running round making good any faults in the stalls and trestles, David felt himself relax. It would all be worth it once the fair got going: the annual event would be a success again.

He glanced upwards and squinted. It was past noon; soon he must see to the other thousand and one things that still had to be organised. He waited until the men had almost finished the second side wall and one half of the roof before making his way along the lane to the busy town.

On a normal day, the centre would be filled with butchers, fishmongers and grocers plying their trade, but not now. In preparation for the fair, many had been moved from their usual premises. Cooks, poulterers and smiths were excluded from the town and must carry on their trade outside the fair's ditch. It was too dangerous to permit fires to be lighted with so many visitors, especially with the number who were bound to get drunk. All livestock was kept out as well, in an attempt to keep the streets moderately clean, but it was not only animals which blocked lanes, and as he went David noted who had allowed garbage to collect. Each would receive a fine if they did not clear it; another duty of the port-reeve was to ensure that those who allowed obstructions to accumulate were punished.

At one corner, near the bottom of the Brentor road as it approached the Abbey, he stopped dead and shook his head.

In a narrow little alley that led between a butcher and cookshop, there was a pile of rubbish. Tattered remains of cloth, ancient and part-rotted sacks, broken staves, and other scraps and debris littered the ground. Shards of broken pottery and poultry bones crunched underfoot, and he accidentally kicked a pot which smashed against the wall. A scrawny dog scavenged, crouching in the dark of the alley, anticipating a kick or hurled stone. Holcroft ignored it. Marching to the cookshop door, he hammered on it.

'Elias? Elias, I know you're in there! Open this door.' He

beat upon the timbers again and shouted, and when there was no response, he took a step back, staring upwards thoughtfully. The little unglazed window above was unshuttered. David picked up a broken spar of wood, hefting it in his hand, gauging the weight, and then hurled it through the opening.

Almost immediately there was a high-pitched shriek, closely followed by a curse. David quickly moved a little farther from the building before his missile could return, as the cook appeared at the window gripping the wood like a cudgel. 'Who the . . .?'

'You know well enough. *Me!*'

'Why, port-reeve! I'm sorry, David, did you knock? I didn't hear, I've been busy, getting ready for the fair, you know. Anyway, what do you think you're doing, throwing blocks of wood through people's windows? It could have been dangerous, you might have hurt someone . . .'

'Shut up, Elias! The fair opens tomorrow, and you've left all your garbage out here in the street. I told you yesterday to clear it, but you've done nothing. If it's still there tomorrow, I'll personally take great pleasure in amercing you. With all this lot, it's got to be worth a good six pennies.'

'Six pennies?' The cook gaped in dismay. 'I can't afford a fine like that, David. Look, couldn't I just move it back in the alley? No one'll see it if I shove it round the corner a bit.'

'No, Elias. Get it all out to the midden.'

'What if I . . .'

The door of the butcher's shop opened, and David winked at its owner, Will Ruby. He was a plump man, and seeing the port-reeve, he leaned against his doorpost and cast an eye up at his neighbour. 'I told you you'd have to clear it, you daft bugger, didn't I? It does my business no good to have my customers walking past your rubbish every morning. I doubt it does much for you, either.'

'Shut up, Will. Why don't you get on and sort out your stall? I'm talking to the port-reeve here.'

'Yes, well, if you'd listened to me in the first place, you'd not have to talk to the port-reeve, would you?'

'Six pennies, Elias,' David repeated. 'That's what it'll be tomorrow, and seeing I'm on my way to the Abbot now, I'll tell him to expect your money.'

The cook let his head droop disconsolately. He opened his mouth to speak, but as he did, David heard a muttered word. The cook glanced quickly behind him, and the port-reeve peered up with interest. Will edged closer and jabbed an elbow into his side, speaking from the corner of his mouth. 'It's that girl, Lizzie. He got her up to his room after drinking with her in the tavern,' he chortled, and strolled towards the fair.

'Elias, you do know all the rules of the fair, don't you? You've got all your things set up in the fairground, have you?' The face above nodded quickly. 'Good.' Then David added suavely, 'Remember, too, that prostitutes are outlawed during the fair, won't you?' Like all fairs, to prevent lewd or bawdy behaviour, and disease, prostitutes and lepers were outlawed. Lepers must stay behind their doors, and prostitutes mustn't ply their trade.

The cook shiftily avoided his eyes. The man was searching for something innocuous to say, and David had an overpowering urge to laugh while the cook squirmed, but before Elias could think of a safe comment, his eyes suddenly widened. He was yanked backwards and disappeared, to be replaced by a young woman with loose brown hair that curled round her shoulders.

'Well, David, do you want me thrown from this house? Where could I go? Would *you* give me a room to sleep in?'

The port-reeve tried to maintain his dignified mien, but when the girl fluttered her eyelashes in mock supplication and held her thumb and forefinger a short distance apart, shaking her head in apparent disgust, he had to relent, relaxing his stern features. 'No, Lizzie, much though I'd like to, I think my wife'd be upset. But remind Elias that Nick Turgys was amerced twelve pennies last year for having whores in his house during the fair. If Elias can't afford six pennies for his rubbish, I doubt he could afford another twelve – not as well as your fee.'

As he moved on towards the Abbey, he was in a contemplative mood. When almost there, he paused a while to watch the latest traders arrive. A long line of merchants was riding up from the western gate, and he could see that they had their wagons and carts filled. One face he recognised: Roger Torre, striding beside a friar. Roger scraped by panning for tin on the moors. He eked out a living by catching rabbits, and rented land from the Abbot to grow vegetables and herbs. He didn't prosper, but he was not so poor as some of the men who inhabited the little stone sheds on the moors. Only the bigger miners seemed to make good money.

David waved to him and carried on. Torre was always keen to drink and exchange stories, and the port-reeve was determined to finish his work and join the moorman in the tavern. He had need of a companion who would not talk to him of garbage, fairs or whores.

Another man was watching Torre and the friar. He stood a little to one side of the port-reeve, partly obscured by drapery hung to celebrate the fair.

It was so many years ago, he had thought he would be safe here, but now his worst imagining was realised as he watched the cleric and his friend making their way to the fair. If he should be seen and recognised, he would be in danger of his life – but what could he do? He had tried to escape before, and that had ended in disaster.

Perhaps even that failure might show him how to avoid justice again. If he dared be bold once more, he might yet be able to get away. He preferred to remain hidden, but if he had no choice, he would act, he decided, and he slipped away down an alley.

Chapter Three

Elias pulled on his hose and left the girl Lizzie in his chamber. Out in the street, he stood and surveyed his pile of garbage with exasperation. It was mad to expect people to clear away everything just because there was going to be a fair. Sourly pursing his lips, he stood for a while assessing how many barrow-loads it would take. He was sure there were more than ten, and the midden lay out at the western edge of the borough. That meant he had at least two hours' hard work.

'God's blood! I'd like to drop it all off on that damned port-reeve's house.'

The idea was tempting, but he discarded it from reasons of practicality. David would be sure to know where it had come from, and too many other people had remarked upon all the muck over the last week or two; if he was to shift it from his alley to another's house, it would take little time for him to be found out. Morosely he fetched his tools and began forking rubbish from the top into his barrow. When it was filled, he set his fork against the wall and started out for the midden.

It was the middle of the afternoon, and the sun's heat was concentrated by the white limewash of the buildings on either side. The walls gleamed so strongly he had to squint. Slouching along reluctantly, he could feel the sweat bursting from his skin. It formed a stream under his shirt, trickling down his spine and soaking into the seat of his hose. At the parish church dedicated the previous year by Bishop

Stapledon to St Eustace, he rested a moment, spitting on his hands and rubbing them. He was used to picking up sacks of flour or carcasses, but walking along pushing his wooden barrow was tiring in the heat. Reaching the midden, he emptied his load into the stinking pool. Then, resignedly pulling his shoulders back, he made his way homewards.

He was on his fourth load when he heard the Abbey bells, and he groaned when he saw the lengthening shadows. Vespers already, and he wasn't halfway through the mound. His irritation made him careless. The wheel caught in a rut, and he froze, eyes wide, mouth pursed into a thin white line as he gripped the solid timber handles, desperately struggling to keep it upright. Then the wheel slipped treacherously on a stone and the whole reeking load slid from the overturned barrow.

Elias fumed. Fists clenched, he kicked the wheel in futile rage. Hearing a man chuckling, he was about to swear when he saw it was a monk. Elias carefully watched till the figure had disappeared through the Abbey's great gate before letting out a hissed oath. He didn't want another fine.

It was almost dark by the time he had completed the eighth trip, and when he got back to the alleyway he groaned. The pile looked as large in the diminishing light as when he had started. He wiped a hand over his brow. 'Tomorrow. I'll finish it tomorrow,' he muttered, too tired to carry on. He was hungry, but his belly craved beer. His attention was drawn up along the road, to where he could see the bush hanging out over the street to advertise the tavern. The alewife had brewed four times her usual quantity of ale in preparation for the fair, and Elias knew she would be happy to let him taste some for a reasonable amount.

He hefted the barrow's handles and shoved it up the alley, round to the yard behind his shop. Then he made his way to the tavern, thrusting the door open with his shoulder and striding through the curtained screens into the room.

This tavern had been a farmhouse once, but over many decades it had been altered. Where a farmer would have sheltered his flocks and oxen, now customers sat at trestle tables on rough benches, while the alewife's girls circled, halting momentarily at tables to dispense ale, then moving on to the next, like butterflies sipping at flowers. A fire glowed in the middle of the packed earth floor, ready to be kicked into life as the temperature fell.

When he walked in, the place was already crowded. Men and women stood talking, one or two children were asleep, wrapped in cloaks by the walls, and a pair of hounds scavenged for scraps among the rushes. He could see Lizzie in the far corner, and thought that after that afternoon she might serve him, but when he tried to catch her eye, the girl didn't notice. There were few seats left, and Elias hesitated in the doorway before seeing someone he recognised: Roger Torre.

'Move on, Roger.'

'Elias? Take a seat. This is a friend of mine, friar. He owns a cookshop.'

'Peace be with you,' Hugo hiccupped happily, sliding up the bench to make space.

'And you, brother,' Elias answered automatically, waving to Agatha, the alewife.

'So, friar,' Torre said, continuing his conversation. 'If the Abbot wants to demand money from me, is that right?'

Hugo had drunk several pints of good ale, more than he was used to, and was filled with good humour. He tapped the side of his nose conspiratorially. 'Abbots and bishops don't deserve your money, nor anyone else's. Many don't even deserve respect. Take the Bishop of Durham – he can't read. He fumbled over his own consecration: couldn't pronounce the word *metropolitanus*, and muttered, "Let's take that as read"! And when he presided over an ordination, he swore when he came to *aenigmate*, that is, "through a glass darkly", saying, "By St Louis, whoever wrote this word was no courteous man"! When we have prelates such as he, how can anyone respect the holy calling?'

'So you think I shouldn't pay, friar?'

'I think ... I think I have drunk enough!' Hugo stood unsteadily and climbed over the bench. 'I need the privy.'

'Where did you pick him up?' asked Elias, watching the grey-clad cleric stumble round the room to the door, one hand touching the wall all the way for support.

But Torre was distracted before he could answer. As Agatha hurried over and thumped a mug before Elias, Torre motioned to the doorway. 'Beware of them, mistress.'

The alewife tutted. 'The watchmen from Denbury? They don't trouble me.'

Torre affably lifted his ale to the one called 'Long Jack', and chuckled when his welcome was ignored. 'I'll go and make sure my friar hasn't got lost,' he said, rising to his feet.

He had only been gone a few moments when Elias saw Holcroft at the threshold. The cook shielded his face, but he was too slow, and the port-reeve sauntered over to him. 'I see your rubbish isn't gone yet.'

'I'll have it finished tomorrow, I promise.'

Holcroft took Torre's seat and waved to the alewife. 'See you do.' As usual at fairtime, many of the faces were unfamiliar to him. He recognised the watchmen, though. They were drinking heavily, standing in a huddle near the fire, and he hoped they wouldn't be drunk all the time. In fairness, he knew they had walked all the way from Denbury, so they must be thirsty.

Every year there were complaints about them. They felt that since they were in Tavistock to protect people, they should be able to demand fees from stall-holders. Sometimes a merchant would complain, but then he might find that his stocks became damaged, or his stall could unaccountably fall over, or perhaps the merchant would wake up the next morning in the gutter with a broken arm. David had heard it all from Andrew the year before, and had tried to get new men from Denbury this time, but as usual no one else was willing. Looking at the heavy-set figures, he thought their faces could have been carved from moorstone slabs. He knew why others didn't put their names forward. Men like these knew how to deter volunteers.

Another group appeared, two rich men and their servant led by a young monk. Holcroft had heard of the anticipated arrival of the Venetians when he met the Abbot's steward earlier, and he assumed these must be the Camminos. If their expensive foreign clothing didn't give them away, the fact that a novice monk had led them to the tavern was proof enough. The Abbot only asked his monks to direct visitors when they were important.

Agatha passed him a mug and nodded to Elias. 'Someone wants to speak to you.'

Nothing loath, Elias left Holcroft and followed after her. In a dark corner of the hall was a powerfully-built figure, thickly bearded, dressed in red leather jerkin over his doublet and shirt, who watched Elias approach with glittering eyes.

'Hello, Elias.'

The cook stopped and stared, almost dropping his mug. 'Christ's blood! Jordan!'

The Camminos' servant Luke pulled a bench over for his master, and waved to the monk. 'Go on, sit, brother.'

'No, I – er – I should get back.' Peter was new to the town of Tavistock, and although his Abbot had asked him to direct the visitors to the tavern when they explained that they had to meet their fellow-travellers, he felt ill-at-ease in a drinking hall. There was too much ribald humour and singing, and the sight of the serving girls made him uncomfortable. 'It's late, I have duties . . .'

'Oh, sit, brother,' Antonio rumbled. 'We may need help to find our way back to the Abbey later. Have a pot of wine.'

Luke rested on the bench gratefully and took a pot from the alewife. It felt good to relax, stretch his legs and drink good English ale. He had spent too many years with his master in Castile and Gascony, and these last few weeks in England had been like a holiday. It was nice to be back in his own country again.

He had been born north of London, near Huntingdon, the son of a cobbler. But he had seen more of the world than his father ever had, especially since he had worked for Cammino. The Venetian had saved his life; when Antonio had found him, Luke had been near the end of his money, and there was little chance that he would have been able to earn any more. The guilds in Gascony, where he had been living, were very strong, and finding work had been all but impossible as a foreigner. Cammino had taken him on and fed and clothed him, and Luke knew he owed his master a massive debt.

Luke's muttered curse made Antonio turn sharply to the door. There, swaying slightly, a benevolent smile fixed to his face, was the friar again. 'Oh, God's blood!'

Hugo was feeling kindly to the world. 'My friend, may I speak with you a moment?'

'No, I have business to attend to. I don't need another lecture.'

'But I want to . . .'

'Enough, friar! Leave us in peace.'

The friar opened his mouth to continue, and this decided Antonio. He stood. 'Come, Pietro, Luke.'

'Father!' his son protested. 'What about Arthur and his daughter . . .'

It was too late, his father was already striding for the door. Luke took Pietro by the arm. 'Come, master Pietro, there will be another time to see her.' The youth shrugged his hand away irritably, but followed his father.

There was a farcical scene in the doorway. Torre was returning, and just as they reached the doorway, he was in their path. Antonio barged past, and Torre turned, arms outstretched as if to demand the reason for such rudeness. An instant later, Pietro also tried to thrust him aside.

But a tin miner was not so easy to push. Torre rotated slowly to study the younger man. Reading the menace in his features, Pietro stepped back and dropped his hand to his dagger, fumbling to unsheath it. It would be demeaning to back down before such a peasant. Torre looked at the knife contemptuously, then brushed past and strode back to his table, sitting by Holcroft.

They had left behind them the dismayed novice standing with the equally confused friar.

Torre took a swallow of his ale. 'What's put the wind in their sails, eh?' Then he saw the monk and muttered, 'Oh, by the cross, it's one of them! You – come here!'

The monk was startled, and Holcroft saw him jerk in surprise at the hostility in Torre's voice. 'Me?'

'Yes, of course you! Who else?' Torre sneered as the youth unwillingly approached. 'What's your name?'

'Peter.'

'Well, Peter. What are you doing here? Are you sent here to spy on ordinary workers for that bloodsucking leech of an Abbot of yours?'

'My Abbot . . .?'

'Is as dark a thief as ever stole a man's livelihood!'

Holcroft stared from his companion to the flushed features of the monk. 'Roger, what in Christ's name are you talking about?'

'Haven't you heard? Abbot Champeaux has decided to steal from me, now he's got the power. He's demanding money for the right to stay where I am, and if I don't agree to pay, he'll take my land from me.'

'Surely he wouldn't do that?'

'I only farm it as a bondman. Now the Abbot wants to change things so the land is a tenement held from him by lease. He wants twelve shillings a year from me just to stay on my own land.'

'Can you?'

'Pay twelve shillings? No, of course I can't. My tinning only brings in a little, and I have to pay tax when it's coigned. The land I farm from the Abbot is poor. It produces barely enough to keep me alive.'

'You could complain.'

'Who to – the Warden of the Stannaries? That's the Abbot now, or hadn't you heard, port-reeve? He's going to steal from us and force us from his land by charging too much. It's just theft, plain and simple. He's devious, like all politicians.'

'No, he's not,' the monk called Peter declared hotly. 'Abbot Champeaux is a fair man. If you speak to him and explain—'

'*Speak* to him? He's a politician – a liar and a thief. If I were to go and see him, I'd be thrown in his clink.'

'The Abbot is reasonable, sir,' the monk protested again. 'He's always upheld the rights of tinners.'

'You would say that – you're not suffering because of his greed.'

Holcroft saw the monk's face whiten with anger, and the lad took a step forward. 'Uh oh,' he muttered, and quickly stood between them. 'Brother, I think this is something we can't resolve peacefully, and I'm sure you wouldn't want to be hauled in front of the good Abbot for brawling in a tavern. Please leave, and I shall keep this man quiet.'

'He's insulted the Abbot with no reason. It's villainous! He's lied,' the monk hissed.

'Yes, but it wouldn't suit the cut or colour of your habit to fight, would it? Come now, let's forget it. It was only the ale talking; everyone knows the Abbot is good and honourable.' Muttering, the youth backed away, then spun around and stamped from the room.

Holcroft gave a sigh of relief. 'What's the point of picking on a beardless youth?'

Torre gave him a cynical leer. 'So you want to protect your position as port-reeve, do you? Does the office matter so much you'll forget your friends for a few more days in power?'

'Roger, if the truth be known, I am heartily sick of the job, and whoever is elected to it is welcome.'

'Yes, you'll give up the money, and the free rent, and the right to arrest and hold people who upset you, with pleasure.'

'All I can do is what I am told,' he said frankly. 'And it's little enough, heaven knows. But I'd prefer to see you free to go to the fair tomorrow and not being held in the clink for libelling the Abbot.'

'You'd take his side against your old friends.'

'No. But I'll be glad to give up all this responsibility and be able to get home at a decent hour like I used to.' And maybe then Hilary would be more friendly, he thought. His wife had been cold and unresponsive for so long now, it was hard to remember when she had last been a true wife to him.

'Oh, yes! You'll be happy to lose all the profits of your work, no doubt.'

Holcroft shook his head. What Torre could not understand was the pressure of the interminable record-keeping, the late hours checking tolls with the prior and others, the planning and administration.

'I can't sit here with you. For all I know you're recording everything I say to report to the Abbot himself!' Torre declared, rising.

'Roger!' Holcroft pleaded, and gestured. 'Come on, sit down. I wanted to see you to relax.'

'Relax with someone else. I'm going to.' Torre stumped away.

'Come, now, Master port-reeve. You'll try some ale? That was good work, keeping Torre and the monk apart. There would have been too much grief from that.'

'Mistress Agatha, I don't know why I bothered,' he said, gratefully taking a fresh ale. He noticed Elias sitting with an unknown companion. Putting the cook from his mind, Holcroft assumed that Elias' friend was someone who had arrived for the fair.

Agatha looked down at him sympathetically. She knew that David had been working madly for the last few weeks, and was about to offer him some words of comfort when she saw new arrivals.

Arthur peered inside, searching for the Camminos.

'Well? Are they there?' his wife demanded.

'Not yet, my dear, but I'm sure they will be,' Arthur assured her. He led the way to the bench recently vacated by the Venetians. It had been a mistake to bring his wife with him. She had wanted to remain at their rented house and supervise its decoration, but Arthur wished her to recover from their long ride, and hoped a pot or two of wine would ease her temper.

At home, he was used to surrendering to her will. Marion was the daughter of a knight, and if it hadn't been for her father's need for ready money, and Arthur's willingness to extend a loan, they might never have wed. In matters of business he could insist on her aid, though, and he was sure that Cammino could be useful. Any contacts with wealthy foreigners were to be fostered, and the mention of a fleet, together with evidence of the acquaintance of an Abbot, meant that Cammino wielded some power. Marion's presence might be useful. 'Come, dear. Would you like some wine?'

Avice sat decorously at the end of the bench, accepting a pot of wine. The Venetian man had looked so dashing in his foreign clothes, she thought, like a squire from a royal court. As her parents spoke, her eyes kept flitting to the doorway.

After serving them, Agatha stood back and surveyed her

domain. When she saw Torre talking to Lizzie, saw his hand on her arm, and the way she giggled and nodded, the alewife's eyes shot to Holcroft. Agatha could see his pain when he saw Lizzie leaving with Torre. It wasn't the first time a man had fallen for Lizzie, and it wouldn't be the last, but Agatha had a soft spot for the port-reeve, and his dismay saddened her.

There was a soft belch at her side, and she turned to see the friar gazing thoughtfully into the distance. At first she thought he was simply drunk, but when he noticed her, he said apologetically, 'Sorry, I wasn't thinking – thought I recognised someone.'

Lizzie straightened her skirts and smoothed them before sitting at the edge of her palliasse to tighten her braids and rearrange them. 'Come on, Roger. I have to get back to the hall or Agatha will throw me out.'

'A moment more,' he groaned, and reached for her.

She stood, chuckling, neatly avoiding his hand. 'No! I have to work. Especially now, with the fair about to begin. I shouldn't really have done this tonight. What if the Abbot should hear?'

'Let him! Why should I care?'

'You may not have to worry, but I do. He could have me evicted. It's happened before.'

He looked up, an angry gleam in his eye. 'You think the port-reeve would report you for this?'

Lizzie shook her head. 'No, he fancies me. David would never report me, but someone else might.'

'He fancies you?' Torre rolled on to an elbow, and his face was serious. 'I had no idea. He must have seen us leave the room together.'

'So what?' She patted her hair and tucked a stray wisp away. 'He doesn't own me any more than you do. I live as I want, and no man can keep me. In any case, he's never so much as touched me. I don't think he knows how to.'

Torre frowned up at her, then at the door. 'Maybe, but I wouldn't hurt his feelings.'

'You were happy enough to in there,' she said tartly.

'That was different: just an argument. But I know David. He's a decent man. I wouldn't want to offend him.'

Lizzie froze for a moment as the bell from the Abbey tolled for compline. 'Listen to that, it's getting late,' she said, hurriedly completing her toilet. 'Look, if you don't want to upset him, don't go back into the hall but go straight to your rooms. If he doesn't see you with me, he'll believe me when I tell him you left some time ago. All right?'

'Good idea.' He climbed up and donned his loose-fitting hose, tying them neatly, pulling on his shirt and doublet, then his red jacket.

She watched him contentedly. He had a good figure, she thought, and he'd been kind and gentle. Hopefully he'd return later on, and if he did, she'd not mind showing him her favours again. She waited till he'd dressed and walked quickly out, then finished her own toilet. A shoe had been kicked away, and she had to seek it, finding it partly hidden beneath the blanket tossed from the bed, before she could follow him. Closing the door, she turned and stopped. Leaning against the door-jamb of the tavern was Holcroft. He stared at her for what seemed a long time, then turned without a word and walked away.

She heaved a sigh, hoping he wouldn't go straight to the Abbot to accuse her, then made her way back into the hall and began pouring ale. When she passed Agatha, she slipped the coin into the alewife's hand. The alewife always had her fifth for room and rental.

He curled his lip at the smell from the pile of rubbish. It stank of putrefaction and decay, a revolting concoction. Leaning against the wall, he waited while his heartbeat slowed and calmed.

It had been easy to waylay him; easier than he'd dreamed.

The burly figure was instantly recognisable, even in the dark with no lanterns or sconces – they weren't allowed during the fair because of the hazard – and although he'd seen the man waiting patiently, he'd done nothing more than duck his head and make a vague sign of the cross.

The killer nudged tentatively at the corpse with his foot. It was almost an anti-climax now he was dead. The action of stabbing him was so quick, and his gasp and collapse so sudden, that he could hardly believe he'd succeeded. There had been no cry, no shriek for help, just a brief, pained gasp, and then he'd dropped like a felled tree. It gave his murderer a feeling of immense power, knowing he could kill so swiftly and easily with impunity.

But he couldn't leave the body here, in plain view for any reveller to discover. He gripped the feet and dragged the figure backwards into the alley. The midden pile would be an ideal hiding place – nobody would want to approach that in the dark in case of stepping in some of its components. He could hear a short scrabbling as he hauled the body and glanced about him with distaste. Rats!

Dropping the feet, he stood a moment staring down at the corpse before kicking waste from the pile over the body in an attempt to conceal it. Satisfied with his efforts, he hurried down the alley, the habit flapping at his heels as he went. At the road he slowed, stuffed his hands in his sleeves over his chest in an attitude of contemplation, and walked out and down the road. When he saw Arthur Pole and his wife and daughter, he was secretly delighted to see that all bowed their heads respectfully and offered him a good evening.

Chapter Four

It was the morning of the fair, and David Holcroft made his way to the Abbey with relief. The previous night had been as bad as he had expected: after all his work, he'd have liked his wife to show some interest in the fair and sympathy for his exertions. Instead she was withdrawn and uncommunicative. They had hardly spoken ten words, and she had soon gone to bed pleading a sickness in her stomach.

At the bottom of the fair's field, he turned and gazed back: everything was settled and organised, and he was sure the Abbot could have no cause for complaint. In the early-morning light, the colours stood out with startling clarity. There was a thin mistiness in the air which gave all a silvery sheen as if bathed in an intense moonlight. Flags hung dispiritedly from their poles in the still air, and there was a feeling of unreality about the whole place, as though it was a ghostly mirage. That would soon be dispelled when the customers arrived and the fair was declared open. Instantly it would be transformed into a rowdy beargarden as voices rose to argue and haggle over the choice arrays of goods. He could already see people making their way up from the town, keen to be the first to see the latest items from all over the kingdom and farther afield.

As the first hammer strokes sounded he nodded to himself. The furnaces of the smiths were lighted, and he could see the pale streamers of smoke rising like conical wraiths, only to dissipate as they climbed higher. This was the true beginning of the fair, he always felt, when the tradesmen and craftsmen began their morning rituals.

And like the determined call of a church's bells, he saw that the ringing and clattering from the anvils worked its own magic on the fair's congregation. The trickle of people heading up to the ground grew into a stream even as he watched, and soon there was a steady river of buyers, hawkers, merchants and entertainers all making their way up from the town itself. It always astonished him how many foreigners the place could hold at fair-time.

He walked with the calm satisfaction that the fair would be a success, but his mood gradually altered as he came close to the Abbey gate. Here he had to wait a moment before being led inside to the large square room beside the gate itself.

Ten constables and twenty-nine watchmen were due to meet him, the complement from the surrounding vills, each man earning two pennies. He had already checked the mounted men the previous afternoon. These, eight all told, were stationed up and down the roads wherever the woods were thickest, to protect any travellers who came to attend the fair from outlaws. Felons often tried robbing merchants: they were easy pickings while tired after a long journey.

The mounted men were always the best, he knew. They were the ones who could afford horses, which necessarily placed them above the average vill watchmen; that was why they earned six pennies a day. It wasn't only the extra expense of looking after a horse that justified the money, it was the fact that they were simply better men.

Nodding at the clerk who kept records of the payments made to the men, and any amercements, he stood as the men filed in. At the sight of the constables, he closed his eyes in silent despair, offering up a quick prayer before opening them again with resignation.

The first that came into view was Daniel, the farmer's son from Werrington. Daniel radiated kindness and goodwill, with the open smile of the pathologically truthful man. He gave the impression of bovine clumsiness and dull-wittedness, and the port-reeve meditated grimly on the devious market-traders. They would all try to pull the wool over this one's eyes.

Next to him were the four watchmen from Denbury, led by Long Jack. David gave them a sour stare.

'Let's see them, then.' The port-reeve eyed the weapons held out for him to inspect. 'What is *that*?'

Daniel was hurt. 'It's my father's sword.'

'Father's? Are you sure it's not your great-grandfather's? I can't see any metal for the rust!' said David in disbelief. He took it and gazed at it. It was so old that the leather grip had worn away, and the wooden handle beneath was rough on his hand. The metal of the tang was sharp, and the pommel had fallen off. In a fight the grip could turn and catch the skin. He tested the blade with his thumb, his expression reflecting his disgust. 'A penny.'

'A penny fine? But . . .'

'If you aren't happy, I can raise it to a day's money. For now, get that thing to the blacksmith and see whether he can put an edge of some sort on it, and a new grip. This isn't just to make the fair look good, it's to protect people – *and* so you can protect yourself. How can you keep the King's peace with an ancient block of rust like that? What have you been doing with it – hedging?'

The watchman shifted uneasily, and mumbled an apology. David shook his head. Any tool was there to be used, in the minds of the peasants of the area, and an old weapon was no more than a good, edged farm implement. It had more cutting power than a bill-hook, and was easier and lighter to carry to a hedge than a heavy axe. While the watchman reddened David moved on to the next man. This one had a cudgel and a welsh knife, one with a good long blade of over a foot. David gave it a grudging nod and continued along the line, making sure that all the blades were strong and sharp, the sticks solid and not cracked.

Almost all were fine, especially those of the men from Denbury, who appeared to have good new blades and oaken clubs.

He watched them go with a lacklustre eye. 'I don't know how people feel about outlaws and thieves,' he said to the clerk as the last one tramped out, 'but personally that lot scares me more than all the felons in the clink.'

Will Ruby sliced through the skin quickly in a long cut round the vent, and thrust two fingers into the capon, drawing the innards out and dropping them into the midden-basket by his feet. Feeling around inside, he located the kidneys where they lay on the back of the ribcage, and tugged them free. He cut through the flesh of the neck and exposed the bones beneath before removing the head. That too went into the basket.

The carcass was tossed onto the growing pile as he reached for the next. Beside him, his wife and son sat on stools, surrounded by a gently billowing cloud as they plucked furiously, stuffing the feathers into sacks. His apprentice was fetching the other carcasses from the wagon stationed by the fairground, setting them out on their hooks or laying them on the boards where the customers would be able to inspect them. Will was pleased to see that the boy had learned how to conceal the worse parts of any joint, and laid out the cuts to best advantage. There was no point in giving a customer an opportunity to argue for a lower price. He nodded approvingly. The boy had gone again while he inspected his wares, and when Will glanced over, he saw that there were no more chickens ready to be drawn yet. His wife and son were still plucking.

The midden-basket was almost full, and he was beginning to feel warm as the sun rose higher. At this rate he would need more than the one basket. A draught of ale would help cool him, too. 'I'll just empty this,' he said to his wife. She hardly looked up, just nodded, as he wiped his hands on his bloody apron and moved off along the stalls carrying the basket.

There was another good reason for taking a walk: to look at how the other stalls had presented their stock to the world. Being butchers, there was the benefit of having no outside competition, because the Abbot promised them their monopoly, but Will knew that all would have bought in extra stock, and he wanted to see how good it looked.

From a distance he stopped and gazed back. His own stall was bright and colourful with its red and yellow awning. He'd picked the colours because they stood out among the greens and blues of the other stalls. The trestle was almost filled to overflowing, and he had enough meat hidden behind in barrels and boxes to supply a lord and his retinue. Feeling satisfied, he carried on, casting an eye to right and left as he went, assessing how others were doing.

The midden lay at the far side of the fairground, and he passed by the new toll-booth on the way. A long queue of merchants from outside the borough stood there, waiting. All had goods to sell, and they grumbled together about the costs. 'A halfpenny for a cart of wheat? It's theft, that's what it is.' A red-faced farmer was insisting that he should have free access because he came from an ancient tenement on the moors and shouldn't have to pay, while his geese extended their necks and waddled nearby, a skinny and mangy dog herding them whenever they strolled too far.

Will barged past the arguing men. It was much like any other year. Prices were higher, but they had been rising since the disastrous famines of four or five years before; at least people could expect to make a profit. There were good reasons for a goose-farmer to want to avoid paying, because from every fourteen birds brought in, one must be given in toll, and that was a heavy price.

Whistling tunelessly, the butcher arrived at the midden. So early in the morning, it was not as violent on the nose as it would become, but there was enough of a rotten stench to make him hurry. In future, he decided, someone else would discard the garbage.

He upended the basket and set off back to his shop. Another basket or two would be needed, and he might as well fetch them now – especially since the journey would take him past the tavern.

It took little time to enter through the town gate and make his way to his shop, where he at once went in and fetched the spare baskets from under his bench. He was still whistling as he slammed the door behind him and moved towards the tavern, but at the entrance to the alleyway he paused.

Shaking his head, he surveyed the pile. It had been reduced, he saw, but that would not satisfy the port-reeve. David Holcroft was easy-going about many things, but the Abbot was his master, and Abbot Robert was known to abhor the messy habits of some of the townspeople. He would be sure to demand that Elias was amerced. Will tutted to himself, and was about to go and beat on Elias' door when he stopped, lips pursed in readiness for a whistle. He could just make out the shape of an old and worn boot, and the sight was strangely out of place. Elias was not the sort to throw out an old boot: he'd be more likely to take it to be mended. Will blinked, peering down into the gloom, then rushed forward, his baskets bouncing and spinning in the road behind him. Under the mound of rubbish he could see the shape of a leg.

Grabbing the boot and hurriedly scraping round it, he stopped with the horrified realisation that there was a body concealed beneath the mound. Seizing the ankle, he hauled, grimly noting that the flesh was as cold as any of the carcasses he handled in his shop. Whoever this was, he was not living. The mound shifted, rags and bits of pastry and bones falling as he dragged the body free. A knee appeared, and a thigh. The hose were sodden and rucked up as he pulled. More garbage slid aside with a revolting sucking noise, and now he could see the other leg. Gingerly, he gripped it and leaned back. A muscle snapped in his shoulder, but still he tugged, and at last the body came free with a slight jerk, and he fell back on his rump. 'Ow! God's blood!'

Standing, he rubbed his backside, then his shoulder, and walked forward to view the red-leather-clad corpse. Staring in horror, he cursed again, more softly now, and swallowed hard.

Sir Baldwin Furnshill winced as a gust of wind threw dust in his eyes, and blinked furiously. 'This fair had better match your expectations, Margaret,' he said as his eyes streamed. 'After travelling so far, first from Crediton to Lydford, and now on to Tavistock, all I wish to see is a comfortable seat and a good trencher of stew.'

'Baldwin, of course you'll find it enjoyable,' she said lightly. Her fair hair was whipping free of her wimple and she had to keep pushing back the stray tresses.

'You do not care, madam, about my soreness or boredom. No! So long as you can feel the quality of the cloths on sale, so long as you can try on the newest gloves, the best shoes, and buy the choicest spices from around the world, you will be content.'

'No,' her husband grunted. 'She won't be made happy by feeling bolts of cloth and trying on shoes; she won't be happy until she's bought the lot.'

Baldwin wiped his face. '*I* will not be happy until we have arrived and I have finally managed to get some rest.'

'In any case, husband, I seem to remember that you first suggested we should come to the fair, so that you could buy some new plates.'

'That's very different. We need plates for when we have to entertain lords,' said Simon. He had not realised how many feasts he would be expected to give as bailiff of Lydford Castle. To be fair, he accepted that a good display of plates could only serve to enhance his reputation as well.

'And we need new curtains and clothing for when we entertain,' Margaret added sweetly.

Baldwin guffawed. Margaret, a slim and tall woman with the fresh complexion of one who had lived all her life on the moors, had gradually started to gain weight. The lines of sadness on her forehead and the bruises under her eyes had faded, and she had regained her sense of humour. After the death of her son, followed by her recent ordeal in Crediton[1], she had lost weight alarmingly quickly. Baldwin had been concerned that she might be wasting away. He had seen other women who had simply lost the desire to live when their sons had died. Luckily, he reflected, Margaret not only had Simon, but also Edith, her daughter. The girl had forced her mother to concentrate on life, for Edith still needed her.

They reached the crest of a hill, and to their left stood a gallows. It looked quite new to Baldwin. He was never happier than when he was at home at his small estate near Cadbury, but in his capacity as Keeper of the King's Peace, he often had to witness the deaths of felons. This gallows was constructed from solid baulks of timber, much better than the ancient device in Crediton, which he was always concerned about lest it might collapse on guards and hangmen. It was most worrying when the executioners leaped up to clasp the bodies, clinging to them until the victim had died. Then the Keeper's eyes always went to the horizontal bar, fearing that it might snap.

A burgess had once suggested that he should stop the executioners performing that final act, and he had been so angry he had almost hit the man. The hangmen were speeding the death: it was no more than Christian kindness to halt the suffering. But the burgess was heavily involved in

---

[1]See *The Crediton Killings* by Michael Jecks, also published by Headline.

the gambling that revolved around hangings, with bets being laid on how long each man would live. He preferred to see them last longer so more bets could be taken.

Baldwin still found some aspects of civil life difficult to accept, for he had not always been a secular knight. He had been a 'Poor Fellow-Soldier of Christ and the Temple of Solomon' – a Knight Templar – and had lived by their Rule, swearing to obedience, poverty and chastity. After seeing his friends die needlessly in the fires when the Order had been betrayed by a malicious and covetous King, he had a loathing for unnecessary pain. He had no sympathy for gamblers who wanted to prolong another's agony purely for profit.

He looked away and down towards the town. At this time of day, in the middle of the morning, many towns would be quiet while people had their lunch, but today Tavistock was beginning her fair, and her streets were thronged with visitors. 'I am glad the Abbot invited us to lodge with him,' he remarked. 'It looks as if bed space will be in short supply.'

Simon drew his horse alongside Baldwin's and followed his gaze. 'From here you can see how big the fair is, can't you,' he said, awestruck.

'Yes. It makes Crediton's look quite small,' Baldwin observed.

Simon waved a hand, encompassing the scene before them. 'This is getting to be a problem. I always receive complaints after Tavistock Fair because Lydford's declines while this one grows. All the tinners tend to come here. It's an easier journey than going up to Lydford, and the Abbot always sees to it that there's more in the way of foodstuffs and supplies.'

'So you're already worried about this fair?' Baldwin teased.

'Worried? No, I intend to spy, to see what they do here that attracts merchants from Lydford,' Simon said firmly. He didn't mention his real concern: he was to meet his new master.

As bailiff of Lydford, Simon was responsible for law and order in the stannaries. He had to make sure that no one smuggled tin; all the tin must be coigned, or weighed, marked and taxed, at the stannary towns of Tavistock, Lydford, Chagford and Ashburton. He also had to calm the incessant wrangles between tinners and landowners, maintain the stannary prison at Lydford Castle, and ensure that nobody broke the King's peace. His master was the warden of the stannaries, and the Abbot had just been granted the post. Simon hadn't met his new master before, and the prospect was daunting.

Baldwin saw his pensive expression, but misread the thought behind it. 'You're already worrying that Tavistock will be a huge success, even before you arrive! Your husband, Margaret, is never happy unless he has something to worry him.'

She smiled at his joke. 'Only the other day he was anxious that his little daughter didn't have enough young friends in Lydford, and then he was troubled she was growing too quickly, and would soon have a husband.'

'That's not fair,' Simon protested. 'I was just saying that . . .'

Margaret listened to their banter with half an ear. She was content that Simon was recovered from his black depression. It was in large part due to Baldwin, she knew. Baldwin's cure for a man with so heavy a weight of misery was to make him laugh, and it had worked better than any medicine. Her husband had aged since his son's death: before he had looked five years younger than his age of thirty-three, but now he seemed older. The lines were etched deeper into his forehead and at either side of his mouth. Though his hair was still almost black, it had begun to recede, giving him a distinguished appearance.

Looking at Baldwin, she could not help but notice the thickening at his waist. Weight was Baldwin's main enemy now. When she had first met him, he had spent many years as a penniless, wandering knight with no lord. In those days, he and his man-at-arms, Edgar, had been forced to live on whatever they could collect for themselves, eked out with a few pulses or a loaf from a farm. Since inheriting the Furnshill estate from his dead brother, he was able to eat well, and his belly was growing.

For the rest, he was an attractive figure, she thought. He was tall, and though his brown hair was shot through with silver, the black beard that followed the line of his jaw was unmarked with grey. But he was not the perfect image of a modern knight. Most men were cleanshaven, like her husband. The old King, the present King's father, had had an aversion to beards and in his day few even wore a moustache. Though times had changed since his death, facial decoration was still rare. It was one concession Baldwin made to his past as a Templar; the knights had always been bearded.

But Baldwin's dress did not impress. He sported an old tunic, stained, worn and unfashionable. His boots had hardly any toe and did not follow the courtly trend for elongated points. That he was capable of fighting was proven by the scar on his cheek, stretching from temple to jaw; but that was the sole remaining evidence of a lively past.

Margaret eyed him affectionately. He was a good friend, honest, loyal and chivalrous. It was only sad that he was still a bachelor. She was sure he wanted to find a wife, but so far he had been unsuccessful. When she tried to interest him in women she knew, her attempts met with failure. None tempted him, not even Mary, Edith's young nurse, who had flirted outrageously when she met him.

That brought her mind back to her little girl. Edith was getting to be a handful now, and it was a relief to have found a nurse who seemed to understand her, and who was willing to indulge her passion for riding over the moors. Mary had been quiet when she had first come to live with them, but now the fourteen-year-old had become Edith's best friend – after Hugh, Simon's servant. He still held a special place in Edith's capricious heart.

'What is it, Margaret?' Baldwin asked.

'I was thinking I should buy you some cloth. That tunic is too old.'

He stared a moment, eyebrows raised, and there was alarm in his voice. 'Old? But this is fine.'

'It's old and faded, Baldwin; it's also too tight round your belly.'

'Um . . . but it *is* comfortable.'

'Comfortable it may be. I'm surprised Edgar hasn't persuaded you to get a new one.'

Baldwin threw a dark look over his shoulder. Edgar had been his man-at-arms since they had joined the Templars together. All knights operated as a team with their men, training with them and depending on them for protection, just as a modern knight would with his squire. Edgar had proved to be an efficient steward as well as soldier, but he had the servant's love of ostentation. If the master displayed grandeur, some was reflected on the servant.

And Edgar wanted magnificent display now. Baldwin had been aware for some little while that his servant had won the hearts of several women in Crediton, although now he evinced passion for one only, a serving girl at the inn.

Edgar looked back serenely, and Baldwin faced Margaret. 'Has *he* put you up to this, Margaret? Has he asked you to persuade me to buy new things? If he has, he might have to find a new post.'

'Do you suggest that I am unable to form my own opinions of a tired and threadbare tunic?' she asked tartly.

'No, no, of course not. It's just that Edgar has been worse than a nagging wife recently, telling me . . .'

'Well, *I* think it's time you bought a new tunic. You can afford it.'

'Simon, give me some support!'

'No,' said Simon with delight. 'My wife knows her own mind, and I'll be buggered if I'm going to get in her way over this: if she takes you to the stalls to find a new tunic, that means she'll have less time to spend *my* money. Meg, you carry on. Make sure he gets new hose, hats, gloves, shirts, cloaks, belts, boots, and anything else that will take time to buy and keep you from your own favourite stalls!'

They had descended to the outskirts of the town, and continued down the street towards the Abbey, passing by the market.

'What's going on there?' Baldwin wondered, seeing a huddle of people.

'Some kind of excitement,' Simon said disinterestedly. 'Probably only a thief or something. Cut-purses always come to the fairs. They know they can steal with impunity in the crowd.'

'Perhaps.' Baldwin noted the heavily armed watchmen, and the burly figure of a man stooping. A group of people muttered nearby. Then he saw the body on the ground. 'Hello? Is someone hurt?'

The bent man straightened slowly. 'You could say that.'

Baldwin studied him. For all the weariness in his voice he had an air of authority, which was emphasised by his somewhat portly figure. That he was prosperous was obvious from the quality of his cloak and hat, and Baldwin assumed he must hold some kind of office. 'Can I help?' he offered. 'I am the Keeper of the King's Peace in Crediton. Do you need some assistance here?'

'*He* certainly doesn't,' said one of the guards and sniggered.

'Shut up, Long Jack,' the man snapped.

Looking down, Baldwin saw what the watchman meant. The body was that of a short but strong man, dressed poorly in faded blue hose and a holed and patched doublet. That the man was dead was in no doubt. Baldwin heard Margaret gasp. The body was headless.

Dropping from his horse, Baldwin glanced round the men in the crowd. 'Has anyone told the Abbot?'

'I have. I am the port-reeve, David Holcroft.'

Baldwin nodded and looked down at the body. 'I am Sir Baldwin Furnshill, here to visit Abbot Champeaux. Has the coroner been called?'

'A man has been sent to fetch him, but it will take at least three days to get him here,' Holcroft said.

'Why so long?'

'There's been a shipwreck. He's been called to the coast.'

'I see. These people – who are they?'

'The neighbours. As soon as the hue was called, I had them all brought.'

'All here?'

'Almost. Only the cook Elias isn't present. He's probably seeing to his wares in the fair.' Holcroft pointed to another. 'He's the first finder: Will Ruby, the butcher. He discovered the body and raised the hue.'

Simon sprang from his horse and passed his reins to Hugh, who remained on his mount staring down distastefully at the corpse. The bailiff walked to Baldwin's side. The neighbours all stood nervously while Baldwin studied them. Simon knew what he was thinking: if the coroner took three days to return, the murderer could be far away by then. If the killer was one of the foreigners and not a portman of Tavistock, he might never be found. Yet Baldwin had no legal right to investigate; that was the preserve of the local coroner.

The men all looked bitter. When a corpse was found, the nearest neighbours must be attached, held on promise of a surety, before they could be formally released. It was the only way to guarantee that they would definitely pay their amercement for allowing a murderer to break the King's Peace.

Looking at the shops either side of the alley, Baldwin asked, 'You are the butcher?'

Will nodded glumly. 'Yes, sir. That's my shop there.'

The first finder interested Baldwin. Will Ruby was a short and strong-looking man, with massive biceps and a belly to match. A thick rug of short, curling hair of a reddish brown covered his large, rounded skull. From the look of his woollen overcoat the knight saw that the butcher enjoyed a profitable business.

'How did you come to find him?'

Will explained about his journey to fetch his midden-baskets. 'I saw his foot sticking from the pile there and pulled it.'

Baldwin listened closely while he looked carefully at the body. 'Do you have any idea who this was?'

Holcroft answered for Will. 'Not with those clothes. He doesn't seem to be from within the port – these things are very foreign.' He frowned, staring at the body. 'I've seen someone wearing clothes like these before, though I can't think where.'

'You think it was someone visiting the fair?'

'It seems likely.'

Simon scratched his chin. 'So where's his head?'

'That's what I'd like to know,' Holcroft said.

'What?' Baldwin asked. 'It is not here?'

'Not in the heap or anywhere nearby. We've hunted up the alley and everywhere, but there's no sign of it.'

'Strange.' Baldwin wandered closer to the pile and stared at it a moment before returning to the body. 'Did you find a knife?'

'Knife?'

'His sheath is empty.'

Holcroft shook his head.

'It is strange that his head should have been cut off,' Baldwin murmured. 'Why should someone do that, I wonder? And why take his knife afterwards?'

'Simon, do you think we could go on ahead if Baldwin is going to . . .'

'Margaret, I am so sorry,' the knight said and leaped to his feet. 'This is nothing to do with me. I am here for the holiday. *We* are here to see the fair. My apologies. It was inexcusable to make you wait here with a corpse. Come, we shall go on immediately.'

Simon climbed on his horse and waited until Baldwin had mounted his own before setting off to the Abbey. The bailiff knew that his friend was always intrigued by crimes, and was surprised at the speed with which Baldwin gave up his questioning. Then Simon saw Baldwin's eyes return to the body and stay fixed there. The knight caught sight of Simon's expression and gave a rueful shrug.

'No, we are here for St Rumon's Day.'

Chapter Five

The Abbot of Tavistock stood in his hall and held his arms
wide in welcome. A cheery, red-faced cleric of middle
height, his tonsure needed no shaving, for his head wore
only a scanty band of grey hair that reached as far as his
temples on either side. All his pate from his forehead to the
back of his head was bare. 'Bailiff, welcome! And your lady,
too. Please be seated. You must be Sir Baldwin Furnshill.
It's a pleasure to meet you at last. Come, please be seated.'

Abbot Champeaux's enthusiasm was infectious. He led
them to a sideboard littered with expensive plate, upon
which stood a flagon of wine and a number of goblets, all
carefully crafted in pewter. Baldwin took one from the
bottler and studied it. There was a hunting scene carved
round it. The Abbot, he decided, was not averse to
displaying his prosperity.

While Simon chatted to his new master, his bag slung
over his shoulder, Baldwin sat and took in his surroundings.
The room was comfortably furnished, with tapestries on the
walls, and padded cushions on the chair seats. A solid
moorstone fireplace took up a large part of the eastern wall.
From where he sat, with his back to the hearth, he could
gaze out through the glazed windows over the fishponds
and gardens. The grounds took up a large area, stretching
to the strip fields. He could see the lazy sweep of the river
as it meandered away from the town.

When he saw a flash of reddish brown, he stiffened. It
was near the water's edge, and he sat up to peer.

The Abbot noticed his concentration, and turned to see
what had attracted his guest's interest. 'Ah, Sir Baldwin,
you have a good eye,' he chuckled.

'It looks a good beast.'

'Yes. We are fortunate in having over forty deer in our
park, though we do sometimes have difficulties.'

'What sort of difficulties?' Margaret asked.

The abbot smiled genially, and there was a twinkle in his
eye. 'Sometimes they manage to escape from the park when
we're trying to catch them. I've been told off for chasing my
venison on to the moors before now. We do try to make
sure that our hounds catch the beasts before they can get
out of the park, but every now and again one of them will
succeed, and what then are we to do? It's hard to keep the
ditches and hedges maintained.'

Baldwin could not restrain a grin. That an abbot should
dare to roam over the chase of Dartmoor to poach, and then
happily confess it, was unique in his experience. 'I should
like to see your pack of hounds,' he said, and the Abbot
nodded delightedly.

'It would be my pleasure. Perhaps I could tempt you to
join me for a hunt as well?'

'I would have to accept so kind an offer.'

Simon patted his bag. 'Would you like to go through the
business of the stannary now?'

'Oh no, Simon. You've had a tiring journey to get here.
Please, *rest*! We can talk about business later. I've been
Abbot here for four and thirty years, and while Our Lord
may decide not to let me carry on for another four and
thirty, I hope that I've a few more years left in me! There's
time for us to discuss our work later.'

Baldwin leaned back in his seat. The Abbot was a good
host, chatting with Simon and his wife and putting both at
their ease. Baldwin had known many priestly men, but this
one, Robert Champeaux, seemed to wear his power and
authority lightly.

And he *did* have authority. Baldwin had spent some time enquiring about his host with Peter Clifford, the Dean of Crediton Church, and had found the time instructive. As Champeaux said, he had been Abbot for over thirty years. When he had taken on the post, the Abbey had been in debt, but now, after his careful administration, it was rumoured to be one of the soundest institutions in the shire.

Abbot Robert had attracted money by improving the fairs and markets, taking business from Chagford and Lydford, and reinvesting the money to buy lucrative offices. He had been appointed controller of all the silver mines in Devon in 1318, and Baldwin understood he had recently extended his management of the mines in exchange for a sizeable loan to help with the war against Scotland. This year, 1319, he had become the warden of the Devon stannaries, *and* keeper of the port of Dartmouth, both highly profitable positions, yet he was content to sit and discuss the quality of cloths in the market with the wife of one of his bailiffs. That displayed a humility and generosity of spirit many other priests would do well to emulate.

There was a knock at the door and a young monk entered, bowing low. 'My lord, the port-reeve would like to speak to you.'

'Please show him in. Ah, Holcroft, you have sent for the coroner, I hear?'

'Yes, sir. And I have attached the four neighbours and Will Ruby, the first finder.'

'The hue was raised, of course, so there is little more to be done. Where is the body?'

'I couldn't leave it there, sir.' Normally a body would be left where it had been found until the coroner could view it. 'It would be impossible with so many people around. I've had it moved to the inn. There's an outhouse there where the coroner can view it.'

'Good.'

Baldwin leaned forward. 'What of the man's relatives?'

'Until we find his head, there's nothing we can do. We don't know who he is, after all.'

Simon waved his goblet questioningly. 'No one's reported a missing man? A wife would recognise her husband's body, after all. You're sure he must be a foreigner?'

'Yes, sir, he must be from outside Tavistock. Nobody's reported a man who's disappeared.'

'That means nothing,' Baldwin said. 'While the fair is on, people will be spending their time in the alehouses and taverns. How many women would be surprised if their husbands turned up late or not at all every night of the fair? This man might well be a resident of the town whose woman thinks he's sleeping off a hangover in a tavern.'

'It's not only that, Sir Baldwin,' said Holcroft. 'The clothes look familiar to me, but I don't remember where from. They're not local; there's no one I know in Tavistock who wears stuff like this.'

'This isn't good,' the Abbot said. He stared wistfully out through the window towards his deer park. Simon guessed that the talk of bodies was distasteful to him – he would rather be discussing his hounds or hawks. 'It will be my court that has to resolve all this, and I don't want a whole group of men from the town penalised when they have done nothing.'

Baldwin nodded thoughtfully. The usual procedure was for the first finder and neighbours to be held against a surety, to guarantee that they would go to court. If no killer could be found, they would all be fined.

'I hear that Sir Baldwin and the bailiff have found many other killers,' Holcroft suggested tentatively.

'You want us to help you?' Simon asked, throwing Baldwin a glance. The knight shrugged.

'Sir, I can do nothing,' said Holcroft plaintively. 'We rarely have murders in the port, and I'm only in this post for a year. I don't know how to perform an inquest or anything.'

'That is down to the coroner,' Baldwin observed.

'Yes, sir, but the killer could be leagues from here before the coroner arrives.'

Robert Champeaux nodded pensively, looking from Simon to Baldwin. 'You would be doing me a great service, gentlemen. Would it be possible for you to investigate this death? It should be the duty of the coroner, but this is my land, and the murder was within my court's jurisdiction. In the interests of justice I feel justified in investigating it swiftly.'

Baldwin stood. 'Come, master port-reeve, let us return to where the body was found.'

'One moment.' Champeaux walked to the door. He held a brief conversation with another monk before returning. 'All should be noted down in case the coroner wants to see exactly what has been said or done. Take young Peter here. He can write down everything for the report.'

As the young man entered, Holcroft shook his head. He recognised the novice who had guided the Camminos to the tavern the night before. Things were bad enough already, he thought, without having an aggressive monk tagging along.

Holcroft led them through the Great Court of the Abbey and out through the court gate – a massive square block large enough to house a small chapel. From there they followed the street northwards until they came to the alley.

Baldwin was pleased to try to help the Abbot, particularly since he was fascinated by the mystery of the missing head, but Simon felt a degree of irritation that they should so speedily have been involved in a murder hunt. He only hoped that their investigations could be concluded quickly. He had left Hugh to help Margaret settle into the room Abbot Champeaux had allocated for them. Baldwin did not bother to ask Edgar to remain. He would not leave his master in a strange town. When they were serving with the Knights Templar his place had been at his master's side, and he took his responsibility seriously. When away from home, Edgar rarely let his master out of his sight.

The servant's expression betrayed only boredom. Baldwin was sure that his keenness in coming to the fair was largely due to his wish to buy a bolt of good cloth for his woman. It was a comfort to Baldwin that his servant was focusing on Cristine at the inn. Beforehand Edgar had pursued an increasing number of women, and Baldwin had become concerned that his servant's peccadillos could harm the respect which was so important to the knight's position.

When they arrived at the alley, the people had gone. Once they had provided sureties, the guards had no further interest in them. The body had been carried away, and only a small pool of dried blood showed where it had lain.

Baldwin stared down at it, shook his head and walked over to the garbage heap. There was a besom with a broken handle leaning against the wall, and he used it to fastidiously disarrange the rubbish and study the contents. 'Nothing here,' he said, throwing down the pole, and strolled back to the bloodstained spot. 'Why would someone take the head?'

'A very good question,' said Simon.

'I reckon he was from outside the port,' said Holcroft, 'and probably only came here to buy or sell something. It stands to reason he knew no one here.'

'If that is so, we should soon find who he was,' said Baldwin. 'His stall will be empty, and somebody will report that, if only the man from whom he rented the space.'

'I've sent watchmen to see whether any stall is empty – but it'll take time with so many to visit. And many stalls have more than one man to serve customers, so they may find nothing.'

'Well, let us see whether we can learn anything from the corpse. You are sure he was not local?'

'Not with his clothes. He must have been a foreigner, murdered by someone he met on the road. They argued; he died.'

'If it was someone on the road, he would have been killed on the road,' Simon said. 'Why should he have been followed all the way to town, where there are watchmen, when he could be stabbed and left hidden somewhere in the country? No murderer would run such a risk.'

'Maybe he had attacked the man who killed him, and left him for dead, then his victim recovered and came here to exact his revenge?'

'In that case, why cut off his head?' asked Baldwin.

'To hide who it was?' Holcroft said, shrugging. Then his eyes widened. 'Maybe it was to *show* who it was! Perhaps someone wanted this man dead, and paid a killer to do it, but wanted the head as proof of his death!'

Simon gave him a look of astonishment. 'What on earth makes you think that someone would ask for a head to prove a murder?'

'It happened to St John,' the young monk interrupted eagerly.

Simon stared at him. He had hardly noticed Peter before. The monk looked as if he was seventeen or eighteen, certainly not twenty yet. His features were drawn and pale, as if he was recovering from a fever, and he had insipid, fair hair. 'I know that,' Simon told him. 'But it's a bit of a convoluted theory to explain this. I don't find it very convincing on an English summer's afternoon.'

'Neither do I,' Baldwin agreed. He looked at the portreeve. 'Where is the body now?'

The disgruntled Holcroft took them up the street and into a tavern. Walking through the screens, Baldwin glanced into the main room through the open door. 'A busy little place,' he observed.

'Yes, sir. And friendly. I was here myself only last night – I never thought I'd be back for something like this.'

He led them out through to the rear. They came into a yard enclosed by a wall of hurdles, with hens scratching in the dirt. A watchman sat on a stool, guarding the outhouse in which the body had been placed, a quart of ale at his side, and an old, rusty spear leaning against the wall. Seeing Holcroft he stood, gripping the spear shaft in both hands.

Inside, Simon was taken by the aroma. There was a delightful scent of apples, and when he looked, he saw a large press. Barrels along the wall gave off a wonderful yeasty smell, and from the potency of the odour, he guessed that a strong cider was brewing.

The body rested on planks laid across upright barrels. Baldwin walked up and stood beside it. In the presence of death, he felt a curious dislocation from his ordinary life. This empty figure was a reminder that life was fleeting. It was also evidence of a brutal murder, and Baldwin knew that if he was careful, he could learn enough from the corpse to help him catch the killer.

The body was still fully clothed. Baldwin called the guard in to help witness their post mortem, and began to undress it, pulling off the red leather jerkin and doublet, then the shirt. The arms were stiff with rigor mortis, but he persevered. After a while the doublet came off, and the hose, then the shirt, and Baldwin could study the dirty figure of a man, a man with strong arms and thighs, who had several minor scars and marks on his torso. 'He wasn't killed this morning,' he declared. 'He must have died last night, for his body is as cold as moorstone.'

'Anything else?' Simon asked.

Baldwin stood, one hand wrapped round his chest, the other cupping his chin while he stared. 'It's odd he has no purse. A cut-purse could have bungled his theft and got into a fight, I suppose . . .' He was silent a moment, then picked up the belt and studied it. The empty knife-sheath interested him. 'Strange, this. It held an ordinary single-edged knife of some sort, with a blade about one and a half inches wide and seven inches long.'

'That hardly sounds very interesting,' Simon observed.

'Look at the quality of the leatherwork. It's very good,

and there is a mark, a coat-of-arms embossed on it.'

'Do you recognise the arms?'

'No, I'm afraid not. That would make life too easy, wouldn't it!' He nodded to Edgar, and the two of them rolled the body over. 'Ah!'

'What?'

'This means that my theory of a cut-purse mucking up a simple waylaying is wrong. A thief might have knocked him on the head to ease his deed, but not stabbed him. Peter, do you have your papers? Then note this. There is a stab wound in his back. It is a little over an inch wide, about two inches to the left of his spine.' He broke off and reached for the shirt. Studying it at length, he dropped it and looked at the doublet and jerkin.

'What is it?' Simon asked.

'He was stabbed, but there is no corresponding cut in his shirt, only a stain. He was murdered while bare-chested, or wearing something else, and for some reason his shirt was put on him afterwards. What could be the reason for that?'

'Why should he be stabbed?' Holcroft said. 'I'd thought he died when his head was taken off.'

'No victim would remain still long enough to allow his head to be swept from his shoulders,' Baldwin said scathingly. 'His head was removed *after* he had died. He was stabbed and killed, and then for some reason his head was taken off and he was dressed in this shirt.'

'What was the point of that?' asked Holcroft.

'A good question.' Baldwin stood considering the body for some time. 'How old does he look to you, Simon?'

The bailiff put his head to one side. 'It's hard to say. Without a head and a face, I don't know.'

'It is hard,' Baldwin agreed. It was hard to tell anything from a headless man. His muscles were well-used, but that simply meant he was probably not a priest. Anyone else would have laboured, whether a knight, butcher, miner, or servant. Baldwin was despondent. What could a man learn from another's corpse when even the identity was a mystery? He forced himself to concentrate. No matter how difficult, he must do his best to discover the truth. Whoever the man was, he deserved to have his murder avenged.

There was not much body hair, but Baldwin had known men in their fifties who had less. 'He was not well-to-do: his hands are dirty with grime, and there are many calluses, so he was unlikely to have been a merchant. The belly is quite large, which makes him appear older, so he was not a poor peasant: he has eaten too well in his life. The skin is not soft like a youngster's, it is coarse. Surely he must be over twenty. Perhaps nearer forty, from the look of his stomach.'

'Why do you say that?' Holcroft asked.

'If he was younger, to be able to afford to fill himself with food and drink he would have to be well provided for, yet this man works with his hands still, so he doesn't appear rich. No, I would guess this man was in his late thirties. Not less.'

Simon averted his eyes. The sight of cartilage and blood, bone and muscle made him want to heave. It wasn't helped by the tang of apples. The musty sweetness of the fruit mixed with the fresh smell of human flesh, like raw pork; the association made the bailiff swallow quickly and move nearer the door.

Baldwin did not notice. Something about this dead man could tell him who the killer was, or if it couldn't, might at least point him towards the killer, and he was determined to seek out any clues.

'That is interesting,' he murmured as he studied the exposed flesh. He squatted near the neck and squinted at it. 'Peter, you should note that I do not think the head was taken off in one sweep of a sword or axe.'

'Why's that?' Holcroft asked, bending over Baldwin's shoulder. Simon winced and faced away.

'See here?' the knight pointed. 'The flesh has been sliced neatly where it has been sawn apart. This was no single blow of a sword, port-reeve. Look here, though.'

When Holcroft leaned nearer he saw that the knight was pointing at a small chip. 'That? It's only a bit of bone!'

Baldwin glanced up at him quizzically. 'Yes, a piece of bone from this man's spine. Don't you see? Ah well, I suppose it's not very important. The killer stabbed him and then cut his throat with a knife. Afterwards he used a heavy but not very sharp weapon to hack through the dead man's neck. He didn't use a knife to sever the bones as he might have done, shoving the point of the blade between the vertebrae and levering the head off, he sliced through the meat, and then used a heavy blade to smash through the bone, just like a butcher.'

'You think it was Will Ruby?' Holcroft gasped in disbelief.

Baldwin shot him a glance and stood up. 'I suspect anyone with access to large tools. This could just as easily have been done with a woodman's axe or a farmer's bill-hook as a butcher's cleaver. In fact, a cleaver is the least likely weapon, for any butcher would have used a sharp blade to cut through bone. This was blunted, and it crushed its way through. No, I do not have any idea who was responsible for this yet. But it is interesting: why *should* the murderer have decapitated his victim?'

Holcroft shrugged. 'I reckon we'll never know.'

Simon could feel a headache beginning. The smell was overpowering, and made him feel nauseous. It was a relief to hear Baldwin murmur, 'Perhaps we should ask the tavern-keeper what he knows of all this. The body was found nearby. Who is he?'

'*She*, sir. She's called Agatha.'

'Fine. Let's go and see what Agatha has to say for herself.'

Chapter Six

The tavern was much like any other. Benches, stools and trestles stood haphazardly on a floor of earth packed so solidly it was as hard as dried and cured oak. A thin scattering of straw lay in discoloured drifts to soak up the worst messes where drinkers had been ill. It was doing a good trade, with men, women and children sitting or standing, all with pots or jugs of ale. A crowd in a corner huddled round a game of merrils, placing bets and heralding each new move with groans or cheers.

Simon glanced round with interest. He felt a loyal irritation to see how well the traders of Tavistock were doing compared with his neighbours at Lydford.

To Baldwin it was merely a hectic tavern. Not as rough as an ordinary alehouse, yet not as exclusive as an inn, it brought the portmen and their families flocking to its hall to sup the keeper's good ale. He saw a woman deftly pouring from a jug. The port-reeve waved to her, and she nodded, then rolled her eyes skywards as another shout went up from the gamesters in the corner. She held up a hand in mute appeal to wait, then walked past them to the rooms at the other side of the screens.

'Sir, I don't think I should go in there,' Peter said plaintively.

'Why on earth not?' asked Baldwin.

'Well, there are lots of women and er . . .' He did not want to admit that the previous night he had almost been involved in a fight. At his shoulder, he was uncomfortably aware, was the port-reeve who had persuaded him to go.

'Don't worry, Peter. I shall protect you,' the knight said drily.

Holcroft led the way to a table, evicting a group of youngsters who had already enjoyed the festivities a little too enthusiastically. They moved off with a bad grace, leaving enough space for the men to sit. Within a few minutes, the alewife appeared.

Agatha had a round face, with apple-red cheeks and trailing brown hair that crept from beneath her coif. Her mouth was fixed in a friendly, professional smile. She walked to their table. Baldwin sat silently while Holcroft asked for ale for them, and explained who Baldwin and Simon were. She shot a look at the monk, and Simon realised that the Abbot had sent the novice not only to take notes, but also to lend his authority to their enquiries.

The port-reeve shook his head as she fled to the buttery. 'Poor bugger. What a way to be killed – and then to be left in a garbage heap like that. Why'd someone do such a thing?'

'When we find the murderer, we shall be sure to ask him,' Baldwin said. 'Perhaps now we should be bending our efforts to that aim. Have you been taking careful notes, Peter?'

The monk glanced up, and nodded quickly. 'Yes, sir. Everything's written down.'

Simon peered at the scribbled writing and was glad he would not himself have to decipher the scrawl. The boy had tried to copy everything down as it was said, and the result was a mess of blots.

'Agatha,' Baldwin said, as the woman returned with a tray of filled cups, 'the body found last night – you have seen it?' She nodded, and he continued, 'Did you recognise the man?'

She wiped her hands on her apron. To Simon she could have been pregnant, her tunic billowed so massively from under her belt. Her gaze darted about the seated men as she spoke. 'It's hard to recognise a man with no head. I think I have seen the clothes before, though.' She glanced at the port-reeve, and Baldwin saw a light flickering in her eyes. 'I don't want to put a man's neck in the noose, but there was a fellow in here last night dressed something like that. He wore a doublet and hose like the ones on the body, but I've never seen him before last night.'

'Of course!' Holcroft exclaimed, and slapped his thigh. He had forgotten the man with Elias – seeing Lizzie with Torre had wiped his memory like a damp cloth cleaning letters from a slate.

'You're quite sure of that?' Baldwin continued. 'It was no one you knew from a previous fair, for example?'

'I can't be certain.' She shrugged and jerked her head towards the guests at other tables. 'It's not as if I was sitting around with nothing to do. At fair-time, there's too many foreigners around to be able to chat to them all. I don't know who he was.'

'What was he doing? Was he alone, or with someone else?'

'He came in alone,' she agreed unwillingly. Agatha did not like to put the blame on anyone, especially when it was a local who was a regular customer.

'Did he sit with anyone?' Baldwin probed.

She was quiet a moment longer, but then she glanced at the port-reeve and the words burst from her in a torrent. 'No, sir. I hate to talk ill of another, but he was here with a local man: Elias. The stranger came in here all alone, but he asked me about Elias, and when he came in, the stranger sent for him. The two of them sat down together, and it was like they were old friends. He was with Elias for some time.'

Simon leaned forward. 'Were they here for long?'

'Long enough for four pints each.'

'Who left first of the two?'

'They went out together, just after the bell for compline.'

'And it looked as if they were friendly?' Baldwin said.

She considered. 'Friendly enough,' she admitted at last.

'Elias was never a great one for talking, but last night he seemed to get quite excited.'

'Excited?' Holcroft leaped on the word. 'Was he excited enough to have a fight with the man, do you think?'

She threw him a bored, casual glance. 'Come on, David, they didn't pull daggers on each other in here, and that's all I know. If they went out and had a fight, I never got to hear about it. I only just caught a glimpse of them going as it was. This is an alehouse; I was serving ale, remember? It's not like I can pass the time of day with all my customers, especially when they're already in a bad mood. He came back, though.'

Baldwin suppressed a grin. The alewife was a shrewd woman to deal with, and wouldn't suffer fools gladly. 'You say Elias returned?'

'Yes. He was out for a few minutes, then hurried back in and had a bit more to drink.'

Simon stirred. 'Did you serve him?' When she nodded, he continued, 'Did you see any blood on him?'

Baldwin watched her carefully. This was important. Killers were always blooded by their victims. The murderer of the corpse in the alley was bound to have been spattered – especially since he had hewn off the head.

She considered, then shook her head slowly. 'No, none at all.'

Baldwin asked, 'Did he bring a bag or anything with him when he came back?'

'No.'

'It means nothing,' Holcroft said. 'He could have left the head in his house or somewhere.'

'Possibly,' Baldwin agreed, but dubiously. 'This Elias – who is he?'

'He's the man who lives next to Will Ruby's shop,' said Holcroft quickly. 'Runs a cookshop. The pile of rubbish was all his.'

'I think we should go and have a word with him, then.'

Baldwin and Simon walked from the room with Edgar. Peter hurriedly stowed away his pen and inks, and was about to chase after when he caught a curious expression on the alewife's face. She was staring at the port-reeve with something like sympathy, while he looked at her with what Peter could only guess was mute appeal.

Elias sat down on his barrel and wiped a hand over his brow before peering up at the sun and yawning. His neck still ached after sleeping on his market stall's trestle, and he was only glad that it hadn't rained.

As another face appeared, he levered himself up and bobbed his head ingratiatingly. His customer reeled off a long order, and Elias blinked as he listened. As the string of instructions ended, he sprang into action and fetched the capon baked in pastry, ten roast finches and a rabbit. This being a fair, he quickly added the prices: eight pennies for the capon, one for the finches, and four for the rabbit, and then rounded up the amount to sixteen pennies. Grumbling, his client paid his money. He knew well enough that although the money was more than he would have to pay in the town normally, it was not so much as a London trader would have charged.

When Antonio da Cammino asked for a mackerel, Elias set it to cook beside his fire. He recognised the Venetian from the tavern the night before, though he didn't know Antonio's name. Antonio's face reminded him of the previous night, and Elias took a long swallow from his pot.

He needed to. Seeing Jordan Lybbe again had been a shock, and then there was the horror in the alley. He wasn't used to such sights. It has been all he could do to pour his drink when he had got back to the tavern afterwards, and not tip the whole lot onto the floor, his hand was shaking so much.

Of course he knew he would have to pay the amercement

for not clearing up the rubbish heap, but he couldn't go back to it. Not now.

Two grimy children turned up, fresh from playing out in the meadows, demanding the price of all of the cooked meats on display, and trying to haggle. Elias was known among the town's youngsters for being generous with his food. He took their money, but gave them a honey-coated roast starling each as well as the thrushes they had ordered. Then the fish was ready, and he served it to the patient Venetian.

Taking the fish, Antonio paid, then stood by the trestle and broke up the steaming, yellow flesh. When he caught sight of Elias' gaze, he motioned to his meal. 'It is all right to eat here, yes?'

'Oh yes, master,' said Elias, and was about to ask where he had come from, for he couldn't recognise the accent, when Antonio waved to catch his son's attention.

Pietro strolled over, Luke behind him, and surveyed Elias' offerings, tossing a coin negligently. He pointed at a cooked leg of lamb, and when Elias had cut off a large slice, the young man flicked the coin down, then stood talking with his father, both conversing in a language Elias couldn't recognise.

The crowd was growing now. Elias had to sit again, uncomfortably aware of the itching in his hands that heralded another fit of the shaking. The acid in his stomach was bubbling furiously like water boiling over a fire, and he took a good swallow of ale to calm it. Sitting under a hot sun, next to his brazier and fire, he felt as if he himself was cooking, and he longed for the hour when he could close his stall and fall on his blanket behind his trestle. During the three days of St Rumon's Fair, he had rented out his shop and rooms, so his stall would be his bed.

He belched and winced, saw the two men glance in his direction. At the expression on the younger man's face he froze. It was a look of contempt so powerful that Elias could

feel himself colouring. He made a deprecating gesture, but
before he could speak, they had both turned and left.

As they made off, Elias found another figure darkening
his stock. 'Yes, sir? Oh . . .'

Friar Hugo held out his bowl questioningly, and Elias
dropped a couple of starlings into it. 'Thank you, my son,'
he said as he walked away in the same direction as the
Venetians.

'Christ Jesus!' Elias muttered, then stood as another
figure appeared. 'Sir, can I help you? Oh, it's you.' At least
he's changed out of the dead man's clothes, he thought to
himself.

Jordan Lybbe grunted, but Elias could see that his
attention was elsewhere, and when he followed Lybbe's
gaze, he could see that it was on the friar and the others.
Without speaking, Lybbe left the stall and walked after
them.

Edgar appeared to lose his lethargy as soon as they entered
the bustling temporary streets of the fairground. All through
the questioning and post mortem, he had been idle, looking
bored with events, but now, as soon as they came upon the
first series of shops, he became alert, casting about him
with the intent concentration of a hound seeking a trail.

His master gave him a long, hard look. Edgar must be
keen on his woman, and that augured badly for Baldwin's
own future. There was a worrying implication: if Edgar was
to marry, would he still want to serve his master? There
was a trend now for free men to leave their masters and buy
property in towns, to become tradesmen. Baldwin did not
know how he would be able to manage his estates without
Edgar by his side, chivvying the villeins and making sure
the business of the estate proceeded smoothly. It was with a
sense of impending doom that he watched his servant.

They passed through the lines of gaily coloured benches
and trestles laden with cloths. Heavy, rough burels were

rare now, though poorer villeins still had uses for the cheap and hairy material. Several of the local traders were selling grey and russet-coloured material alongside 'dossens' – the cheaper bolts of twelve yards length and one yard in width. Baldwin saw a monk discussing the quality of bolts with a dealer, and assumed that the thoughtful-looking cleric, who shook his head in disagreement only to put in a counter-bid, must be the Abbey's almoner.

Peter, when Baldwin caught a glimpse of the lad's face, was enthralled, staring about him with wide-eyed fascination. The youth had never been to a fair. Never before had he seen such a variety of goods; it looked as if the produce of the whole world was here, and all in profusion. They walked past glove-makers, tailors, cordwainers and tanners. There were candles, soaps, herbs of all kinds, spices all set out in pots, and seeds from as far away as Constantinople. Each alley held new attractions and wonderful exhibits. It irked the young monk that Baldwin did not let them pause until they came to the cattle-market.

Here they watched for a few minutes as a huge red-brown beast was led round the ring. Its mad black eyes glared at the spectators while they watched, and the bargaining began. Peter stood open-mouthed while the calls were shouted out. A deal was soon agreed, and the bidders all moved forward to pay for their share; under the fair's rules it was illegal to hoard any provisions within the town in case a trader should try to gain a monopoly and thereby cause a dearth. Anyone who put in a bid for the meat of an ox must be allowed a share to prevent any single dealer controlling all meat.

Peter was aware that the others were moving on again, and he trailed after them. He'd not realised how diverse the world was, and he murmured a quiet prayer to himself as he hurried on. A short way along the street, he stumbled and dropped the leather packet holding his quills and inks. He had to stoop to pick them up, and when he stood up again, he found he couldn't see the others any more. He stared about him with sudden anxiety.

Peter had only been a monk for a short time, and was still serving his novitiate. He had been at the Abbey school for some years, but had spent little time outside the Abbey itself. Now for the first time he was alone in a fair, and the mass of humanity was fearsome. He gathered up his package, but then stopped.

In front of him a young couple had appeared. He knew Pietro da Cammino from taking him to the inn the night before, but he'd never clapped eyes on Avice Pole.

Peter was young and impressionable, brought up to revere and idolise the image of the Madonna, and to his eyes Avice Pole was an angel. She was as fine and beautiful as the Abbey church carvings of Christ's mother. Her wide-set green eyes and a slightly tip-tilted nose gave her an air of amusement, as if she could see the best in everyone and everything in the world. She looked a kind and generous soul, he thought.

The novice watched as she passed. Pietro saw him but ignored him: he was only another monk, and there were enough of them at fair-time in Tavistock, especially with the mendicants, who spent their time alternately preaching and begging; but Avice beamed at Peter as she swept by, and that simple recognition melted his heart.

Then two irritable men brushed him aside. One was Antonio, but he didn't know Arthur Pole. In their train came Luke, who cursed him, and then he was alone once more. He was suddenly aware that the others must have moved on, and was about to set off after them when two more men hurried by, one of them a friar.

Peter didn't care. His mind was fixed on the graceful creature who had smiled at him.

Luke felt a quick discomfort when he realised he had shoved a monk from his path. It hadn't been intentional; he had thought it was just another cheaply dressed peasant. He'd only caught a glimpse of the robe before he elbowed the lad out of his way. By the time he'd spotted the tonsure it was too late.

But there was no time for regrets. Antonio da Cammino, his master, was displaying his annoyance by staying close behind his son and the girl, and Luke was hard pushed to keep up. The crowd that filled the alleys was bunched around particular stalls, and at each knot Antonio was slowed. As soon as he could, he forged ahead, trying to close the gap between himself and his son, and each time there was another delay for Luke, who was forced to batter his own way through. It was tiring – and more than a little ridiculous.

Luke set his jaw as he pushed through yet another group. Now they were entering a new lane, and here at last the passage was almost clear. He could breathe a little easier, and lengthened his stride.

The girl's father appeared a self-important little man to the servant – strong, but soft with easy living. Antonio and Arthur Pole hardly glanced in each other's direction, and Luke wasn't surprised. In his experience parents were rarely eager when their children found their own companions. Fathers were keen to arrange alliances in which wealth could be married to wealth, but neither Antonio nor the girl's father knew anything about the other. Their children had met and agreed to walk together almost before their parents had realised what was happening. Now they strolled side-by-side, neither one speaking but both greedily absorbing their children's words in case of an indiscretion.

Luke sighed. It was no surprise that his master should be worried. The very last thing he needed was for his son to start an amorous affair. Especially if it became serious.

He gave Pietro a shrewd look. Luke had never known him to get attached to girls before. That he should do so now, and with the daughter of a burgess was surprising:

Pietro knew how little time they had in Tavistock. But the servant had seen growing signs of rebellion for the last few months.

It was always the way. Sons would seek their own amusements, and Pietro had apparently decided that this girl was interesting – or possibly something of a challenge, Luke amended. The lad certainly seemed taken with her – he could hardly take his eyes off her. The servant eyed the girl appraisingly. Pietro had chosen well. She looked vulnerable, ready for a serious, mature attack from a worldly squire like Pietro. His stories of foreign travel, with his fashionable and expensive dress, should make his charms irresistible.

Luke had some experience of young and impressionable women. At one point he had married one, though he had left her behind when the French approached.

That was some years ago, when he had been living in the eastern marches of Gascony. He had scraped a decent enough living there, and if it hadn't been for the French attacks and their capture of swathes of the English King's territory, he would be there still. But the French were known to dislike those who had allied themselves to the English, and as soon as the first heralds appeared near his town, he had saddled his horse and escaped. Under the urge of homesickness, he had made for Bordeaux, to a place where he would hear English voices again, but the citizens of the town weren't charitable, and for months he had been close to starvation, begging and trying to find work, before he had met Antonio and his son.

He looked at his master again, seeing the bristling anger in Antonio's rigid shoulders, and shook his head. The girl might be worth a tumble, but he wondered if Pietro had realised how his father felt.

Chapter Seven

Peter caught up with Baldwin and the others near the leather-goods stalls. The next section included the poulterers and butchers. Will Ruby was there, and Baldwin saw that he watched the group with eyes that betrayed his anxiety.

Baldwin stood at the entrance of the lane where the cooks plied their trade and looked down the narrow way. There was an open space here where children ran, playing chasing games, while parents looked on indulgently. Rich and poor mixed together, all drinking or chewing their food.

Simon felt his purse. The smell of cooking was making his mouth water. Onions and garlic, pepper and meats of all kinds were boiling or roasting all round as he moved in among the stalls, and he eyed the offerings with an appreciative eye. It had been a long time since his breakfast.

Holcroft led the way. He walked quickly, but Simon could see that he was observing the people and wares on offer as he went, and the bailiff was impressed by his dedication. The man obviously took his responsibilities seriously, and was always on the lookout for an infringement of the fair's rules.

Elias saw Holcroft appear and groaned to himself. He had been about to leave for a few minutes, to go and duck his head in the water trough in the cattle pens. His skull was a thick, dense boil of pain and he longed to lance it. With the blazing sun overhead being reflected from white tunics and bright awnings, he had to squint to try to lessen the agony.

'Hello, David,' he said, trying to sound cheery. 'How are you today?'

'I'll be better when I've got your money.'

'My money? But why's that?'

'You know why. I warned you about the garbage.'

'Oh. Well, I tried to get it cleared, but you've got no idea how long it took. I wheeled ten loads over to the midden and then—'

'Quiet, Elias,' Holcroft rasped. 'I'll get the beadle to collect the money next week. I don't care what your excuses are. Especially since—'

Baldwin smoothly interrupted him before he could give away any details of the dead body, pointing to a pie and asking, 'What is in that one?'

Holcroft subsided while the cook reached over and picked up the golden crust and eulogised its filling of goose and ham.

'It sounds very good. I might take one. First, though—'

This time it was Baldwin's turn to be interrupted. A heavy-set watchman broke through the crowd and went to the port-reeve. 'There's a deal being arranged between the King's official and a horse-dealer. You're needed to witness it.'

'Oh, God's blood!' Holcroft muttered. As port-reeve, it was his duty to validate any large transactions. There were heavy fines for a trader who did not have him witness their business, for the Abbey's portion depended on the port-reeve's mark on the papers.

He threw a harassed look at Baldwin, who said understandingly, 'Leave it to us. We can let you know what is happening later.'

The port-reeve nodded, his eyes going from Simon to Baldwin, while the watchman tapped his sword hilt irritably, then looked at Elias. 'You tell these gentlemen the truth, Elias. They're here on the Abbot's authority. If I hear you've been talking rubbish, I'll come and check all your stock for weights, understand? And for every pie that's under you'll get a day in the pillory.'

His mouth wide open with dismay, Elias stared as the port-reeve marched off with the watchman close behind. 'What was that all about?'

'Elias, you have the shop next to Will Ruby's, don't you?'

The cook shut his mouth with a snap. Baldwin could see he was nervous, and his hands shook with the occasional twitch of the heavy drinker. That, the knight thought, would explain his pale complexion. Baldwin did not drink to excess, and held little regard for those who did. They were invariably foolish or stupid, to his mind. In his experience only those who had lived through a severe shock or those who were weak in spirit would resort to drinking excess-ively. Elias looked a rather pathetic creature, the kind to crumble at the first blow of fate. His face was skinny and freckled, under an unruly mop of reddish-brown hair. The thin nose and close-set eyes made him appear shifty, and fleshy pink lips gave him an unwholesome appearance as if he was suffering from a disease.

'Where were you last night, Elias?' Baldwin asked.

'Why? Who are you?' he demanded, glancing at Peter as the monk spread paper and began to write.

'I am Baldwin Furnshill, Keeper of the King's Peace in Crediton, and this is Simon Puttock, bailiff of Lydford Castle. The Abbot has asked us to investigate a murder. Where were you last night?'

'I was here.'

'Where were you before that, Elias?'

'It took ages to get all this ready.'

'I see. Let me tell you where you were, then. You were at the tavern near your shop, weren't you?'

'If you know, why ask?'

Simon grated, 'Elias, we're working for the Abbot, trying to get to the bottom of a killing.'

He sulkily looked from one to the other. 'All right,'

he said ungraciously. 'I *was* at the tavern.'

'That's better. Who else was there?' said Baldwin.

Elias winced as a sharp pain stabbed at his temple. He sat on his barrel and screwed his eyes into slits as he stared up at the Keeper. 'It was the start of the fair – there was loads in there.'

'Whom did you recognise, Elias?' Baldwin asked less gently.

'Several of them: the port-reeve himself was there later. Four watchmen from Denbury were all sitting at a table; the one who came for David just now was one of them. Torre, from Ashburton way, he was there, and a merchant with his wife and daughter. Oh, and three men with a monk guiding them, though they didn't stay. I'd never seen them before.'

'What did they look like?' Baldwin asked.

He shrugged. All visiting merchants looked the same to him. He began repositioning some of his pies and meats. 'They were here – you only just missed them. I reckon they're father and son. They look sort of similar.'

'The man you were sitting with,' Baldwin said, watching the cook's face closely. 'Who was he?'

'Sorry?'

There was a note of uncertainty in his voice that caught Baldwin's interest. 'In the tavern you were sitting with a man for a goodly time. You had many drinks with him. Later you left the tavern with him. Who was he?'

'No one . . . It was just someone who came up to me and wanted to talk.'

'You left the tavern together, so where did you go?' Simon pressed.

'We didn't go anywhere. He happened to leave the place just as I was going out to the privy, that's all.'

Baldwin stared at him, and Elias' eyes dropped. 'He is dead. Murdered.'

The cook dropped a pie. He stared at the knight with his

mouth open in shock. 'No! He . . . he can't be!'

Simon watched him, puzzled. Elias had not been surprised to hear that there had been a murder, but his shock
on hearing about his companion was surely unfeigned.

'You spent the evening with a man in a red leather jerkin,
and left the tavern with him. And now we find a man in a red
leather jerkin has been murdered and hidden in your
rubbish. So *who was he?*'

Elias retreated under the blast of the knight's sudden
bellow. 'Sir, I . . .' Elias shivered. This questioning was
confusing him, and he regretted the ales he had drunk the
night before. The two men standing so aggressively before
him, the one dark and angry, the scar on his cheek shining,
the younger one, the bailiff, a sinister grin on his face as he
watched Elias squirm, both made him fear for his freedom.

But he had no idea how to escape from them. He felt like
a rabbit caught in a snare: he could try to pull away, but only
at the risk of harming Jordan. Yet if he were to stay silent
without an attempt at protecting himself, he might get
arrested.

It was obvious that someone would have seen him
leaving, but how could he have known that the body would
be so quickly discovered, and that he would be linked to
Jordan so easily? He shook his head, trying to clear it from
the fog that thickened his brain. It was impossible to tell
them the truth. That way led to ruin. An escape occurred to
him. 'Sir, I don't know who he was.'

'You're lying,' Simon said. 'We already know he asked for
you. You expect us to believe that he knew you, yet you
knew nothing of him?'

'It's the truth,' Elias protested stubbornly.

'No,' said Baldwin shortly. 'It is not true. You knew him.'
Elias shook his head. To Baldwin he looked as determined
as a mule. On a whim the knight lowered his tone. 'Why
should a man stab his victim and then cut off his head?'

'His head was off?' Elias curled his lip in revulsion.

'More than that,' said Simon shortly. 'His head was taken away. We don't know where it is.'

Elias shivered suddenly as if attacked with an ague. Baldwin was convinced he wasn't acting. There was nothing new in a man being murdered with a knife – almost all murders were committed with knives or daggers. But removing a victim's head was a different matter.

'Who would . . . Why?' the cook stammered. 'I mean, what would someone do that for?'

Simon crossed his arms and leaned against the awning's support. 'That's a good question,' he said.

'Elias, why will you not tell us who the man with you last night was?' Baldwin asked.

'I don't know him,' Elias asserted doggedly.

The knight surveyed him quizzically. 'You were with the man for ages. It is obvious you must have known him. Yet you continue in this ridiculous denial. Perhaps we should remove you to the gaol so you can reconsider.'

They both saw the fear and doubt twist the little man's visage. Simon felt only contempt. The cook was weak. For some reason he was scared of letting the truth come out. But his very weakness was what made Baldwin doubt that Elias was capable of murder. He found himself recalling the corpse. It was strong and square with a barrel chest, the body of a man in his prime of health and strength. In life he must have been a little over middle height. His shoulders and biceps marked him out as a powerful figure.

The knight considered the frail man before him. Would so pathetic a character be capable of murder, he wondered – especially the murder of a strong man who was fit and healthy. Baldwin had met enough cut-throats who were willing to slip from a darkened alley to overcome their prey, but Elias did not have the air of one of them. His expression was not guilty, merely determined.

Baldwin had seen that expression before, and for a moment he wondered where, then it came to him. He had once caught a boy in one of his meadows, terrified sheep running all around. A lamb had disappeared, and the enraged knight had accused the lad of theft. While defiantly denying all complicity, the boy had refused to say what had happened. It was only later when Baldwin had found the missing lamb, dead and partly eaten, that he had discovered the truth. The lad's dog had chased the sheep and lambs. It had captured one of them and run away with it. But the dog was the boy's only friend and companion. He would prefer to be punished himself than see his dog killed.

The knight stared thoughtfully at the cook. He would not arrest Elias yet, he decided. There was no logic to his decision; it was based solely on his sense of justice. Elias was no footpad. Surely whoever had killed and decapitated the body, leaving it in the rubbish, was no weakling but a strong and powerful man in his own right.

No, he thought. He would leave the cook for now. If there was any more definite evidence against him, he could arrest him later. For the time being, Baldwin was content to keep an eye on him.

But when he reached the end of the alley in which Elias' stall lay, he couldn't help feeling he was taking a risk. 'Edgar,' he said to his man-at-arms, 'I don't think Elias is the killer, but he knows *something*. Stay here and keep an eye on him. I don't want him disappearing.'

Lybbe was in two minds which group to follow. Avice and her father were heading off towards the spicers' area, while it looked as though the Italians were returning to the Abbey. While he stood wavering, he caught sight of the friar.

Hugo was a few yards from him, his bowl loose at his side, peering after the Italians with a doubtful set to his features. Lybbe watched him with increasing interest. He had noticed the friar ahead of him all the way since he had left Elias' stall, but hadn't realised that the cleric was stalking the same prey. Discovering someone else curious about his quarry made him feel relief bordering on euphoria. If the friar held doubts about them too, Lybbe couldn't have been completely wrong.

If it had been a priest, Lybbe wouldn't have considered telling the man anything, but this was a grey friar, a Franciscan. He knew well enough that the Order had its black sheep, but this wandering friar looked honest with his grubby habit and battered collecting bowl. He had the appearance of a man who took his duties seriously. Lybbe wondered whether he could confess to this one, and tell his story. The Franciscans were notorious for giving light penances on the basis that a light penance which would be performed was better than a strict one which could be ignored at the peril of the soul concerned.

Hugo raised his hands in indecision, and let them fall with apparent despondency. Lybbe, watching him closely, saw his irresolution. Slowly the cleric trudged back up the hill, away from the Poles and Camminos. As he neared Lybbe, the merchant started as he realised who it was; that decided him.

'Brother friar, would you like something for your bowl?'

Hugo glanced up at the quiet voice. 'Thank you, but I have everything I need.' Then his eyes widened. '*You!*'

'Brother, would you hear my confession?'

Holcroft nodded as the details were read out, and took the official stamp from his purse. He thumped it into the molten wax almost before the clerk had finished dripping enough on the parchment, and snapped, 'Is that all?' before stalking out.

He had intended to find a tavern to quench his thirst – he had no wish to see the bailiff or knight again immediately, but he had to pass by the horse-market. Here he idly whiled away some time watching the creatures being paraded round the ring before being put through their paces. It was always exciting to see the farm boys racing their mounts up and down the fields to demonstrate their speed and stamina.

Turning to fetch himself a cool quart of ale, he found a small knot of watchmen standing behind him. He almost walked straight into them. Giving a gesture of annoyance, he motioned to them to get out of his way, but they stood their ground, and with a sense of distaste, he saw that it was the men from Denbury. 'Well?'

'Sir.' It was Long Jack. His dark eyes were filled with a reserved concern. 'There's been a robbery.'

'Well? Get the details and find the felon. God's blood, do I have to do everything around here?' Then he froze as he noticed the man's face. 'What is it?'

'You'd better come with us, port-reeve.'

He followed behind. If it was bad enough to make Long Jack fearful, it must indeed be a dreadful act. He found himself holding back as the men forged a way through the crowd, unwilling to encounter whatever evidence they might force upon him. First a murder, now a robbery, and both had to happen in the year when *he* was in charge.

To his surprise he found he was being taken towards the butchers. The bull-baiting pen was empty now – the wounded cattle were being slaughtered and new ones had not yet arrived. The men took him up the alley to Will Ruby's stall. Here they stood back respectfully, leaving space for the port-reeve to enter, and after throwing them a suspicious glance, he sidled behind the trestle table and went to the sheltered space behind.

Ruby lay on a low palliasse, pale-faced, while his wife silently held a damp cloth to his temple. When they heard Holcroft approach, she leaped back, and her husband snatched up a club studded with nails from beside his makeshift bed. Seeing the port-reeve, he let it fall shame-facedly.

'What in God's name is all this about?' Holcroft demanded, astonished. He had never seen the butcher behave like this before. It was out of character, even if he had been robbed.

'Sorry, David. It's this attack, it's made me a bit twitchy.'

'Who was it, did you recognise him?'

Ruby gave him an odd look. 'No, I never saw him before.'

'What did he look like?'

'Didn't the watch tell you?'

'Tell me what?'

'Port-reeve, it was a monk! A damned monk robbed me!'

Chapter Eight

Abbot Champeaux waved the men to seats. Peter nervously hovered at the door, unsure whether to enter the Abbot's private chamber, and was delighted, though secretly fearful of committing a *faux pas* in such company, when the Abbot beckoned him in and motioned him to a seat.

Simon walked in after his friend and was surprised to see him halt only a few steps inside. Then he saw why. The Abbot was sitting at his great chair at the head of his table while the servants busied themselves preparing bowls, towels and water for washing. At the Abbot's side was Simon's wife, and next to her was another woman.

The bailiff had always thought his wife to be the most lovely woman he had ever seen: Margaret's body was slender but strong, her face still free of wrinkles and un-marked by the grief that so often made features prematurely haggard, and her thick golden hair gleamed like a flame in the summer sunshine. But the woman next to her was beautiful in another way.

As the Abbot introduced him to the lady, Baldwin stood fixed to the spot. He could see red-gold tresses protruding from her coif, which contrasted with her bright blue eyes. Her face was regular, if a little round; her nose was short and too small; her mouth looked over-wide and the top lip was very full, giving her a stubborn appearance; her fore-head was broad and high: but the knight considered the sum of her imperfections to be utter perfection.

'Jeanne? Surely that is not a local name?' he asked.

She smiled, and he was secretly delighted to see how her cheeks dimpled. 'No, sir. I was named in Bordeaux.'

'Are you staying in the Abbey?'

'The Abbot has given me a guestroom near the court gate. It is where I used to stay with my husband when we came to the fair.'

The Abbot interrupted. 'You may know, Sir Baldwin, that as Abbot of Tavistock, I hold a baron's rank. I have to maintain some knights to supply the host in time of war. Sir Ralph was one of these. It was nothing to arrange for a room to be available for his widow.'

'Widow?'

'Sir Ralph de Liddinstone sadly caught a fever earlier in the summer.'

Fever, Jeanne thought, hardly described the raging agony of his last days. She had never thought that so hardy a man could collapse with such speed. But she was grateful that he had.

Her husband had been a brute. She could admit it now. Ralph at first had met her ideals of a truly courteous knight, being kind and thoughtful, loving and gentle – but that had changed when she had been unable to bear his children. He blamed her for it, as if she was deliberately witholding his heir from him. Each time a friend of his had announced another child, Ralph had looked on her more blackly, until at last he had hit her.

That first time her shock had been so great she hadn't really felt any pain, but from then on he had taken to drinking ever more heavily, sulking in his hall, and afterwards, as if as a diversion from bedding her, he would punch or kick her, once taking a riding crop to her bare back.

No, Jeanne was grateful that God had taken him from her.

Baldwin saw the fleeting sadness in her eyes. 'My lady, I apologise if I unthinkingly reminded you of—'

'It is nothing,' she said lightly, giving him a look that

made his heart swell. 'It is all over. And the Abbot here has been very kind.'

'My dear, I have done nothing. The Abbey has a duty to provide hospitality.'

'Abbot, you have let me stay in my home, you have loaned me your steward to make sure the house is well run during the harvest so we have food for the winter, and you have made me your friend. That is more than nothing.'

Baldwin nodded. Many abbots or priors would want a widow out so that their lands could be more efficiently controlled by a man. It confirmed the impression of kindness and generosity he had earlier formed of the Abbot. 'So, er, are you here for the fair?'

'Yes. My husband and I used to come here every year for St Rumon's Fair, and the Abbot was good enough to ask me again, even though I am a widow now.'

Margaret saw with near disbelief that her friend Baldwin was more keen and interested in this woman than in all the others she had paraded in front of him over the last years. She gave a tiny sigh of frustration that all her work had been wasted, but then studied Jeanne carefully. Apparently he was attracted to this red-haired woman from Liddinstone: if she could make Baldwin happy, Margaret would do all in her power to make sure he won her.

Seeing Baldwin was awestruck, Margaret turned to her. 'Jeanne, I have to make several purchases at the fair, and my husband and Baldwin are poor company, especially when they have the excuse of a murder to investigate. Would you mind joining me in search of cloth and plate?'

Jeanne threw a quick glance at the knight, who stood uncertainly. She could see that he was fumbling for words, and the sight of the knight's shyness was a balm to her soul after years of being told she was worthless because she was barren. 'I would be delighted.'

The Abbot was old now, older than many, but he had not missed the interest in Jeanne's eyes as she surveyed

Baldwin. It would be pleasant indeed, he felt, if St Rumon's Fair could unite a couple such as this. He usually ate with his monks in the refectory, and he would often invite visitors to join him there, but it would not be conducive to the monks' concentration to have women in their midst, and it would be equally unthinkable for the Abbot to leave them in a separate room, so today he had decided to invite his guests to eat with him in his hall. Now he wondered whether this decision could lead to a fortunate outcome.

'So, Sir Baldwin, have you enjoyed any success?'

'Um? Oh, we have found out a little, but what we have uncovered appears only to add to the muddle. We think the murder happened around compline – the man we *think* was the victim was seen leaving the tavern just after the bell tolled. But we still cannot confirm who the dead man was.'

'At least that diverts attention from us,' the Abbot said, nodding to Jeanne. 'We were here with my Venetian guests as the compline bell rang.'

Jeanne asked, 'Does no one recognise him?'

'Not with his head gone. He was a merchant as far as anyone knows, and you know the number of merchants who come here for the fair. Until we find his head, it's hard to prove who he was.'

'Good God! So we may never know who the poor soul was,' sighed the Abbot.

'That is possible. Still, we have made some little progress,' Baldwin said, and told them about their talks with the alewife and cook.

'Does that not give you cause to arrest Elias?' the Abbot asked uncertainly. 'If he left the tavern with the man, and the man was not seen alive again, surely that makes it all the more likely that it was him who did the murder.'

'The more I consider it, the more I think Elias is unlikely to be the killer. He can't be so stupid! If he was to murder, why would he leave the body so close to his shop? If he wanted to hide the body, he would take it inside, surely, and conceal it more effectively. And if he did stab the man and cut off the head, he would have been covered in blood, but he returned to the tavern with no such stains or marks on him. Then again, if he did kill, where could he have hidden the head? The alewife said he returned quickly after leaving.'

'There are some things we could check,' Simon said thoughtfully. 'We could search his house. If he had little time to hide the head, surely it would be inside. Perhaps we will find blood or something else incriminating.'

'That is a good idea,' Baldwin said. He looked at the Abbot. 'Could you arrange for us to do that?'

'I shall speak to Holcroft and tell him to have a watchman join you,' he said. 'For now, don't look so fretful! You can only do your best; and it's difficult to see how you could be expected to resolve a murder when you don't even know who the dead man was.'

Margaret saw Baldwin smile politely, but she knew him too well to believe that it was genuine. The knight disliked puzzles. He always wanted to find the truth in any situation, and she was convinced that he was irritated by the paucity of facts upon which he could build a case. She saw him open his mouth, but before he could speak there was a knock at the door. A monk opened it and stood back to let the visitors enter.

Peter was standing near the door, and when he looked up he saw the Venetians. Seeing them reminded him of the girl, and the memory brought the blood rushing to his face. He hardly heard the Abbot's introductions.

'Ah, my friends, please meet Antonio da Cammino and his son Pietro, from Venice. They have been visiting the Bishop of Exeter, and came here to see the fair and discover whether they might be able to profit from it.'

As he went round the people in the room and introduced them all to the Italians, Margaret noticed that the youth made no attempt to display interest. He hardly bothered to meet the gaze of the men as he was introduced, and soon walked to the window, peering out with apparent petulance.

His father was plainly disconcerted at such rudeness, and threw a despairing glance at his son's back. Margaret walked over to divert him. It would be inexcusable for the two to argue in the Abbot's chamber. 'Sir, have you just arrived?'

'No, I have been here for a day already.' She was surprised that he spoke perfect English, with only the faintest trace of an accent. He saw her confusion, and his face lightened. 'You are surprised to hear me speak your tongue so well? I was born in this country. My father was a merchant and lived here for long periods while I was young. I learned English before I learned my own language.'

'And you come back to England often? Are you on business now?'

It was hard to place his age, she thought. His looks were timeless, with an easy poise that was entirely foreign. His eyes wrinkled with a charming, and flattering, appreciation. 'Yes, I am here to discuss matters with the good Abbot.'

'But you will have some time for diversions?' she asked. 'To visit the fair and see the things on sale?'

'Oh, yes! I have already been to the fair to see what kind of goods are offered. It is more varied here than many other fairs, especially in Venice.' His eyes left her and went to his son, who stood with his back to the people in the room, one arm resting on the wall by the window.

'And you, Pietro?' she asked as he turned to face the others.

'Me, *signora*? You ask about diversions? There is nothing I want in this town, save one thing,' he said quietly. 'But I am not allowed that.'

'If all you can do is carp and moan, leave us and seek your own amusement! Do not insult the Abbot's hospitality,' his father said coldly.

There was silence in the room as the two men eyed each

other, the son pale, the older man with an angry gleam in
his light grey eyes. The youth shook his head in a quick
gesture of despair, and walked from the room.

The Abbot poured Antonio wine and waved him towards
a seat, and the man gave an embarrassed shrug as he
accepted it. 'I must apologise for my son. I am sorry he was
so ungracious, my lord Abbot.'

'The young are so often difficult to understand,'
Champeaux observed.

While the men chatted, Margaret sat in a corner with
Jeanne. The men's conversation revolved around the
business of the fair, and she was uninterested. Matters of
finance, such as how many visitors were likely to come over
the three days of the fair, how many horses would be sold
and whether the King's own cloth procurers would deign to
arrive, were of supreme unimportance to her. For Margaret,
the only interest in the market lay in seeing all the goods on
display, and buying something for her daughter back at
Lydford.

'Were you married to Sir Ralph for long?' she asked
tentatively.

'For five years, I think.'

'You must have found the moors a strange sight after
Bordeaux.'

'I did, although there was a memory of it for me. I was
orphaned when I was young, and my uncle took me to live
with him in Bordeaux, but before that I had lived not far
from Tiverton to the north, so seeing Devon again was to
see the land where I should have been living if my parents
had not died. The only hardship was living so far from a
town, but I soon became used to it.'

Margaret nodded. She could imagine that for a town-
dweller the move to the wilds of Dartmoor would have been
hard. 'When I return to Lydford, you must come and visit
us. It is hard for a widow when so few people live nearby.
You will make new friends with those we know in Lydford.'

'That would be very kind of you,' Jeanne said, and her gaze fell upon Baldwin. When she glanced back at Margaret, her eyebrow was raised in a silent question, and Margaret had to stifle a giggle. She had no idea her plan was so transparent.

'Do you have any children?' she asked, and saw a shadow pass over her new friend's face.

'No, none. It has been the regret of my life.'

'We only have the one. Our son died this year,' Margaret said softly.

This was the first time she had felt able to leave her daughter behind since her son, Peter, had died. When he had gone, she had almost suffered a brain fever, especially since she had felt as if she had also lost her husband. Simon had always been a model husband, but he felt the lack of a son very acutely. When Peter had been born, Simon was delighted, seeing in his boy a future companion who would carry on his name, and perhaps begin a dynasty that could become a noble family. The shock when their son had died had been all the greater.

She glanced at him. Simon was listening to the conversation and adding his own comments. The men were talking about tin now, and she could see that the Abbot was pleased with what he heard from his bailiff. Simon, she knew, was respected among the miners because he had shown himself to be shrewd and fair, upholding the rights of the tinners whenever he could, but punishing them when they tried to overstep the mark. Seeing the Abbot treating her husband's remarks with such respect made her feel a glow of pride. Abbot Champeaux was an important man in Devon.

Baldwin, she could see, was still worrying at the problem of the murdered man. She wished they would return to discussing the killing; it was vastly more interesting than this talk of metal and wool. Her attention wandered to the anxious features of Antonio da Cammino.

He was staring at the door through which his son had left, and looking at him, Margaret could feel a little of his pain. Margaret was a sensible woman, born and raised on a farm, and she had seen how young creatures could turn on their parents. Seeing Antonio's expression made her remember that no matter how careful were the parents, their children could always prove to be a disappointment. Fleetingly she wondered how her dead son might have turned out.

Simon saw the sudden dullness in his wife's eyes and quickly left the conversation, bringing the bottler to top up her wine.

While he spoke to Abbot Champeaux and Cammino, Baldwin noticed Margaret and Simon together. They looked happy with each other again, now that both had overcome their sadness. He could watch the affection between Simon and his wife with pleasure, but it sometimes reminded him of his own loneliness. Then he caught a measuring look from Jeanne.

It made him consider his position. When he had joined the Templars he had taken the vow of chastity. Yet since his Order had been destroyed by the Pope's avarice, he considered his oaths annulled. The Pope had demanded obedience, and had then betrayed his knights, so how could the oaths of poverty and chastity be valid?

Baldwin was proud not to have succumbed to lust as so many of his peers did so regularly, but he could admit to himself that now he was adrift in the secular world, without the great purpose of the Templars to order his life, he felt the same urges as his fellows. He wanted a wife for a companion. And he wanted a son to continue his name.

His attention was drawn back as the Venetian spoke. 'My lord Abbot, I hear that a man has been found dead. Is that right?'

'I fear so, Antonio. He appears to have been killed out near the tavern on the Brentor road.'

'A great shame, the poor man,' Cammino said, shaking his head.

'Yes. I am fortunate indeed to have Sir Baldwin and Simon here. They are experienced in finding killers. I am sure they will soon discover the murderer.'

'Yes. Of course.' Cammino was thoughtful for a moment, then he glanced at the door. 'My lord Abbot, ladies, Sir Baldwin, Simon – I fear I should find my son and ensure that he is not making a fool of himself somewhere else.' He took his leave of them, his servant following him through the door.

When Baldwin caught a glimpse of the Abbot's expression, he saw that it betrayed relief. Champeaux made no effort to hide his feelings. 'It is well said that a man's worst enemy is his son – the son always knows how to hurt. So, Sir Baldwin, is there anything else you will need to conduct your enquiry?'

'Hmm? Oh, no.' The knight's gaze was firmly locked on the door through which the two Venetians had left. 'No, I think I have everything I need, thank you.'

'Good. In that case, let us dine. I know *I* am hungry!'

Holcroft walked slowly and deliberately on his way to the brewers' stalls. More than before, he felt he needed a drink, and not a weak ale.

A monk had robbed Will Ruby! The idea was mad, yet Ruby had been convincing. He had seen the Benedictine, had bowed to him, acknowledging the man, and as soon as he passed, had been struck on the head. While he was on the ground, stunned, his purse was grabbed, there was a flash of steel, and he had lost his money. At the time he was glad that the blade had cut only the thongs of his purse and hadn't stabbed his heart, but as he said to the port-reeve, if this was to get out, there would be danger for any monk in the town.

That was the rub, and Holcroft knew it. It was

inconceivable that a real monk could be guilty, it had to be someone masquerading. But if this got out, people would at best look askance at a monk in the street. If he didn't let it be known that someone was dressing in monk's garb to steal, the man could continue unimpeded, but if Holcroft did, it would be impossible for a monk to walk abroad – at the fair almost everyone was a foreigner, and few would know one of the real monks.

He sipped at his beer. The story would be bound to get about if there was another theft; he was lucky that the first man to be attacked was a townsman wary of causing offence to the Abbot. The next merchant to be robbed was likely to be someone from out of town, and then the news would become common knowledge, and when it did, there was the risk that a mob could form. Tavistock had ever been a quiet, safe town, with few of the riots so common to great cities like Bristol and London, but Holcroft knew perfectly well that there was resentment among some of the population at the wealth of the Abbey. Like dried tinder, mutiny required but a tiny spark to ignite an all-consuming flame, and news that a monk was robbing people could be that spark.

He had no choice: he must tell the Abbot. Finishing his ale, he set the empty pot back on the table and stared at it. When he glowered around him there was no sign of a Benedictine habit, which was a relief, but that only meant that the thief was somewhere else, waiting to strike the first passer-by with a filled purse.

Holcroft set off towards the Abbey with a heart that had sunk so far it felt as if it was dragging on the ground behind him.

In the fairground the excitement of the morning had died a little. Now the visitors walked more speculatively, with less urgency, as they realised that there was plenty more for all to buy and no need to rush to get stock from the first stall to display something suitable.

People strolled along the thronged streets and alleys, measuring the wares, assessing their worth and comparing the goods from one stall with those of the next.

Elias could see how the customers wandered from one place to another, and was glad that he sold meats and pies. With his business, people wanted what he had or they didn't. There was none of that seeing something on one trestle, then rushing back to another merchant and telling him that the same cloth, or gloves, or shirt, could be purchased for at least a penny less five stalls up. For Elias, it was a simple case of 'What's in that pie? Oh, good, I'll take one.'

He sat on his barrel and rested his back against the pole of the awning. A jug of ale in his lap, he gradually allowed the warmth of the sun to ease his eyelids shut. It was so good to sit and soak up the heat.

Elias had married, but his wife had died in childbirth with their second child. His first had succumbed to a strange disease which made him short of breath and sneeze in the spring, and though Elias had thought that he should be safe enough when he got to ten years old, the cook had returned home one afternoon to find his boy lying blue-lipped and pale in the hall, gasping sporadically for breath. Panicking, Elias had rushed to the Abbey, and begged the doorman to fetch a monk to help, but by the time the man had found one, his boy was dead.

The cook sniffed and took another long draught of ale. It had been hard, but after burying his wife and child, he had settled into a routine. Working hard to keep his business going took up most of his day, and then there was always the tavern and Lizzie or another girl. All in all he was reasonably content.

The barrel rocked and he came to with a sudden alarm. Standing over him were two of the men from Denbury. His startled gaze went from one to the other.

'Elias, we think you need your stall looked after carefully,' said Long Jack.

The second man smiled. In a way, that was more terrifying than anything else. His teeth were black stumps, and his breath was as foul as the devil's own. 'Long Jack's right,' he leered. 'Otherwise you might find all your pies and things trampled on the ground. You wouldn't want that, would you?'

Chapter Nine

It was gloomy here. The sun was beyond its zenith, and buildings shadowed the packed dirt of the roadway. Laughing men and women trailed idly, most drifting back towards the town, the excitement of the first morning of the fair beginning to pall in the middle of the afternoon. They had already sated themselves in viewing the range of goods available; now was the time to return to inn, tavern or rented rooms to prepare for the evening's entertainments.

In the gloom of a doorway, Pietro da Cammino waited nervously, leaning against a wall and glancing up and down the street with anxiety creasing his brow as the people trickled past, one or two casting an uninterested glance in his direction.

His father couldn't understand. He was too old. Pietro had listened to Antonio telling him time after time how he had wooed Isabella, his mother, all those years before, and how proud he had been to win so handsome a woman, yet Antonio could not understand that Pietro had found the woman he needed at last. Even her name, Avice, sounded unique to the young Venetian. The name matched the girl; both were rare and exotic.

She was beautiful. Pietro was smitten on the ride into town, but when he mentioned her to his father, as they returned to their room from seeing the Abbot after their abortive visit to the tavern, Antonio had immediately expressed his reservations.

'No, Pietro. She's not right for you.'

'Not right?' He could still feel the disbelief. 'What does that mean? She's well-mannered, beautiful, healthy, and her father has money! No other woman could be so ideal for me.'

'That's not the point. We are here only long enough for me to persuade the Abbot, you know that. There is no time for you to court her. No, leave her alone, and we will find you a wife when we return home.'

'Home? I know all the women at *home*! Avice is the woman I want.'

'Yes? And how will you win her hand? You are prepared to stay in this country, are you? What would you do when I left?'

His father had been amused, his tone patronising, but his conviction that Pietro was wrong made his son determined. Antonio had no *right* to prevent him choosing the woman he wanted; he was old enough to choose for himself.

'I'll stay here with her if I want!'

'Without my money to keep you?'

'*Your* money?'

Antonio had frozen at that, his confidence evaporating at the sharpness in his son's tone. He took a deep breath and spoke placatingly. 'Pietro, you must see that this is impossible. We must be gone within a few days. What if something goes wrong? You would still be in this country – at risk.'

'I am willing to take that risk: I want her.'

Their servant entered, pouring ale from a jug. Antonio had sipped and pulled a grimace. 'This tastes like something the dogs have passed!'

His son shrugged. Antonio had always disliked ale, but refused to pay English prices for wine. It was exorbitant in this godforsaken land.

Pietro hated quarrelling with his father for there were bonds of loyalty between them that went further than the usual ties of blood. His mother had died when he was not yet two years old, struck down by a runaway wagon in a narrow alley in Florence. The boy had grown up without even a memory of his mother, and had depended on his father more than anyone. It had made their relationship unusually close.

But that very closeness was now suffocating him. He longed to escape from his father's rule and create his own life, rather than always being an associate in Antonio's schemes. And Avice was his concept of perfection.

It had been a sheer fluke that they had bumped into her this morning at the fair. Even his father could not then refuse to talk to her and her father, and Pietro had walked with her while their parents had followed.

It had been wonderful, just being with her. Even her kindness to the monk was an indication of her generosity of spirit. But afterwards his father had not changed his mind. 'Pietro, just think what you are risking! You know what almost happened in Bayonne. Your life could be in danger.'

'Father, I *love* her!'

'You only met her yesterday. Today you love her; tomorrow you may loathe her. She's pretty, but she's not worth dying for.'

Pietro didn't have to accept his father's commands any more; he was old enough to know his own mind. He cursed under his breath. His father had always ruled him: he never had any say in their fortunes. What Antonio demanded was what he expected; what Antonio demanded was what he got. The wishes of others were irrelevant. Pietro felt suddenly very alone. If Avice did not accept him, what would he do? He had made his position clear to his father – if she did not accept his wooing, he was not sure he could apologise to his father and beg forgiveness. Antonio was too proud to accept him back without an apology, but Pietro was not self-confident enough to be able to do that whole-heartedly.

There was a giggle from further along the road, and his

head snapped to the sound. He recognised her even from that simple explosion of mirth.

At first he saw nothing. Where he stood was in shadow, and after glancing upwards, he was blinded. In the road all seemed gloomy and dull, it bent and twisted away, sinuous as a snake, and seemed to grow ever more dingy as it wound its way further up the hill, erratically making its way north. It was from that direction that he heard her voice, and he wondered what could have made her so cheery. There were too many people in the street, and he could not see past them to Avice. Then at last he caught a glimpse of her between other, irrelevant figures, and he felt a quick pleasure. Seeing a man at her side, he stiffened with jealousy – until he recognised her father.

Arthur Pole nudged his daughter as the figure detached itself from the wall and stood as if wondering whether to approach or wait. 'See what you've done now?' he murmured.

'Oh, Father! It's hardly my fault. I haven't led him on or anything.'

The merchant eyed his daughter with good-humoured cynicism. 'Oh? And I suppose you didn't tell him where we were staying, is that right?'

'He *would* keep asking,' she said serenely.

'Avice Pole, I don't know what will become of you.' Her father took a deep breath and cast a sidelong glance at her. 'You know your mother is set on John and . . .'

'Father, I don't want to argue about it,' she said firmly.

Arthur Pole blinked slowly in exasperation. In his house he knew that his servants called him the 'scold's saddle', and he often felt he deserved it, for no matter how often he tried to impose his will on Marion, his wife, he usually tended to be pulled round to her point of view. She overrode his objections and forced him to agree with her. It was much easier and created a better atmosphere in his home if he surrendered.

When he looked at Avice now, he could see in her the woman he had married – and yet Avice was more than that. With her fine features and wide-set green eyes, she was more beautiful than even Marion had been. Her face was perfect, with high cheekbones, a healthy pale complexion dotted with small freckles, and marred only by the pugnacious set of her chin. As he glanced at her, he saw her eyes light with glee at the sight of the Venetian. There was little doubt that she had her heart firmly set on the boy.

'Master Pietro,' he called coldly. 'What a coincidence you should be here.'

'Hello, Pietro,' Avice cooed, and her father shot her a glance. She was growing too fast, he thought. Her tone held just the right note of flattering pleasure and promise. Arthur determined to set her maid to watch her.

'Sir,' Pietro said, then bowed. 'Miss Avice.'

She preened – she positively preened herself, Arthur saw. One bow and his daughter lost all control. He set his jaw. It was all too likely that this jackanapes Venetian was only after one thing, and Arthur Pole would protect his girl against a predatory foreigner. 'Can we help you?'

The boy was dressed outrageously, in a manner which would have been ridiculous for an Englishman. At least that must count against him. The Venetians, with their fleet of ships and vast financial resources, could afford pretty much what they wanted, and now, with the money being generated in England, they could behave as they pleased, but the rich red velvet of the boy's cloak, the fur lining of his hood, the hose of green and red, all pointed to an opulence which was outlandish, and more than a little embarrassing. Arthur felt sure his girl could not be attracted to such a vain boy for long.

He was wrong. The startling flamboyance of Pietro's dress was the very core of his attractiveness to her. Avice eyed his costume with unconcealed delight.

'Sir, after meeting your daughter this morning I have not

been able to forget her, and I came here to wait, hoping I
might be able to catch a glimpse of her.'

'I don't think—' Arthur began haughtily, but Avice cut
him off as their door opened.

'What a pretty speech, but I hope you have not been
chilled by the wind. Pietro, you must come inside and warm
yourself by our fire. Would you join us in a drink? We have
some very good wine from Guyenne. Father, if you could
see to our guest's needs, I shall join you shortly. First I must
go and tidy myself.'

He gave her a longsuffering look as she walked away.
Waving Pietro into the hall, Arthur stood a moment, listening. He could hear her footsteps on the hard floor. As she
turned the corner of the corridor to make her way to her
room, he heard her suddenly rush. Her sedate walk had
been only a masquerade, hiding the urgency of her mission,
and as soon as she knew she was out of sight, she had
hitched up her skirts and run.

Her determination, even at the risk of upsetting her
father, made him eye the Venetian sourly, but the boy kept
his gaze fixed firmly to the door where Avice would
return. Arthur cleared his throat irritably, and at last the
Venetian gave a start and recalled the presence of his
host.

'Well, Pietro? Would you like some wine?'

'Yes, please, sir. Some wine would be very pleasant.'

His apparent nervousness endeared him to the merchant,
and Arthur nodded to the steward. 'Bring wine and three
goblets.'

'This is a very splendid house, sir,' Pietro said hesitantly
as the servant departed.

Arthur could hear the tremble in his voice, and felt
warmer towards the lad. He could remember his own court-
ing of Marion, and the gut-wrenching horror of being alone
in the same room as her father under similar circumstances,
terrified lest an unwary word should offend and blight his

chances. 'We were lucky to be able to rent it at short notice,' he said diffidently.

'It's not your own?'

'No, we only come every second year to the Tavistock Fair. There's no need to come more often than that. What would I do with a place such as this for the rest of the time?'

'And your good lady wife? She is with you here?'

'No, she is at the fair, buying many things she needs at home. She'll be back later. Where are you staying? Do you have your own house?'

The Venetian shook his head. 'No, we are staying in the Abbey while my father negotiates with the Abbot. Abbot Champeaux has a good-sized flock of sheep and wishes to guarantee the best prices for his wool. My father has ships and could help transport the wool abroad, and with his banking interests we may be able to help the Abbot in other ways.'

That gave Arthur pause for thought. The boy was off-hand about his father's work, but he knew his position in the world. If Antonio had a banking business and access to ships Pietro's family were not only prosperous, they were affluent. Arthur had met some bankers, mainly from Florence and Genoa, and knew how much wealth the city-states had accumulated through their dealings with the east. If this young man was the son of a banker, he would be a far more useful son-in-law than John of Hatherleigh. Marriage into a baronial family was one thing – getting Avice connected with a foreign trading business was another. Arthur began to see possibilities in Pietro. It might even persuade Marion to change her mind.

'And what then?'

'My father will return to Venice.'

The servant returned with his tray and set it down on a table. He passed the wine to the Venetian. Arthur took his own and gulped greedily. If there was one thing he would never get used to, it was this ritualised process of purchasing a husband for his daughter. He loathed the thought that it must inevitably lead to his pure and sweet Avice being tied to some callow youth he had no knowledge of, like John, purely because he was titled. What if he was the kind who regularly beat his woman? What about this Venetian? He shot a glance at Pietro. It was so venomous that the young man spilled wine over his lap. He was still staring at it in dismay when they heard the steps in the corridor.

Arthur was pleased to hear Avice's hurrying feet slow as she approached the doorway. By the time she came into view, her breathing had almost steadied. Arthur sighed when he saw the crimson tunic shot through with golden threads that shimmered in the candlelight as she walked. It was, he knew, her favourite dress, and it showed off her colours to perfection, the crimson glinting just as did the auburn tints of her hair as she walked past sconces and candles.

She ignored her father, preferring to speak directly to Pietro. Arthur knew all her moods, and today he could see she was minded to win the heart of the youth.

He was still eying Pietro appraisingly when he heard his wife's voice. His eyes shot guiltily to the doorway as she came in.

Marion stood taking in the scene a moment. Avice met her steady gaze defiantly. Looking at the Venetian, Marion saw his ardent expression, and her own face hardened.

'My dear, let me present Pietro da Cammino. You remember, we met him and his father on the ride here.'

She inclined her head gracefully. 'I was not expecting to find a guest. Please forgive me for not being here to greet you.'

'Don't worry, Mother. Father and I have entertained him.'

'I am sure you have, Avice,' said her mother with honeyed irony. 'And now, sir, I am sure you will excuse us, but we have many purchases to sort through. Avice, please come and help.'

'Can't your maid help you, Mother?' said Avice coldly.

'I would prefer my daughter to show her excellent taste,' Marion said, and only someone who knew her could have told that her gentle voice hid a steel resolution.

Avice sat still, inwardly raging that her mother should demand her attendance as if she were a mere serving girl. She was tempted to refuse and continue speaking to Pietro, but she knew that her mother would wait, outwardly patient, until obeyed, and eventually Avice *would* obey. She had no choice while she lived under the same roof.

But she could demonstrate her rebellion, and she did so now. She stood, and smiled dazzlingly at the Venetian, curtseying politely, before turning and leaving the room, ignoring her mother.

Marion had not finished. She turned to her husband. 'It is always nice to meet new people, Arthur, but you must be careful now Avice is betrothed. It is best that there is no hint of scandal, for that might endanger her reputation, and the young wife of a noble can't afford a stain on her character.'

She swept out, and when Arthur saw Pietro's face, he felt a quick sympathy. The boy looked devastated. 'My apologies for that, my friend,' he said kindly. 'My wife holds strong feelings when it comes to her daughter. It is no reflection on you, of course.'

Pietro hardly heard him. Marion's meaning had been all too clear to him. Avice was betrothed! His argument with his father was in vain. He couldn't have her anyway.

Then a firm resolution strengthened him. He could not have mistaken Avice's mood. She wanted him as much as he desired her. He *would* win her. He *must*.

Rising, he thanked the merchant, explaining he had business to attend to.

In the street, he stared back at the house before turning

to walk down the hill towards the Abbey. After only a few
yards there was a whistle, and he spun to see his father's
servant leaning negligently in the shadows against a wall.
'What are you doing here, Luke? Father told you to check
on me, did he? You can tell him that his precautions seem
unnecessary.'

Luke glanced at the building with frank amazement. 'She
rejected you?'

'Oh no. Not she.' Pietro gazed into the distance as they
began walking back to the Abbey. 'She seems as interested
in me as before. No, it is her mother who wants to keep me
from her.'

'Do you know why? Has she heard something about your
father?'

'Be still!' Pietro hissed. 'Don't say such things even in the
street!' He continued more calmly, 'No, I don't think she
has heard anything about Father. She's just got someone
else in mind for her daughter.'

'If you're sure.'

'Don't worry about that. If anyone had heard about my
father, the Abbot would have been told. There's no risk –
when her mother hears about our negotiations with
Champeaux, she'll probably fall over herself to try to get
me back to woo her daughter.'

Jordan Lybbe leaned against the pole of the awning and
yawned. The day had been busy, and he could nod with
inner satisfaction as he saw how his stock had been
depleted. Now the throng before his stall was reducing, and
he had time to rest a little.

The pair of men came along the little alley where his bolts
of cloth were set out, talking to all the other traders. Lybbe's
boy, Hankin, watched them approach with eyes like saucers.
They strode with cudgels in hand, and Hankin saw them
taking money from all the stallholders.

'Good day, gentlemen. How can I serve you?' he began,

but he was thrust aside. The watchmen wanted his master.

Lybbe sat on a box and waited while the two surveyed the produce in his stall. He radiated comfortable enthusiasm, as if hoping for a sale.

'You have good cloth. Is this the first time you have been to Tavistock Fair?' one of them asked.

Lybbe nodded, beaming. 'Bonjour.'

The two looked at each other. 'You understand English, don't you?'

'Pardon?' After so long his Gascon accent was perfect.

Long Jack frowned. He hadn't met a stallholder who couldn't speak English before. He spoke no Gascon or French, and the breakdown in language wasn't something he'd anticipated. Gesturing with his cudgel, he indicated all the merchandise. 'This! It's all good cloth. You've got to pay us for looking after it. You understand?'

Lybbe nodded and ducked his head, smiling. 'Oui, c'est bon, n'est-ce pas?'

'This is a waste of time,' Little Jack said to his companion.

'Just take one of the bolts, then. We haven't got all day.'

Little Jack moved towards a rack of cloth and selected one. Lybbe nodded happily, and Little Jack turned to leave the stall. Instantly a thin cord whipped round his neck, and he was jerked backwards, off balance, held by the throat with all his body's weight drawing on the thong. He gurgled and gave a hoarse cry, the muscles on his neck standing out as he fought for air.

'Now then,' he heard an amiable voice say beside his ear. 'You weren't trying to take a present from an honest trader, were you?'

The watchman scrabbled with his hands to tug the ligature free, dropping cloth and club together.

Lybbe continued cheerfully, 'I like giving presents, but only when I'm ready. I don't like people trying to force me into giving them things; I don't like that at all. So when I let you go, you'll just walk out into the street quietly and we'll say nothing more. And if anything happens to my stock in all the time I'm here, I'll be visiting *you*. You understand? I'll come to ask you why such a big strong watchman like you couldn't stop someone stealing my stock, or burning it, or just tipping it into the mud. And I'll ask you all about when you were near my stall, so I can find out when the people did the damage. And I might just get angry then and lash out at someone. Anyone who's close at the time. Know what I mean?'

He shoved, releasing his cord at the same time, and the man staggered forward until he came to a halt against a trestle. Choking, he stood rubbing his throat, hatred glittering in his eyes. Lybbe twirled the leather thong round his finger. 'Like I said, anything strange happens round here, and I'll be along to see *you*. Got that?' He picked up the cudgel and weighed it in his hand meditatively. Then he tossed it to Little Jack. The watchman managed to catch it before it struck him in the belly, but all the time his eyes were fixed narrowly on the short figure before him, as if trying to fix the man's features permanently in his memory.

Chapter Ten

Margaret had invited Jeanne to accompany her on a visit to
the fair, leaving Baldwin and Simon to join Holcroft, who
awaited them with the watchman Daniel. The port-reeve
was frustrated at having to assist the knight from Furnshill,
for he had many other duties to see to, but the Abbot had
been quite definite even after hearing about the attack on
Will Ruby. 'This is a murder,' he pointed out, 'and you must
help Baldwin and the bailiff if you can. The attack on Ruby
is secondary; it can wait.'

With Hugh, Simon's servant, in tow, Margaret led her
new friend up the hill, past the alley where the garbage was
still heaped, past the cookshop and the tavern, and on up
towards the fairground.

Margaret often went with her husband to Lydford Fair,
but Tavistock Fair was on a different scale. The number of
stalls was daunting, and many carried goods from far afield.
She stared around her as they passed, but it was only as
they came to the food-stalls that she began to study the
goods in earnest. She had almost run out of spices, and
needed to replenish their stocks.

Hugh stood resignedly as his mistress haggled with stallholders. In a short space of time he was laden with baskets.
Oranges and almonds, loaves of sugar, packets of ginger
and cinnamon, mace, cardamom and cloves, were all piled
into his baskets until he complained at the weight.

Margaret turned her nose up at goods she could buy at
Lydford. Mustard, salt and saffron were all ignored, as was

pepper, but to Hugh's dismay she slowed at the barrels of fish, and he was delighted when he heard Jeanne attract her attention to the cloth-sellers.

'Didn't you say you needed new material?'

Soon Margaret was casting a speculative eye over the bolts on display. 'It has to be the right colour for him.'

'For your husband?'

'No,' she said, feeling a purple silk with a sad covetousness. It would have to go to a woman more prosperous than she: Simon would never agree to such an expense. 'For Baldwin. He has no decent tunics.'

'You have taken it upon yourself to buy him new clothes?'

Margaret smiled at the note of surprise. 'There is no one else to do it for him.'

'He has no woman?'

'He's never married, and he rarely meets women of his own rank to woo. And he's far too honourable to take a peasant.'

'Oh.' The simple expression carried an undertone of interest.

'I would be grateful,' Margaret said innocently, 'if you could help me – what colours do you think would suit him?'

Jeanne threw her a curious glance. 'You know him much better than I.'

'Yes, but sometimes another opinion can help greatly.'

'Really?'

Jordan watched the three approach and moved forward to the trestle. 'My ladies, you must surely want to see the best in the fair. For two such beautiful ladies, only the finest wares will do. Come and see the bolts here.'

Margaret inclined her head at the compliment, and she and Jeanne followed him to the makeshift shed he had constructed behind the table between two wagons. Here they found racks set out with the choicest materials. Cloth of gold, gauze, and fine woollens from the Flemish towns were displayed, and Margaret gasped when she saw the fine colours.

'There are cloths here that will make you both look like queens,' Jordan said confidently. 'Look at this.' He pulled out a deep blue material. 'Could any lady want a finer wool for a tunic?'

'It's not for us that we're looking,' Jeanne managed when Jordan drew breath. 'It is for a man.'

'Excellent, my lady. And your husband must be a strong and noble gentleman, I am sure – and a man with a wonderful eye for beauty. This would be the perfect thing.'

She eyed the crimson cloth in his hands, then looked at Margaret. 'What do you think my husband would need?' she asked, and giggled. Margaret grinned, then both were rocking with gales of laughter while the stallholder and Hugh exchanged uncomprehending stares.

Elias' door was unlocked. Inside it was as black as a cellar; the shop's entrance faced east, and the meagre light from the waning sun missed the interior completely. Baldwin waited while the port-reeve cursed and muttered, trying to light tinder from flint and his knife. As soon as the flames spluttered fitfully into life, he lit a candle, and the room was filled with a yellow glow as he handed it to Baldwin.

Holcroft had not wanted to check on Elias' house like this. He had the soul of a free portman, and this felt like trespass. The fact that the Abbot himself had ordered it did not help. Abbot Champeaux did not own Elias' house any more than he owned Holcroft's. The borough was a free entity, and while the Abbot might possess the rights to the court, that did not mean he owned the justice dispensed in that court, only the profits accruing from it.

Baldwin accepted the candle and studied the room carefully. Sleeping rolls and blankets lay on the floor. Elias had rented out every inch of spare space for the duration of the fair, but his lodgers were presently at the ground, and the house was deserted. Only their unwashed smell remained, overwhelming the more wholesome tones of cooked food.

To Peter it was an unexceptional place, constructed of timber with cob filling the panels. The shop windows – two large shutters which opened outwards to form tables on which Elias could display his wares – lay at either side of the door. Apart from a number of tables and benches, there was little furniture. The floor was covered in straw which, from the look of it, had lain there some time.

There was no obvious place Baldwin could see where a hole might have been bored to conceal the missing head. The walls were thin, so he set the watchman to clearing the straw and looking underneath for a secret cache.

He walked through the low doorway into the back room. Here was all the paraphernalia of a cookhouse. A brick oven stood at the back, furthest from the street. Pans, dishes and bowls were stacked on the table that lay along one wall. At the opposite wall was a staircase, each step formed from timber cut diagonally to give a triangular section and then nailed on two rails. Baldwin clambered up it to reach the small chamber upstairs. A bed sat in the middle, the linen curtains hanging loosely, none tied back. There was a musky scent from the herbs laid under the straw mattress to keep the fleas at bay. A chest stood at the foot of the bed, and when the knight peered inside, he found spare sheets and clothing. Nothing more. A few rolls of bedding lay on the floor.

Simon had followed him, and stood in the doorway while Baldwin stared out into the street.

'Not very prepossessing, is it?' Simon said.

The knight waved a hand curtly round the room. 'I was just thinking that this man must live alone. He can hardly be married in a place so sparsely decorated.'

He gave the place a last cursory glance and descended. The room reminded him of his own, similarly spartan chamber, and he was struck by an odd sense of sympathy for the lonely cook, living above his shop, without even the comfort of a woman – the comfort of a woman like Jeanne, he found himself thinking, and roughly forced the memory of her face from his mind. 'Holcroft?'

The port-reeve scurried through from the front room. 'Yes, Sir Baldwin?'

'Elias – is he married?'

'Widowed. She died in labour. Then his son died.'

Simon had followed them, and heard this last. He saw Baldwin's quick glance, and smilingly shook his head. He was over the death of his son, and hearing mention of another's loss couldn't hurt him.

The knight turned back to the port-reeve. 'Has Elias no woman?'

'Only the girls from the tavern.' He recalled the night before the fair. 'One in particular, I suppose – Lizzie. She was here with him yesterday afternoon.'

Peter glanced about him. After the opulence of the Abbey, he found this little shop with its smell of unwashed bodies distasteful.

'We should speak to her as well at some point,' Baldwin murmured. He looked round the room again, noting the trivets and pans, the large bowls and dishes. 'Is there any sign of him hiding something in here?'

'None. I've even had a look in the oven and firebox.'

'Ah, well. I suppose we should be glad of the fact,' Baldwin said, and walked to the back door. 'What's out there?'

'His yard.'

Baldwin opened the door and went out. Simon walked with him and saw him standing and gazing around carefully. The knight looked like a short-sighted and absent-minded monk who had mislaid something. When the bailiff studied the area, he saw the general rubbish of years. There was a loose pile of logs under a haphazardly thatched roof, a small shed that looked like Elias' privy, a little series of raised beds planted with leeks, onions and garlic, brassicas, beans and worts. In a small section fenced off with hurdles, chickens scratched and clucked quietly. The plot was separated from the alley by a paling fence.

'Nothing here,' Baldwin said, turning to leave.

'Wait a moment,' Simon said. By the logs was an old wooden box. Striding over, he lifted the lid and picked up a heavy-bladed bill-hook that lay within. 'Baldwin?'

The knight took the tool from him and hefted it in his hand. He met Simon's gaze. 'It could be,' he agreed.

'It's hard to tell, but the staining on the blade—'

'Yes, it looks like blood.'

Simon peered round the little garden again. He walked to the bed furthest from the house and squatted, staring down at the soil. Tentatively he reached out and touched it. There was a shallow depression in the ground. 'Daniel, fetch a shovel,' he called.

'What is it?' Baldwin asked.

'That soil has been dug over recently,' the bailiff said with certainty. 'I recognise the look of it: when miners fill in their holes, it dips like this.'

Daniel was not happy with his task. He brought the spade and began digging, but with little enthusiasm. The job of watchman was something he enjoyed for the money – it was not his plan to investigate murders or to seek out parts of dead people. His distaste for his task made him slow as he gradually went deeper, and when he felt the shovel strike something that gave way a little, he recoiled from the hole, staring up at the Keeper with despair in his eyes.

Baldwin took pity on him and gestured the man aside. He discarded the shovel, reaching down with his bare hands to scrape the earth away. Soon he could see a sack, and he tugged it free. Pulling it from the hole, he set it on the ground and glanced at Simon, who gave an unwilling grimace. Baldwin cut the string that bound it and the coarse material fell away. Peter winced and turned away, swallowing hard to keep the bile at bay.

'You were right, Simon,' Baldwin said.

'Yes.'

Holcroft said thickly, 'No, we were all wrong. That's not the merchant who sat with Elias. It's a man from Ashburton way: Roger Torre.'

Baldwin stared from him to the head. 'Are you sure?'

Holcroft nodded. Behind him, Peter staggered to the fence, his eyes shut.

'Perhaps that's why Elias was shocked when we told him his friend had been killed,' Simon mused. 'If he knew the corpse was Torre's, our words must have made him think his companion had been murdered as well.'

Baldwin nodded thoughtfully. 'It would explain his dismay.'

'The body was in his alley, the head in his garden. All the evidence points to Elias,' said Simon.

'True, but Elias had no blood on him when he returned to the inn.'

'I know. Perhaps his friend did the killing, and Elias had nothing to do with it, but that's not my concern. I was thinking, with all this evidence against him, the mob will be convinced he did it. What then for his safety?'

'You are right. We should make sure Elias is safe.'

'With the head here there's enough to arrest him. He'd be safe enough in the clink.'

'And a while in there might persuade him to tell us about his friend,' Baldwin agreed. Hearing retching, he raised his eyebrows. 'Peter? Are you all right?'

In view of Peter's evident inability to take notes for a while, he was despatched to the Abbey to inform Abbot Champeaux of developments. When he had gone, Holcroft gingerly took the sack from Baldwin.

'This Torre – did he have a wife or family? Was there anyone who might be able to recognise him from this body?'

Holcroft scratched his jaw. 'Not really. He wasn't local. Only came into town occasionally.'

They walked through the cookshop to the street. 'So that is why he was not reported as having disappeared,' Baldwin said. 'There was no one to miss him, poor devil.'

'No, sir.'

'Did you see him at the tavern?' Simon asked.

'Yes, he was there when I arrived; we drank together for a bit.'

'Did you see him get into a row or anything?'

'Well, he did have a problem with those Venetians staying with the Abbot. They were rushing out in a hurry, just as he was coming in and the youngster pulled his knife. But it was only a silly dispute, nothing much. Nothing to kill for. Torre just looked at the lad and walked away.'

'But the boy had almost drawn a blade,' Baldwin mused. 'Italians can take such matters seriously. And they are prone to subtle means of revenge.'

'Was Torre alone after that?' Simon probed. He was sure the port-reeve was holding something back. He had a shame-faced look to him.

'He went with Lizzie for a while.'

'This "Lizzie" is the same girl who was friendly with Elias?'

'She's a prostitute in the tavern,' Holcroft explained.

The knight said, 'Did you see Elias when he and his friend left the tavern?'

'No, sir, no I didn't. Why?'

'Because the alewife told us that Elias and his friend left, then Elias came back shortly afterwards. If he and Torre both enjoyed this girl "Lizzie", Elias might have become jealous. It has happened before. This might well give us a motive for the murder. Let us go and see her now.'

Holcroft swallowed hard. If Sir Baldwin could believe that Elias might have killed just because another man had taken Lizzie, what would the knight think if he heard about

Holcroft's own feelings towards the girl? 'Sorry, sir, but she's not here now. All prostitutes are outlawed during the fair.'

Baldwin asked blandly, 'Really? You think she's left the town, then?'

'Yes, of course.'

'Where does she usually live?'

'At the tavern.'

'Fine. Well, let's go there, put this head with the body, and find out where she has gone.'

While Holcroft went out to reunite Roger Torre's head with its body the others entered the tavern. It was busy as usual, and Simon had to force his way to a table. To his surprise, Baldwin stood talking to the watchman in the doorway before joining him. A few minutes later, the alewife appeared and took their order.

By the time Holcroft returned, his hands thoroughly washed, he was in need of strong ale. Carrying the sack with its revolting contents had been deeply unsettling.

Before she could hurry away with their orders, Baldwin asked Agatha, 'Mistress, you have a girl working for you here, called Lizzie. I would like to speak to her.'

'I'm sorry, sir. This is fair-time. She's not allowed in while the fair is on.'

'She is not here? That is a great shame. Do you know where she has gone?'

The alewife frowned, her attention moving from Baldwin to the port-reeve. 'No, I have enough to do trying to keep my customers happy without worrying about the likes of her.'

She stormed out, and Holcroft stared pointedly at the knight. 'See? I told you she wouldn't be around. Prostitutes and lepers are banned during the fair.'

'I have a feeling that Agatha could help us more if she wished,' Baldwin said mildly. There was a delay for a few minutes, and then the alewife returned, carrying mugs and a jug. She set them down, mouth tightly pursed. 'Agatha,' Baldwin said persuasively, 'could you rack your brain to try to think where Lizzie might be staying now?'

'I can't think,' she said firmly.

'I see.'

She gave him a suspicious look, which turned to anger as Daniel walked in gripping a smiling young woman by the elbow.

'What are you doing with her? What right do you have to—?'

'Sir Baldwin, I caught her trying to escape through the back door after this alewife had spoken to her,' Daniel announced.

'Thank you. Mistress, please fetch us another jug of ale, We will not keep your servant long.'

Holcroft was gaping. 'But . . . but what are you doing *here* still, Lizzie? You were supposed to have gone hours ago.'

Simon glanced at him. 'It's all very well to ban prostitutes from the town while you hold your fair, but where do you expect someone to go when they have no relations and nowhere else to run to?'

'Agatha has some explaining to do,' Holcroft said heavily. 'So do you, my girl.'

'No, not really,' said Baldwin reasonably. 'After all, the whole idea is that prostitution should not be rife during the fair, and Agatha stopped Lizzie from plying her trade. However, being a Christian soul, she did not throw the girl out on the street. I think the Abbot would be delighted to hear that she had shown such mercy.'

Lizzie looked pointedly at the watchman's hand on her arm. Baldwin waved dismissively. Daniel let her go and sat next to Holcroft.

'Lizzie, I am trying to find out who might have committed a murder,' Baldwin said, and explained about the body. As he spoke, Agatha returned and set a jug down, keeping an eye on Lizzie all the while. Simon could see she was nervous that she might be arrested and fined for keeping prostitutes during the fair. His attention returned to Baldwin as the knight continued, 'He must have died not far from the inn's doors. Did you hear or see anything last night? Someone calling for help – a struggle?'

'No, sir. Nothing.'

'Agatha? What about you?'

'Me, sir?' She threw Lizzie a quick look. 'No, nothing.'

'I see. Were there many people in here last night?'

'I've already told you who was here and who wasn't,' the alewife snapped. 'Look, I'm busy. There are people here who want serving, and you asking questions isn't going to help me pay my rent.'

Baldwin watched her as she flounced off among the throng, then looked up at the girl. 'Lizzie, please sit down. This will not take long, but it would be discourteous to expect a woman to stand while her questioners all sit.'

Daniel moved over – a little too enthusiastically for Baldwin's taste, and the knight threw him a sour look.

For the first time, Baldwin studied the girl. If he had to guess, he would say that she was a little over twenty, and very attractive; she had not yet lost the sheen of youth. She was a brunette, and her hair was chestnut with auburn tints where the light caught it. Her face was square but very feminine, and her lips were full and seemed to smile with an easy joy. Baldwin could easily understand how she could entice the men of the town. All too often he had noticed the harsh measuring look in the eyes of other women of her trade, but in Lizzie's brown eyes all he could see was an ingenuous happiness which surprised and warmed him.

'You work from here?' he asked. Her eyes went immediately to Holcroft. 'Er, Lizzie, I think the port-reeve would agree with me that the Abbot will not need to know too much about where you live and how you work. Abbot Robert is concerned about the murder of a man, and other things really do not worry him. Oh, and I seem to recall that the port-reeve will be retiring soon, and making way for a new man, is that not right?'

Holcroft gave a shrug. 'I reckon the Abbot couldn't care less about minor offences when he has a dead body to account for, and there's no need for me to trouble him with things he's not worried about – and yes, I do retire in a few days, so I'm not going to make difficulties.'

'Lizzie?' Baldwin pressed gently.

'I usually live here, yes. Sometimes I go away, but I often help Agatha with her cooking and brewing, and she lets me sleep in a room out at the back.'

'Not just sleep, neither,' said a man passing by the table.

She glanced up quickly and retorted, 'You keep hoping, John Bacon. When your todger's grown large enough to please me, maybe I'll think about showing you what I can do for you.' She turned back to Baldwin apologetically. 'Sorry, but Bacon's always like that.'

Baldwin coughed, and felt his face redden. His only compensation was that he could almost feel the heat radiating from the face of the port-reeve. It was plain enough that the girl could see his confusion. She leaned forward to rest a cheek on her hand, and the movement pulled her tunic tight over her breast. He found it difficult to keep his eyes on her face as she looked innocently at him. Her eyebrow flickered upwards, just the once, in a quick movement he could have easily missed – but her expression showed she knew he hadn't. 'Um. So who, er, who was here last night?'

'Last night? Oh, there were lots of men,' she said, and he was sure she was teasing him. 'Elias, and Will Ruby, the port-reeve here . . .' Baldwin noted the comment. She was bright enough to make sure that the port-reeve was implicated '. . . and lots of others. Elias spent time talking to some stranger, and there was a father and his son from foreign parts, some watchmen, a friar, and Roger Torre, and . . . Oh, I don't know who else.'

'It is Torre we are interested in,' Baldwin said. 'How well do you know him?'

Her mouth widened into a broad grin. 'What do you want to know?'

'Lizzie, Torre is dead.'

Her amusement vanished, and her posture changed. 'You think the dead man was Roger? That's daft . . . I can't believe it.'

'It's true.'

'Well, why wasn't it announced immediately? Everyone's been thinking it was a stranger.'

'Because with his head off we couldn't tell,' Holcroft said bluntly and took a long pull at his ale.

She stared. Everyone in the tavern knew the body was headless, but it hadn't occurred to her it might be Roger. 'But *why?*'

'That is why we are here,' Baldwin explained. 'We know he was with you last night. We are trying to find out whether he said something, or maybe you saw somebody arguing with him – anything.'

'If it's true, let me see his body.'

Baldwin waved a hand, and Daniel stood. He walked to the door. After a moment Lizzie followed him. A few minutes later, she was back, her face pale.

'Drink this,' Baldwin said, pushing his pot towards her.

She accepted it gratefully. Picking it up in both hands she drained it. When she set it back down on the table, Baldwin could see that her hands were shaking. 'It's Torre all right,' she said harshly. 'And the only man I know who could have done this was *him!*' She pointed a quivering finger at the port-reeve.

Chapter Eleven

Arthur Pole swirled the wine in his goblet and stared into it thoughtfully. His wife sat serenely in her favourite position by the fire, stitching at a tapestry. Outwardly she was calm and spoke with what might have sounded to an outsider to be indifference, but Arthur knew otherwise. This was her tone of sweet reasonableness. It was the one she used when she wanted one of the servants to understand very clearly what she expected. Arthur knew she used it on him as well when she thought he had failed her in a spectacular manner.

It was unfair. He had done nothing today to merit this treatment. As far as he was concerned, he'd tried to keep that blasted Venetian from his daughter. Cammino had not appeared on his doorstep at Arthur's invitation: it was all down to Avice. She had contrived it, not him.

Arthur was used to being treated as a delinquent by his wife when she considered he had fallen below the high standard of so important a merchant and Guild member, and he had grown inured to a daughter who thought of him only as a personal bank with unlimited resources and no interest charges, but it rankled that his wife should lecture him on the type of man he should be thinking of for his only child.

'John would be a very good match for her,' Marion was saying as she imperturbably finished a stitch and selected a fresh thread. 'True, he has no money himself, but his father, Sir Reginald, owns a good portion of land and four villages. Avice will be well provided for. And Sir Reginald has connections to the de Courtenay family as well, so John will make the perfect father to her children.'

Her husband looked up to see his servant waiting by the door. He drained his cup and motioned for a refill.

Marion noticed the movement. 'Haven't you had enough, dear? You drank a lot with that man earlier.'

' "That man", as you call him, is the leading cloth merchant in Winchester. He could be worth a small fortune to me.'

'I should hope so, the amount you spent on wine for him.'

'How do you expect me to make friends and fresh contacts in business if I don't sometimes buy them presents? Have you learned nothing about business in the time we have been married?'

'Oh, yes. I have learned much since you married me,' she retorted tartly. 'I had to, I wasn't used to such things before.'

Arthur took the goblet from his man and jerked his head to send him from the room. He recognised the acid preamble to the usual complaint, and did not want it witnessed.

'After all, husband, when I wed you I was the daughter of a knight.'

'Yes, dear.'

'He came from an old family. I was lucky he agreed to let me marry you.'

'Because I was only the son of a cobbler.'

'You were of . . . lesser nobility,' Marion nodded, adding complacently, 'But I could see you were an honourable man.'

Arthur felt stung into retaliation. 'I was already wealthy, and your father needed money.'

'That had nothing to do with it.'

'Marion, your father couldn't afford to feed you.'

'That is untrue!' Her eyes blazed with indignation.

Arthur put his goblet down. 'My only saving grace was the money I had amassed over the years. If it wasn't for that, your father would have refused me. He needed my money.'

She looked at him with cold fury. Marion was not a hard woman. She had married Arthur when he was still relatively unknown, and had learned to accept some of the curious attitudes and beliefs he had held, but gradually over the years she had managed to educate him to a level of gentility. He could never aspire to being a real gentleman, since he didn't possess nobility of birth, but for all that she was quite sure she could improve her family's standing in their town, and one method of achieving that was to make sure that her daughter married well. It was important, not only for Marion, but for Avice herself. How much better it would be for her if she could marry a man with status. Her father could provide the money.

She swallowed her pride – Holy Mother, how often she had needed to do that over the years! – and forced herself to nod understandingly. 'Arthur, you are a good man, and your business skills have made you successful, but can you not see that what I want for Avice is what is best for her and for her children?'

'She has no children.'

'The children she *will* have. She *must* be in a position to look after our grandchildren. That means she must find a husband of suitable rank, and the only one we know of is John.' It was true, she knew, that John was ignorant and more than a little stupid, but what could one expect from a rural squire? He was really little more than a farmer.

But he was related to the de Courtenays, and that counted for a lot.

Marion stitched on in silence for a moment while she considered. It would be a significant achievement to once again have nobility in the family. And Avice could not wish for a better mate. None of the greater families would countenance having the daughter of a trader attach herself to them, and she was lucky that John had accepted her.

Marion watched her husband affectionately. He was staring sulkily at the fire and refusing to meet her gaze.

'Husband, you know that it is best for her that she marries into a good family.'

'I would prefer her to be happy.'

'*I* am happy.'

The softness of her tone made him look up, searching her face for a trace of falsehood. 'But she seems set on this Venetian, and from the way he's mooning around, if he doesn't love her, I don't know what love is.'

'That is not love, just infatuation. They will both grow out of it,' she said confidently. 'Arthur, we know all about John and nothing about this other boy. Which is the safer partner for our daughter?'

'Did you know that Pietro is the son of a banker? The father is negotiating with the Abbot even now.'

She paused while she absorbed this. 'Perhaps so, but money is not the only issue.'

'Marion, some of these Italian bankers are extremely rich. With that kind of money Pietro could *buy* a knighthood, maybe even a Dukedom.'

'A new title isn't the same as an ancient one,' she protested uncertainly.

'And how do you know the Venetian isn't from a titled family? Many of these Italian bankers come from noble stock.'

'I hardly think . . .'

'If he is, we are losing a good man for our daughter, aren't we?'

'What do you suggest we do, then?'

'Only this: that we find out what we can about the Camminos. I shall set the groom on to this. Henry's always been nosey. He'd love checking up on them.'

Marion considered, then nodded agreement. 'If you think it's worthwhile, husband.'

Arthur watched his wife as she returned to her

needlework. She appeared content, and when she glanced up and saw his look, she smiled again. He returned to his staring at the fire; he would never understand women. Still, he resolved to have enquiries made about the Venetians as quickly as possible. If he was to bow to his daughter's wishes, he would first have to make sure that she would not later have cause to regret her choice.

Margaret took the cloth from the merchant and held it up against her body while Jeanne considered it. Then they both began giggling again. Jordan kept his pleasant expression, but it was becoming a little fixed. When he glanced at Hugh, all he could see was a morose scowl, and he had to wonder to which of the two women the miserable-looking sod belonged. If his wife had possessed a servant such as that, he swore, he would dismiss the creature immediately.

Hugh was weighed down with the mass of foodstuffs and his arms felt inches longer. The gaiety of the women was incomprehensible to him, and he didn't trust the salesman, either. Jordan Lybbe seemed too pat, too smarmy in the way he sang the praises of the pair as they held bolts of material against themselves. It was bordering on the familiar, and Hugh was deeply suspicious. The man almost seemed to be flirting, and what made it worse was that the women gave every appearance of loving it.

Hugh glanced up and down the alleyway. The day was drawing in, and people were clearing from the pathways between the stalls, preparing to return to their rented houses, or rooms at inns and taverns, some to get back to their warm beds in the straw over the horses. Firstly, though, all would be looking forward to the entertainers who inevitably tagged along in the wake of the fair. In the alcoholic haze in many rooms tonight, people would be blearily watching fools performing acrobatics or singing, and few if any of them would remember a thing about it in the morning. Their only reminder would be the size of their hangover and lightness of their purses.

He could visualise it only too well, and he wanted to be a part of it. But there was precious little chance that he could enjoy any of the festivities while his master was the guest of the Abbot. It would be unseemly for a bailiff's servant to cavort with jugglers or dancers while staying in a convent.

As another gale of mirth rang out, he carefully set the baskets on the ground, leaning against a pole. Here he could feel the last gleam of the sun, and he closed his eyes and enjoyed the faint warmth. It was rare enough that he had time to sit in the sun nowadays. That had all stopped once he left home to earn his own living. Before that he had been first a bird scarer, throwing stones at the pigeons and crows, and sometimes getting a lucky hit and food for supper, until he was eight and old enough to become a shepherd, and if the winter months were cold and cruel – working in the snow trying to find missing animals and protecting the young lambs from foxes, buzzards, crows, wolves and all the other animals which preyed on the long-legged and stupid creatures – the summer months more than compensated. Then he could sit in the pastures with his pouch of food and a skin full of ale, and doze in the sunlight while the young sheep continually circled their grazing: walking and cropping, walking and cropping.

In his mind's eye he could see the pasturelands now, as if he was back on the hill near Drewsteignton, the forty-odd animals in front of him, their jaws moving rhythmically, taking a slow step at a time as they followed after their leader. The vision was so strong, he felt he could almost reach out and touch the nearest sheep.

Then he snapped back to wakefulness as he heard the voice.

'My friends say you're from France. That right?'

Hugh looked first to the women: they were silent but unharmed. The merchant had been talking with such concentration he had not noticed the three men who had stealthily encircled him. Hugh moved quietly behind the pole, his hand falling on his old knife and testing it in the sheath.

'They reckoned you couldn't understand English. Said you had problems with it before.'

They had timed their attack perfectly, Hugh saw. The clothseller and the women had been busy at the back of the stall, and it was hard to see the lane now, they were so far from the trestle at the front. If they were to call for help, it was likely they would be unconscious and their attackers far away before anyone dared to enter and find out what was happening. Not many people would care to risk their lives to protect another stallholder. Hugh stood still, and so far as he could see, none of the men had noticed him.

The leader of the three, the one who had spoken, hefted a large blackthorn club in his hand, and let it rise and fall two or three times. 'Let's see if this teaches you the King's English, you foreign bastard. Get him, lads!'

The two men at either side of Lybbe reached out to grasp him, but the merchant was too quick for them. He sprang forward, knocking the leader's cudgel aside and gripping the man's wrist. Ducking under his shoulder, still holding his arm, Lybbe twisted, wrenching the man's arm back. The leader was now bent over in agony; Lybbe took the club from his unresisting fingers and rested it on his attacker's shoulder, pushing the man away from him and forcing a little gasp of pain from his lips.

'I understand English well enough, I reckon,' Jordan said coldly. 'It seems your friend didn't, though. I told him I'd get angry if anything happened to my things here, but he obviously didn't get my meaning.' He twisted the arm and held it higher, and the leader's legs crumpled as he tried to stop his shoulder being prised from its socket. 'I wonder, do *you* understand me? If I have any more of this, I'll have to keep lifting your arm up, and then you'll need to see the monks to get it mended. It might take some time.'

Watching him, Jeanne was transfixed by shock. There was an acceptance of violence in his action, a precision in his slow torturing of the man, that sent a feather of horror tickling down her spine. She had never before witnessed such intentional cruelty towards another person. Her own suffering at the hands of her husband was a different matter, for she had known that she could cope with it – and a part of her even accepted it as her due for not being able to give her man the children he craved – but this deliberate infliction of pain on another made her soul cringe.

Long Jack walked forward stealthily, lifting each foot and setting it down silently. He had been left to guard the front of the stall in case the merchant's cries of fear and groans of agony should attract other stallholders to his defence, and he had heard the first sarcastic jibes of his friends, but when all went silent, he had become anxious. Spying on them through the curtains of hanging cloth at the rear, he could see Lybbe gripping the man in a painful armlock.

'Do you want to find out how long it will take to mend a broken shoulder? It's excruciating, so I'm told,' Lybbe continued conversationally, lifting the arm higher. Another cry of pain broke from his victim.

Long Jack pushed through the materials, using his cudgel to move the cloth aside as he came closer, ever closer. There was no sound but the rasping breath of Lybbe's victim and the cold tones of the merchant. Long Jack got to the edge of the last hanging screen of material, and took a deep breath as he prepared to rush forward.

That was when Hugh hit him over his ear, and he fell like a pole-axed steer.

The sudden crack, rustle, and groaning sigh as the man fell made Lybbe look quickly over his shoulder. Hugh shrugged, and the merchant nodded. 'Your last friend seems to be having a sleep now. What's your decision, friend?'

'I give in, I surrender,' the man gasped.

Lybbe eyed him contemplatively, then kicked him hard in the base of the spine. The leader fell prostrate before the other two, who stared at their friend with angry consternation. 'Get that garbage out of my stall, and don't let it back here,' Lybbe rapped out. 'You're lucky. There are two of you, and two pieces of excrement to take away, so go!'

Hugh watched as the two men circled warily round the merchant and grabbed their friends. The unconscious man was dragged away, his head bumping gently over each tussock of grass, while the other had to be helped to his feet, cradling his sore arm, and led off.

When they had disappeared, Lybbe tossed his new cudgel up, spinning, and caught it again. 'And now, ladies, after what you have gone through, and especially since your servant here has just saved me from a beating, you can have your choice of cloth for half-price.'

Simon and Baldwin stared as Lizzie hurled her cup at Holcroft's head. He ducked and it hurtled past him, shattering against the far wall.

'Murderer! Killer! Coward! Why did you have to kill him? What had he done that many others hadn't already – eh? Was it because you were so weak you had to kill him? You never dared speak to me much before, did you?'

Baldwin prepared to grab her in case she flew at Holcroft. 'Lizzie, please, be quiet and explain yourself.'

'Quiet? Why should I be quiet? I accuse him, that man, our port-reeve, of killing Roger.'

'Why?'

'Because he's always wanted me, ever since he first saw me in here. Because he spotted me going off to my room with Roger yesterday, and was waiting at the doorway when I came out. He didn't come into the tavern afterwards – he must've hurried after Roger and killed him.'

Baldwin glanced at Holcroft.

The port-reeve sat with his head lowered as if expecting

another missile. He had never anticipated that Lizzie would accuse him of murder. Hearing her denounce him gave him a fleeting terror, as if her contempt had scalded his very soul. But somehow it made him feel easier, as if her outburst had destroyed his infatuation completely, leaving nothing, not even regret, in its wake.

The loathing in her voice had cured him of his love for her, whatever its cause. He lifted his head and met Baldwin's gaze steadily.

'She's right. I did want her, and I was devastated when I saw her leaving the room arm-in-arm with Roger. But I swear I had no part in his death.'

'You were there waiting when I left my room,' she blazed.

'Yes, I was. If I'd wanted to kill Roger, I would've been out in the road to ambush him.'

'Oh, rubbish. You had time to chase after him, to stab him and—'

Baldwin held up a hand. 'Please, Lizzie, you have done enough guessing and accusing already. Calm yourself. Agatha – more ale! Now, Lizzie, tell us exactly what happened when you, er, finished with Torre.'

She glared at Holcroft as she spoke, her voice still trembling with anger. 'I heard the bell for compline, and realised we'd been longer than I'd intended, so I got up and dressed while he was still in bed. When I told him that Holcroft here fancied me, he said he had had no idea. He was upset, thinking he might have made the port-reeve miserable by taking me from the tavern so obviously, especially since Master Holcroft had been arguing with him. That argument must have been very nasty, that's all I can say!'

'Yes, and what then?'

Under his patient questioning, she organised her thoughts. 'He dressed and went out. I was still braiding my hair and putting it right. I put on my coif, and had to retie my apron, and I'd missed one of my shoes, so I had to find that, and then I went out. As I was shutting the door, I saw him, Holcroft, leaning against the doorway to the tavern.'

'So he was at the back door to the screens?'

'Yes,' she snapped, irritated by the interruption. 'He was stood there as I came out. When I walked towards him, he turned round and went away.'

Baldwin nodded. 'Holcroft?'

'That's all true enough. I had been waiting a while. I remember the sound of a door opening and slamming, and when I looked, I saw Torre. He saw me at the same time, and hung his head as if he was ashamed, and hurried past me. I waited some time longer, and was about to go back in when Lizzie came out. She looked right through me.' He sipped his drink. 'I decided to go home.'

Simon cleared his throat. 'Which way did you go, Holcroft?'

'Straight up the hill towards Brentor.'

'So the other way from Torre.'

'He must have run after Roger and killed him!' Lizzie proclaimed.

'Was Torre a fool?' Simon asked caustically. 'Was he deaf? Are you telling us you think a man would walk down a road in the middle of a fair at night-time, and not turn at the sound of approaching feet? If he heard someone running after him, he would have readied himself in case he was to be attacked.'

'Not Roger. He knew his way around the town, he'd been here every year for ages. If he heard someone coming down the road after him, he'd just think it was someone in a hurry.'

'You've just told us that Roger was nervous at the thought of upsetting Holcroft here,' Simon pointed out. 'If that's so, he'd certainly have kept an ear out for any steps hurrying after him – unless he was a complete idiot! Who would turn his back on a man who thought his woman had been stolen?'

'I wasn't his woman,' Lizzie said lamely.

'And what of Elias?' Baldwin asked. 'You were sleeping

with him earlier in the afternoon, weren't you? Could he have become jealous of Torre for having you?'

'Jealous – what of? I'm no one's wife; no one owns me, I live as I wish. Why should Elias get jealous of me?'

'Elias left the inn while you were out with Torre. He scurried back in later. It could be that he followed Torre and murdered him. He had to drink some ales quickly to calm himself, or so some have reported.'

Lizzie stared at the knight as though he was mad. 'Elias – *kill*? If you believe that, you'll believe me when I say the sky's green. This man here was the jealous one, not Elias. The baker just got lonely sometimes, and he'd ask me for company. No, Elias wouldn't kill. This man was the one who wanted me all to himself.' She rose, gazing scornfully at the port-reeve, who stared back with a hurt surprise. 'Anyway, I have work to do. I can't sit here dreaming all day, and as far as I am concerned, I don't want to sit anywhere near *you*, David Holcroft, ever again.' Spinning quickly, she flounced from the table.

'Now, David,' Baldwin said kindly. 'I suppose you realise we have to know all about this? I can promise you that if it has no bearing on the killing, it will go no further.'

Holcroft gave a bitter smile. 'Now Lizzie's made up her mind, it'll be all over the town. The Abbot's bound to hear – and my wife.' He sighed.

'Well, Sir Baldwin, it's a brief enough story. I was married when I was very young, and my wife is five years older than me. It was my father's wish that we should be wed, for her father owned a good portion of land out towards Werrington, and that together with my family's holding would have made a sizeable farm, but shortly after we married, my father died, and what with the debts he had at the time, the holdings were ruined. They had to be split up, and afterwards there was less than when we married. Still, I grew to love her, and I was content.

'But lately she's become reserved. It's hard for me to get

a word out of her, and at night she's always tired, or has a headache. This has been going on for a good two months. Maybe it's my fault. They say a man should beat his wife, but I never have.' He continued tiredly, 'I've always worked hard at my trade, but three months ago she started complaining because she never saw me. I couldn't stop, not with the job of port-reeve as well.'

There was a moment's pause while Holcroft collected himself.

'I already knew Lizzie, and as you can see for yourself, any man would want her. Every time I saw her she asked how I was, and always had time to listen. She seemed to care. I suppose you could say I got infatuated with her. At first I'd come here for a quick drink on my way home, but recently I've been coming here just to see her. She takes an interest. It made her really desirable.' He took a long swallow of ale and met their eyes defensively.

'What did you argue about with Torre? Was it her?' Baldwin prompted quietly.

'No, Roger didn't know about my feelings for her – Lizzie herself has told you that. No, it was the monk.'

'Monk? What monk?'

Hesitantly, Holcroft told of Peter and the near-fight with Torre.

'What was Torre on about?' asked Simon with incomprehension. 'The Abbot seems a kindly man, not the sort to upset anyone.'

Holcroft gave him a hard look. 'Robert Champeaux became Abbot here when the place was falling apart. The monks had no money, and everything they tried to do drained more of their resources until they were near desperation. Then Champeaux took over. All at once he found old papers which gave the Abbey certain rights, and he quickly took these up. He borrowed money, loaned money, made profits which he ploughed back into new schemes, ever increasing the Abbey's reserves. I believe he *is* an honourable man, and all he wishes to do is make sure that the Abbey is strong and protected for the future, but there are many who take a different view. They think he's like all the others – simply lining his own pockets at the expense of all the townspeople.'

'And Torre thought that?' Baldwin probed.

'Yes. He thought the Abbot was victimising him. Roger simply couldn't understand that the Abbot would have treated anyone else exactly the same.'

'How was Torre treated?'

'Fairly enough. Roger was one of the Abbey's bondmen – a serf. The Abbot is gradually letting men take on the land with leases for several years, because that way he can charge them annual rent, but he can also get them to pay him extra with the amount they make. He was trying to get Roger to take on a lease, same as everyone else; the trouble was, Roger didn't see it like that. All he could see was that he was being forced into a deal that would cost him many shillings a year to grow the food he depends on. That was why he hated the Abbot, and that was why he insulted him in front of the monk.'

'This monk you say was young Peter?'

'Yes. The boy is still a novice. He was happy to defend his master, just as any young squire or man-at-arms should. I don't know how the Abbot would feel, but he should be grateful that one of his own would want to uphold his name and honour. Anyway, I had to stand between them and suggested the monk should leave before he got into a tavern brawl.'

'And Torre relaxed then?'

'No, Roger thought I was on the Abbot's side and didn't want to stay with me afterwards. That was why he left me and went off with Lizzie.'

'Fine. So later, you went to wait at the door.'

'Yes,' Holcroft agreed heavily. 'I saw Roger leave, and he pushed past me, sort of embarrassed. I just stood there until

Lizzie came out. Then I went off home.'

'On your own?'

'I doubt whether anyone saw me. If they did, I wasn't looking. I wasn't in a good mood.'

'Why? You knew she was a prostitute,' Simon pointed out.

'I don't know. Look, as I've said, my wife won't talk to me any more, and Lizzie was sympathetic. You may think it stupid, just a puerile infatuation, but it felt real enough to me. Seeing her go off with Torre brought it home to me. I wanted to make her feel guilty, waiting there by the door. But I swear I had nothing to do with his murder.'

Baldwin nodded. 'Now Lizzie has accused you of murder, you can hardly help in the inquest. Whatever we found with your help would be disbelieved. It would prejudice any findings.'

'You will have to tell the Abbot.'

'I will tell him nothing. All he needs know is that a woman from a tavern became hysterical and shouted your guilt. That is no proof, and I do not expect it to affect you. But it does put us in a difficult position. If we were to find the real culprit with your help, some might be willing to assume you had sought a scapegoat to protect yourself, and if people are prepared to believe that the Abbot is devious,' he held up a hand to stop the port-reeve's protestations, 'they might also spread rumours that an innocent was hanged to protect the Abbot's man – if, that is, we ever do find someone to accuse.'

Holcroft nodded slowly. 'In that case, I shall return home now. You can always contact me there.'

Simon watched as he stood and made his way out through the door. 'Poor devil!'

'He'll recover. Holcroft will soon pass on his responsibilities to another, and then he'll have time to resolve things with his wife. All he can do now is go home, and that's the one place he can never find any sort of peace. What it must be, to be caught in a loveless marriage.'

'It happens often enough,' said Simon, with the

insensitivity of a man who loved, and was loved by, his wife.

'Yes,' Baldwin agreed, thinking of Jeanne's bright smile. Somehow he was sure she could never be as cruel as Holcroft described his wife. He pushed the picture from his mind. 'I think we should see to Elias now, don't you?'

Chapter Twelve

Edgar was sitting at a bench, a mug of ale in one hand, a small pastry in the other. He had an air of contentment. The knight kicked his seat. 'Eating? I thought I told you to watch Elias?'

'He's there,' Edgar said, pointing with his pie. 'He's not once been out of my sight.'

Baldwin looked. Elias was standing chatting to a bearded man and a friar. 'Come on, let's get it over with.'

As they approached, the bearded man faded into the crowds, but the friar remained. Baldwin walked straight up to the cook.

Elias stood resolutely. His face had taken on the same mulish aspect it had held before. 'Yes, masters? Do you want to buy a pie now?'

'Elias, we have been to your house, and we found something in your yard.'

Baldwin watched him closely as he said this. If there had been even the faintest stiffening of his features, the most momentary movement of his eyelids or twitch of his hands, Baldwin would doubt his strengthening conviction that the cook was innocent, but there was nothing. If anything, Elias looked amused.

'Well, I don't have to clear my yard when there's a fair on. You can't amerce me for that!'

'We found a head buried in your yard, Elias. Torre's head.'

Elias caught at the trestle-top and gaped. 'Torre's head in my yard? Sir, I had nothing to do with it – *I* didn't kill him.

Why would I kill Roger? We never had a cross word. Why, even the night he died, I was sitting with him. Ask Friar Hugo here, he was there with us.'

Baldwin motioned to Edgar. 'I'm sorry, Elias,' he said stiffly. 'There's nothing else I can do. With the body in your alley and the head in your yard, we have to arrest you. I do this with the Abbot's authority.'

'Speak to the friar,' Elias begged desperately.

'Friar?'

Hugo had seen much of England on his travels, and he was wary of knights. Many of the men he had met who bore swords were little more than robbers themselves, and some openly committed felonies. Yet the tall, dark-skinned man before him looked different. There was no ostentation to his dress, and Hugo got the impression that compassion, not violence, lurked behind the shrewd dark eyes.

'Sir, he's telling the truth. I had gone to the tavern with Roger Torre, and this cook joined us.'

'Was this before compline?'

Hugo bobbed his head shyly. 'Sir, I had been there some while with Torre, and by the time Elias arrived I had drunk quite a lot of ale.'

'Then it's no good, Elias. Your alibi is too weak. Edgar, take him to the gaol.'

Baldwin watched while the protesting cook was taken away, held between Daniel and his servant, and when they were out of earshot, he looked at the friar again. 'Before you protest, friar, I agree. I don't think he is a killer – but what will the mob think when they hear the head was found in his yard?'

'I see. It seems harsh to gaol him just because of the mob doubting his word.'

'Better to be harsh now than see him hanged by hot-heads,' said Baldwin. 'And now, is there anything you can tell us about that evening? You say you were with Torre – did you see anyone threaten him, or overhear anything which might help us find the killer?'

Hugo gave him an apologetic look. 'Sir, the ale in that tavern is very strong. I'm not used to such powerful drink, and for most of the evening I wouldn't have been able to hear someone talking to me directly.' He quite liked the look of this knight, but he wasn't going to speak of the other man – not yet. If he was wrong, Hugo didn't want to see an innocent man sent to the gibbet on his evidence. And what evidence did he really have? Just the fact that he thought he recognised a face from years before.

No, he decided. He would wait and consider, and if he became certain, he would tell the knight. Not until then.

With a quick glance after the cook, he walked away.

Baldwin watched him go with a feeling of anti-climax. He was sure that the friar knew something, and that he had been close to telling the knight. 'No matter,' he muttered to himself. 'I will find out another way.'

Peter dithered in the street. He knew he shouldn't be here, but after hurrying back to tell the Abbot about the head, Champeaux had sent him off to find Baldwin, and he was dawdling on his way. He had much to consider.

His vows were to be made soon, and after that he would be committed to God. Once he had entered the gates of the Abbey that last time, he would be lost to the world. From then on, he would no longer be of the material, corporal world, but part of God's kingdom. His body would have been left at the Abbey gates; only his soul would enter.

All he had ever wanted was to be a man of God, but now secular interests were distracting him.

The monks of the Abbey were a mixed bunch, ranging from the completely other-worldly, whom he could hardly understand as their thoughts were so concentrated on the life to come, to the frankly dishonest. These last consorted flagrantly with the people of the town, chatting to them through the Abbey's gates when they could, and sharing ale and gossip; some of them dallied in alehouses and taverns when they should have been at their work. It confused the young man, whose vision before coming to Tavistock had been of a dedicated community serving God and God alone. Here, under the relaxed management of Abbot Champeaux, the monks appeared to work as hard to earn money as they did to earn their place in Heaven.

No matter how often he tried to tell himself that the behaviour of the others was irrelevant, that it was for him to live as he knew he should, looking to the future in Heaven, interceding for the people of the world, and praying for those who had already died that they might be granted entry to Heaven and not hurled into the pit – he sometimes had doubts.

He had been told that doubts were necessary. It was only through facing doubts that a man of God could recognise his own failings and come to that state of grace in which he could serve his Lord fully. One had to confront one's weaknesses before one could give up the world and live solely to pray and save souls.

But Peter was assailed by doubts of a virulent nature. He had thought that his weakness was his laziness, that he might find himself unable to wake in the middle of the night for the service of nocturns, or, worse, might fall asleep in the middle of them. This dull aching desire was something he had never considered.

Yet it was there, and now it appeared to be taking over his entire concentration. Where before there had been only the bitter-sweet adoration of his God, now he found his thoughts always turning from his duties towards the gorgeous, scented figure of Avice Pole.

He shook his head harshly, like a dog drying itself. This was all wrong. He was about to dedicate his life to God, and every time he tried to consider the great burden he was taking on, Avice Pole's face insidiously intruded. The way that she held her head, the way she walked, the slight

narrowing of her eyes as her mouth widened in a grin, all
were indelibly printed on his mind, and he was finding it
harder and harder to shake them free.

A door opened, and he felt an overwhelming urge to flee
as he recognised Avice, as if she was sent to lure him from
his vocation.

She came out with a maidservant – and she looked at
him with a kindly warmth.

Peter felt his heart dissolve into molten lead. It was heavy
with longing, burning with lust for this woman. For a
moment he wondered whether the stabbing agony was
proof of his own death, but then the instant red-hot flush
that scorched his cheeks made him realise that dying would
be preferable. It would not be so embarrassing.

Avice stifled a giggle. Her maid clucked with disapproval,
but the girl could see nothing wrong with talking to a monk,
especially one who was so obviously tongue-tied with
adolescent yearning for her. He was endearing, she thought.
Like a puppy.

'Hello,' she said.

Peter swallowed. He felt as if a large stone had
materialised at the base of his throat. All he could manage
was a grunt.

She began to walk, her eyes on him the whole way, and
as if hauled along by a rope, he found himself trailing beside
her, half unwillingly, half drunk with pride that she should
want him to join her.

At home she was used to lovers who waited hopefully
outside her door. That the monk might have been simply
walking past with no knowledge that she lived there did
not occur to her. Avice assumed, not vainly, but simply as
a matter of logic, that he must have been waiting to see
her, and she was determined to repay him for the compliment. She talked kindly to him, prattling about the
excitement of the fair, telling him of her purchases and
what she must still look for, and he drank in her words like

a wine, and was drunk with admiration for her.

Avice had no idea how total was his ardour. She had grown up in Plymouth, where there were many young men, and she was used to their adoration. In the small town there were no competitors to her beauty matched with her father's wealth. To her, it was merely a whim that she should reward his worship. She had no realisation that a few words from her could cause him to reconsider his vocation, that over the space of a few short yards she would convince him that he could not renounce the world and hide from such tender beauty as she possessed. If she had understood the turmoil in his heart, she might have relented and been curt to him, as a kindness. But she could not appreciate how a young man's desires could be lighted; still less that a monk was a man, possibly a man of even more passion than the weak, vapid youths of her home town.

Peter was fired with adoration. He would give up his cloth, leave the monastery and become an ordinary man: he would marry this woman.

For Avice it was all the more gratifying to receive his attentions because he was a monk. If even a man of God should recognise her beauty, she felt in her youthful arrogance, she must be destined for a great marriage. She couldn't possibly wed John, he was a slob. He had no understanding of art or beauty. No, Avice must find a husband with whom she could create a dynasty. With that gratifying thought her mind turned once more to Pietro.

She was resolved to marry him. She was convinced that he and his father were rich, and that her mother could not object to the match when she saw the true value of the Venetians' estates. For Avice it was irrelevant. Pietro appreciated her – something of which John was incapable.

They were approaching the tavern. Avice remembered the place with fondness, now that the mistake of the previous evening was cleared up. She could recall the doubt and upset while sitting there for so long, waiting and waiting for Pietro to arrive, and then realising he wasn't going to. It had been terrible – the worst night of her life. But his apologies had been so fulsome this morning that she had forgiven him.

She could just make out his figure standing opposite the tavern, and she smiled inwardly. Peter mistook her expression as being on his behalf, and he sighed happily. This, he thought, was the woman for him. She was so kind, so soft and gentle, she would be the perfect wife, an angel on earth. When he was ill, her cool hand would caress his brow; when he was well, she would be a staunch friend and the mother of his children.

He was reflecting happily on his fortune in finding so wonderfully beautiful a mate when he saw the Venetian. The monk was feeling a spark of irritation that the foreigner should interrupt his walk with his woman, when his muse gave a small gasp of delight, and his dreams shrivelled in the heat of his dismay: he had a competitor, a man who was not sworn to chastity. In that second Peter made the decision that would change his life.

Avice hurried forward, her steps light now as she saw her man, and her maid had to collect her skirts in her hands to keep pace. Peter halted, his belly churning.

'My lady, I am honoured to meet you again,' Pietro said softly. 'May I join you?'

'No, you mayn't,' her maid declared hotly. 'She doesn't talk to every foreigner in the town, not when she doesn't know them.'

'Don't worry,' Avice said, her eyes fixed on her lover. 'He has met my parents. Father let me walk with him this morning.'

Her maid muttered darkly, but dared not gainsay her charge. She knew perfectly well that her lady could have a will of steel when it pleased her.

Pietro glanced behind her. 'Who is the little monk?' he asked patronisingly.

His tone stirred her caprice. She turned and waved. 'He is an admirer of mine, no mere monk. I may marry him.'

'Marry him? A monk?' he sniggered.

His amusement stung. 'Monk he may be, but he would give it all up for me.'

'Oh? And what of the noble John?'

'*Him?*' she said scornfully. 'He revolts me. He's a fool, a buffoon. My mother likes him because he is related to a lord, but he is nothing to me. No, I will not marry him. But a young monk? What better proof of devotion could there be, than that a man should give up his religion, his life, everything for his woman? I think he is rather noble.'

'You think so?' Pietro studied her smiling face. It had been bad enough to hear that she was betrothed to a squire, but her denial persuaded him. Yet now she asserted her passion for a feeble monk! He looked back at Peter, suddenly filled with an unreasoning hatred. No boy would come between him and Avice, he resolved. If he was prepared to renounce his calling for a woman, he was no monk, and his cloth wouldn't protect him.

Avice saw his stare, and felt convinced that this man would fight for her if he had to. It was deliciously stirring – and pleasurable.

Abbot Champeaux bowed, smiling, as the Venetian walked from his hall, but by the time he had returned to his table his face had become thoughtful. Cammino's idea *was* interesting, he acknowledged. His proposal to export the wool from the Abbey's flocks by galley instead of slow cogs could well increase their profits. The Venetians with their fast vessels could move it over the Channel to France in half the time – if the weather was good enough – and Antonio appeared keen to form a close alliance with the Abbey, promising loans at low rates if he won this deal.

Yet Antonio da Commino was the very kind of man Champeaux had learned to distrust. The Venetian appeared to have few opinions of his own; he moulded his every word to suit his prospective partner, and Champeaux had the feeling that if he was to say that all merchants and bankers should be hung and drawn, the other would wholeheartedly agree.

The Venetian had made a great play of his contacts, giving the name of the Bishop of Exeter as someone who could confirm his probity and integrity. Perhaps, Abbot Champeaux mused, Antonio had expected to be taken purely at his word; perhaps an Abbot *should* trust to a man's honour – but Champeaux was too wily in matters of business. Something had struck him as false, and as he already had a man going to Exeter, he had sent a message to Stapledon to confirm Antonio's credentials. The reply lay on his table. Stapledon's steward apologised that the Bishop was away, and denied any knowledge of a Venetian called Cammino. The Bishop had never, to his knowledge, had any dealings with such a man. Abbot Champeaux was forced to conclude that he was the target of a trick. It made him determined not to accept the Venetian's offer.

The Abbot stared up through the window towards the west. The sky was purple and golden above the hill, an impossible mixture of colours, and once again he thanked God that his predecessors had chosen to have the Abbey's precincts facing westwards instead of east. He knew it was because of the flow of the river and the lie of the land, all logical, sensible reasons, and all unutterably mundane, but they gave him this magnificent view of the setting sun, and for that he was enormously grateful.

Robert Champeaux had much to be grateful for. He had a good, thriving Abbey, excellent farmland, a prosperous borough, and the conviction that he would be viewed as a patron of the Abbey after his death, which was an honour he had struggled to achieve all his life as Abbot.

The Abbot had always wanted to leave his mark on the Abbey. To him it was a sacred enterprise, one which required all his efforts. The Abbey was a crucial part of the fight against evil, an essential fort in the spiritual conflict, and he intended leaving it in so strong a position that it would last for a thousand years. That was his legacy to Tavistock: a religious institution that would rival the best and strongest in Christendom. If he could have his way, he would like to be remembered on the same basis as one of the founders of the Abbey.

That was why Holcroft's words had unsettled him. It was inconceivable that a monk could attack and rob a man, but Champeaux had evidence from a reliable witness, and as the arbiter of justice in the town, he couldn't ignore what he'd been told. He knew of Will Ruby, the butcher was known as a decent man by all who passed his shop. It would be different if the allegation had been made by a feckless individual like Elias, but when a man like Ruby spoke, only a fool would ignore his words. If Ruby said that a monk had robbed him, unpalatable though that news might be, the townspeople would think it was true, and that could be enough to cause a riot.

Champeaux stood and wandered over to the window, frowning. He must tell the bailiff and his friend, no matter how potentially dangerous the information could be. If they were to come across the story later, they would be justified in being suspicious about his motives for concealing such important evidence. It was distasteful, but necessary.

His decision made, he returned to his desk and sat. His musings were interrupted by a monk tapping at his door. It opened to reveal Margaret and Jeanne.

Margaret had left Hugh to transport their purchases to their chamber next to the Abbot's hall. The servant had said nothing, merely turned and shuffled off with his load like a long-suffering donkey, but Margaret refused to be influenced by his mood. Jeanne had made some good recommendations, and between them, the two women had overloaded Hugh with materials bought at great discount from the curious trader.

The Abbot was at first baffled by their torrent of chatter. 'Ladies, please, one at a time,' he protested as they burst out with the story of their adventure.

Jeanne dropped into a seat as Margaret explained what had happened to them. Now she had a chance to collect herself, Jeanne found her humour falling away like a cloak. She had an irrational loathing for the stallholder: irrational because he had been protecting himself and his goods, and it was the right and duty of any man to protect himself and his property. Yet something about him as he had stood in that vengeful pose had fired a hatred within her, as if it had stirred an ancient memory.

Robert Champeaux greeted Margaret's story with appalled astonishment. It seemed impossible that such an overt attack could have been perpetrated during his fair. As she finished reciting her tale, he found he had to close his mouth; it had fallen wide open in his dismay. 'But ... are you both all right? You were neither of you hurt?'

'No, no, Abbot,' Jeanne said gaily. 'We were fine, it was only the two trail-bastons who were hurt – and their friends, I suppose, if only in their pride.'

'This is dreadful,' the Abbot insisted. 'That men should dare to commit acts of such outlawry, and during the fair too – where were the watchmen?'

Margaret threw a quick glance at Jeanne. The widow was about to speak when Baldwin and Simon entered.

Simon greeted his wife with a suspicious narrowing of his eyes. She looked too cheerful for his purse to have been undamaged after her foray into the fair. Margaret interpreted the look and grinned broadly. 'No, I spent less than you would have expected, husband, but only because of the attack.'

'Attack?' Baldwin asked sharply. 'What happened?'

His face registered his shock as he heard their tale. Simon merely dropped into a seat and nodded. 'I've seen Hugh in action before.'

'Is that all you can say?' Baldwin demanded. 'This is terrible! What if Jeanne or Margaret had been hurt?'

Margaret heard the order of the names and glanced at her new friend. To her pleasure she saw that the widow too had noticed.

Simon shrugged. 'When you're raised as a farmer out in the wilds, you soon learn how to fight. Hugh was trained by protecting his sheep from wolves on four and two legs. If he ran, his father would beat him, so getting into a fight was at least a way of avoiding a thrashing. He learned how to fight well, and not to lose. I pity the man who tries to harm him while he's got a weapon of any sort to hand.'

'And you are sure you're both all right?' Baldwin asked the two women.

'Yes, we're fine,' Jeanne said. Margaret knew there was no need for her to answer.

'You say this merchant sold you his goods at a low price?' Simon pressed relentlessly. 'Does that mean you spent less, or that you bought so much more that you ended up losing all your money?'

'We spent little, especially when you see what we bought,' Margaret beamed.

'And you, Sir Baldwin,' Jeanne added, 'will soon have a new tunic and cloak.'

'A new tunic and cloak?'

He looked so crestfallen that even the Abbot burst out with a guffaw. 'Sir Baldwin, how could you refuse new clothing from two such kind patrons?'

'With difficulty.'

'I fear I will have little to do with it,' Margaret said. 'Jeanne wishes to do all the work herself.'

Simon saw the quick look Jeanne gave his wife and correctly surmised that this was news to her, but he was also pleased to see that she appeared more than happy with the offer. 'Yes, Sir Knight, if you will allow me, I would like to.'

'I would be honoured, my lady,' he said self-consciously.

The Abbot was still considering the problem at the fair. 'Where were the watchmen when these men committed this outrage? I will have to make sure that the men on duty are punished for allowing this.'

'Don't be too hard on them,' Baldwin said as he sat near Jeanne. 'How many hundreds of stalls are there here? You have people from all over the kingdom and over the sea visiting your town. Do not be surprised that there is a minor incident.'

'You are right, especially since there is a more serious matter to attend to. You found the head, Peter tells me,' the Abbot said slowly, 'but it belonged to the man called Roger Torre.'

'Yes. The head was buried in Elias' garden, but we still have no idea why Torre should have been killed. We have arrested the cook.'

'So you *do* think Elias was the killer?'

Baldwin shook his head. 'I can't believe he did it. He is too weak, and I don't think he had time. What is more, he could not have committed this murder without getting blood on him. No, I find it hard to believe that Elias had anything to do with Torre's death.' He explained that they felt Elias would be safer in the goal, and the Abbot nodded understandingly.

'That was a good idea. The mob here can be as unpredictable as the citizens of London. Anyway, there is something else you should know. A man has been attacked by someone in a Benedictine habit.'

'Surely the fellow's brains are addled?' Simon protested when the Abbot had told them Ruby's story. 'Who could accuse a monk of something like that?'

'Sadly, all too many people could believe the worst even of Benedictines. There have been too many tales of men of God becoming outlaws recently, and there are plenty of examples of monks who have chosen to ignore their oaths of chastity and take women. Only a short time ago I heard about a brother who was found abed with a married woman. It's something which always gets bruited abroad, when a monk goes to the bad, and people then look on all as being corrupt and venal.'

'Do you think one of your monks could have done this?' Baldwin asked, toying with his wine. 'Or is it a counterfeit?'

'A few yards of cloth is all that's needed to imitate a monk,' the Abbot pointed out.

Baldwin noted that he did not definitely deny that one of his monks could have committed the robbery. 'You have many men in cloth here.'

The Abbot shot him a glance. 'We are a good size,' he admitted. 'Twelve monks including myself, and another thirty lay brothers and pensioners who also wear the cloth, but I doubt that any of them could have committed a felony like this.'

'No, of course not,' Baldwin said calmly, and the Abbot returned to musing about Elias.

'I'm pleased the cook is behind bars. You may not be convinced of his guilt, but why should someone else put the head in his yard?'

'My question is, why would Elias himself have put it there? Only a fool would bury it so near his own home.'

'He had no time before returning to the tavern,' the Abbot suggested.

'But he did afterwards. Why not dig it up and take it to the midden, and throw it in? At least that way there'd be nothing to connect it to Elias.'

'Did you find a habit in his house?'

'No, my lord Abbot. But we weren't looking for one.'

'If he had one, he would have hidden it,' the Abbot decided.

'I suppose so,' Baldwin agreed reflectively, 'but what interests me is why he is shielding the man he drank with that night.'

The Abbot nodded absently, signing to his steward for more wine, and Peter appeared with a pewter jug on a tray. He poured wine for his master and guests, but then stood before Champeaux, staring at the ground, his hands clenching and unclenching at his side. 'My son, is there something the matter?' the Abbot asked gently.

'Could I beg a moment of your time, my lord?'

'Friends, please excuse me.'

Baldwin watched with interest as the Abbot left the room with the monk, passing through the door behind his little dais, into his private chapel. The bailiff was less inquisitive than the knight, and walked over to chat to his wife.

It was some minutes before the monk reappeared, sniffing and wiping at his face. Behind him, Abbot Champeaux followed hesitantly. He went to his chair and sat, taking a deep draught of wine before staring contemplatively at the door through which the novice had left. 'There are many things in this life which don't make sense,' the Abbot observed.

Baldwin looked at him in surprise. Champeaux had lost his genial good humour. He looked sad and old. 'Is something the matter?'

'There are times when my cross is heavy indeed.'

Baldwin nodded, and turned to talk to Jeanne, but every now and again he found his attention being drawn to the distracted Abbot, who gazed at the door and drummed his fingers on the table before him.

Chapter Thirteen

Hugo walked through the crowds peering about him as he sought the man again. Since Elias had been taken, he had wandered among the throng looking for the bearded man, but he had disappeared.

The friar was uncertain if he had done the right thing. Perhaps he should have trusted the tall knight and told him all he knew, but what if he was wrong? It was dangerous to trust to memory, especially after twenty-odd years, but how much more dangerous *not* to report it? Then there was the bearded Jordan: telling Baldwin must surely result in Lybbe's death. Yet Hugo would have to inform Jordan that Elias had been arrested, in case he had not yet heard.

He pensively carried on down towards the square as he thought through his difficulties, and there he forgot his troubles in fascination at the plays and acrobatics displayed.

One of the hardest duties of a friar was finding new material for preaching. He, like the other members of the friars minor, believed that preaching dogmatically was pointless when the audience was largely uneducated. He was always on the lookout for material which would bring home moral points simply. It was with this in mind that his attention wandered over the people watching the miracle plays.

It was almost night when Marion Pole set her needlework aside and threw her husband an anxious glance. 'Where could she have got to?'

Arthur put his pot down and shook his head. 'She must have chosen to watch some of the entertainments. Perhaps she has gone to a tavern.'

'You don't seem very concerned about your daughter. She's only young.'

'But clever enough to escape danger.'

'You may think so, but I'm not convinced of it.'

'Marion, she will be fine. She doesn't often get the chance to see a fair.'

'Husband, have you forgotten about her and that foreigner? What if she is holding a secret tryst with him even now?' Her face hardened. 'You don't think she intended that, do you – that she went out hoping to see that Venetian again?'

'Marion, Avice is in the company of Susan. That maid would tell you anything that happened if it was remotely indecorous.'

'But what if your daughter was to commit an indiscretion?' Marion asked, her face blank with horror.

'Woman, are you suggesting that Susan would allow her charge to have a tumble in a common alehouse? Or do you think Avice could couple in the street without her maid noticing? Don't be so ridiculous.'

'But Arthur, what if she's been attacked? You hear such dreadful things about fairs, especially large ones like this. What if—?'

'What if the sky should fall in or the sun forget to rise in the morning,' he snapped. 'Don't be stupid, woman – she told you she would be gone for some time. It's not compline yet. If something was to happen to her, Susan would stop Avice being harmed, and if she failed, I have Henry watching them both.'

'Henry?'

'Yes. And if our groom saw anyone trying to threaten our daughter, he would die rather than see her come to any harm. You know him as well as I do. So,' his voice rose, 'by

God's own blood, will you stop worrying and leave me in peace for a while? I have enough to think about with all the business I am conducting at this fair without your inane chatter!'

In his room, Antonio da Cammino paced angrily as the light faded outside and the monks entered to light the place. It was difficult to keep a calm exterior while these innocent fools went about their business, but he kept a tight rein on his tongue as the men slowly walked round with their candles and tapers, setting the waxen tubes down and lighting them. He even managed a smile of gratitude as they finished and left him alone.

Only then did he allow himself to consider his son again. The cretin had been behaving like a love-lorn squire from a courtly tale. Antonio walked to the window and stared out. He had meant what he'd said: he would not wait while his son indulged his whim for a girl. There were plenty of pretty maids at home; there was no need to seek one here in this godforsaken backwater.

From his room in the southern perimeter wall of the Abbey, near the Abbey bridge, he could look out over the river to the pastureland beyond. Cattle stood idly. A hog grunted at the edge of the trees, and he could hear doors slamming and people calling out as the town settled for the night. Whistling and shouting showed that not all were ready for their rest, however. Some of the youngest were looking for entertainment, and were determined to find it: there was a pattering of feet under his window as somebody rushed down the riverside path.

After his years in Gascony, Antonio was astonished that so small a borough could accommodate so many people. Obviously all the traders stayed with their goods, as there were not many who could afford to rent a room and hire staff to guard stock every night, and there was a large tented encampment east of the fairground where many of the excess people slept, but there was still a huge number who found houses in the town itself.

Of course, Tavistock was not in the same category as Orléans or Paris in France, or the English King's fairs at La Rochelle, Bordeaux, Winchester and London, but it still had a huge attraction for many people. They flocked here, yet Antonio could not understand why.

It was not that the town was easy to get to. For the most part the roads were poor, although Antonio thought they all were in this benighted kingdom. It could hardly be the climate, for though it had been warm and pleasant enough today he knew that here, near what had been the King's forest of Dartmoor, the weather was apt to change in minutes from sunny and bright to gloomy, wet and miserable.

Antonio turned from the view and walked back to the table, resignedly pouring himself a large mug of ale. He disliked the weak and chilling, belly-filling flavoured water the English peasants lived on. The Abbot, he knew, kept a good cellar of wine, but that was for his own use, and though the Abbey had a duty to provide hospitality to travellers, the Abbot had no compunction charging his guests for the wine they drank. It was a sign of parsimoniousness that rankled with the Venetian. His money was tight enough as it was. He preferred to force himself to consume this unwelcome brew while dreaming of the strong red wines of Guyenne.

Abbot Champeaux was an odd fellow, he thought. Seemingly genial, he had a hard streak when it came to business. Antonio had hoped that his offer would have been taken up faster than this, and that he might have been away from here within a day or two. Instead it appeared that the other man needed time to consider his proposals. All it entailed was a monopoly on wool for three years, which was hardly a great period, and his offer of cheap loans should have made the Abbot snap up the offer.

Antonio hoped that the deal would go through. He needed the money that the wool would bring, especially after the

fiasco in Bayonne where they had been chased out by a
horde of angry townspeople. The resulting chase had
almost cost them their lives. Luckily Luke had thought to
cut the reins of the pack-horse, and without the slow beast
to hold them back they had evaded capture. Not that
Antonio had thanked his servant. It had been his duty to
save the goods. Still, there was no getting away from the
fact that when a knight, three squires, and two men-at-arms
were thundering after you, it was better to cut the traces
and one's losses to stay alive.

He looked up at the sound of a door opening and shutting.
After a few moments, he heard the light step of his son, the
heavier tread of Luke.

'You deigned to return, then? How kind of you. Perhaps
you would like me to kill the fatted calf?'

His sarcasm had no effect on the good humour of his
son. 'Father, you may be irritated, but I have had a pleasant
evening and I will not allow you to spoil it. Come and pour
ale, Luke. My father needs something for his digestion.'

'No, we're due with the Abbot, and we're already late.
You can drink when we are with him. At least there we'll get
good wine, instead of this muck.'

He scowlingly pulled on an overtunic and coat, giving his
son's attire a swift appraisal. Pietro had dressed well for his
girl. He wore tight hose under his shirt and short tunic, and
his best fur-lined cloak: he would do for their host. 'Come
along, then. I don't want to see the Abbot upset because of
your lateness.'

They crossed the Great Court, past the stables and store-
rooms, past the sties and kennels, and entered the Kitchen
Court. Walking through it, they came to the prayle – the
yard before the Abbot's lodging, where he kept a small
orchard and garden, secluded from the busyness of the
Great Court, in which he could sit in peaceful
contemplation.

The Abbot's hall was in a building that formed a part of

the Abbey's main perimeter wall. They entered and
ascended the stairs to his rooms, following behind an
elderly servant.

'My apologies, Father,' Antonio said as the door swung
open. 'My son forgot the time, and has only now returned. I
trust we have not delayed your meal?'

'Not at all, not at all. Please, come in and take some wine
with us.'

While the wine was poured, Antonio surreptitiously kept
an eye on the others. The bailiff, he knew, was married to
the blonde woman, but the knight appeared to be paying
great attention to the widow. Antonio stored the information
for future use. It was always best, as an international trader
and merchant, to log any points that could be of interest. If
he was questioned, as he often was, about who knew whom
and whether they were friendly towards each other, tiny
snippets as to who was wooing which lady could be useful.
Dealing with officers of kings he always found distasteful,
but sometimes giving away gossipy items about people as a
spy was the only way to avoid the more penal rates of tax.
And sometimes information like this was useful locally; after
all, any lord in the area could have an interest in someone
as important as the Keeper of the King's Peace.

The servants were seated at a second table nearer the
door. He saw Pietro frown as a monk entered with the
knight's servant, Edgar, who stood surveying the room
before walking to his own place between Peter and Hugh.

At his own table, the Abbot sat to one side, giving pride of
place to Baldwin, his most important ranking guest. Antonio
and his son took their seats near Baldwin, next to Simon
and Margaret, while Jeanne was placed beside Baldwin at
Abbot Robert's insistence.

Jeanne gave a bright smile of apparent pleasure as the
Abbot helped her to her seat, but in her heart she would
have been happier to curse him. Champeaux's motives were
transparent, and she didn't want a new husband yet.

It was not that Sir Baldwin de Furnshill was unattractive.
While he was chuckling at a quip from Margaret, she took
the opportunity to study his profile. He was quite comely,
she thought – a strange mix of Norman and Celtic, with his
swarthy skin and dark hair. The scar on his cheek gave him
a reckless, devil-may-care air, though she was sure it didn't
reflect his nature. He appeared too solid and considerate.
From the short conversations she had held with him, it was
obvious that he was concerned for those poorer than himself, although his reticence about the Church was curious
to her. She didn't know he had been a Templar, and since
the destruction of his Order had held the Pope and his
cardinals in low regard.

It was a pity, she felt, that she had not met Sir Baldwin
before and got to know him. Now, under the gaze of so many
others, especially the bailiff's wife, she felt as if she was
being forced into a courtship for which she wasn't ready.

The bowl arrived, and she dipped her hands in it, taking
the towel and drying them. Afterwards she caught
Baldwin's eye, and saw that he was nervous, too. Jeanne
was offended. What reason did *he* have to be nervous? The
man should have found her perfectly desirable; she wasn't
too old for him, surely? That Baldwin might be experiencing
similar qualms as herself made Jeanne quite annoyed – and
then she saw him give a quizzical look, and almost laughed
out loud as she recognised the irony.

Their predicament was largely due to the matchmaking
zeal of Margaret and the Abbot. Their attempts at subtlety
were a farce, Jeanne thought, without rancour. They were
trying, no doubt, to help their friends find happiness, though
how curious it was that they should think they knew the
key to other people's contentment.

As if by agreement, both chose not to speak to the other.
It was not a conscious decision on either side, more a
reaction to the air of anticipation in which they were
watched.

Margaret noticed the apparent coldness between the two. During the course of the meal she had seen that Baldwin and his elegant neighbour spoke little if at all, and she felt a growing frustration that her hopes might be thwarted, for she was keen to see him marry someone who could provide him with company and children, and this was the first woman in whom he had displayed any interest. That they should suddenly have developed a frostiness was worrying. She cast a quick look at her husband to see whether he had also noticed, but he was talking to Antonio. She heard the Venetian say:

'You mean to say that the dead man was not the stranger, as everyone thought?'

'No, sir. The man who was killed was a local farmer by the name of Roger Torre. He was in the tavern as well that night.'

'But I thought ... I assumed he must have been identified. How could you have been so mistaken?'

'Yes, why could you not tell at once?' Pietro frowned. 'Did no one bother to view the body?'

'Of course,' Simon explained patiently. 'But the killer had cut off the corpse's head and hidden it. It's hard to recognise a body when there is no face.'

Pietro and Antonio exchanged a baffled look. It was the father who stammered, 'His head? Why ... I mean, why should a man do that to his victim, bailiff?'

Jeanne pursed her lips in distaste. 'It seems a particularly cruel thing to do to a victim: take the life and then desecrate the corpse.'

'That's what worried us as well. It makes no sense.' Simon broke off a piece of his bread and chewed it meditatively. 'We have arrested the man in whose yard the head was buried.'

Baldwin was glad that Simon carefully avoided suggesting he thought Elias was the murderer. Enough people would be bound to assume his guilt without their help. He waved a hand, vaguely encompassing the borough outside the Abbey. 'There is no need to worry all the traders. I daresay it was a dispute of some sort, which quickly led to blows, and for some reason the killer decided to take the head.'

'A curious trophy,' Antonio mused.

'I expect you saw the dead man yourself, sir,' Simon continued, thinking of Elias' words. 'He was in the tavern at the same time as you.'

Antonio shrugged. 'The tavern? Which tavern?'

'The one on the way to the fair. You were there, weren't you? Torre was the man you barged into as you left,' Baldwin said, and was surprised when the old Venetian stared at him with suspicion.

'Do you suggest that *I* was involved in this dreadful act, Sir Baldwin?'

The Abbot interrupted soothingly. 'The knight suggested nothing, Antonio. He was merely commenting that you might yourself have seen the man.'

'Has the man confessed yet?'

'No,' said Baldwin, returning to his food. Looking up, he noticed a strange expression on the Abbot's face as he watched Antonio: suspicion mixed with a certain hardness. As Champeaux caught his eye, his face relaxed once more into genial hospitality. 'More wine, Sir Baldwin?'

'Thank you.' Baldwin waved the bottler on to Jeanne, whose goblet was almost empty. He was intrigued by the look on the Abbot's face. It evidently betrayed some inner concern, but what that concern could be, he had no idea. Then he recalled that Roger Torre had made allegations against the Abbot just before he died. It was hardly conceivable that Robert Champeaux himself could have been involved in the murder, but he could have come to hear about it – there was always the confessional. That made him think of the monk. Baldwin found himself surreptitiously watching Champeaux and the novice Peter.

Antonio was eager for any information about the murder, but that was no surprise. In Baldwin's experience any murder attracted great public interest, and when it was as bizarre as this, with a decapitated corpse and a head found hidden in a vegetable garden, any man would be keen to know all the details. When he glanced over at Jeanne, however, he saw that the talk was offending her.

She sat stiffly as the discussion ranged over the mystery, rarely looking his way. It made Baldwin a little sad. He had thought she was interested in him when they had first met, but now she concentrated on her food and rarely even glanced in his direction. The knight saw her eyes flit quickly towards Margaret, and then he understood. He had been aware for over a year of the solicitous marriage planning on his behalf which the bailiff's wife had undertaken. It was as plain as a battle-axe in a church that she had decided the knight had found his mate; intuitively, he guessed that for her part, Jeanne de Liddinstone was fearful of being paired again so soon after losing her husband.

But she was very attractive; the ideal vision of a knightly lady. And the way her nose wrinkled when she laughed, the coy manner she had of peeping at someone from the corner of her eye, her intenseness when she listened, head set to one side as if he was the only person in the room, all made her desirable. That she was young and healthy merely added to her allure.

Looking up, she saw his expression, and he was about to glance away, embarrassed to be discovered studying her, when she smiled, and suddenly he did not mind Margaret preening herself at the other side of the table.

He was startled from his thoughts by the Abbot leaning towards him. 'Sir Baldwin, would you like to arrange to come hunting with me?'

'Yes, indeed – but do you not have other duties with the fair? It would be kind of you, but surely you have enough to do without seeing to the comfort of a wandering guest?'

Champeaux shrugged. 'My life is one of constant toil with God's work: *Opus Dei*. Yet if tomorrow I have to celebrate our founding saint, I can take time the day after to relax. There's little enough for me to do, in any case. The fair runs itself, with the port-reeve taking most of the burden, so all I am expected to do is wait here in case I'm needed, and usually on the third day of the fair I'm not. It's too quiet. Will you join me?'

'I would be delighted, Abbot.'

'Then that's settled.'

The meal ended soon afterwards. Compline was not for another hour, but the Abbot had many duties to attend to. As his guests prepared to leave, Baldwin found himself alone with Jeanne. Simon and Margaret pointedly waited at the door, looking at him.

He could not simply walk away as if she did not exist. 'My lady, I . . . er . . .'

Once he began, he had no idea how to continue. Aware of the interested expression on Edgar's face, he found himself colouring, and felt a rush of irritation. He was a knight trained in warfare. All over the known world he had travelled without fear, purely because of his prowess with lance and sword; yet now he was flustered, embarrassed and nervous simply because of a woman. It was insufferable.

But of all the knightly skills, the one he needed most now was the one in which he had never been instructed. Squires were taught courtly manners and how to behave with women, but he had learned his knightly skills as a warrior monk. There had been no place for the soft art of courtship when he had taken his vows.

Jeanne saw his pain. 'Sir Baldwin?'

'Lady, I wanted to . . . er . . .' He wanted to apologise if she had felt pressured, to make her know that he held her in high regard. Yet to say so would imply that she had felt such pressure, and what if she had not? Suddenly he was hemmed in with doubts. 'Lady, I . . .' Then inspiration struck. 'Would you like to walk for a little? The evening is clear and warm, and I would be honoured to accompany you, if you wouldn't feel my company to be boring.'

She glanced at the door. Antonio and Pietro stood talking, openly watching her. Near them were Simon and Margaret. The bailiff's wife wore a look of approval, and Jeanne saw her give a quick nod as if in encouragement. It decided her. 'I fear I would feel the cold.'

Instantly she saw the sadness, and loneliness in his eyes as he nodded gravely. 'I understand. I will not trouble you again.'

'But if I could send someone to fetch my cloak, I should be all right, shouldn't I?' she said quickly, and was surprised at her own pleasure at the thought.

Baldwin could not prevent himself standing a little more erect with pride as he walked with her to the door. Then he became aware of his servant at his shoulder. 'Um, Edgar? I think you may leave me. I shall not need you.'

Edgar looked at him blankly. He disliked leaving Baldwin unprotected. But as his master stepped out of the room and Edgar heard his steps echoing along the passage and out of the building, he shrugged. There could be little enough danger from the pretty widow, and what danger there was, Baldwin would be certain to enjoy.

Chapter Fourteen

At the fairground, Jordan Lybbe bundled up the last of his goods and tossed them into his makeshift shed. Hankin leaned against the pole supporting the roof with his arms crossed. His work done for the day, he was finding it difficult to keep his eyes open, and Lybbe gave him a friendly clout over the shoulders. 'Don't worry, boy! You can soon shut your eyes and get some sleep. Stay in there tonight. When you wake up I'll have your breakfast ready.'

He watched the lad affectionately. Hankin was only ten years old. Lybbe had saved him when his parents had died of a fever, over in Gascony. The town had been unwilling to take on an orphan, and it had been difficult for the English boy in a strange land with no friends. He had become like a son to the lonely Lybbe.

As Hankin went inside with the cloths and made himself a bed of rugs on the grass, Lybbe stood and breathed in the clear evening air.

A breeze flapped the pennants and flags, whipping away the thin grey coils of smoke from the fires out behind the ground where the tents and wagons stood. Fires might be illegal within the fairground itself, but men still needed to keep warm. The wind brought the tang of burning faggots with it, and hints of cooking, making Lybbe's empty stomach rumble. Although it was chilly, it was a relief after the heat of the day. The coldness reminded the merchant of his youth here in the town.

He stood in the alleyway between the stalls and stared up

at the heavens. The sky was a deep blue, with a thick
sprinkling of stars shimmering and dancing high above.
Lybbe was not given to contemplation, but when he saw
those glittering specks, the thousands upon thousands of
pin-pricks of light high overhead, he felt an awe and
reverence for God.

Slowly he began to make his way towards the town. The
fair was quiet now, but just beyond its ditch were small
groups sitting at fires, warming their hands and chatting
easily about the day's business. At this time of evening, all
the customers had gone and the only people remaining
within the perimeter were the stallholders or their guards.
After standing all day and shouting their wares, most were
exhausted, and needed to rest their feet and throats. They
drank from pots of ale or cider, talking in muted voices as
they stared wearily at the flames, preparing for the night.
Lybbe knew a few, and called out to them as he passed,
feeling again the gratitude that among so many visitors he
would be unlikely to be recognised, especially with his
beard. He looked nothing like the youth who had been
forced to leave after the murders.

At the entrance to the fairground he paused. Lybbe had
expected to find Elias waiting, but the cook was nowhere to
be seen. There was no hurry. Lybbe found a log to sit on in
the darkness under a low eave and folded his arms
contentedly.

Elias had been shocked to find Lybbe back in Tavistock.
The last time they had met, Lybbe had been a fugitive, an
outlaw, and Elias had given him food and a bed while they
planned how to effect his escape – the only alternative was
the rope. That had been almost twenty years ago now, and
Lybbe had been surprised by the force of the emotion he
had felt when he had once more entered his town, the place
he had known as home.

Once he had got over his initial disbelief, Elias had been
effusive in his welcome, insisting on purchasing ever more

ale, but Lybbe had an aversion to drinking too much. He was nervous of talking too loudly or unwarily, and knew how ale could loosen tongues.

It had alarmed him when the watchmen had attacked him. He had assumed they were seeking him out for his crimes; it was only as they pounced that he realised they wanted to scare him after his refusal to submit to their extortion. In any case, Jordan Lybbe had a loathing for men who tried to coerce others into giving up their goods for no reason. He had put up with enough of that before, and wouldn't accept it any more.

He found it worrying that Elias was late. After a separation of twenty years, he would have expected punctuality. There was so much still to talk about. Probably it was the horror of the previous night catching up with him, he thought.

Elias had been terrified. That was why Jordan had sent the cook away before he had swapped clothes with the man – and before he had hewn off the head. Elias wouldn't have been able to cope with that. It couldn't hurt the dead man, but it could protect *him*, Lybbe.

Hearing steps, he glanced quickly down the street, but it was a couple. Peering, he recognised one of the women who had witnessed the attack on him.

Baldwin did not know Lybbe, and had all his attention fixed on the woman at his side. Jeanne was giggling at a quip from him, and Lybbe smiled at their self-absorption. It was good to see two people so happy in each other's company.

To the knight, the fair was not as impressive as one of the huge ones in London or Winchester, but it was not so daunting either. The fairs at Smithfield and St Giles were massive, attracting so many people they were quite fearful to the country knight. He sought a quiet and restful life, and Tavistock was better suited to his tastes.

There were a few people still wandering among the little

lanes and alleys, and Baldwin kept his sword-hand free. It
had been drummed into him continually while undergoing
his training that he should always be ready to defend himself and others who might need his aid, and with so many
strangers in the town he felt a vague unease without his
servant near to hand.

'You have never been married?' she asked.

'No. I spent my youth in Outremer, in the Kingdom of
Jerusalem, and then in Cyprus and Paris. I only returned
to England four or five years ago when my brother died
and left the estates to me. Before that I was without a
lord or master of any sort – marriage was out of the
question.'

'You could have married when you returned.'

'There has never been the time. As soon as I came back,
I was asked to become the Keeper of the King's Peace, and
since then I have had little time to seek out a wife.'

She threw a quick look at him from the corner of her eye.
The idea that this knight should have been so continually
occupied that he had no time left to find a woman was
preposterous. He was a knight; he could make time to do
anything he wanted.

'It wasn't only that, though,' he confessed, seeing her
shrewd glance. 'I am not a youthful knight, am I? Women
expect young, chivalrous admirers, not hardened old
warriors with few graces like me.'

She gave him a look of mock disgust. 'Oh, Sir Knight,
you're right! You are so ancient and grizzled, how could any
maid look upon you except with pity?'

'You see? Even *you* can't treat me seriously,' he grumbled,
but there was a vein of sadness in his expression which
gave rise to a feeling of tenderness in her breast.

She tried to quash it as soon as she was aware of it,
reminding herself that she did not need this man, and if he
was still alone after so long, he must be dull indeed, but his
loneliness touched her. 'I am surprised you weren't married

when you were younger. Have you given up all hope of finding a wife?'

'It was not possible. At first there was the distraction of war, then the long process of recovery and at last the poverty of being a lordless outcast.'

Jeanne looked up at him. The starlight was kind to him, smoothing out the lines of pain and making him look younger. His hair gleamed in the grey light, giving him an air of quiet dignity, but there was suffering in his voice when he talked about his past. She couldn't understand what made him so bitter, but she'd seen impoverished knights, as had everyone in Europe. All over Christendom there were knights who had lost their lords, whether from arguments, or because their masters had died, or from some other reason. Once they were without a home, they became wanderers, without income or patron, and with no source of food or even a bed. They were sad men, often proud and haughty beneath their dishevelled exterior, who had been struck down by a quirk of fate. Many resorted to villainy, robbing to live.

Jeanne had never considered them before, but now found herself wondering how these knights survived. How would her own dead husband have reacted if he had not been able to inherit his lands and money but had been forced to seek a new master, only to find that his new lord was bested in battle, or killed, or died of a fever, and the son was not keen on keeping his father's old retainers? She had little doubt that her husband would have taken to the woods, become a renegade and outlaw, and died young, hanging ignominiously from a tree. The thought made her shudder.

At once Baldwin was solicitous. 'Are you cold? Would you like to return?'

'No, Sir Baldwin, I am fine, really. Please, tell me about your home – about Furnshill.'

His voice softened. 'It is an old house, long and narrow, on the side of a hill. There are woods behind and to either side, and a stream which starts from the ground near the house. I have good farmland, with several vills and bartons, and the villeins keep the house filled with food even when they have taken enough for themselves. On a clear day, I can sit before my threshold and look out over the hills for miles, and see almost nothing except trees and my fields.'

'I should like to see it.'

He glanced across, surprised. 'Would you? You would be very welcome. I shall ask Simon to bring you the next time he comes, if you wish.'

'That would be very pleasant,' she said.

'And what of yourself? A woman like you could find another husband with ease.'

His boldness made her stammer. 'Me? I . . . It is good of you to say so, but there are many widows, and more young women. Why should a man look to a woman of nine-and-twenty when he has his pick of younger ones? Anyway, I am content.'

Baldwin was about to answer when he noticed another couple. To his surprise he recognised the young monk and a girl; a maidservant stood nearby, clucking with disapproval. 'I think we might have happened on a sad event,' he murmured as they approached.

Avice was staggered at the effrontery. 'You would like to marry me? *You?* And where would you have me live – in the gatehouse with the other guests?'

'No, my lady, I will find us a house. It needn't be too large for only we two.'

'Oh yes? And how will you, sworn to poverty, buy food for us to live on? If your Abbot allows you to live outside the Abbey . . . *Can* he do that?'

'But it is arranged! I haven't taken the vows yet. My Abbot has agreed that I may leave the Abbey,' Peter said desperately, confused by her rejection. He could not have mistaken

her feelings, not when her smile at him had been so kind
and sweet earlier that morning. She must be displaying
anger because her maid was there, he reasoned. 'All I have
to do is tell the Abbot when I am to leave.'

'You may leave the Abbey when you like if you are so
incontinent you may not swear to chastity, but don't expect
me to accept poverty for no reason. The thought of it!
Quitting my home to live in a hovel like a peasant!'

'Leave us a moment,' Peter said to the maid.

Avice stamped her foot. 'Let her alone! She's my servant,
and if I wish her to go away, *I* will order her, not some
impecunious monk!'

Avice was aggrieved that this scrawny little clerk should
dare to embarrass her in front of Susan. Although she had
proudly boasted to Pietro earlier that she had won the heart
of the monk, she'd not realised her victory had been so
complete. When she'd said that he would give up his service
to God, she had been trying to make the Venetian jealous,
nothing more. To be confronted with the adoration of the
pasty-faced cleric was alarming; no, more than that – it was
fearful. What would happen to her soul if she were to tempt
a monk from his vocation, she wondered distractedly. The
thought lent venom to her voice. 'Leave me alone, I don't
want to see you again.'

'But lady, I . . .'

'I wouldn't think of having you for my husband if you were
the only man in Christendom, not if you were wealthy
beyond equal, not if you were a king. To shame me in the
street like this! No, go! Leave me alone, and never speak to
me again.'

She swept on; the monk stared after her, his mouth open
with utter dismay, but she didn't look back. Uppermost in
her mind was the long prayer she would have to say before
retiring to bed, and the apology and confession she must
offer to the priest at her next Mass. She was shocked,
horrified, that the silly boy could think she would be

prepared to give up her life and become his wife. 'Who does he think he is?'

'He thought he was the man you loved,' said Susan curtly.

'Don't answer me back! Keep a civil tongue in your head or I'll see to it that you leave my father's house.'

'It was your flirting that ensnared the boy, not my words. If you want to snap at someone, bite she who caused your troubles – *you*!'

'Be quiet!'

Susan shrugged, but without concern. She knew her mistress was making an empty threat; she would not give up her maid, not that she had much choice. No matter how much her father wanted to please her, he knew Susan had been picked by his wife, and Arthur would not risk offending Marion just to satisfy his daughter's caprice.

As the boy hurried past, Baldwin called to him. 'Peter? Are you well?'

Peter's visage was a picture of devastation. He stared without recognition at the knight, backing away, his mouth moving but no words coming. Suddenly he spun round and fled off, straight up the hill away from the town.

Baldwin made as if to run after him, but Jeanne laid a hand on his arm. 'Leave him. I think he has a degree of pain and suffering that no words can heal.'

'But what could have caused it?' Baldwin asked.

Jeanne motioned towards Avice's speedily disappearing back. 'I think you need ask her that. It was she who talked to him just now, and surely she must know what has cut his heart in two.'

Baldwin stood a moment undecided. 'What could a young girl have said to have wounded a monk so grievously?'

'I can think of a few.'

'That is hardly likely, surely.'

She made an exasperated gesture with her hand. 'A young man is a young man, whether he wears the clerical

garb or not. Just because he has a black habit doesn't mean
he can't feel the same lusts as a normal boy.'

'But a monk!' Baldwin fell silent, deep in thought. He
could remember a time when he was younger, recuperating
in Cyprus. There had been a girl to tempt him then, and the
anguish he had endured after giving her up was painful to
recall. 'I suppose he is a novice still and has not taken his
vows.'

'Perhaps. But I think it would be more pleasant to go
home the way we came rather than following after either of
them, don't you?'

Baldwin stared up the street as if seeking the monk, and
nodded.

Hugo left the last of the revellers and walked back to the
little house where he had lodging. It had not been a fruitful
evening. Whenever he had seen a possible new theme for a
sermon, the killing intruded on his mind, and the face in
the tavern. It was frustrating – and worrying – and he
prayed for guidance as he walked up the hill.

A short way from the fairground, he saw two women
approach. He did not recognise Avice, although her face
seemed familiar to him, but when he saw the cowled figure
that hurried from the shadows towards her, he was
surprised. It was a young monk, who addressed the women
with apparent familiarity. Avice clapped her hands with
delight, and allowed him to join her.

Hugo watched, stunned, as the three passed by him. No
monk should be so familiar with a woman. There were no
lights here, not with the strictures for safety imposed by the
watch, but the three passed close enough for the friar to
recognise Pietro's face, and Hugo felt the chill of horror.

A lad who could steal a Benedictine habit and wear it in
public, laughing as he polluted it by wooing a girl, was
capable of anything.

*   *   *

Elias sat in his cell and wrapped himself in the rough blanket the watchman had sold him. The cell was a mere ten feet square, and Elias had been in it once before. That was twelve years ago now, when he had been found selling pies containing meat that had gone off, and he had spent a morning in the clink before being hauled off to the pillory, where the 'putrid, stinking and abominable meat' pies were burned beneath his nose. It was a salutary lesson for a young cook, and had ruined his business for some months.

It was not a serious crime. He had known as soon as he was caught exactly what would happen. It was a common enough sight to see a baker, cook or brewer being locked in the pillory for a day after adulterating their produce with cheap ingredients, or some which had gone bad. He'd known the risk and accepted it, because the pigeons had been too expensive to simply throw away, and he hadn't expected anyone to realise there was anything wrong with them – he'd used his spices more liberally than usual to disguise the rotten meat. It had been typical of his luck that a couple of youngsters and a woman had been ill after eating them.

But he couldn't fool himself that he would get away with a day in the pillory or stocks with this. Why Lybbe had decided to hide the head in his garden he couldn't understand. It was madness! Yet he realised Lybbe might not have known where else to hide it. He'd not been to Tavistock for many years, and wouldn't have wished to wander round the town hunting for a suitable cache.

Outside he occasionally heard the steady tramp of boots as the guard walked past, and the man's shadow crept along the inner wall of his prison thrown by a blazing torch on the building opposite. It was one of only a few kept lighted to make escape difficult. Elias could see the market-place outside in his mind's eye. It was a large area, roughly triangular, where the tinners regularly came to coign their metal and buy provisions. He'd always viewed it as a pleasant part of town, even after his previous confinement; it always seemed so busy and bustling.

His head drooped. He had done nothing wrong, but he was to stand trial for murder. He had no doubt of that after seeing the grim expression on Baldwin's face. It was unjust, unfair, but he knew life was often both. Shivering, he pulled the blanket tighter round his shoulders and pessimistically considered his future.

One thing he was determined on: he would not betray Jordan. In all likelihood it would do no good. It would only mean that both would hang. There was no point in dragging Jordan in and seeing him die too. Elias was a realist, and knew that Lybbe had no chance of escape if he should be called before a judge or coroner. That was the irony of the whole affair: his only protector was the one man he could not call, the only one who was in mortal danger should he be discovered. In any case, his word would be disbelieved, so his alibi for Elias could not help.

At the sound of scratching, he tutted and huddled deeper into his blanket. It was just his luck to have to share his cell with a rat. The scratching came again, and he jerked awake. At the barred window was an indistinct, crouching shape. Elias could just make out the head of a man. 'What?' he asked irritably. 'You want to gloat at a man's misery, do you? Bugger off! Leave me al—'

There was a low chuckle, and he felt the skin on his neck stand vertical. 'What are you doing here? God's teeth, Jordan! What if someone sees you?'

'Hush! Nobody'll see me. What are you doing here? I thought you'd been waylaid when you didn't turn up. I've only just heard you were taken by the watchmen.'

'They found the head.'

Lybbe felt the breath freezing in his chest. 'They found it? Christ's blood!'

'Yes, but don't worry. I'll—'

'You'll what? You mustn't die on my account, Elias. Oh,

Good God, how can *You* let this happen?'

Elias gave a wry smile at the bitter tone of voice. '*He* didn't; *you* did. If you want someone to blame, blame yourself for putting the damned thing in my garden.'

'I must surrender myself. Admit to what I did and explain why.'

'You think that'll help us? This is England, Jordan, not some wonderful place like the preachers talk about, where there's justice and fairness for all and no one can be hanged and quartered on a whim.'

'I can't let you die without trying to save you, Elias.'

'You can't do *anything*,' the cook pointed out wearily. 'If you confess to what you did, they'll hold you too, and when we go before the judge, we'll both be hanged. What good would that do? Leave me to my fate. At least if I say nothing, they'll have to prove me to be a liar. Find me a lawyer and get him to stand and defend me. That's the best thing you can do.'

'I can't leave you there alone to hang in my place!'

'If you give yourself up, we'll both hang anyway. At least this way it's only one of us. Think of your mother, Jordan. What would she have preferred?'

'She was your mother too, Elias!'

'I know. Would she want both her sons to die, or just one so that the other can live? I'm not sacrificing myself, Jordan, I'm doing the only thing which makes sense.'

'They'll rot in Hell for this, I swear.' Lybbe fingered the hard wooden grip of the dagger at his belt.

'Do nothing, Jordan. Don't put yourself in danger again, not for me. What would be the point? Just find me a lawyer so that I can defend myself.'

'I will, but I – someone's coming!'

'Go, go now! And don't come back. Nobody knows who you are yet, so you're safe. If you come back you could be seen, and then where would we be? Go, in God's name, and leave me alone!'

Lybbe slipped silently into the shadows as the feet approached, and retreated around the wall. As soon as he was out of sight, he darted over the road and hid in a gloomy alley.

Peering cautiously round the corner, he saw a monk striding purposefully up the road. The man had his hood over his head, and Jordan was surprised. Most went with their heads bare in the warmth of late summer. There was something else that looked incongruous, but before he could put his finger on it, the figure had hurried away.

He was about to go back to see his brother when he heard more steps approaching. This time he saw the heavy-set figure of a watchman. He heard the man snort, hawk and spit. 'You awake in there? If I have to stand up all night to guard you, I don't see why you should sleep comfortably, Elias Lybbe. Wake up, you bastard!'

'All right, Jack. I'm awake.'

'Good. Make sure you stay that way, or I'll have to prod you with this.' There was a quick movement, and Jordan saw the figure thrust something between the oak bars of the window. There was a short cry. 'Yes, well, if you sleep, that's what you'll get, so stay awake. I'll be back to make sure you are.'

Jordan's anger rose as he heard the blow struck, and he sprang forward, reaching for his knife, but the man had disappeared round the opposite corner of the building before he could even draw his blade. He stepped forward quickly, but as he came level with the cell window, he stopped at the sound of his brother's voice.

'Jordan, don't be a fool!' Elias hissed. 'Do you want to hang? Go now, and don't come back. The only thing that makes this bearable is knowing that at least you're safe. Don't make me feel I've died in vain. Go!'

And for once the older man obeyed his brother, but as he took his leave, all thoughts of Elias temporarily fell from his mind. He could not forget the sight of the monk hurrying up the road. Then he realised what had looked so incongruous: the monk had been carrying a cudgel. Almost unconsciously he followed after the cowled figure.

Chapter Fifteen

Arthur yawned and poured more wine, and was pleased to hear the door slam. 'And where have you been?'

'Father?' Avice walked in, her maid remaining at the door, and threw herself at Arthur, sitting on his lap and hugging him. 'You should have seen the jugglers and musicians! They were wonderful. There was a woman there, she had the sweetest voice, and she sang all about Judas and how he was lent thirty pieces of silver by Jesus to buy food but got robbed, and betrayed Jesus to the lord of Jerusalem to get back the money – oh, it was so sad!'

She sat up, and he could see a tear running down her cheek. 'There, there, child. It was only a song. Maybe they shouldn't let musicians play in the town if they are going to upset the women.'

'Oh, but it was so beautiful, Father. And the others all sang about kings and queens, about Arthur and Guinevere, and one had songs all about the King, our King's father.'

'Yes,' Arthur said heavily. 'No one has any songs about the new King yet, do they?'

'Father, don't be so nasty. I'm sure everything you hear about him is untrue.' She got up, looking down at him affectionately. 'I'll go to my bed now. You should go up soon too. You look tired.'

'I am,' he admitted. 'But I have a little more to do.'

'Oh yes?' she said, glancing pointedly at the goblet and jug.

He slapped her rump. 'Yes, little shrew! Don't look at my

wine like your mother. You are getting more like her every day as it is.'

'I am not!' she declared hotly, but kissed him and left the room. Her maid stood aside, curtseyed, and followed her charge.

It was a few minutes later that Henry walked in. Arthur waved him to a seat where a flagon of ale stood warming by the fire. While the man took a long draught, Arthur drummed his fingers impatiently on the arm of his chair. 'Well?'

Henry was a wiry, short man with his face pitted and scarred from a disease in his childhood. He gave an expressive shrug. 'She met him early on, but not for very long. Afterwards she just walked round the town, watched the dancers and acrobats, then went out to the fairground.'

'She met no man there?'

'A couple of monks. The first had some words with her, but she sent him off with a flea in his ear.'

'Why? Could you hear what they said?'

Henry gave him a long, cold look. 'If I was close enough to hear what was said, I'd have been close enough to be seen, and Avice knows my face. What would you want, that I could hear what was said and be told to leave her alone, or that I kept back and could stay with her to protect her from footpads and thieves?'

'You are right, of course. Continue.'

'The monk ran off to the north, and your daughter carried on round the edge of the fairground. Further on, she met another monk, who had his face covered with his cowl against the cold, for the wind was chill. Your daughter told Susan to leave her for a while, and he walked with her for some time, talking. She left him when she decided to come home.'

'It must have been getting late by then.' Arthur frowned. 'And it was another monk?'

THE ABBOT'S GIBBET   183

'It was late. I heard the compline bell ringing as we went back down the road to town. He must have been known to her, for she was civil enough to him. Not like the first one.'

Arthur stared at the flames. 'Another monk,' he repeated. 'Henry, you may think me paranoid or just an old fool, but what was a monk doing out of the Abbey at compline? The monks are all supposed to be in their church.'

'Perhaps the Abbot had given him a special mission, sir.'

'If he was performing a duty for the Abbot, what was he doing chatting to my daughter? Henry, this second monk: was he tall, short, fat, thin, broad, narrow? No! Before you answer, think. Specifically: was he like Pietro?'

'The Venetian?' Henry asked sneeringly, but then his brow furrowed. There was a faraway look in his eyes for a minute or two, and he took a drink from the flagon gazing into the middle distance. 'It couldn't be, surely. In body I suppose he was very like the boy, but would he dare to emulate a priest?'

'I think the bastard would impersonate the Pope to get his hands on my blasted daughter!' Arthur snapped, and sat back, glowering. 'In the name of God, don't tell my wife about this. If Marion was to hear of it, I shudder to think what she'd do.'

'Do you want me to stay with Mistress Avice when she goes out in future?'

Arthur slumped limply in his chair. 'Yes, do that. And in the meantime, I shall have to do some other work.' Other work about summed it up, he added to himself. If his daughter was so set on the lad, he would have to speed up his enquiries about the Venetians staying with the Abbot, and see whether they were as prosperous as they appeared. 'Henry, tomorrow, as soon as it is light, go to the Abbey and see if you can find a monk to talk to. Learn all you can about this boy and his father. I must know what sort of men they are.'

* * *

He'd done this often enough in the last two years, and he knew his business. It was late, but that should help. His victims would be the more insensible from tiredness and drinking. The first places to check were the taverns and alehouses which lay dotted all over the town. Here would be the drunks, the men who could be quickly subdued, struck once on the head and then relieved of all their spare money and any valuables.

It was urgent that he should get as much as he could as quickly as possible. He could kick himself for his error, but it was hardly a surprise he'd killed the wrong man. It was so dark without sconces or torches. When he'd seen the burly frame, he had instantly assumed it was Lybbe; it was not his fault that Torre looked so similar in the dark. When he had struck, the man's back was to him, and he hadn't bothered to check his face. There hadn't seemed to be the need.

But he felt stupid about the mistake; and his own danger was doubled as a result. Not only was he still at risk in case Lybbe might recognise him, now he must keep one step ahead of the knight from Furnshill over Torre's death.

There was an increased anticipation as he waited. His desperate need to escape from the town fuelled his tension.

He'd decided not to go to the tavern where he had attacked Will Ruby. There might be a watchman posted to catch him. No, tonight he went further up the hill, past the cell and on towards the fair. Here there were several alehouses which even now, late in the evening, were filled with merchants and tradesmen spending their earnings on wine, ale, and women.

The first one he came to had a handy, quiet alley alongside it, from which he could see the whole of the front of the place and most of the street in both directions. He installed himself in the darkness at the entrance and leaned against a wall, idly swinging his club. There was plenty of time. He had all night, and his patience was up to the task.

At breakfast the next day, Baldwin was pleased to note that
Jeanne appeared happy to see him. Simon watched his old
friend walk to the table and take his seat beside her. When
Margaret nudged him delightedly, he grumbled cantanker-
ously, 'I know, I have eyes in my head!' But she could tell he
was relieved as well.

The knight glanced at Jeanne. 'No Abbot this morning?'

'You haven't been to the fair before, have you, Sir
Baldwin? No, well, today is the Feast of St Rumon, and the
Abbot will be with his monks. They will hold an extended
service to the honour of the Saint, and a Mass for the
founders of the Abbey.'

Baldwin nodded. In the Abbey Church there were
shrines to its chief benefactors. Not only St Rumon, but also
Ordulf and his wife Ælfwynn, the two founders, Abbot
Lyfing, who rebuilt it after it was razed by Vikings, and
Eadwig, who gave his manor of Plymstock to the monks.
All were remembered with reverence and gratitude.

'The Abbot has a great number of duties to attend to,'
Jeanne continued, 'in honour of the patron saint of the
Abbey. Merchants and craftsmen bring offerings to St
Rumon's shrine, and some always wish to speak to the
Abbot to make sure that what they have given will earn
them their due reward.'

'I am sure the Abbot discharges his duties honourably
and to the satisfaction of all who go to the church,' Baldwin
said lightly.

'Yes. Abbot Champeaux is a good and kindly man.'

'I am sure he is,' Baldwin agreed. 'I am glad you live on
his land. He must be a good lord to his bondmen.'

At that she laughed. '*I* am lucky, yes, but you wouldn't
hear many of the other people living on his land say as
much. Did you hear about Torre?'

'Only that he had argued with a monk the night he died.'

'Abbot Champeaux is a generous soul, but he is determined to make sure that his lands pay. He's converted some of his serfs into tenants: rather than having to provide him with service in his fields and paying him a small rent, he has given them leases so that they are better able to farm for profit.'

'Why should he want that?'

'It brings in more money to the Abbey. Look at Torre. The Abbot was going to make him take a lease, and that would have meant that instead of a few pennies each year, he would have to pay twelve shillings to the Abbot. That was being generous, for now Torre has died, he will get that from the new tenant, but the Abbey's almoner thinks he will earn more, probably a pound each of pepper and cummin as well as the money.'

'So that was what Torre was complaining about. He was to win more freedom, but would have to pay for the privilege.'

'Yes.'

Baldwin chewed thoughtfully. 'And the monk, Peter, was defending his lord, and that was why he came close to fighting the miner.'

'Do you still doubt that Elias was the killer?'

'I cannot believe it was him. If he had a motive for killing Torre, why should he wait until now to do it?'

'Surely he might have bottled up any slight until the fair so that there would be a confusing number of people around?'

'It is possible. He doesn't strike me as a fool, and that would involve a certain cunning. But I still believe that if Elias did have a part in this murder, it was as an accomplice. It is the other man I want to meet, the man he is shielding.' And unless he tells us who that was, Baldwin admitted to himself, there is little chance of clearing up this mess.

* * *

The Abbey's wall had several gates. There was the small one beneath the Abbot's lodging, the water-gate which gave onto the Abbey's bridge, and the court-gate – a great block with rooms above that took the bulk of the traffic to and from the Abbey. It was here that monks with little to do would pass their time talking to travellers.

Arthur had asked him to get information, and the groom knew where to go. Henry walked towards the open wicket-gate in the massive oak doors. There were already a couple of hawkers standing there, chatting to a monk, who rested on a shovel and eyed the passing crowd. Even this early people choked the street on their way to the fair.

In his hand, Henry carried a large pitcher of good Bordeaux wine. He leaned against the wall until the hawkers had moved on, and then greeted the monk. 'Brother, my master told me to thank you and the Abbey for allowing him to come to the fair. He sends you *this*.' He flourished the wine.

'For us?' the monk said dubiously, taking the pitcher and sniffing at the open mouth. His mood quickly improved as he smelled Arthur's good wine.

'Try some,' Henry urged. 'It is my master's best.'

The monk eyed it, then Henry, then the pitcher again. At last he made up his mind, set the shovel against the wall, and took a quick sip. 'It's good,' he breathed.

Henry glanced behind him. There were many visitors in the Great Court, and no one was paying any attention to the pair at the gate. 'I've never tried my master's wine,' he said sadly. 'He always tells me it's too good for a groom.'

'That's typical.' The monk shook his head. From his accent Henry was pleased to hear the soft burr of Devon. Henry was sure he must be a lay brother, a local peasant offered free food and lodging in the Abbey's precinct in exchange for taking on much of the laborious work so that better-born brothers could spend their time in study and contemplation without the need for excessive manual work.

'The poor never get to taste the better things in life, do they?' He looked over his shoulder, then suddenly thrust the pitcher at Henry. 'Here, *you* try some.'

Henry took a long pull at the wine and passed it back, smacking his lips. 'It's fine, isn't it? I can see why my master keeps it for himself.'

The monk weighed it speculatively in his hand. 'Your master said it should go to the monastery, or to the Abbot?' he asked seriously.

'He said it was for the Abbey, to thank the monks.'

'In that case, since I am a monk . . .' his new friend said gravely, and upended the pitcher again. 'But it would be greedy to have it all,' he added, and winked as Henry took it back again.

'Is it very busy in there? You have a lot of guests.'

'More than usual,' the monk agreed, wiping a dribble of wine from his chin. 'People from all over. The bailiff and his wife, a man from Crediton, a . . .'

Henry waited while the monk told him of all the visitors. When he mentioned Venice the groom jumped on the word. 'Where's that? Is it near York?' he asked innocently.

'No, it's foreign. Somewhere south of Gascony,' the monk said knowingly. 'Outlandish, though. You should see the way they dress.' He shook his head and drank again.

'What are they here for? I'd have thought they'd go somewhere else if they wanted to buy things.'

'Oh, no. They're here to negotiate with the Abbot. They want to arrange to buy all his wool over the next three years at a fixed price. That way the Abbot knows how much he'll get in advance, and it'll make his work a little easier.'

'I see. They'll be here for some time, then.'

'Oh, I don't know. I reckon as soon as they have their contract they'll be gone. They seem to have other business to deal with, according to my friend who works with the guest-master, and want to leave quickly when the Abbot has agreed their contract.'

'They must be rich to negotiate with the Abbot.'

'They *say* they are.'

Henry's ears pricked. 'You think they aren't?' he asked, feigning disinterest.

'Something's not right about them. They say they are merchants and bankers, and such men are very well-off. But these fellows, they have very fine clothes and their saddles and harnesses are good quality, but their horses are cheap creatures.'

Henry could understand the distinction. His master often played the host to affluent men, and as a groom he knew that those who sported good clothing owned the best horse-flesh as well, and spent fortunes on finery for their animals. There was no point in a first-quality mount if it was made to look like a broken-winded nag by cheap saddle and harness. The wealthy flaunted their money. He recalled the Camminos' arrival in town. 'Why should that be?'

'They said they were robbed, but if they were, why wasn't their money and plate taken? And if someone took their horses, wouldn't they have taken the saddles and equipment as well? I think these men aren't as well-heeled as they would have the Abbot believe. Still, it's none of my concern.'

Henry stayed until they had finished the pitcher between them, but there was little more to learn, and he left the monk, now with every appearance of contentment, to make his way back to his master's house. En route he saw a familiar figure, and dawdled to study him.

It was the young Venetian, Pietro, and his servant. The pair waited a little to the north of the tavern, standing in an alleyway in the shadow of a large house. Henry was not sure, but he had a feeling that they were waiting for some-one, and as he watched, he saw the figures of Avice and her maid approach. When he noted how the young girl's face lit with joy at the sight of her lover, Henry looked on grimly. His master would have a problem in persuading her to leave the Venetian alone.

He realised that the four were continuing down the hill towards him, and he turned to hurry away before he could be seen, when he tripped. Another hurrying fairgoer had stumbled into him, and Henry stifled a quick curse at the man as he recognised the young monk Peter. The groom scrambled to his feet and hurried to a wall, glancing up the road. He was amazed to see the monk standing before his master's daughter. Also watching was the old friar, from the other side of the street.

'My lady, I must demand that you—'

Henry saw Pietro take a casual step forward. 'If you are prepared to renounce your vocation, your habit is no protection. Leave my lady in peace!' he said, and suddenly his hand whipped out and slapped Peter on the cheek, almost spinning the boy completely around before he fell to the ground.

Peter lay sobbing with fury and jealousy, while Avice and Pietro stepped past. He could not even muster the energy to call out; he was exhausted – and ashamed of his action. The day before, life had seemed full of promise; his future was mapped out for him, and he knew his vocation – and yet now all was ruined. He was in love with a woman who spurned him, his life's ambition was destroyed, and his hope for happiness had been crushed beneath her dainty heel.

He felt a hand grasp his elbow and he was hauled to his feet. 'My son, my son, what is all this?'

Peter wiped his eyes, smearing dirt over his face. 'Friar? It's nothing. Nothing.' His eyes followed Avice as she made her way down the hill with her squire. 'How could she prefer *him*?'

Hugo patted his shoulder. 'It is better that she should choose a man such as he rather than persuade you from your calling.'

'But he . . .'

'What, my son?' asked Hugo patiently.

Peter set his jaw. 'He might be a murderer!'

'What?' Hugo took an involuntary step back.

'Yes! I was there – you were, too! In the tavern on the night that man was killed, you must have seen it. When the man was in the way, that Venetian puppy almost drew his knife.'

'That means nothing. He didn't actually draw it and—'

'But what if he waylaid the man later? What if he stabbed him? That would mean Avice was going to wed a murderer!'

Henry heard the words. He saw Hugo shake his head and advise the novice to be careful to whom he made such wild accusations, but the boy was not of a mind to be placated. 'She is not for you, my son. You have a calling. You have to forget the passions of the flesh if you are to become a good monk.'

'I won't be a monk. I have already told the Abbot.'

Hugo rested a hand on his shoulder with compassion. 'Before you make a decision like that, you must reflect long and very hard. God has sent you this temptation to test your resolve. Can you really fail Him so easily?'

Peter shook the friar's hand from his shoulder. 'I love her.'

The friar shook his head in sympathy as the boy, head bowed, walked down towards the Abbey. Hugo had been lucky – he had never suffered from lust, and found it hard to understand the torment of others. For him, adoration of Christ's Mother was enough.

Henry took his chance and walked to him. 'Friar? Is the monk all right?'

Hugo glanced at him. 'He is not harmed,' he equivocated. 'Those foreigners should be less arrogant.'

The friar put the young monk from his mind. He still wanted a theme for preaching, and he spoke absently. 'It is not only them. Arrogance is not the preserve of Venetians.'

'It is typical of foreign bankers.'

'Bankers? Are they bankers? I thought they were only

merchants.' Hugo suddenly stopped dead in the street and gave a little gasp of pleasure. It might be a well-worn theme, but at last he had an idea for a sermon.

Chapter Sixteen

Baldwin and Jeanne walked a few steps behind Simon and his wife, partly out of self-defence. While behind them, the knight felt that he was not quite so much under constant observation.

It was always the way, he knew, that a wooing couple would be subject to continual scrutiny, and the slightest failure of manners or courtly behaviour would render the squire open to the most vicious of verbal leg-pulling, or worse. It was not all on one side, for any girl offering what might be considered by parents and friends to be overly indecorous or flirtatious comments would be severely reprimanded. He had hoped that if he was to find a woman to court he would at least be able to do so without the embarrassment of a friend listening nearby, and no doubt storing up each foolish word or misused phrase with a view to reminding the knight later when he was in a defenceless position.

He was painfully aware that his servant and Simon's were both behind him, and that was almost more appalling than Simon and Margaret being within earshot in front. Baldwin had recently been given enough proof that Edgar had enjoyed the companionship of several of the younger women of Crediton. His martial appearance and easy flattery seemed to win them over, although Baldwin could not understand why. Only the week before he had heard his man paying court to a hawker in the street, and Edgar's expressions of amazement at the girl's beauty (although to

Baldwin's mind she was rather plain) won him a dazzling beam of happiness and every promise of more than a mere discount.

Flighty talk of that nature, which to Baldwin was little more than lies clothed in politeness, was irritating to him. It was meaningless. He would prefer to be able to make an unequivocal statement of affection to one woman he loved, and remain on terms of honourable politeness to all others than have to make even one gut-churningly embarrassing statement that was untrue. Baldwin was a knight, and the soft nature of a campaign to win a woman's heart was a mystery to him. One thing he had already discovered was that wooing a lady was not so straightforward as setting his horse at an enemy and charging. A certain subtlety was required which was alien to his soul. With a feeling of defeat, he wondered whether he should take advice from his servant. Edgar knew how to fight this kind of battle.

Once inside the fair, the women naturally gravitated together, and Simon moved to his friend's side. Baldwin ignored his leer and wink, and the elbow jerked into his side, maintaining what he hoped was a dignified silence.

Simon grinned wickedly, enjoying his friend's discomfort. 'Have you had any more thoughts on Elias?'

'I am afraid not. Until he realises his own danger, there's little we can do to force him to reveal the other man's identity.'

'Your mind has been on other things, I know,' Simon smirked, 'but one thing did occur to me. Elias is weakly in build, while Torre was barrel-chested and powerful. The clothes put on Torre fitted him, but they wouldn't have fitted Elias. The man with Elias must have been the same in shape as Torre.'

'Yes, but how many hundreds here have a similar build?' Baldwin eyed the latest counter at which the women had paused. It held expensive gloves, and he felt a glow of sadistic pleasure as Margaret excitedly discussed them with the stallholder. 'Why has Elias remained silent? That is what puzzles me. Do you think the man with him was the murderer?'

'Perhaps. From the descriptions, he might have been similar in size to Torre, and the clothes bear that out, if indeed he swapped clothes with the corpse. Also, if it was he who killed and decapitated Torre, it would explain how Elias could have reappeared in the tavern without a mark of blood on him.'

'But what sort of hold could the man have over Elias that would persuade the cook to keep silent when his life is at risk?' Catching a glance from Jeanne, Baldwin felt a burst of irritation. He needed time to figure out the best manner to court this lady, yet he was forced to concentrate on catching a murderer. For a moment he felt an unreasonable loathing for Elias. It was the latter and his damned silence which was causing him this problem. If it weren't for him, Baldwin would be able to join the women and perhaps buy a present for Jeanne. 'And what possible motive could the man have?' Baldwin continued. 'He was new to the area, only a traveller, or so the alewife implied. He was certainly no local man, for she did not recognise him.'

'A personal slight, an accident – who knows? Maybe we should go to the tavern again and ask there; maybe meet up with Holcroft and see if a night in the clink has loosened friend Elias' tongue.'

'Oh, I suppose so,' Baldwin grumbled. 'If that pathetic damned cook would only speak, we could stop wasting our time. Why didn't he just tell us what happened?'

They walked over to the women. Jeanne instantly turned to Baldwin questioningly. He shrugged apologetically as Simon explained, then added, 'I think Simon is right – we should go and check on this.'

To his surprise, she nodded understandingly. 'Of course you must.' He looked so chagrined at going, she wanted to give him a hug, like a mother cuddling a recalcitrant child.

She gave him an encouraging smile instead. 'It would be boring for you to trail after us anyway, going from stand to stand looking at clothes and boots. No, you both go, and we'll see you later.'

Jeanne was no fool, she had seen the expression on Simon's face as they were talking, and knew how shy the knight was. The bailiff had been ribbing him unmercifully, that she was sure of, so as they turned to leave, she called them back. 'One moment, Simon – surely when your wife has so much to buy you wouldn't leave her with only a little change? Your purse is full, and hers is almost empty – won't you give her your money?'

Simon stared open-mouthed. 'My money? But—' As Jeanne held her hand out he retreated, walking into the grinning Edgar, who quickly caught the bailiff's arm and led him back. Under Jeanne's firm gaze, he felt he had no choice but to untie his purse-strings and remove all the coins. 'Don't spend it all on sweetmeats,' he said gruffly, and jerked his arm free. 'Come on, Baldwin. Let's leave these beautiful thieves behind and seek a good, honest murderer.'

They left Hugh with the women, looking mutinous at the thought of the goods he would have to carry again, and walked away with Edgar, heading through the main gate and down to the market-place. Here Baldwin strode up to the cell's window and peered in. He saw the cook huddled uncomfortably in the corner, wrapped in his thin and thread-bare blanket, shivering.

Passing the market area, they had to push past the crowds which had already collected to watch the jugglers and acrobats. Minstrels were tuning their instruments, one woman singing in a high, nasal voice. Then, at the far end, they saw the friar.

Hugo was standing on a barrel to preach. 'God teaches us that there is a fair price for everything, and it should be enough to allow a man a profit. But He teaches that if a man makes too much profit, that man is actively pursuing avarice, and that is a sin. That's why our laws prevent you from hiring more staff than you need, or anything else that might give you an advantage over others in your trade. It is why you mustn't overpraise your work to the detriment of that of other people.

'It is why usury is such a unique sin, for usury adds nothing to man's well-being. Bankers add only to the misery of the world, because they lend money and charge interest on that money. What does that benefit mankind? If you are a cordwainer, you help us by making us shoes so that we can walk far without hurting our feet; if you are a cooper, you allow us to store our food and drink so that we don't starve during the winter; if you are a weaver, you make cloth for us to clothe ourselves; if you are a farmer, you provide us with food that we might eat. But what do bankers do? They make nothing, provide nothing, add nothing to the good of men.'

Baldwin muttered, 'He'd best be careful. We don't want the rabble roused.'

'He knows what he's doing – he'll be on to why avarice is so bad soon. I've heard this kind of lecture before,' said Simon. 'Come on, let's get to the tavern.'

They passed on, and so missed the end of Hugo's sermon. Later, Baldwin would come to regret that.

Inside the tavern there was a pleasant odour from a pottage cooking in a huge three-legged pot over the fire. The bailiff snuffed the air appreciatively. If he had not eaten before leaving the Abbey he would have demanded a bowl of the thick broth. As it was, he asked the serving girl to fetch ale for him and Edgar. Baldwin was not thirsty.

There was quite a crowd, with traders and buyers sitting and haggling over their deals, families taking their ease while their children ran about between the legs of farmers, merchants and tinners. Baldwin could see a group of watchmen in a corner, and he studied them with interest.

One appeared to have hurt his arm, for it was held close to his body in a sling. Another was looking extremely pale and shaken.

'Simon, do you see those men?' Baldwin hissed.

The bailiff grunted. 'What of them?'

'Margaret and Jeanne told us last night of the attack on the cloth merchant, don't you remember? One man was left unconscious, another with his arm badly wrenched.'

'You think they're the ones?'

'They look like them, don't they? What are watchmen doing threatening traders in the fair?'

'If it *is* them, perhaps they had a good reason to . . . I don't know, maybe they were collecting unpaid tolls.'

Baldwin gave an exasperated grunt. 'Remember what Jeanne and Margaret said? Those men made no mention of tolls – they said they wanted to teach the stallholder English or some such nonsense. Anyway, it would be the port-reeve's beadle who would go to collect money, not the watch. No, those men have been up to something.'

Agatha appeared with a jug and two large pots. She set them on the table, but before she could leave, Simon said, 'Agatha, have you heard that we have arrested Elias?'

'Yes, and it seems about as stupid as everything else as far as I'm concerned.'

'Why?' Baldwin asked.

'Because he's no killer. Elias is foolish sometimes, and he can be a right whining pest, but stabbing someone in the back? Never!'

'The evening Torre died, we know Holcroft was here, because Lizzie saw him waiting for her, so it's not likely *he* could have killed Torre, no matter what the girl thinks.'

'What Lizzie thinks is her affair. I never thought the port-reeve was responsible.'

'But Elias was with this other man. How big was he – about Torre's size?'

'Maybe.'

'You see, we think Elias would not have killed the man on his own, if he *did* have a part in Torre's death. He and his friend left here together, according to you. At the worst, he killed Torre with an accomplice. We think it's more likely than him stabbing Torre on his own.'

She shrugged. 'That's for you to find out.'

Baldwin leaned back and eyed her searchingly. 'Agatha, how quickly did he come back into the tavern after walking out with his friend?'

'It was only a few minutes.'

'Are you quite sure? The killer of Torre would have needed plenty of time. Could you be mistaken? Could he have been out for a while?'

He waited expectantly, and let out a sigh of relief when she slowly shook her head. 'No, I don't think I made a mistake. He was only gone for a little bit.'

'So, Agatha, it's possible that his friend was the man who undressed Torre and put his own clothes on the corpse. Would his clothes have fitted Torre, from what you saw?'

She again paused, holding his gaze, before giving a quick nod. 'I suppose so.'

'Good. That being the case, we need to find Elias' friend. It's more than probable he was the killer.'

'Ask Elias.'

'We *have*,' Simon protested wearily. 'He won't tell us.'

'Make him, then.'

Simon gritted his teeth. 'Did you notice Torre argue with him?'

'With Elias' mate? No, not at all.'

'But you did see Torre argue with others?'

'Oh, yes. He'd had a few ales, and he was in the mood for a fight.'

'Who did he fight with?'

Agatha said cheerily, 'Everyone: he had a go at the monk, and David, and some strangers as they were leaving.'

'But not with Elias or his friend?'

'No, not them.'

Baldwin was frowning at the alewife. 'Mistress, we know there were others here that night. You mentioned a merchant. Do you know where he lives?'

'He's over there if you want him.'

Following her pointing finger, Baldwin saw Arthur Pole sitting alone at a table. Before him was a pot of wine, and he was studying a sheet of paper. 'Yes, I think we should speak to him now,' Baldwin said.

Arthur glanced up as they stood by him, and hearing who they were, he gestured to the bench opposite. 'How can I help you, gentlemen?'

The knight thought him pompous. His dress was not overly showy, but the squirrel fur at his collar was a sign of his wealth. 'Mr Pole, we are trying to discover what happened on the night Roger Torre was murdered.'

'I thought you'd arrested someone for that.'

'We have a man in gaol, but he is at best an accomplice, not the killer. We would like to know what you saw that night. What time did you arrive here?'

'It was a little before compline. The bell had not yet tolled when we entered.'

'How long did you stay?'

'Only a short time. We had been invited by a Venetian merchant whom we'd met on the journey into town.'

'Antonio da Cammino?'

'Yes,' Arthur confirmed sourly. 'His son has formed an affection for my daughter. It is a problem, for both seem wilful in this and I don't know what to do for the best.'

Baldwin nodded. If Pietro was pining for a woman, that would explain his behaviour in front of the Abbot. 'When did they arrive?'

'They left before we arrived – which I must say was rude, bearing in mind they accepted my invitation.'

'Did they explain why they left?'

'No – but the alewife here told me it was because they

were offended by a friar. I think it was likely the same friar who had preached at Antonio on our way in. You know what these mendicants can be like. Antonio was unlucky enough to be the target of this one's speech, and I suppose seeing him in the tavern again was the last straw. He chose to leave before he could be publicly humiliated.'

'Did you see anyone arguing or fighting in here that night?'

'Nobody, no. It was quite late, and people were already beginning to settle for the night. Everyone was tired from travelling. Anyway, we left a little later ourselves.'

'Before the cook?'

Arthur shrugged. 'I don't know him. The only man I noticed walking out before me was the port-reeve. I don't think anyone else did before us.'

'The dead man went from the tavern a little while after the compline bell rang. Did you hear it as well?'

Arthur hesitated. 'I think I do remember it, yes. Oh, of course! It was when I heard it that I asked the alewife whether she had seen the Venetians. That was when she told me they had gone. So we finished our drinks and left.'

'You may well have left here before the dead man. I assume you know where the body was found, in the alley between the cookshop and the butcher's. Did you see anything suspicious?'

'No. We only saw a monk on our way back.'

'A monk? Would you recognise him again?'

'No, he had his hood up, covering his face. All I know is, he was coming out of the alley as we emerged from the tavern, and as we passed him, we all gave him a polite greeting.'

Baldwin leaned forward. 'Did he look large in body? Was he well-built?'

'Oh no, he was quite slight. Not a large man at all. And now you must excuse me. I have to go and – er – see my groom.'

Simon watched him walk to the door. 'His groom?'

'I wonder if the port-reeve can corroborate Pole's words,' Baldwin said.

'If you want to ask him, he's just walked in.'

Looking up, Baldwin saw the cheerful figure of the port-reeve at the door. Holcroft glanced around the room, and seeing the bailiff and his friend, he walked over to them. 'A good morning, sirs.'

'How are you, port-reeve?' Simon asked.

'Rushed off my feet. I've left the fair to get a few minutes' peace – it's mayhem up there – but apart from that, I am very well.'

Simon felt his eyebrows rise at the enthusiasm of the man. Holcroft could almost be a different person from the one who had ducked under Lizzie's pot.

Seeing his expression, the port-reeve explained. 'My wife – I told you she has been reserved for some weeks – well, now I know why! I had to tell her about Lizzie before it got back to her from one of her friends, and she was very understanding. She's only been behaving like this because she's pregnant again, and it was worrying her. Now she's herself once more, and I can't tell you how much better my household is!'

'I am glad to hear it, port-reeve,' Baldwin smiled. 'By the way, tell me: those men – they are watchmen, aren't they?'

Holcroft sat beside Edgar. Following Baldwin's look, he found himself peering at Long Jack. 'Yes,' he said, adding resignedly, 'What have they been up to now?'

'They've been brought to your attention before?' asked Simon.

'Those buggers are brought to the port-reeve's attention every year. There's nothing they could get up to would surprise me.'

'I see,' Baldwin murmured with interest. Then, 'David, we are sure Elias wasn't the murderer. If he had something to do with it, he was not alone. Elias is shielding someone, and we need to find out who and why. Did you recognise the man he was drinking with?'

'I hardly even noticed him. I was talking to Torre.'

Baldwin moved his stool so that he could lean back against the wall, and thrust his hands into his belt. 'Torre came close to blows with the Venetians staying with the Abbot—'

'With the son, anyway,' Holcroft corrected.

'Thank you. As you say, with young Pietro. Then he tried to pick a fight with a monk, and finally he argued with you. At the same time, he was angry with the Abbot.'

'You're not suggesting that the Abbot might have had something to do with his death?' Holcroft asked, appalled.

'Hmm? Oh no, of course not,' Baldwin said. A devil made him add: 'But I suppose the possibility should not be ignored.'

Simon tried unsuccessfully to prevent a grin. 'But we also have the curious treatment of the body.'

'Ignore that. Once we know who wanted Torre dead, we can look at why the killer mutilated him. The trouble is,' he went on, shaking his head, 'there really doesn't seem to be a serious motive for murdering the man. Not from all we've so far discovered. We must be missing something.'

'What has Elias said?' Holcroft asked.

'Nothing yet,' Baldwin said heavily. 'We'll see him again shortly, but he seems intent on martyrhood. You know him, Holcroft. He is a widower, you said, so scandal couldn't be at the bottom of it – he is not trying to protect his wife. Is he the sort of man to have a secret that could embarrass any family he has still living? Has he something hidden in his past that could ruin his reputation?'

'Elias? No, he's not imaginative enough.'

'And what could be worse than being hanged as a murderer?' Simon said with disbelief.

'You are quite right,' said Baldwin, shaking his head with disgust. 'But why should he let himself be hanged without bothering to defend himself? There must be a *reason*!'

As he spoke he saw the four men in the corner rise and make their way across the room. The knight watched them idly. They looked like ordinary watchmen, except they had an extra hardness about them. To a man who had fought in the wars against the Saracens, it was easy to recognise the latent violence that lurked in their powerful arms and forbidding features. One of them, who was shorter than the others, with light brown hair and a face burned brown by wind and sun, held his eyes with an unmistakeably threatening stare as he approached the doorway. Edgar, seeing the fixed expression on his master's face, turned in his seat and followed Baldwin's look. The watchman gave him a malevolent leer before traipsing out after his colleagues.

Holcroft was happily sipping his ale, his mind clearly back at his home with his wife. Baldwin nudged him. 'Those watchmen – there was some trouble at the fair yesterday.' He explained about the attack on Lybbe.

'I wouldn't be surprised at all if it was something to do with those buggers. They always charge protection money from the stallholders, but no one will ever point the finger. If someone has been able to turn the tables on them, so much the better. Maybe in future they'll behave.'

'I doubt it,' Baldwin said, thinking of the mindless cruelty he had observed in the ruthless dark eyes of the last man to go out.

Chapter Seventeen

Leaving Holcroft to finish his drink, the two friends left the tavern and walked back up the hill to the gaol. They skirted the market square, keeping away from the crowds which thronged the streets.

At the clink was a watchman, sitting on a three-legged stool, gripping a polearm and wearily resting his head on his forearms. When he looked up, Baldwin saw that it was the same guard who had helped them find the head.

'Daniel, we want to talk to the prisoner. Release him.' Standing stiffly, the watchman walked to the door. Baldwin gave him a sympathetic look. 'Have you been here all night?'

'No, sir. That was Long Jack. I took over at dawn. But the town is so full, the only room I could get was in an alehouse, and that on the floor.' He rubbed at his back bitterly. 'There were drinkers there all night, and I hardly got any sleep.' He unlocked the door and released a blinking, cold Elias into the sunlight.

'Elias, we want to ask you some more questions about what happened at the tavern on the night Torre was killed,' Simon said.

The cook walked determinedly to a patch of bright sunlight at a wall, leaning against it and enjoying the warmth like a hound in the sun. Baldwin took up his station at one side while Simon stood before the little man.

'Elias, who were you drinking with that night?'

'I've answered all the questions I'm going to.'

'When we last spoke to you we thought the dead man

was the one you were drinking with, and we didn't believe you when you said you didn't know who he was. Now we know it was Torre who was killed, and we can only assume that either you or your friend murdered him. Can you run fast?'

The question made the cook stare. 'What?'

'If you can, I suppose it's possible you could have stabbed him, ripped his clothes off, dressed him in new ones, hacked his head off, hidden it, and run back to the tavern, but I doubt it. No, I think it's more likely that your friend killed him, with or without your help, that he carried out his revolting deed while you hurried back to the tavern and consumed several ales to soothe your shattered nerves. That seems more likely to me.'

Elias turned away again, his mouth shut. It was as he had feared: even without telling them who was with him, they had guessed enough to assume that both of them had been involved in killing Torre. There was nothing to be gained from Jordan confessing. It would only result in both of them dying. Better that he should keep silent. That way only he would die: his brother would live.

Baldwin glanced at his friend, who gave a helpless shrug. The knight stared up at the sky, searching for inspiration. 'Elias, you are keeping quiet to protect someone else. Who, we don't yet know, but we will. You must think he is guilty, for why else would you seek to keep his identity from us? Yet you know that you are putting your neck in a noose by doing so. That shows great courage and integrity, but consider: if you had nothing to do with this murder, and you think your friend did it, what is the point of your dying? It would be better for all concerned that he should be caught. If he cut off the head and hid it, he was surely trying to leave the evidence pointing at you, wasn't he? Why not become an approver and inform on him? If you tell us who did do this crazy act, at least your neck would be safe.'

Elias remained mute, and Baldwin threw him an

interested look. 'Elias, we're sure you didn't do it. The shirt that the man was wearing was not yours – you're too small to own something that large. So who *was* wearing it? We can only assume it was your friend in the tavern. Has he threatened you? If so, I will make sure you are protected, understand? But I can do nothing if you refuse to help me.'

'Elias, talk to us,' Simon said, almost pleading. 'Let us help.'

'You can't do anything.'

'What do you mean?' Baldwin demanded. 'We don't think you killed Torre. Tell us the truth and we will find the man who *did*.'

But the cook would answer no more questions. He remained stubbornly mute, and at last even Baldwin gave up, irritably waving him away. Elias turned, once, and gazed at Baldwin as if tempted to speak, but even as the knight met his gaze hopefully, the moment passed. The cook disappeared inside, still silent.

'Look, if the damned fool wants to kill himself, why should we stand in his way!' Simon muttered angrily as Daniel relocked the door.

Baldwin shook his head. 'For one simple reason: while Elias is in there, the real murderer is free. The law, and justice, demand that we bring the real killer to book. I just cannot understand why he insists on maintaining his silence.'

'There must be a powerful motive for him to keep his mouth closed when he knows it's his neck at risk. I'd not have thought he'd be so brave.'

'No, it doesn't seem in character.' Baldwin began to walk back to the fair, his brow wrinkled with concentration. 'Something must have scared him into this crazy bravery. What, though?'

'Right now I don't care!' said Simon positively. 'I want to get my purse back from Margaret before it's been completely emptied.'

They made their way along the alleys and streets, shoving past a crowd gawping at a group of acrobats. A little band of tin miners stood in a corner, trying to shout the lines of a mystery play over the gasps and claps of an audience who were watching men walking on their hands and leaping high into the air to land on one another's shoulders. Simon gave them hardly a glance. He knew the tinners had paid to sponsor plays at the religious festival; they thought it would curry favour with their new warden, the Abbot. For the bailiff the plays were largely unintelligible, and he gave them a wide berth whenever he could.

At the fair once more they barged their way in among the crowd. With unfettered access to his purse, Simon was convinced that his wife would gravitate naturally back to the stalls selling cloth, so he headed in that direction.

The array of cloth on sale was a surprise to Baldwin; he had not expected such a choice. Expensive scarlets, woollen cloth that gained its particular softness from being dyed in grains, camlet made from scraps of wool, and coarse-woven russets were displayed hanging seductively to show off their colours. Dark blue, blue-black, green, red, violet – all colours were available, and trade was good, it appeared, from the number of people staggering away under the weight of bolts.

Baldwin acknowledged to himself that he had not seen such variety since his time in Paris. Linens, muslins, canvas, worsteds, fustians, even cloth of England, the hard blanket used under saddles, were hanging and limply fluttering in the light breeze. Peasant women and ladies huddled with bored husbands or excited, chattering maids to handle the offerings. A few even bought some.

In the lane, the daylight was excluded by awnings and the draped goods. It made the pathway sombre, although the gay colours attempted to give it a festive air, and the knight found himself responding with a gloominess of spirit. Above and outside the fair, the sun shone brightly in a clear sky with only pale wisps of clouds that could not dim the heat of the sun, yet down here, with the chilly breeze from the south and the shade provided by the tradesmen's stalls, all was different. It was as if the fair itself existed outside the reality of the world, was a distinct creature in its own right, one which could alter the brains of men and women alike. There was a hushed thrill in the crowd, a tension, which put Baldwin's teeth on edge. He disliked crowds at the best of times, but this one, whose sole reason for assembling here was to buy fashionable gear, felt febrile and manic.

Two women clung to the same bolt of cloth and berated the seller, hurling imprecations as each tried to pull the bolt away from the other. At another stall Baldwin saw a lady shove a poor woman aside to buy the cloth she had been fingering. The woman stumbled and fell against a pole, and sat rubbing her flank, staring with huge scared eyes at the people pushing and shouting. The sight made his blood suddenly chill.

It was the fair. People had an urge to purchase things no matter what the cost. The atmosphere made women who usually would welcome each other with a polite greeting, see their neighbours as competitors in a struggle to the death.

Baldwin walked over to the fallen woman and helped her to her feet, then escorted her through the throng, back to the stall; he stationed her by the cheaper cloths which she would be more likely to be able to afford. She ducked her head in gratitude, but he did not notice, he was already on his way. He had an urgency about him; he wanted to find Jeanne and Margaret and leave this frenetic buying spree.

Further along the lane, things improved. Here the cloths were of a uniformly better quality, and although some peasants wandered by to investigate, clucking and shaking their heads in disgust at the prices like so many hens, most of the customers were more opulently attired women looking for material for new clothes for themselves, their husbands or children.

It was here that they found Margaret and Jeanne. At the entrance to a small stall, with a great trestle table laden with velvets and scarlets, they almost passed a quivering mound of cloths.

'Sir? Sir, don't go!'

Simon halted and slowly turned to face the quaking pile. Round it peered the anxious face of his servant. 'Hugh, what are you doing under all that lot?' he asked with disbelief.

'Your lady, sir. She told me to carry all these things back to the Abbey, for her and for Lady Jeanne.'

'Say nothing,' Simon told Baldwin.

'Me? I wasn't going to!' the knight protested innocently.

'Where are they now, Hugh?'

The bailiff walked in behind the table. Here he found Hankin, and gave him instructions to help his servant as the cloth had been bought from his master. The boy scampered up, nothing loath, for the morning was proving very dull. When he had taken two of the smaller bundles from Hugh and lightened his burden, the pair wandered off to the Abbey.

Meanwhile Simon followed the sounds of excited chattering, and pushed through the materials hanging like curtains at the back of the stall, Baldwin and Edgar in his wake.

Today Jordan was more cautious. At the first sound of voices, he moved to the corner, and when he saw booted feet approaching under the draped cloth, he grabbed his cudgel. When Simon came through and saw his wife, he stopped dead at the sight of the armed stallholder.

'Who are you?' Jordan demanded.

'I am bailiff to the Warden of the Stannaries, who is the Abbot. Who are *you*?' Simon demanded gruffly, eyeing the cudgel suspiciously.

As Baldwin entered behind Simon he saw Jeanne give him a smile, and he returned it warmly. Her apparent

pleasure made his sullen mood evaporate, and he could turn
to the merchant with a new lightheartedness.

Jordan stood stock-still, his cudgel now negligently
dangling, but he was in a turmoil. He recognised the bailiff's
tone of authority, and for a short moment, as the knight and
his servant appeared behind him, he thought he was about
to be arrested: a vision rose in his mind's eye of the gibbet
on the hill at Forches Field. Then he made himself relax as
he saw the bailiff's wife move to her husband, and Jeanne
began to show Baldwin her latest purchases. Jordan took a
short step back, increasing the space between him and
them.

As he did so, Baldwin noticed his movement and glanced
up. For an instant he saw naked fear in the stallholder's
face, and the sight made him wonder.

'Baldwin, this is the brave man who had to defend himself
from those three bullies last night,' Jeanne said.

'You were fortunate, from what we heard,' Baldwin said.
Ah, so that explained the man's fear. It was caused by having
three men, all strangers, appear in his stall only the morning
after the last attack.

Jordan shrugged. 'It's one of those things.'

'Did you recognise who the men were?'

'Oh yes. They were all watchmen. I've seen them around
here since. They want black rent – money to protect goods.
If someone doesn't pay, they'll damage the stuff themselves
– they've fleeced most of the other merchants here already.'

'Well, I think you've demonstrated that you don't need
help to protect your things, anyway,' Baldwin laughed, but
he noted what the stallholder said. It bore out his thoughts
on the men in the tavern.

Meanwhile Jeanne held up a heavy cloth. 'Look at this.
Don't you think it would make a wonderful tunic?'

'Hmm?' He studied the bright red velvet. 'It would suit
you perfectly, my lady. The colour would set off your
complexion.'

'Then if my knight thinks so, I should buy it, shouldn't I?' she said, dropping him a mocking curtsey.

Baldwin considered. 'No, my lady. If I think so, *I* should buy it for you.'

'You can't, Sir Baldwin. It's far too expensive – I couldn't allow it.'

'Then refuse it when I give it to you,' he said lightly, and pulled coins from his purse as he approached Jordan.

The stallholder took it from him. 'The whole bolt?' he asked hopefully.

'Yes,' said Baldwin with reckless generosity.

'No,' said Jeanne with the determination of a woman who was used to counting her money. She instructed Jordan to cut off six yards, and watched as he began to unravel the material and measure it against his stick. When he had enough, he marked the cloth with a little piece of white chalk and called out to his boy.

'I sent him away to help my man with the other purchases,' Simon said.

'Ah, no matter,' Jordan said, hiding his annoyance that another should give orders to his assistant. He went to the trestle to fetch his scissors, but couldn't see them. They weren't on the table itself, nor under it, and he muttered angrily to himself. Scissors were expensive, and he was always going on at Hankin to look after them, but now once more they appeared to have disappeared. Returning to the waiting group, he gave an irritated shrug. 'My lad seems to have taken my scissors with him.'

'Have you nothing else?' Baldwin said.

'Oh, yes, I have a knife.' Jordan pulled it from his belt, made a fold in the velvet where the chalkmark lay, and began to cut carefully along the line.

Baldwin counted out his coins with that faint shock that assails a man who after making a rash promise pays the reckoning. He had no idea that cloth could be so expensive. Jordan had separated the material from the bolt. He set the knife aside and folded up Jeanne's piece, shaking out wrinkles and creases as he went. When he was finished, Baldwin took the bundle and passed him the coins.

While Jordan pushed them into his purse, Baldwin's eyes dropped to the table. The knife lay on its left side, and the hilt was plainly visible to him. It was of wood, and there was a motif cunningly carved into it. 'That looks a good blade,' he said.

'I've had it many years. I always carry it with me.'

'Oh? Is it English?'

'No, I bought it in a fair in Rennes from a Spaniard. I think it was made by a Moor.'

Baldwin picked it up. It had a good weight and feel to it, solid and balanced, and had a long blade, wide at the base and narrowing to a point.

It was hard to imagine it slicing through Torre's neck, but Baldwin recognised the crest on the handle; it was the same as that on the sheath they had found with the body. 'Edgar? Come here a moment,' he called, hefting the knife in his hand, holding Jordan's gaze. 'I have wanted to speak to you for some time,' he said quietly.

Peter shuffled through the long grass, head down as he contemplated the ground before him. After the last few days he couldn't stay: he'd have to go. There was no choice involved: it was simply the inevitable consequence of his actions and the turn that events had taken. Although Avice had rejected him, he was too unsettled – and ashamed of his carnal weakness – to remain.

Out here, in the orchards beyond the perimeter wall of the Abbey, the sun dappled the ground through the apple, pear and cob trees. The grass would soon be cropped when the sheep were released back inside, but for now they had been removed so that the fruits could all be collected, the ones on the ground as well as those on the trees. The Abbey depended on the orchard to stock the undercrofts for the winter and fill the barrels with cider.

All round him was the crackling sussuration of the tiny, black and yellow pods of the vetch bursting. A cricket gave an experimental rasp, quickly accompanied by another, but both died as he came near.

This was one of the last days of summer, and Peter was reminded how gorgeous the world could be in the midst of his desolation. It felt as if God Himself was mocking him, sneering at his misery. The fault, Peter knew, was his own, and he cringed at the fact that his God was aware. He would have to leave the Abbey and the protection of the Abbot and find a way of earning a living somewhere else.

It was not easy to see how he could. Peter had been a student at the Abbey school for many years before he had taken the tonsure. Many boys from the town attended the school, although most went on eventually to become merchants or knights. Some even entered Parliament to help advise the King. For Peter, after seeing how the monks lived and served God, the decision to remain had seemed natural. Like the brothers, he wanted to dedicate his life to praying for the dead and ensuring that their souls were saved. That was the duty of the Abbey, to intercede for all Christians who had died; they were spiritual warriors, the saviours of the human race.

And now Peter had to accept that he wasn't worthy. How often he had heard those words said of others, and felt the smugness that his own relative success gave him. Perhaps, he wondered, this was all God's punishment for his sinful pride. He should never have considered himself better than the unfortunates who failed by discovering their own weaknesses. He was no better than them; he'd simply managed to cling to his belief in his own vocation . . . out of arrogance.

Kicking at a stone, he watched it bounce and spin away. It reminded him of himself: insignificant, meaningless. He was of no more note than a pebble in the eyes of the world.

As he approached the river, a loud metallic clattering made him stop and look up. A dragonfly, vivid blue in the body, darted hither and thither, patrolling its territory near the pond which lay in a bend. It was perfect in design and beauty, and Peter was overwhelmed with the magnificence of a God Who could create so wonderful a creature. The novice had always wanted to understand more about the world around him, and it was a source of shame to him that he could not continue his studies within the Abbey.

Slumping at the river bank, he hugged his legs, morosely gazing out over the pasture opposite, contemplating his future. It was bleak. He had no craft or trade. There were few enough apprenticeships in the town, and he was too old already for most of them. For a man of nearly nineteen, the only career he was capable of taking on was probably that of soldier. At least with that he would have a guaranteed portion of food and ale, and a bed at night.

He stood and continued his aimless wandering. The idea of soldiering was not one that attracted him, and not only because his sedentary lifestyle unsuited him for the rigours of fighting. He had an aversion to the principle of making an oath to obey the orders of an earthly baron now that he had enjoyed serving an Abbot.

Another sudden noise drew his attention. There was shouting and banging coming from near the market. His feet had brought him back to the road that led westwards from the town, and he gazed one way and then the other, undecided. There was a temptation to leave Tavistock behind, to simply disappear and seek his fortune, whatever it might be.

But he couldn't. He had nothing – no money, no job, no enthusiasm; he had truly lost everything. There was nothing for him to do, nowhere to go. He felt utterly alone. Whereas he would gladly have given up his vocation to wed Avice and would have been content to live with her in poverty, her rejection of him was so total and uncompromising he felt that there was little reason for him to carry on living.

His head dropped to his chest and he walked miserably towards the town and back to the Abbey. As he approached it, he saw a little crush of townspeople, some waving sticks and broken pieces of wood. From this distance, it could have been a group of merry-makers, but even as he looked, he saw youths picking up stones from the roadside and hurling them at the Abbey's gates.

Quickly he turned his steps away, back up the hill towards the fairground.

Behind him he heard a shout, and when he looked, he saw some figures hurrying after him. He took to his heels, his heart pounding. All too often the townspeople enjoyed ridiculing the young novices when they had a chance, but this was no party in the mood for fun. This was a mob in search of victims.

Before him he saw another black habit, and he sped towards it. Glancing behind, he saw that his pursuers were gaining on him. Panting in the heat, he picked up the hem of his habit and pelted after the other brother.

Chapter Eighteen

When her daughter walked in, Marion laid aside her work and studied her. To her chagrin, she was aware of a sense of pride in the way that Avice held herself. Her carriage was as haughty as Marion's own, and her regal entry, ignoring her parents and walking straight to a bench and sitting, was a masterpiece of contempt.

Arthur for his part was sad to see her so openly mutinous. His daughter, whom he adored with all his soul, for whom he would gladly lose an arm if it would make her happy, was treating him with as much respect as he would give a beggar in the street. And all because of that *Venetian*. He sighed, and threw a glance at Henry, who stood by the wall. The groom was indifferent; he had performed his duty as he saw it, and was waiting to provide the necessary evidence when called.

There was no gloating in Marion's voice, only calm sympathy. 'Avice, we wanted you here because we have been finding out what we can about this swain of yours. This Pietro da Cammino.'

Avice looked up and met her mother's gaze. 'And what have you discovered?'

Her father glanced at Henry once more. 'Avice, his father is negotiating with the Abbot, but there are other things you should know.'

'I assume this is your spy – let him speak!' Avice said, staring at Henry.

The groom winced. He'd expected this duty to be painful,

and his young mistress was not of a mood to ease his task. 'Miss Avice, I did go and try to find out what I could, not because I want to upset you, but because I wouldn't want you to be unhappy.'

'Hurry up, man! She wants to know what you've found,' Marion snapped.

'The father and son are staying with the Abbot while they conduct business with him. They say they are wealthy, but others think they aren't. It could be that they are trying to con the Abbot out of his money.'

'Rubbish!'

'Their horses are of poor quality – how many wealthy men would tolerate ponies like theirs?'

'Maybe their own horses went lame.'

'Perhaps. But some say the boy is dangerous. He drew a knife against the man who died near the tavern. Some people think he was the murderer.'

'Some "people"? Which people?'

'Among them, monks.'

Avice's mouth fell open with dismay. 'But, how?' she said, then rallied. 'If a monk thought that, he would tell his Abbot, and the Abbot could hardly let a man suspected of murder stay as his guest. I don't believe you!'

'Avice,' her mother protested, 'Henry wouldn't lie to you.'

'He would if he thought you wished him to. He would if he thought you were determined to see me unhappy for the rest of my days and married to John.'

'Mistress, I have not invented this. It's what I heard a monk say.'

Suddenly her voice sharpened. 'A monk – or was it a novice? Was it the boy who asked me to run away with him? It was, wasn't it? It was that fool Peter!'

'Who it was doesn't matter, girl,' Arthur rumbled, but she ignored him.

'That's all the evidence you can collect, the jealous, unfair and biased view of a boy who wants me himself so much he'd perjure himself to his God! Yet you can't prove Pietro isn't rich! That he and his father are guests of the Abbot must mean that Abbot Champeaux himself thinks them honourable, and yet you are prepared to spread malicious lies just to convince me I'm wrong – well, I won't listen to this. I know what kind of a man Pietro is, and I will marry him.'

'You can't, Avice. You will wed John,' her mother reminded her.

'I will not. I have been a dutiful and obedient daughter, but I will not agree to this. It's my life, and I would prefer to go to the cloister rather than harness myself to John until my death.'

She swept to her feet and flounced from the room.

Arthur shook his head. 'Not the result we desired.'

'She will come round,' Marion said, but with more confidence than she felt. 'Henry, tell Avice's maid to come and see me right away.' When he had left the room, she continued: 'Arthur, until this nonsense is finished, Avice must be confined to the house. We cannot have her wandering where she will with this Venetian vagabond. Who knows where her folly might lead her?'

'Oh, very well,' he said and stood.

'Where are you going?'

'Back to the tavern. I've had enough of all this.'

'You don't mean you support her in this capricious flouting of our will?'

'*Your* will, not mine. All I want is to see her happy.'

'So do I, Arthur. I simply do not believe she will be happy with this boy.'

'Perhaps, but right now, I don't know that she can ever be happy with John either. You call it capriciousness, but I wonder whether it is equally capricious to wish on her a marriage with a man whom your daughter finds contemptible.' And before she could answer him, he had left the room.

Outside the house, he reflected a moment. His words would have hurt his wife, but he could not regret them. She was waging a vendetta against the boy based on her own desire for Avice to marry into a knightly family. It was a natural enough wish, he acknowledged, but he would prefer his daughter to be happy rather than trying to force her to begin a dynasty. He hesitated, then made off down the hill towards the tavern. If he could not find peace in his own house, he would seek it elsewhere.

They were gaining on him. Peter was convinced he was about to be attacked, and his flesh cringed at the thought of what the youths would do to him when they caught him.

The monk heard the noise, too. Seeing the baying mob, he ducked sideways into an alley. Peter saw him disappear, and marked the spot. Panting, he ran close to the buildings at the side of the road. If he could just get to the alley, he might be able to follow the other monk without his pursuers seeing him.

He didn't recognise the monk – he was too far off, but Peter wondered whether it was one of the lay brothers. There were so many who laboured in the fields, or kept the smithy and mill working, Peter could not remember them all. The figure of this one looked familiar, but he could not place him.

Coming level with the alley, he risked a glance behind. The bend in the street hid the mob from view. He nipped in, only to meet a man stepping out. In one hand he held a black habit, bundled loosely. In the other was a heavy stick.

Peter stared. 'What were you doing wearing that?' he demanded, but he saw the man heft his stick, and the monk retreated, his eyes fixed on the cudgel with horror. Hearing a shout behind him, he spun, just in time to see the jeering pack running past. Suddenly he was less scared of them; suddenly they looked like his protectors, and he opened his mouth to shout, but before he could, he was yanked backwards into the dark maw of the alley. The youths ran off up the hill, oblivious to Peter's panicked defence.

The fire smoked badly in the tavern, and Arthur coughed when the fumes got to him. It made a change for him to drink ale, and he enjoyed two quarts before deciding he should make his way home. He settled with the alewife and began the walk up the hill to his house, his cheerfulness fully restored. Surely it would all work out all right – they would soon leave Tavistock, and Avice would be away from the malign influence of the Venetian. Maybe she would even come to like John after all.

His wife was not so wrong, he thought with alcoholic optimism. It was right that she should want the best husband she could find for her girl, and although John was ugly and less prepossessing than an ape, he did have the attribute of breeding. It was merely a pity that Avice was too young to see that. She would come round – *probably*, he amended with a burst of realism.

The street had cleared, and he could see a group of cheerful boys waving sticks and shouting. The sight made him a little nervous. Youths these days so often seemed prone to violence at the slightest provocation, and it was not unheard of for a man to be attacked merely for glancing at a lad. He kept his eyes steadfastly fixed to the ground, walking faster as he passed beyond them. Further on, his steps faltered at the sight of a familiar figure.

Pietro was lounging on the opposite side of the road from the house, staring at the window of Arthur's upper rooms. His attitude was that of a man who has made a purchase and is waiting confidently for his servant to bring his bauble to him. Arthur's sense of well-being evaporated as if driven off by the breeze that gently shivered the flags in the street. The alcohol which had filled him with happy contentment now fuelled his anger.

The arrogant puppy! What nerve, to blockade his house

like this. It might be the way to steal a man's daughter in his own barbarian land, but Arthur would be hanged rather than let him win over Avice by such overt means.

'What are you waiting for, sir?'

Pietro spun around, shocked out of his pleasant reverie. He had been trying to compose a poem to Avice – he couldn't run to a tune – and had forgotten that here he would be on plain view to all. At first he could only gaze in astonishment at the furious merchant. Arthur was bristling like an angry terrier, and Pietro half expected to see his hackles rise and hear him growl.

'Well?' Arthur hissed. 'Do you expect me to call Avice and have her tossed to you like scraps to a wolf? That's what you look like, an evil predator who would rend my daughter from her family. You have disordered the peace of my house, upset my daughter, possibly harmed the match between her and the son of a knight, and dismayed my wife. And now you have the bald nerve to stand at my door as if you have the right to expect that she should come to you.'

'Sir, I only hope for a glimpse of Avice, that is all,' Pietro protested. 'I love her—'

'Love! You've no idea what the word means. If you *loved* her, you would let her marry the man to whom she is betrothed, and stop worrying her! She will marry a squire. Are you a squire? John belongs to an ancient family, he's related to an earl – are you?'

'Sir, my father is prosperous, and he can—'

'Prosperous? What is *money* to me? I have money and to spare, I have no need of *money*.'

Pietro could feel his face reddening under the onslaught. It was not that the abuse was unjust; on the contrary, the man's concern was all too well-justified, especially with his own father's lack of money.

'And where is the proof of your affluence, eh? How can I trust your word?'

He could not. That was the rub. Pietro and his father had

been forced to scrape along for quite some time now.

'Avice will marry a man who can provide for her, a man who will have a decent horse and the money to keep it, a house and servants, with land enough to ensure she will always have food,' Arthur thundered, 'not some jackanapes in fancy clothing with a broken-down pony!'

Pietro winced and stepped back. His retreat fired a cruel pleasure in Arthur's breast. With inebriated enthusiasm he followed the dumbstruck lad like a fighting knight who sees his opponent falter.

'I do not believe that you and your father are genuine. I think you are shams – fakes, and I shall warn the Abbot that you are trying to defraud him.'

Arthur saw with anger that the lad didn't even try to defend himself. Anyone accused of such crimes should instantly deny them, but this fool was taking every word as if they were all true . . . *all true*. Arthur gaped. Until now his words had run away with him; he had intended only to persuade Pietro that he was not welcome around his daughter, but this lack of defence must mean that his suspicions were closer to the mark than he had thought. If this was so, the Camminos were worse than even Marion had assumed.

He needed say no more. Pietro threw him a look in which loathing and fear were commingled, then turned on his heel and stalked off towards the Abbey.

One thought was uppermost in Pietro's mind. Avice had promised she would go with him, but if she heard Arthur's accusations, would she change her mind? At the least she would doubt him. Pietro gritted his teeth. He wouldn't – he *couldn't* – let her hear what her father believed. She would never look at him again.

Yet he couldn't just run away to elope with her. His father would never agree. No, he must stay.

He had come to this decision when he rounded the last bend in the road, and saw the mob at the gates to the Abbey.

* * *

Abbot Champeaux had spent much of the morning in the Abbey Church with the people who wanted to make offerings at the shrines to St Rumon and the founders of the Abbey; he still had many other duties to attend to. There were the alms to be given, and not only food, because five and twenty years before he had assigned money to buy shoes and clothing for the poor. The almoner had purchased a quantity of cloth for those who could not afford it, and money and bread must be given to the lepers in the maudlin, the only benefit to them of the fair since they were outlawed for the duration. It was all a heavy drain on the Abbey's resources, especially the eight bushels of wheaten flour which would be cooked into loaves for the poor and the wine which would be drunk by all the monks. Abbot Champeaux sometimes felt that the most important thing in his life was money. It guided his thoughts almost every hour of the day.

When he first heard the shouting, he thought it was just the noise from the fair borne on the wind. It was only when it grew loud and he heard anxious cries from inside the court and the ponderous creak and slam of the great gate that he hurried out.

Lay brothers stood wringing their hands as he approached. 'What is the meaning of all this noise and disturbance?' he demanded.

'Father Abbot, there is a riot!'

The Abbot closed his eyes for a second. Other abbeys and priories had suffered mutiny, but he had never expected to have one here. Tavistock had always been treated leniently by him – his taxes were fair, his demands few. There was no reason for the townspeople to revolt. 'Do we know why?'

'No, Abbot. The mob just appeared at the gates, demanding the Venetians.'

Champeaux gazed at him blankly. It seemed

incomprehensible that the town should have taken against the Camminos. Walking to the Court gate, he went to the wicket and pulled the bolt back. When a monk ran to prevent him; he gave a curt order to leave him alone. Hiding was no way to stop a rabble. Throwing open the door, he walked out.

It was only a small gathering, he saw, maybe forty all told. Some held clubs and sticks aloft, but more gripped jars of ale or wine. They had been shouting and making threats, but as he appeared, the noise faded. Those at the front were slowed and went quiet at the sight of the most powerful man in the town. When he glanced round at the faces, most of them red with ale and heat, none of them would meet his eye. They gazed at the ground and shuffled.

Gradually the atmosphere changed as those at the back of the mob realised something was happening. The rowdy chanting became a sequence of shouts, and then a general mumbling. Soon that ceased, and the road was engulfed by stillness.

'My friends, what are you all doing here?' he asked quietly, and in the silence his voice carried clearly and echoed back from the houses opposite. 'This is the Feast Day of St Rumon – the Abbey's saint, and yours – and you come here drunk, yelling and cursing as if you wish to pull down his own sacred shrine. Do you think your saint would love you and protect you as he always has done if you were to desecrate his Abbey?'

'We wouldn't do anything against St Rumon,' someone called, and the Abbot peered through the crowd, trying to see who it was.

'No? But you come here, armed with cudgels to beat at his door.'

'Only because they locked the doors against us.'

'What else could they do? What would you do if an armed mob appeared at your door – invite them in? Come, what is the point of all this disturbance?'

At once many voices were raised, and the Abbot could hear nothing. He held up a hand. 'One at a time, please! Now – *you*, you tell me what this is all about.'

The man he pointed to, a miner, met his gaze resolutely. 'Abbot, we know you've got Venetians with you. They're known to be criminals, felons. We came here to demand that you throw them out.'

'You demand that I throw out guests, when my duty of hospitality requires me to look after them?'

'Your duty doesn't demand that you protect usurers and thieves, Abbot.'

There was an angry murmuring, and Abbot Robert held up his hand again. 'Who among you accuses these men?'

'We were told,' the miner stated, but behind him Champeaux saw men shamefacedly letting their weapons drop, and others surreptitiously hiding them from sight.

'My friends, these men *are* here, but they are harmless. I assure you that they are innocent of any crime against me, against the Abbey, or against the town.'

'Isn't it true they're trying to make you sell them your wool?'

'No one can force me to sell my fleece. If it will make you comfortable, I swear I shall sell them nothing. There! You can have no quarrel with these men, and neither do I. Now disperse, before the watch comes to beat you away. I will have no fighting at my door, especially on St Rumon's Day. My monks have enough to do without mending your bones!'

It was a bold demand, but the crowd had lost its collective will to violence. The Abbot had seen such groups before. They gathered where there was too much ale, and a single man could rouse them to rage in a moment, but all too often another strong-willed man could cow them, and the faces here were more embarrassed than brutal. The Abbot took advantage of the sudden lull to make the Sign of the Cross, and that was enough to end it. As if it was an accepted signal, the crush thinned as men sought entertainment and more ale.

Heaving a sigh of relief, the Abbot watched as they faded away. It was a good-sized group, he thought to himself. If they had truly wanted to cause havoc, it would have been difficult even for the watch to dispose of them. He was doubly glad that he had been able to disperse them before they committed any acts of violence upon the Abbey or his monks.

As the men wandered away up the hill, Champeaux leaned through the wicket-gate and called to the gatekeeper, 'Open the gates and let them stay open.'

As the great oaken doors rasped wide on their iron hinges, he glanced back. There were only a few pots and sticks to show where the crowd had been. He should have told the rioters to take away their own rubbish, but he reflected that it was all for the best that he had not. One such demand could have been enough to swing their mood back to violence again.

He was about to return to his study when he saw two figures hesitantly approaching – Pietro and his servant. The Abbot waited, outwardly calm and patient, but inwardly seething, sure that they were somehow responsible for the eruption.

'Are you all right?'

Pietro entered first, pale and wary. 'Yes, my lord Abbot, I'm unhurt.'

'What caused this madness? Did you see what led to it?'

'No,' Pietro said, and there was a baffled look to him which brooked no debate. 'I was returning when I saw the men here, and I hid from them.'

'I did,' said Luke, and he cast about him fearfully. 'There was a friar in the market-place giving a sermon about usury, and he quoted my master's name as a usurer. It was him who incited the crowd to fury, my lord Abbot.'

'Who gave my name? What's the matter?' called Antonio

genially. He had been taking a nap when he heard the row from the main gate, and had missed most of Luke's words. 'What have you been up to now, Luke?'

'A friar?' Champeaux repeated thoughtfully. Friars had often caused problems before through overzealous preaching, but this was the first time it had happened in Tavistock. 'Antonio, there is nothing for you to fear. A few hotheads, that is all.'

'Fear?' Antonio gazed at him blankly. 'Why should I fear?'

'Master,' Luke burst out excitedly, 'it was that same friar – the one we saw on the way here, and again at the tavern. He was talking about usury and rousing the people against the sin, as he called it.'

'It seems as if it's impossible to escape the prejudice of the uneducated,' Antonio said loftily.

'This has happened to you before?' Champeaux asked.

'Yes, in Bayonne,' Antonio said.

'But master, he was talking about *you* – he gave your name, he described you. The mob was after your blood!' Luke cried. 'I thought we were going to be lynched.'

Pietro stared at Luke. He quickly turned to the Abbot. 'My lord Abbot, I think it is dangerous for us to stay here now, and not good for the Abbey if we are likely to create disturbances by remaining. Perhaps it would be better for all if we were to leave.'

'We can't, Pietro,' said Antonio. 'Not yet.'

The Abbot shot him a look. It was clear enough what was on the Venetian's mind: the deal for the fleeces. 'I am sure you would be safe enough here, my friend, but if all that holds you back is our negotiation, I am afraid that I must refuse your offer.'

Antonio started. 'But, Abbot, you . . . Is my offer not high enough? If I were to increase the amount . . . ?'

'No, Antonio. I had to give my word to the mob to stop them from their mad rampage.'

'But, Abbot, surely . . . surely your word was given under

duress. There's no need for you to be bound by it . . . and think of the profit it would give you!'

'My word is my word, Cammino,' the Abbot said, and though his voice was calm, it held a steel edge. Antonio lifted his hands and let them fall in a gesture of defeat. He was stunned at the sudden reversal of his fortunes. This was the second blow in a year. He turned from the Abbot to glower balefully at the gates, now open. Apart from the debris, there was nothing to show that a few minutes before the rabble had congregated to bring about his ruin.

'In that case,' Pietro said, with a glance at his father, 'I think we should leave immediately. If we remain we will only cause more trouble.'

'Very well, then. Go with my blessing,' said the Abbot agreeably.

He watched as the three made their way across the courtyard to their rooms, and was about to return to his study when something made him glance back outside.

There, strolling down the hill, were Simon and Baldwin with the women. Champeaux waited for them to arrive, but his eyes narrowed as he saw another man pelting past them down the hill. Soon the Abbot could make out the figure of Daniel. The fair-headed man dashed into the courtyard and cried breathlessly, 'My lord Abbot, you must come! It's Peter – he's . . . he's dead!'

Chapter Nineteen

The Abbot had a sense of unreality as he stood in the alley staring down at the slumped figure clothed in the black habit of his Order. People clustered at the entrance to the alley, craning over the crossed polearms of two watchmen to peer at the body. Beyond, men and women strolled past, uninterested, as they made their way up to the fair or returned from it to their lodgings for a meal.

Champeaux had seen many dead bodies in his life – monks who had expired from fevers, old age, or occasionally famine, but there was something unutterably sad about this death. Peter was so young. He should have had many years to live, for he was healthy enough, and he might have become a good monk if he had resolved his problem with the girl. All men who entered the cloister were forced to come to terms with their vow of chastity, and Champeaux was convinced that the youth would have been able to as well. It was one thing to be tempted, but if one had to be, it was better that it should happen before taking the vows so that the problem could be confronted and the firm decision taken beforehand.

He was only glad that Baldwin and Simon were on hand. The knight was already crouched by the figure, staring at it with a strangely sympathetic expression.

'How did he die, Sir Baldwin?'

Baldwin hardly looked up. 'His wrists are cut.'

The bailiff watched as Baldwin gently rolled the body

over, examining Peter's back and maintaining a commentary on what he saw.

'He's not been dead long: his body is still warm and the blood hardly clotted. There is no sign of a wound in his back or anything to suggest that he was murdered. Only the cuts on his wrists. It is . . .'

'I know, Sir Baldwin,' said the Abbot quietly. 'It looks like suicide.'

The knight said nothing, rolling the body over onto its back once more and holding an arm up to study the scored flesh.

Simon said, 'His hands are clenched as if he was preparing to fight.'

'All of us are bled for our health,' said the Abbot slowly. 'He would know that clenching the fist makes the blood flow faster.'

The knight nodded. 'It was merciful and swift. The boy would have lost consciousness speedily with both wrists opened.' He looked up at the grieving face of the Abbot, adding softly, 'He would not have suffered, my lord.'

'Thank you for that, Sir Baldwin. I would not wish to think he had been in pain for long, the poor fellow. It is bad enough that he should have contemplated such an evil act, such a sin against his God, without having to suffer for it.'

That, they all knew, was the nub of the issue. Suicide was a crime against God: an act of violence condemned by all. It meant a suicide could not be buried in a church or churchyard.

'Why should he have done this?' Simon wondered.

The Abbot was silent a moment. He could not discuss the novice's confession of lusting after the girl. 'He was not in the Abbey last night,' he admitted at last. 'I think his mind was disturbed.'

'What will you do with him?' asked one of the watchmen standing nearby. 'Leave him out at the crossroads?'

There was a greedy delight to his voice that made the

Abbot snap his head round sharply. The watchman was smiling, pleased to see that even a monk could fall to utter disgrace, and for once Abbot Robert permitted himself a burst of anger.

'You think that because he has suffered the torments of evil, a slow and dreadful torture you cannot imagine, that he should be deserted like a felon? You think his soul should be cast aside because of the pain he has been forced to endure? You yourself, aye and your family, your children, your parents, all of you, are protected by the monks of this Abbey giving themselves up to God, and you dare to crow when one of us finds the agony too great! This man was taken by God. He committed suicide after days of struggling with the devil within him, while his mind was unbalanced, and that was an act of God. God chose to take him to Himself. How *dare* you suggest he should be treated like an unshriven felon! Peter will be buried with honour in the monks' graveyard, the same as if he had died in any other way, and you can tell your friends that!'

Simon was stunned to see the Abbot's sudden emotion, and the watchman was equally shocked. He withdrew, muttering apologies, and the Abbot gave a great sigh, as if he had exhausted his final energy with his explosion. Champeaux glanced down at the body once more. 'Oh, Peter, Peter. Why should you have come to this?'

The bailiff wanted to lead the Abbot away. The death of the monk had shaken the older man to the core of his soul, and his sadness was unbearable. Simon was about to propose that they quitted this miserable place when he caught sight of the stick.

It was a plain oaken cudgel, with a large ball for a head, which rested at the foot of one of the walls only a few feet from the alley's entrance, Someone could have tossed it in, he thought, a passer-by with no further use for a heavy piece of wood like this. Yet Simon knew that no one would discard such a useful weapon. A good defensive tool like this would be kept and cherished until it became old or rotten.

He held it to the light and studied it. There was no sign of cracking, no dents – it was in fine condition. The ground here was a matter of a yard or so from the corpse, and Simon gave it a measuring look. The cudgel could have been brought here by the monk, dropped while he prepared to destroy himself, and had lain here forgotten while the lad watched his life-blood trickle and gush from his wounds. Simon had never seen the monk carry a cudgel, but many men would, and he had no doubt that a monk could get hold of one as easily as a serf. His gaze sharpened. If Peter had taken this with him, could it be possible that he was the monk responsible for the reported thefts? Might Peter have been the one who struck Will Ruby down? There had been other men too who had been attacked – could Peter have been the robber?

The watchmen converged on Jordan Lybbe's stall and shoved past the boy at the front. Long Jack grabbed his arm and hauled him after them: Hankin had no time to call out, let alone scream. He wanted his master, but Lybbe wasn't there, and Hankin knew he had no protector without him.

Other stallholders, who had all paid their protection money, had been expecting this. It was well-known that the watchmen had been trounced by Lybbe, so it was inevitable that while the merchant was away from his stall, it would be visited again. Those nearest turned their faces away and concentrated on their business. There was no point in being beaten to protect another's goods – especially when the owner was an accused felon and outlaw. News travelled fast among the community of traders.

'All this is your master's, isn't it, boy?' Long Jack said, waving an arm round the goods on display. 'It all belongs to Jordan Lybbe, this. Well, no longer. Now it's ours, and we're taking it.'

Hankin stared up at him, a young boy gripped by a man

representing authority – a watchman. His master, the man he looked on as a father, had disappeared, and these men were going to steal all his goods. Hankin was scared, but Lybbe had saved him, had rescued him from starvation when his parents had died. The boy had no family, only Lybbe. He had no loyalty except to Lybbe. And these men intended robbing his master of everything he owned.

His right arm was gripped by Long Jack, but he could still reach his small sheath-knife with his left: he snatched it from its scabbard and jabbed it into Long Jack's arm. The watchman shrieked, let go of the boy, and stared uncomprehendingly at the gash as his blood dripped. 'You little bastard!'

Hankin scrambled back into the recesses of the hanging materials. He still feared the grim men, but thrusting his knife into Long Jack's arm had given him a sense of satisfaction that even a thorough beating couldn't erase. He could defend himself. Deep among the bolts of cloth, he crouched, his knife poised, waiting.

Will Ruby was furious when his apprentice broke the little knife. The thin-bladed tool was one of his favourites, and he always used it when he had any fiddly jobs to do, such as cutting up young coneys or hares. The fool should never have tried to use it to pry apart the bones of a goose's neck. It was no surprise that the blade had snapped in half – it was far too weak for a job like that.

There was a cutler in the fair, and Will decided to go and see what the man had on offer. If there was anything like his old knife, he would buy it. He'd made enough already to be able to afford it, and he felt he deserved a present after the two consecutive shocks of finding the headless body, and then being attacked. He gingerly touched the lump on his head. It was still sore, but at least no harm seemed to have been done. No harm other than losing his favourite knife because of letting the apprentice look after things while he went to rest his headache, anyway.

The route to the cutler took him past the cloth-sellers, and he nodded and smiled at the people he met, most of whom he knew from his shop. It was always best to appear to be cheerful and friendly; customers preferred to deal with happy men rather than morose ones.

A small crowd was gathered at one point, blocking his passage. Everyone was staring at one particular stall. Ruby followed their gaze and stopped dead.

The watchmen huddled round the merchant's awning, Long Jack with a tourniquet bound above his elbow. At his nod, the men cautiously entered. Ruby frowned when he heard a high scream, then curses, and a boy was dragged out between two men, Long Jack following with a knife in his hand.

'What's all this about?' Ruby asked his neighbour.

'It's the man's stall, the one who's been arrested. I reckon those swine are going to make sure they get as much money as possible now the owner's gone.'

'What about the boy?'

'He wanted to protect his master's stuff, daft little sod.'

Two members of the watch had the boy gripped hard between them, stretching him over a barrel. Another stood with his club in his hands, watching the crowd with a sneer, while Long Jack untied his heavy leather belt. He raised it and brought it down on Hankin's back.

Ruby could see the agony in the lad's strained muscles as the leather cracked on his frail body. But no one stirred in the crowd as Long Jack raised his arm again, preparing to strike. There was merely a hushed expectancy, and then a kind of mass sigh as the belt came down on the child's thin form.

Ruby knew the watchmen. They had extorted money from him for the past three years at fair-time. All the traders knew how they made money for themselves, but there was no one to complain to. The Abbot must know how they abused their position, but he took no action, and there was hardly any point in a portman trying to stop them if the Abbot would not support him.

The strap rose again, and Ruby saw the sweat break out on the boy's face. He looked as if he was pleading with the crowd, begging one of them, any of them, to help him, but all those he stared at glanced away, with a kind of shame. Ruby felt his headache renewing its force, the pain increasing with each lash of Long Jack's belt.

Then he could bear it no longer. The pain in his head, the agony on the boy's face, the sense that the port was being overrun with injustice in the form of watchmen who used violence for no reason, that the town was degenerating into a cesspit of murder and felony . . . made his blood suddenly boil.

He growled – he actually growled! The sound made him feel a sudden animal delight in battle, and he leapt over the trestle. Grasping the belt from the watchman, he kicked the man's legs away, and he fell. Ruby was already on the others. For a moment, they stared as he screamed abuse, as dumbfounded as a farmer who sees his mildest pig become a mad boar, but when he laid about him with the belt, they moved. The guard with the club caught the full weight of the buckle over his forehead, and collapsed like a pole-axed steer, but by then the other two were already out of range. They let the lad fall, weeping, and withdrew to a safe distance, one laying his hand on his knife.

Ruby dropped the belt and knelt by Hankin, murmuring to him softly, and the two men glanced at each other. They were about to rush at the butcher when a voice made them stop.

'Bugger this! Let's get the bastards!'

The watchman drew his knife. 'Who dares attack us? You?' he asked, pointing with his dagger at a grim-faced cobbler.

'Yes, me.' And before the other could respond, the

cobbler had thrown himself forward. The watchman stepped back, but his sneer of contempt changed to a look of concern as he realised that the cobbler was not alone. The crowd, which had averted its eyes as the boy was thrashed, had seen the hated watchmen forced to retreat by the brave actions of one man. Now, even as the cobbler jumped into the fray, his neighbours followed, and instead of one headstrong opponent, the watchman found himself faced with thirty moving forward inexorably. He waved his dagger uncertainly to hold them at bay while he fell back, his friend at his side.

But before they could move far, the cobbler had gripped the man's arm, immobilising his knife-hand, and the mob moved in, grabbing both men and dragging them to the awning poles. The two were lashed to it, and Long Jack and the guard were hauled and bound to another. Then, while all four howled with impotent fury, they were thrashed with belts, and when the traders got tired of that, they fetched rotten fruit and pelted the bullies with it.

Ruby was oblivious to all this. Cradling Hankin's frail body, he carried him past the screaming watchmen and was about to return to his own stall when he was stayed by a hand on his arm.

'Is the child all right?'

'Yes, brother.' Ruby had not spoken to Hugo before, but recognised the friar. 'Beaten, but not too badly.'

'Why did they do it?' Hugo asked, shaking his head.

'They knew his master was locked up.'

'Who? The man who owns this stall?'

'Yes, friar. Hadn't you heard? It was Jordan Lybbe, the outlaw. He's been arrested – everyone thinks he must have murdered poor Torre.'

'Jordan Lybbe an outlaw?' Hugo repeated with horror. 'But he can't be!'

Simon studied the club speculatively. A man dressed as a

monk had robbed men in the town and attacked Ruby. It was possible that Peter had been the thief. If so, maybe it was for the best that he had taken this way out of a disgraced life.

Catching sight of the Abbot's face, Simon was sure that he had already reached a similar conclusion without seeing the club. His face was pained, but set into a firm blankness, and the bailiff wondered what he had heard in confession when Peter had demanded his talk the previous evening. Baldwin had been interested in the lad even then, Simon knew, and the bailiff wondered at the acute suspicion his friend had shown.

Simon didn't want to add to the Abbot's sorrow, but he was the warden's own bailiff. He could not allow this evidence to be hidden. 'Sir?'

Abbot Champeaux turned to him enquiringly, and when he saw the club his eyes widened, and he cast an involuntary glance at the body which told Simon he had guessed the same.

'What is it?' Baldwin asked, grunting as he got to his feet. 'Ah – a cudgel, and a solid one at that. Where was it?'

As Simon explained, the knight listened carefully. 'It was there?'

The bailiff nodded. 'He must have been sickened by what he had done, and tossed it away from him. Or maybe he dropped it there as he came into this alley, filled with his determination to end himself.'

'Perhaps,' Baldwin said, but without conviction. 'Why here?' he wondered, squatting by the wall. 'Let's suppose it was his.' He walked to the entrance to the alley, swinging the club, and let it fall. It struck the damp soil of the alley and fell over. 'It couldn't have fallen from his hand, then.'

Simon saw what he meant. The cudgel had lain at the wall opposite the body, and the boy would hardly have let it fall there and then crossed the alley to kill himself. Yet it could not have bounced there as he slumped down.

The knight walked to the body and tossed the stick towards where it had been found. 'He could have thrown it away.'

'Perhaps he was revolted by what his club had done and hurled it from him?' the Abbot supposed.

'It's possible, but if that were so, wouldn't he have thrown it harder and further? And why come here to die? Suicides hang themselves or cut their wrists at home. What could bring him here?'

'He had the mind of a monk,' said the Abbot. 'He didn't want to pollute the Abbey precinct with his blood.'

'If he had such a mind, why kill himself and endanger his soul by such an affront to God?' Baldwin asked curtly.

He squatted, staring at the wall and the fallen cudgel, then down at the body, before giving a short exclamation. Slowly, reverently, he uncurled the fingers of Peter's hand. He studied the hand with intense concentration, and as the Abbot made to leave, he looked up. 'Abbot, could you come here, please?'

'What is it, Sir Baldwin?' the older man said, his voice betraying a degree of asperity.

'This,' Baldwin said quietly.

Simon saw a series of deep slashes that cut the palm and fingers. He winced at the sight: he could imagine the pain of the blade cutting so deep into the flesh.

'Well, Sir Knight? Am I supposed to be interested in the last madness of the boy? He is dead, and these marks and mutilations are of no concern to me now,' the Abbot said brusquely.

'They should be. I have only ever seen this kind of mark on men who had tried to defend themselves against an attacker. Why should a suicide slash at his hands? But a man who is set upon by another with a knife will often grab at it to keep the blade away, and as the attacker pulls the knife back . . .'

'He was attacked?'

'Yes, Abbot. This lad is no suicide. These marks show he tried to protect himself against his killer. My lord Abbot, Peter was murdered!'

'Who could do such a thing?' Abbot Robert whispered, horrified.

Baldwin shrugged. 'That I don't know. Perhaps the man who has been robbing, and perhaps it was the same man who killed Torre. That could explain why the cudgel is here: because Peter saw the thief in the alley, and maybe the robber dropped the club to hide his guilt, and then couldn't find it again, or ran away as soon as he had killed the boy. Perhaps he wanted to implicate the boy in his own crimes. It is no matter – what *does* matter is that Peter was murdered, and didn't commit suicide.'

'Sir Baldwin, you give me a crumb of hope in the midst of all my despair.'

'We still have to seek his murderer.'

'Who could it be? Who would dare such a crime?'

'We have arrested the man who had the knife from the sheath on Torre's body. It is possible that he could have killed Peter, but . . .'

'What, Sir Baldwin?'

'He was with Jeanne and Margaret for some time before I had him arrested,' Baldwin said slowly. 'I would be surprised if the novice could have been here for long without being discovered: this alley is well used. Yet our man has been in prison for over an hour already. We must go and see whether he can shed some light on this. There is another thing: this monk was keen on a girl.'

'I know it,' the Abbot admitted. 'I tried to persuade him out of his infatuation, but it was no good.'

'Last night I saw him north of the fair. This lad was scorned by her, and it looked as though his heart was broken. I think we must see the girl and ask her what was said and why she chose to refuse him so forcefully – perhaps she can give us a clue.'

'What possible clue could she give you?' the Abbot asked.

'She was scathing towards him. Perhaps this was not the act of a mad felon but there is a more prosaic reason for the boy's death. What if he had a rival? Might not that rival have decided to dispose of her other suitor?'

'If Peter's rival knew she had spurned him, there would hardly be a reason to kill Peter,' the Abbot said reasonably.

'True, but she was so disdainful of him, I have to wonder what she knows of this. Something surely made her react in that way to him. He seemed so sure of her feelings, and must have been utterly devastated when she rejected him so cruelly. We need to question her.'

'Go and speak to her with my blessing. I can tell you where she lives – Peter told me who she was last night.' The Abbot's voice hardened. 'But first interrogate the man in the gaol and find out what he has to say for himself.'

Chapter Twenty

'How did they realise you were involved?' Elias asked.

Jordan shook his head. 'The bailiff came to buy cloth, and like a fool I cut it with the knife I used on that man. The knight knew it from the emblem.' He was standing at the unglazed window. The room stank of faeces. His brother hadn't bathed, and Lybbe could smell his sweat, all the worse for his fear. There was a bread-crust on the floor, which had been nibbled by rats, and a bucket with water. A box of ashes formed a crude privy. The window at least offered a little fresh air, and Lybbe leaned gratefully against the bars. 'It was my own fault. I should never have come back, but I couldn't help it.'

'Why did you? You must have known you were walking back to the Abbot's gibbet!'

'Bayonne was good enough to me, I suppose, but I'm a moorman. Could you live in a land, even the most beautiful place in the world, and not look at the moors ever again? Dartmoor isn't just a place: if you're born here, it's in your bones. I've missed it ever since I left. And I missed you, too, you daft bugger. After all, you are my brother.'

'I'll tell them what happened.'

'It's a bit late to worry about that,' Jordan said. 'I'm sorry I brought you into this, Elias. I should have stayed away.'

It was too late for regrets now. He couldn't accept it was his fault things had come to this, but he needed time to think, to find a way out of the morass into which he had fallen. His greatest concern was the boy. What would become of poor Hankin? he wondered. He had saved him when his parents had died, and now his stupidity would lead to his second orphanage. For the first time since he had rescued Hankin he felt the weight of his responsibility. He didn't even know if the lad was safe – there were so many dangers for a youngster at a fair.

But it was hard to think of anyone else while he could feel the shadow of the Abbot's gibbet. In his mind's eye he pictured it again, but now he saw it with a body already dangling – his own. His voice was heavy. 'Don't worry, Elias, I'll tell them everything. There's no need for you to suffer for me any more.'

'You'll both tell us what happened,' Simon said sharply from the doorway. 'Come out, Elias; you too, Lybbe.'

They followed him into the sunlight. A motley crowd had already formed, patiently waiting to hear what the second man had been arrested for. Baldwin eyed the townspeople carefully; he didn't want any more rioting. He was glad that Edgar had waited at the gaol after escorting Jordan Lybbe there; he felt unarmed when his man wasn't nearby.

Simon read his expression correctly, and inwardly cursed the inevitable curiosity of the townspeople; there was always the risk that a hothead might decide to free men considered innocent, or organise a lynching mob. He glanced about him. Next door to the cell was a little room used for meetings by the burgesses of Tavistock. It would do for their enquiries. He led them inside and sat on a stool as the others filed in. Baldwin and Edgar took up stations at either side of the door, the watchman Daniel with them. Simon surveyed the two men before him.

Elias was a scruffy, tattered scarecrow, with wide, fearful eyes and pale face. Lybbe stood with casual resignation, feet apart as if preparing to resist an onslaught. He looked to the bailiff as if he had expected to be caught, and was ready for his trial.

'Elias,' Simon began. 'You called this man brother – why?'

Lybbe glanced wrily at Elias. 'I *am* his brother. I left here many years ago and went to live in Gascony, but recently I came back to see him. It has been a long time since we last met.'

'Did you kill Roger Torre?'

'No,' Lybbe said flatly. 'He was dead when we found him.'

'You'd better tell us what happened.'

'It takes little time. We were drinking in the tavern that evening. I hadn't been able to warn Elias I was coming here for the fair, I wasn't even sure he was still alive, but I found the tavern and decided to try it.

'The alewife told me Elias often came in, and I waited to see if he would turn up. He did, and I sent the alewife to ask him to join me. We talked for a good long time, and then he suggested that we could go to his house and get some food. I was happy to eat, for I'd not had anything all day, so we upped and left. I remember that the compline bell was ringing as we went out. Elias had told me about this pile of rubbish he had to move or be fined, and I asked how much of it there was, because after we'd eaten I could help him ferry it to the midden. So he took me up the alley to show me . . .'

'It was in there we found Torre,' Elias continued. 'He was lying in the pile. I tripped over his arm.' He shuddered.

'He was laid out face down, like someone had just dragged him in by the heels and covered him with the muck,' Lybbe explained.

'On his face?' Baldwin interjected, with a keen look at Lybbe.

'Yes, sir. On his face.' Lybbe sighed. 'He was dead, but his head was still on his shoulders.'

'Why did you behead him?' guessed Simon.

Lybbe squared his shoulders with resolution. 'I thought – I still think – he died because someone mistook him for me. I'm sure they meant to kill me, not Torre.'

Simon leaned forward, staring at him intently. 'Go on.'

'Sir, I have lived in Gascony for twenty years, trading at the markets and keeping a shop in Bayonne. Last year Bayonne had a great fair, and people travelled there from all over Christendom, to buy or sell their goods. The Venetians came – the Camminos. They stayed with the Abbot himself, arranging to buy pewter from all the sellers in the town, always at good rates, using the guarantees the Abbot extended to them.

'All during the fair there were problems. Men were robbed, knocked out in the street and their purses taken. Those responsible were never found, although several were held. On the last day of the fair, a man was attacked – a merchant from the north. I suppose he'd heard of the robberies, for he was on his guard and managed to draw his knife to defend himself, but he was stabbed to death.

'Well, the townspeople were furious. They took to the streets, intimidating anyone they thought could be responsible. The Abbot agreed when the Venetians said they were scared and wanted to leave. I think he thought having them in the Abbey might tempt a few of the hotheads to attack the place.

'They rose early the next day, and rushed off before dawn with their servant, taking all the pewter with them, to the shame of the Abbot. The hue was raised and a posse set off after them. Luckily other travellers had seen them passing, so the men knew the direction to take. The criminals only escaped by releasing their packhorse with all the pewter. Lightened of their load, they could gallop off, while those in pursuit, whose horses were already well nigh exhausted, could only watch as the gap between them widened.'

'They weren't caught?'

'No, sir. Now, when I was sitting with Elias in the tavern, we saw three men enter. They came in and sat down to wait for the alewife to serve them, and because she stood with us, they became impatient. I caught a glimpse of the older man's face, and I thought I recognised him, but I couldn't think where from. I was sure it was not a face I remembered from here. A few moments later, they all left the inn. Only later did I recall their faces from Bayonne.

'It was when we found the body; Elias noticed that the dead man was the same size as me – he had a similar build. Looking at him, lying there, he said it could have been me. That was when I realised where I knew the men in the tavern from. They were the Camminos – the thieves at Bayonne.

'I suddenly thought to myself, what if they had spotted me first? They would know I was a risk to them, as I might recognise and denounce them. If they were trying to defraud someone here as well, they might have felt safer killing me so that I couldn't bear witness against them. In the dark they might have thought this man *was* me! If they had seen me in the tavern, saw my face, realised I was in Bayonne when they were, they might well have decided to silence me for ever by waiting to spring an ambush.

'This all passed through my mind in a trice. I was sure the man had died in error; and I was equally sure that the men in the tavern were responsible. But at least they now thought I was dead.'

He halted, and Simon prompted him to go on.

'Well, sir, I told Elias what I thought, but he could hardly keep his teeth from chattering, he was so upset. I suggested he went back to the tavern and had another drink to steady his nerves.'

'Why didn't you raise the hue?' Simon grunted.

'I couldn't get the idea out of my mind that they'd tried to kill me – and once they learned they'd made a mistake, they might try again. But I had no proof! I could hardly ask the port-reeve to believe that the Abbot's guests were murderers, could I? And if I did, they might find a way to kill me before I could have them arrested. I just didn't know what to do – but then I thought, what if they *don't* find out they killed the wrong man? What if I could hide the identity of the victim? I couldn't conceal the whole body, for if I did that they might think they'd not killed me, that I'd managed to crawl away and recover . . . but if the identity of the corpse was hidden, they might leave me in peace until I could show they were the killers. Then it came to me, I suddenly saw how I could hide their failure: I could change clothes with him. I went back to the alley and swapped his things for mine. But his face would tell the lie. I had to hide his face.'

Lybbe looked up, pale but defiant. 'I wasn't trying to upset the King's Peace. Only I knew the secret of these three men, and I wanted to expose their villainy. I needed time to find out what new crime the Camminos were involved in. Look – Torre was dead already, and what I did couldn't hurt him. But his head wasn't easy to get off.' Lybbe paused to get a grip on himself. 'I cut with my knife, but I needed something stronger. I went to my brother's house and found a billhook, and used that to hack his head off, then covered the body again, but carelessly so it would be easily discovered.'

Baldwin stared. 'Did you not think that taking off the head would make the killer suspicious?'

'I had no time to think. All I knew was, they mustn't find out I was alive.'

'You could have called the watch and had the men arrested immediately. Why this ignoble charade?'

Lybbe was quiet a moment. 'Like I said, they were staying with the Abbot – they were his friends. And anyway, I've been attacked twice already by the watch. How could I trust them? If the Venetians were to pay them well enough, the watch might agree to arrest me instead of them.'

'I see. Continue.'

'The head was the last thing. I had to hide it. In my brother's garden I found a sack, dug a hole and buried it. After that, I went back to my stall.'

Simon confronted the baker. 'Elias, why on earth didn't you tell us all this? Why put your life in danger to hide something that was none of your doing?'

'I was scared. I thought you'd assume we'd both killed Torre, and there was no point both of us dying, so I thought I might as well take all the blame rather than see us share it.'

Baldwin nodded slowly. That much made sense. He considered, then looked back at Lybbe. 'Why did you leave the sheath with Torre but take away the knife?'

He grinned mirthlessly. 'Because I am a fool, Sir Knight. I dressed him in my clothes first, and then when I wanted to cut off his head, I realised I'd left my knife on the belt. Rather than remove the lot, I just pulled out the knife, intending to take the sheath later, but I was so shaken up afterwards, I forgot. I shoved the knife in my belt as I dragged his body to the rubbish pile and then went off to bury the head. When I realised I'd left the empty sheath with the body, I foolishly decided to leave things that way. I'm not soft, Sir Baldwin, but that day's work has haunted me since.'

'And these thieves – the men you think killed Torre. Who were they, again?'

'They call themselves "Cammino".'

Edgar and Daniel took the brothers back to the gaol, and when they had gone, Simon glanced at the knight. 'What do you think?'

'I think it is preposterous. Why go through this charade when all they need do was report finding a body and tell what they knew about the other men?'

'You heard what Lybbe said about the watch.'

'Yes, and that was untrue. He said he arrived here the day Torre was killed. The watchmen tried to extort money from him the next day, so it was a lie to say he was scared of them at that point – unless . . .' His voice trailed off as he stared unseeing through the open door. It faced down the road towards the town. In the distance he saw a figure, the port-reeve.

'What is it?' Simon demanded as Baldwin strode off.

'A thought. Come on, hurry up!' the knight cried over his shoulder. The bailiff cursed, but set off after him.

The port-reeve had hoped that the earlier questioning would be enough. He had several transactions to witness, and tried to mask his impatience as the knight hurried to him.

'Holcroft, you have lived here for some time, haven't you?'

'All my life.'

'Did you know Elias had a brother?'

'Yes, of course – Jordan. Left here, oh, years ago. At least twenty.'

'Why did he go away?'

The port-reeve pursed his lips. 'He was an outlaw. He joined a band of trail-bastons, a group that murdered and burned their way round the north of the county. He was only found because the gang got into a fight with the people of Tiverton, and the town won. They chased the men for miles, but the crooks were lucky. One of their band was found in a church, claiming sanctuary, and agreed to approve. He gave all the names of the men in the gang, and was allowed to abjure the realm. One of the names he gave was Jordan Lybbe's.'

'How did Lybbe escape justice?' asked Simon.

'Easy. He came home before news of the battle reached here. Took some of his belongings and disappeared. A ship left the coast shortly after, and it was said that a man looking like Lybbe had gone aboard just before it set sail.'

'I see. Well, thank you, Holcroft,' said Baldwin.

He left them, and Simon shook his head. 'So that's why he preferred this elaborate hoax rather than calling the watch.'

'He knew his life would be forfeit if he was discovered in the kingdom again. If he called the watch and was recognised, he would be hanged.'

'And so he will!'

'Yes,' Baldwin agreed, but he was perplexed. 'But why

should he remove the head and hide it? If he had nothing to do with the murder, he'd have just left town while it was dark.'

'Maybe he thought that would be viewed as an admission of guilt.'

'But if he thought that, he'd have just left the body as it was. There must have been a reason for him to remove the head.' Baldwin put his own on one side. 'The alternative is, he was the killer: but why should he kill Torre? We have no motive for him to have done that.'

'Maybe Torre recognised him.'

'If he had, wouldn't he have shouted it out? The watch were in the tavern, so were many others. If Torre had recognised Lybbe, he'd have made a row.'

'Unless he thought he could blackmail Lybbe into paying him for his silence.'

'In that case, Torre would have gone to speak to him, but no one saw them talk.'

'We haven't asked anyone whether they spoke,' Simon pointed out reasonably.

'True. But also, if Torre realised who Lybbe was, he surely wouldn't have gone out with Lizzie. He'd have stayed inside where he could keep an eye on his investment, whether he had spoken to him or not. This all makes no sense.'

'Are you saying his story was true and the Venetians did it?'

'I don't know, Simon. But it makes as much sense as Lybbe being the killer.'

They left the gaol and went back down the hill again. The house to which the Abbot had directed them was a pleasant block not far from the tavern, and Baldwin thumped heavily on the door as soon as they arrived. A harassed maidservant appeared, and Baldwin strode past her into the hall.

Inside a woman sat placidly sewing at a tapestry. She

looked up in some surprise at the sound of footsteps ringing on the stone flagging, and then her face sharpened. 'What is the meaning of this intrusion? Do you have business with my husband, because if you don't I'll call for the watch this instant!'

'My lady, excuse our abrupt entrance,' Baldwin said smoothly. 'It is the young lady we wish to speak to, the girl who has befriended the monk Peter. Do you know where she is?'

Marion studied him coldly and set her tapestry aside. 'What would you want with her?'

'Lady, the boy has been found murdered, and we must find out whether she can help us find the killer.'

'Murder? My daughter knows nothing about this. I cannot allow you to question her.'

'We must.'

'You will not, on my honour! If you wish, you may speak to my husband, but—'

'We are here,' Simon interjected, 'on the Abbot's orders. It is very important that we speak to your daughter instantly.'

Mistress Pole scowled, but consented. The Abbot's will could not be denied. She sent the maidservant to fetch her daughter. In a few moments she returned, but alone. 'Mistress, the door's locked, and she won't answer.'

'Let me try,' Marion said, and lifting her skirts, she hurried from the room. Simon glanced at Baldwin, and they followed after her.

'Avice? Avice, open this door at once!'

She pounded on the timbers with the flat of her hand, and Baldwin could see that she was beginning to panic. He muttered, 'God's blood!' If there was one complication he did not want, it was that the girl might have run away with her beau.

'Lady, excuse me.'

He looked at Edgar, and his manservant rushed at the

door with his shoulder. It shivered, but the timber was strong. Baldwin joined him. Under their combined weight the door and frame shattered, and Baldwin tripped over a broken spar to fall flat on his face. From the floor he could see that the room was deserted. The open window told the story of Avice Pole's escape.

Behind him he heard a stifled laugh. 'Simon, if you think this is funny,' he said coldly, 'next time *you* can charge the door.' He slowly got to his feet, wincing at the bruise on his shoulder. It felt as if he had broken it at the same time as the door. When he looked at the jamb, he saw that the door had been bolted on the inside.

'What in the Devil's name is the meaning of all this?'

Simon turned to find a florid-faced man gaping at the devastation. There was a strong smell of alcohol as he entered the room. 'I return to my house to be told that strangers have forced their way in, and then I find that they've destroyed a door! What's this all about, eh? Who are you?'

Baldwin dusted his knees and stepped over the wreckage. 'I am Sir Baldwin de Furnshill, and this is Simon Puttock, bailiff of Lydford Castle. We are investigating the murder of Roger Torre and a novice monk on behalf of the Abbot.'

'What has this to do with me and my family?'

'Arthur, these men wanted to speak to Avice, but she's gone. Arthur, she's run away!'

'What?' Her husband scanned the room, his eyes returning to Marion's face with fright. 'When? I mean, how?'

'She's disappeared. It must be Pietro!'

'I'll have his blood if he's harmed my Avice!'

'We don't know for certain it was him,' said Baldwin.

'*You* may not, *I* do! I want him whipped – God's blood! What if he's . . . If he's polluted her, I'll have his—'

'Husband, the least we can do now is consider how to find her and bring her back.'

'Find her? Of course we'll have to find her, woman!'

Baldwin took the sputtering, furious merchant by the arm and began to direct him back towards the hall. His voice was low and calm, talking with an unhurried steadiness that soothed the irate man. 'You mentioned the Venetian. Was that the younger man? I thought so, yes – it was Pietro. Avice was in her room? Fine, I see. There was little more for a concerned father to do, other than manacle her to a ring, and that is not the way to earn the love and trust of your daughter, is it? Of course not . . . Ah, here we are.'

They had arrived once more in the hall, and Baldwin directed the now compliant father to a seat, then sent the maid for wine and water. Marion sat, hands in her lap, while she considered her husband. She had told him it wouldn't work, she'd said they should pack immediately and leave, but he had refused because of his business. He had all the furs still, he hadn't managed to sell them yet, and he had to remain in Tavistock to try to get rid of them. 'She'll be all right locked in her room,' he'd said. This was how all right she was, Marion thought bitterly. Probably ruined already, and John wouldn't want her like that. He came from an old family, and they would expect any woman he chose to be pure, no matter how rich her parents.

The wine arrived, and Baldwin filled a goblet, nodding to the man to drink. Arthur lifted it to his mouth with shaking hands, sipped, then put it down. His Avice had run away, it was inconceivable!

'Sir, when was your daughter last seen?' Baldwin asked.

'I don't know. Marion?'

'About the middle of the morning.'

'Thank you, madam. And she had been forbidden, I assume, to see this boy again, is that right?'

'Yes,' Arthur said heavily. 'We told her this morning. You see, we'd checked up on him and his father, and they were not as they portrayed themselves. The pair of them had made out they were prosperous, yet I know that they only have poor riding ponies. Would a wealthy man stint on his horse-flesh like that?'

'I see.' Baldwin chewed his lip. There was one thing that concerned him more than any other. 'Tell me, do you know of any reason why he should have decided to run away with your daughter now?'

'Yes. I saw him this morning, arrogant damned fool!' Arthur explained with a sidelong glance at his wife – he hadn't told her this yet. After seeing Pietro, he had been so angry that he had gone straight back to the tavern. 'I informed him he would not be able to see my daughter again, that he was not suitable for her as far as I was concerned.'

'I see. What did he do after you spoke with him?'

'He scampered off towards the Abbey. After what I said, I assumed he'd never dare to show his face again.'

'Do you have horses kept here?'

'Yes, there are stables at the back in a yard.'

'Has your daughter's gone?'

'I don't know – follow me!'

He rose and hurried out to the screens. The back door gave onto a small yard with stabling on the left. While he went to question the groom, Baldwin cast an eye upwards. There was a ladder leaning against the wall. 'That's how, then,' he said to Simon, jerking his head at it.

'Not the most difficult inference you've ever made,' Simon muttered.

There was a cry from the stable, and they ran over to the entrance. Inside they found the merchant bending over a squirming figure. 'The bastard tied up my groom!' Arthur bawled indignantly.

The knight bent over Henry and cut the cords binding his arms and feet. Edgar helped him to his feet and with his help Henry was taken to his palliasse and laid down on it gently. The knight stood at his side.

'Can you tell us what happened?' Baldwin asked.

'I was clobbered, sir,' Henry said painfully. 'Someone belted me from behind.'

'Did you see who it was?'

'No, sir. All I know is, I was out here seeing to the horses, and next thing I had a headache and was trussed like a capon.'

'You didn't see which way they went?'

'No, sir.'

'Did you hear anything? Screams or shouting?'

'Do you mean,' Arthur said, drawing himself straight with indignation, 'do you mean to suggest that my daughter might have willingly eloped with this Venetian jackanapes?'

'It is possible,' said Baldwin, raising a hand to cut short the angry expostulation that Pole's daughter would never connive at such a betrayal of her parents' wishes. 'At this moment we don't even know for sure that Pietro da Cammino is involved. We shall leave you now, and go to the Abbey to question him.'

'He won't be at the Abbey – I tell you he's run off!'

'In that case, when we have made sure he is not at the Abbey, we will organise a search for him – and her.'

'There is one more thing, Sir Baldwin. If the Abbot doesn't believe this, tell him that his guest, that bastard Pietro, has been impersonating a monk.'

'What?'

'My man saw him last night. He was dressed like a Benedictine, wandering round the town. My daughter met him, and he wooed her under the protection of holy garb.'

'God's blood!' Simon breathed. 'Was *he* the thief?'

Chapter Twenty-One

Simon and Baldwin sent Edgar to get their horses saddled and bridled, and ran across the court to the Abbot's lodging. A monk told them he was in his private chapel, and they had to wait, chafing at the delay, while another monk went in and asked the Abbot to see them.

'My friends – do you have news from the girl?'

Simon told of the missing girl, and the Abbot froze. 'But . . . the Venetians have gone.'

'When?' Baldwin asked quickly.

'After the rabble came to the gate. Both Pietro and their servant were terrified by the appearance of so many ruffians calling for their blood. Someone had roused them against bankers. Pietro insisted that they should leave. His father was unwilling at first, not wanting to lose his deal with me, but I refused it, and he agreed to leave then.'

'It would appear that Pietro had an ulterior motive. The crowd at the gate gave him his excuse, and he took his chance.'

'Sir Baldwin, you must find them.'

'We shall try, sir. But where they could have gone is a matter of guesswork. We will need to hunt them down carefully.'

'I shall come to the yard with you. It's impossible for me to join you on the Feast Day of the Abbey's saint, but at least I can make sure you are sent off with as many men as possible.'

So saying, Abbot Robert led the way out of the room. A

monk was outside in the Prayle, and the Abbot called him over, telling him to prepare men to join the hunt. He scurried off and the Abbot and the others continued on their way.

Edgar stood waiting with the horses, and Baldwin took the reins from his servant. 'The trouble is, we have no idea where they might have gone. Do you have a hunter used to tracking animals?'

'I do, but he's not here, he's out working.'

Simon said, 'Surely they'll make straight for the coast? Plymouth would be best for them.'

'Perhaps,' Baldwin mused. 'But the port there is very small. The chances of finding a ship before we catch up with them are remote, unless they have a ship waiting.'

'Did they leave in a great hurry?' Simon asked the Abbot. 'What about their clothes and belongings – are all gone?'

'I don't know, I . . . You,' he called to a lay brother. The man ambled over, a spade on his shoulder like a weapon. 'Go to the guest-master and find out whether the Venetians left anything behind. Quickly, brother!'

The man dropped his shovel and hesitated, wondering whether to pick it up. Catching sight of the Abbot's face, he let it lie and ran off. The Abbot sighed. 'Only a few hours ago all was normal. It was merely a hectic Feast Day for St Rumon, and now I have lost a novice to a murder, a pair of guests are to be hunted like venison, and—'

'My lord Abbot!'

Champeaux glanced at Baldwin with surprise. 'Eh?'

'Hunted! Your hounds!'

He stared for moment, then groaned and slapped his forehead. 'I must be the greatest fool alive!' and dashed off towards the River Gate. A few moments later he returned with a man, narrow-faced, and with a sallow complexion. Bright blue eyes glittered under dark brows. 'This is my berner, the master of my scent hounds.'

'Berner, you have harrier hounds?'

'We have – twenty couple.'

'Could they chase men?'

He chuckled. 'They could chase an ant from its smell.'

There was a commotion from the guests' quarters, and when they turned to see the cause, they saw the lay brother coming towards them at a run. 'Abbot, the servant is still here!'

Seeing the berner shrug and start to make his way back to his beloved hounds, Baldwin called to him, 'Master berner, bring ten couples here immediately, and a horse for yourself. We shall be hunting men.'

Simon turned to the monk. 'Where is he?'

'In the guestroom.'

'Good. Come on, Baldwin.'

Guests could be placed in various parts of the Abbey depending upon their rank and importance. Those of lowly position would stay in the communal accommodation above the Great Gate itself, while the most important would stay in the Abbot's own private rooms alongside his hall. For others, when this was already being used, there was the main guest block overlooking the river, and it was in this building that the Venetians had been placed. Simon walked up the stairs to the first floor, and only when he arrived at the door did it occur to him that the man inside might be desperate and dangerous. He was uncommonly glad to hear the steady steps of Baldwin and his man behind him as he reached for his sword and tested the hilt in his hand. He glanced at the knight, then opened the door in a rush and burst in, drawing his sword as he went. He fetched up against a wall, holding the weapon before him.

'The sword is unnecessary, Simon,' he heard Baldwin murmur as the knight walked in.

In the far corner of what was a broad and long room, he saw the servant Luke folding clothes and stowing them into a light cloth bag, suitable for dangling from a saddle. The man stared in astonishment, eyeing Simon as if doubting his sanity.

'You are the servant of Antonio and Pietro da Cammino?' Baldwin asked, walking quietly towards the man. He nodded, which was a relief to the knight, who had feared that he might not speak English. 'What is your name?'

'Luke, sir.'

'Good. Luke, do you know where they have gone?'

'No, sir,' Luke said, his gaze still fixed upon Simon as the bailiff carefully felt for his scabbard and thrust his sword home. 'They collected their things and went; I don't know where.'

'Did you help them pack?'

'Yes, sir. After the shouting and everything at the gate, Pietro came straight up here, and told me to pack his things.'

'How did he seem?' Baldwin asked.

'Very upset, sir. Flustered and cross. He said I must prepare to leave immediately, and from his look I imagined something must have happened.'

Simon shook his head. 'They already have a good head start on us, let's get going.'

His friend shook his head and held up a hand. 'Wait, Simon. Let's not rush off before we have to. The hounds aren't ready yet, and we don't have a posse. Now, Luke, you say Pietro was flustered and angry. Did he give you any indication what had angered him?'

'No, sir. He only said that he'd been a fool, and went out as soon as I'd started packing his things. Then he came back a little later with his father, and Antonio seemed depressed. He said nothing to me at all while he was here, just paced up and down the room.'

The knight remained staring fixedly at the servant. 'When you were in Bayonne, weren't you attacked by a mob there?'

Luke nodded. 'Yes, it was fearsome, being chased like

that. We had to leave almost immediately.'

'Did you know Pietro saw Avice's father today? He told Pietro to leave and never see his daughter again.'

Simon interrupted, 'Baldwin, is this really necessary?'

'Pietro must have seen the girl at some point, or how would he know she would go with him?'

'Fine, so the lad went to see her, and when she told him she'd be happy to go away with him, he came back here and prepared to leave. Can we get a move on now?'

'But there was this crowd at the Abbey gates, Simon. Was that just a fortuitous coincidence? And the mob dispersed as soon as the Abbot spoke to them. Did Pietro and his father really feel so threatened that they had to leave immediately? If he knew Avice would go with him anyway, what was the hurry? He could surely have waited until dark and gone then.'

'Baldwin, you're quibbling over details, and all the time they're getting further away. Come on, let's be after them!'

'Patience, Simon. Now, Luke, I do not believe that Antonio would have rushed off just because of a crowd making a noise. He would be safe in the Abbey here. Why would he agree to go in such a hurry? Enough hurry, for example, to leave *you* behind, Luke,' Baldwin finished imperturbably.

Luke stared back. He knew he had to make the choice whether to protect his masters and hide their secrets, in which case he might be viewed with suspicion and possibly even accused with them, or discard them utterly and protect himself. He glanced quickly at the bailiff.

Simon gave an exasperated groan and dropped onto a bench. 'I assume you have some reason for wanting to wait? Maybe the lad was in a hurry to go because he had killed the monk, and now we know he abducted the girl—'

'Simon, we know nothing of the sort! There is nothing to connect him to the murder of Peter, and we don't even know that she wasn't a willing accomplice in their departure. At this moment we know nothing about the matter.'

'Sir, my master Antonio was accused by the girl's father of being a fraud, of inventing a bogus scheme to steal from the Abbot.'

'That made him suddenly run away?' Simon asked dubiously.

'Sir, I refused to go with them. I'll tell you all I know, but only if I can be exempted from blame for what they have done.'

Baldwin nodded. 'Speak!'

'I first met Antonio and his son two years ago in France. They had lost their servant to a disease, and they were glad enough to have me instead.

'Last year we went to Bayonne to the fair, staying in a small inn. At the time, I thought it was to find new stuffs to sell, for they had made a fortune out of selling a great stock of Toledo metalwork, but then I began to have doubts.'

Simon was interested despite himself. The servant's story was halting, but the bailiff could see that he was coming quickly to his point.

'Antonio spent much time talking to the Abbot there, and whenever I overheard them, it was always about the same thing – how Antonio had a fleet and was looking for the best suppliers of goods to transport to Florence. It sounded strange to me, for I had never seen any evidence of a single ship, let alone a fleet.

'Then one night Antonio came to me and instructed me to pack everything and prepare to leave. I thought he had lost interest in the Abbot and wanted to avoid his bill for stabling and food, so I did as I was told, but when I heard Antonio talking to his son, he was scornful and contemptuous. I had no idea why; I just did as I was told. When all was packed, Antonio himself led the way to the stables, and I found that a pony had been laden with other stuff, but I thought it was just the things that Antonio had bought from the fair. It never occurred to me . . . Well, I'll come to that.

'We walked the horses from the stables behind our inn,

and once we were outside the town, rode off. Some twenty
or so miles farther on, there was another inn, and we rested
there for a morning before setting off again, but before we
had gone far, there was a sound of charging horses behind
us, and when I looked over my shoulder, I saw a knight and
others racing along. Antonio saw them at the same time,
and cried to us to whip up.

'I didn't know what was going on, but if they were after
us, whether they were outlaws or lawful posse, I didn't care:
I didn't want to be caught by so many warlike men miles
from anywhere. Just like the others, I clapped spurs to my
mount and tried to escape. But the pony was a heavy
burden. Its load was too heavy for it to hurry, and the men
were gaining on us. I tried whipping it, but although I cut its
hide in many places, it couldn't keep up. In the end I let it
go.'

'And?'

Baldwin's voice was quiet, but it shattered the silence like
a mace hitting glass. The servant looked up again. 'Sir, when
Antonio saw what I had done, he was in a towering rage. He
said, "What was the point of stealing all that pewter if you're
going to let them take it all back?" I was horrified: I'd had
no idea he was stealing it. Maybe there are some things I've
done in my life I'm not proud of, but I'm no thief, and the
thought of robbing so many, and all under the Abbot's
guarantee . . . It was like stealing from the Abbot himself.

'We carried on, and Antonio managed to trade a few items
and keep us from starving, and I had thought when we came
here to Tavistock, it was so that he could start to rebuild his
business. When he came in this morning, just like he had in
Bayonne, I realised he was doing something wrong again,
and I decided to leave them. If they want a hemp necklace,
they're welcome. I don't!'

'And,' Baldwin prompted, 'what else? Come, we know so
much already.'

Edgar was standing at the door, and through it he could

see the hounds milling in the court. Men were arriving; the mounted watchmen placed around the fair to protect travellers had been called to form the posse. He considered telling his master, but seeing Baldwin's concentration, he remained silent.

'Sir, Pietro met this girl, Avice, and fell in love with her – and, I think, she with him. He arranged to meet her in the tavern, so that he and she could allow their fathers to talk and discuss business, with the hope that both would find the other amenable to their marriage, but to Pietro's disgust, his father insisted that we should leave. Sir, while we were in Bayonne, there was a merchant we saw several times. He was in the tavern that night too. When Antonio saw him, he rushed out, almost knocking down a man coming in, and Pietro all but drew his dagger to strike the man down; it was only me holding his arm that stopped him. Outside, Antonio told us that he'd seen the merchant from Bayonne. Pietro hadn't, but Antonio was absolutely certain, and he told us to avoid the tavern in future so that we could not be recognised. Then he and I returned to the Abbey.'

'And Pietro?'

'He remained: he said he wanted to wait for his girl and parents, hoping he would be able to talk to her or persuade them to go to another tavern.'

'So it *was* him,' Simon breathed.

Baldwin scratched his chin reflectively. 'What else?'

Luke was committed now. He closed his eyes briefly, then held Baldwin's steadily as he completed his story. 'Sir, this morning Pietro was in a rage about a monk who had been "pestering", as he called it, his woman. He went out to see her, and when he came back, like I say, he was pale and anxious. I didn't want to question him – I know what he's capable of. He can have an evil temper. Now I hear the monk's dead.'

'And you have formed your own conclusion, obviously,'

Baldwin said, and stood. 'Very well, Edgar, I can hear them;
there's no need to wave like that. Luke, you will remain here
until we return. Come along, Simon, what are you waiting
for? We have men to catch.'

In the court they found the Abbot talking to the berner
with men cursing and swearing at the hounds, which
slavered and slobbered at the horses' hooves. Abbot
Champeaux himself seemed unaware of the mayhem, and
Baldwin assumed that he was so used to hunting and the
din created by his harriers that this was an almost relaxing
sound to him. The knight asked the Abbot to see to it that
Luke was held, then prepared to mount his horse.

The knight was pleased to note, as he swung his leg over
the back of his Arab mare, that the hounds all appeared to
be from good stock. They were of a good tan colour, and
larger than his own, with wide nostrils set in long muzzles,
and all had powerful chests with strong shoulders and hips
that pointed not only to their being able to maintain a steady
speed, but also to their ability to bring down heavy game.
Baldwin did not miss the heavy hunting collars, all of thick
engraved leather, that the Abbot had invested in for his
pack. The collars were not overly ostentatious, they weren't
studded with silver or even iron, but the knight could see
that they were expensive, and the sight made him give a
grin. The Abbot was proud of his harriers.

Baldwin hoped that his pride would today be justified.

'You will send these to the Abbey for us,' Margaret stated,
preferring to assume the man's compliance than offer him an
opportunity to refuse. Miserably, he nodded. He had already
been forced to bargain away more than he had intended, and
it was worth agreeing just to dispose of the harpy.

Jeanne kept a straight face as Margaret sternly instructed
the man, but as soon as they had gone a little way along the
alley, she began to giggle. 'The poor devil was glad to see
the back of you.'

'I'd have been worried if he wasn't,' said Margaret complacently. 'That could only mean he thought he had the better of the deal, and I wouldn't want him to make too much profit from me. I haven't been too hard on him – he was happy enough to agree to my conditions in the end.'

'Of course, my lady,' Jeanne said, giving her a mock curtsey. 'He should be grateful that you deigned to visit his stall, let alone graced him with your business.'

'The cloth will suit my sideboard.'

'Yes, and the other will look good on you,' Jeanne said.

Margaret laughed. She had convinced the man that dealing with the bailiff of Lydford's wife was potentially good for his business, and he had initially scrambled to show her the choicest materials he had, but his enthusiasm for the talk had waned when he realised that her aim was to win the best cloth for the price of the cheapest. 'It's not my fault,' she said. 'I was raised as a farmer's daughter, and we were taught to bargain and save as much money as we could. My mother would have been horrified to see me throwing away good money just because I couldn't be bothered to haggle a bit.'

'If she was like my uncle's wife in Burgundy, she'd be just as shocked to see you spending so much on a few choice materials.'

Margaret ignored the tone of mild reproof, her interest fired by the comment. 'Your aunt and uncle raised you?'

'Yes, after my parents died, they took me with them.'

'It must have been a great adventure to go so far,' Margaret said, with a trace of jealousy. The furthest she had travelled was to Tiverton.

'Not for a girl of only three years. I had no idea what my home was like, I hardly remembered the house, and within a short space I had forgotten what my mother looked like.'

'Surely not!'

Jeanne glanced at her, hearing the note of disbelief. Too late she remembered that Margaret had a daughter, and gave an apologetic grimace. 'I'm sure if I'd been a little older I would have been able to recall her face, but I was very young to lose both parents.'

'Of course. But tell me, wasn't your uncle sad to see you marry someone who lived so far from him? It must have been an awful wrench for you to have lost two families when you married.'

Jeanne surveyed a stall of hats. 'Not really, no. Having lost my parents, I did not much mind losing an uncle. And he didn't miss me. As far as he was concerned, I was a constant drain on his purse, and little more. It can only have been a relief to him when I left. He'd invested a lot of money making sure I was well turned out, and primed in etiquette and the proper manners for my station in life. When I was snapped up by Ralph de Liddinstone, I think Uncle saw that as proof of success in some way: he'd got rid of an expensive member of his household. It was the same as if he'd sold off one of his more useless serfs to a buyer for a reasonable sum.'

There was a note of sadness, of accepting a miserable position with equanimity, and Margaret suddenly felt she had an insight into the woman's life. Margaret had always been loved, from the day she was born by her parents, and latterly by the man she had wed and their daughter; Jeanne had never known such all-devouring love. She had been unwanted as a child, but her uncle had accepted her when she was thrust upon him, and when he could, he had disposed of her as quickly as possible, to a man who apparently had not loved her, but had instead treated her like any other possession, something to be thrashed when recalcitrant.

It made Margaret push her arm through the other's in a sympathetic gesture, and though Jeanne looked quite surprised, she was obviously grateful as well.

They were still linked arm-in-arm when they came across a small group of actors in a miracle play, and both stopped as if by mutual agreement to watch.

The story was so badly acted that Margaret was not sure what it was about. At one point she felt that it might be about the Last Judgement, but it was hard to be sure, partly because she had never been educated, but also because she found her attention wandering during sermons – that was when her daughter began to lose interest in proceedings, searching around for something to do, and she made it hard to concentrate.

Jeanne was unimpressed by the play, but someone in the crowd caught her attention.

It was a man, probably only in his early twenties, who stood with his son at the edge of the audience. All the time the actors were speaking their lines, he pointed to them, explaining what was happening, and when his son complained of not being able to see enough, he caught the child up and sat him on his shoulders.

Unbidden, the thought came to her mind that Baldwin would be as gentle and kindly if he were a father. It made her give a quick smile.

There was no point in giving the harriers a scent of Antonio's or Pietro's clothing; they would be on horseback, and the chance of a hound catching a whiff of the men was remote. Instead, the dogs were given an old saddle-blanket from Antonio's stable – one which had been worn by his horse. The berner was dubious, thinking that his harriers might confuse the beast with another horse, but it was the best they could do. When the hounds had all snuffed the blanket, the berner shouldered a large leather bag and mounted. The hunt moved off into the street.

The traffic had been so great that the hounds could not discern the trail, and Simon glanced at Baldwin. 'If they went to the moor we'll have time to find them later. I would suggest either the road to Brentor or the coast. Surely they would try to escape by one of those routes?'

'I think so. We'll head to Plymstock and see what we can

find; if nothing, we can double back and test the road to Brentor, and the moors last.'

So saying, Baldwin called to the berner, and the cavalcade set off at a lively canter, the harriers moving like a solid mass. They reminded Baldwin of a swarm of bees; each was individual, but acted as a part of a whole. Tails up and wagging, they gave every appearance of delight at being released from their kennels and having a new quarry to chase.

The road led past the Abbey's orchards and fish-ponds, and soon they were out of the town itself. At their left lay the midden reeking with the town's waste, and townspeople were at its edge, hurling rubbish in and retreating swiftly. The noisome stench wafted over the road, and Simon was amused by the reaction of the riders. Some fell silent, a few covering their faces with their hoods, while others resorted to earthy humour, chortling at the disgust of their companions. Simon himself disliked the smell, but was used to it; Baldwin, he saw, curled his lip in disgust – the knight was from the country, and this putrefying stink was never so concentrated where he lived. There human waste was collected in ash to dry and lose its virulence until it could be spread on the fields to help the crops grow.

Baldwin was glad to be past the midden. The country air smelled sweeter beyond it, as if nature had put up an invisible barrier on the distance that man could pollute the atmosphere. Now instead of that malodorous reek, he smelled the fresh-cut grasses in the meadow, the sweet scent of herbs and occasionally the clean fragrance of wild garlic.

They rode on until they had travelled over a mile, and in all that distance the hounds picked up nothing. The berner worked them well and had them circling at either side of the road in case their prey had left it to avoid leaving a trace, but the harriers sniffed for a while, then returned to him, heads cocked on one side in enquiry, tails wagging slowly, and finally Simon had to admit defeat. 'Let's try the Brentor road,' he said.

The berner waved ahead. 'There's a track up there takes us back to Hurdwick. We can pick up the Brentor road there, rather than going all the way back to Tavistock and up.'

Simon nodded, and the berner spurred his horse on, calling to his harriers as he went. The rest of the posse trailed after.

After the events of the last couple of days, Baldwin was relieved to have some physical task to perform. It left his mind free to roam: at first over the things he had heard from the Venetians' servant, but soon his thoughts turned back to Jeanne.

She was so beautiful, she was daunting. Baldwin was convinced she reciprocated his feelings, but it was hard to imagine why – he was not arrogant enough to lie to himself, and he knew that he was hardly the perfect suitor. He had only a small farm and estate, held under his duties of service to his lord, and even his manner of dress – and here he glanced down at his worn but comfortable tunic with a wry grimace – was an embarrassment, as Margaret had pointed out to him.

The berner led them off to the right at a fork, and they were on a smaller, grassy track that wound between thick hedges and ditches until they came to a crossroads where the berner took the harriers north. This trail soon turned back to the northeast, so that they were heading back almost parallel to their first route from the town. It passed by several small vills and bartons, and when they came to another crossed road, the berner let the dogs circle in case they might find a scent, but again they betrayed no excitement.

'Berner,' Simon called, 'is this the Brentor road?'

'No, sir,' the berner called back calmly. 'This is the road to Milton Abbot, but I wanted to make sure the buggers hadn't come here instead of up to Brentor.'

Simon nodded. The berner obviously knew his business, and was checking all the roads which radiated from Tavistock. The abbey town sat in its valley with roads leading to north, east and west, though none south over the moors at the other side of the river, and the berner was working each trail as if it was the worn path of a deer in his search for the Venetians. They set off again to the next road. This was the one which led up the hill towards Brentor.

The berner set his harriers to test the road, egging them on with enthusiastic cries and whistles, and waited while they milled at the crossroads. Simon watched, the tip of his tongue protruding between his lips in his eagerness to see them take off, but then he sighed as dogs began to stop and sit and scratch. All around him, Simon could sense the men relaxing in their seats, letting lances fall a little from the vertical, slumping, one or two chatting. 'Looks like we should have gone for the moors instead,' he said to Baldwin with resignation, but before the knight could comment, the berner edged closer.

'Look at her, sir.'

Following his pointing finger, Simon saw a bitch trotting slowly up and down a little distance away from the others. She paused, glancing back at the pack, her head set to one side with a comical expression of doubt, her brow wrinkled.

'She's just found the trail of a fox or something,' the bailiff said dismissively, and turned to Baldwin.

To his surprise, the knight could barely control his excitement. Baldwin often hunted with his own hounds, and he recognised the signs. The bitch was dubious because of the strength of other scents, and he watched with bated breath. 'Master berner?'

'Yes, sir, I reckon so. The bastards came this way,' the man said, after a scathing look at Simon.

The bailiff stared from one to the other. 'You can tell from a dog doing that?'

'She's the best, sir. She's just making sure, you'll soon hear.'

All at once there was a sharp yelping from her, which was taken up by the other hounds in the pack as they joined her, urgently setting their noses to the dirt of the road and sounding off as they caught the elusive scent. The barking and howling took on a persuasive quality, and the men all round began shifting in their saddles and gripping their arms more firmly as they saw that the hounds had the trail at last. Suddenly the pack moved.

It was an awesome experience for Simon. He had never before joined a large hunt, and seeing the magnificent creatures in full spate was a little like watching the torrent in full flood rushing down the Lydford Gorge. The leader of the pack set up a long baying howl, then went silent with a dread purpose as he began to trot northwards, the rest taking up position behind until he was the point of an arrowhead of harriers making off. As younger hounds caught up with him, the leader snapped at them over his shoulder, and hurried his pace. Others increased their speed to keep up, and there was soon an inevitability to their onward rush, which was made menacing by its sudden silence. The harriers were reserving all their strength for the chase and would not sound out again until they had caught their prey and held it at bay.

The berner whipped his mount without another word, his face showing his excitement, and when Simon glanced at Baldwin, he saw the same look on the knight's face. 'Come on!'

It was like starting a horse race. Clapping spurs to his rounsey's flanks, Simon felt the power surge through his horse's hindquarters as it sprang forward with a sudden explosion of energy, and he had to crouch and grip its flanks with his knees to keep his seat. From behind him he heard the clatter of horseshoes on stone, then a quick scattering of hoofbeats on the densely-packed earth of the roadway as riders kicked their mounts and found their own position in the mêlée, each man thrusting others from his path to make a clear space in which his horse might be able to forge ahead. A horse reared at his side, but the rider remained in control, and forced the animal to twist in mid-air, forelegs flailing, until it was facing the right way, and then he gave it its head.

The discordant, stumbling sound of many horses falteringly finding their pace gradually settled into a rhythmic drumming as they all cantered in unison, and suddenly the sound became a solid thundering. To Simon it was as if the horses were copying the pack. The harriers had formed a solid wedge-shaped group, the leader out in front, while the men behind formed another behind the berner. Baldwin, he saw, was restraining his Arab, which wanted to gallop off. She had the power and speed to overhaul any other mount in the group.

There was an awesome noise: leather squeaked and harnesses jangled as they rushed on, ever faster, the wind hissing and booming in Simon's ears and all but deafening him, the clap and snap of cloaks as they billowed in the wind like sails, and over all the pounding, unified and terrible in its violent force, of the hooves hammering the ground beneath them. For a short second, the bailiff wondered what he would feel like seeing a chivalry of mounted knights charging towards him, but thrust the idea aside. His concentration was needed merely to stay on his beast.

They began to climb a hill, passing Forches Field where the Abbot kept his gallows, and rode over a short plain. At the far side, the hounds streamed around a loudly cursing farmer on a wagon, who struggled to keep his ox quiet as the harriers darted to either side of him, only to have the following riders gallop past. When he glanced back over his shoulder, Simon saw a man barge into another as they both tried to take the same route, and one fell, arms widespread, into a hedge, his horse continuing on alone, stirrups flying and bouncing by its side as it struggled, wild-eyed, to keep its place among the others.

Now they were on the great plain of Heath Field near Brentor, and the conical rock that gave the village its name stood stark on their right, the church at its summit a comforting sight in the bleak surroundings. Still they thundered on, the harriers as silent and daunting as the Devil's own wish hounds in their implacable purpose.

Baldwin could not help a smile of contentment as he felt the urgent desire of his Arab to overtake all others in this race. He had been formed for just such exercise, he felt. The hunt was the only way of life for a man, with the blood rushing as fast in the veins as the air past the ears, the thrill of the search for the quarry, and the skill of holding the mount under control all combining to make it a uniquely exciting experience.

Yet the end of the chase would be the capture of two men, he knew. And their capture might shortly after be followed by their death, hanging from the rope at the Abbot's gibbet. The thoughts circled in his brain, the glorious, hectic delight of the charge; the ghastly end for the quarry.

There were so many lives bound up in this affair: those of Peter and Torre, Avice and Pietro, Antonio, Elias and Jordan. Lybbe was likely to hang for his past offences, and if Pietro was found guilty, as Luke's evidence suggested, of killing Torre and possibly Peter as well, he would die too.

But Baldwin was niggled by something. There was a clue he had missed, something vital that would shed light on all that he had heard today.

Chapter Twenty-Two

At last there was a ripple of music from the harriers.

'Listen to that!' the berner called excitedly. 'We have them now. They can't escape.'

Baldwin nodded agreement. He had rarely heard hunting hounds give voice so strongly, and when they did, it was a sure sign that their quarry was near at hand.

He looked about him as they raced on. They had taken the north-western route after Brentor, and now they were passing on the old road under Lydford, towards the moors. The weather here was gloomy, with thick clouds grey and dull overhead. It was hard to believe that in Tavistock the weather was calm and bright with few clouds in a deep blue sky, looking up here and feeling the damp chill in the air.

Baldwin could recognise most of the countryside from his trips to see Simon, and this part was familiar. They were riding at an easy canter to save their horses, and he had time to study the land. Ahead, a little to the right, there was a low hill with small cairns on its summit which Baldwin recognised as White Hill. Just left was Doe Tor, with the great mound of Great Links Tor rising behind. The posse was chasing along a narrow valley with a stream trickling quietly at its base, with Sharp Tor rising before them. Even as he looked, he saw the faint smoke of hoofbeats in the dry dust ahead of them.

There were tiny figures on the beasts. It was hard to see while pounding along so steadily, but he was sure that there were three mounts – so Avice *was* with them, he noted. The sight gave him added enthusiasm for the chase. He glanced to left and right, and saw that the others too had seen their prey.

'Once they're in among the rocks it'll take ages to fetch them out,' Simon called, and Baldwin nodded grimly. If Antonio and his son were of a mood to fight, it would be the devil's own job to dislodge them. Their only hope was that the three riders were more tired than the posse. But although the horses they pursued showed signs of exhaustion, it was clear that the Venetians would gain the security of the rocks before they could be headed off, and Baldwin swore under his breath.

But he had reckoned without the Abbot's harriers. The berner called to them, whistling and singing to them in a curious, high-pitched voice, and the pack suddenly streaked away. The men had to whip their horses to try to keep up, but it was in vain. There was no way to catch the racing hounds. Baldwin saw the Venetians glaring over their shoulders, their faces showing both rage and fear as they assessed the distance between them and their pursuers, while beside them the girl lurched along on a mare. 'No,' Baldwin said between gritted teeth, 'it's not like Bayonne, where you escaped because you had gone with time to rest your mounts before your pursuit could catch up with you. This time your horses are as tired as our own, and ours are the better bred. This time you won't get away.'

They did have one last, desperate throw to make. Just as in Bayonne they had distracted the posse by releasing a packhorse, now, as Baldwin watched, he saw the girl's horse sheer away and turn off to the north. The knight refused to be tempted to hare off after her, and bellowed over his shoulder to the two nearest men to follow her and bring her back. The others carried on.

The Venetians reached the rocks, and now found another obstacle to their escape. All around the tor was a clitter of small stones, on any one of which their horses might break a leg and fall. They could not keep up their mad, break-neck pace.

But the harriers could. With thickly padded paws they feared no stones or rocks, and they scrambled up and over the boulders with the eager enthusiasm of hounds who see their prey at last.

'Come on!' Simon roared, and the posse set itself at the hill.

Baldwin heard the tone of the baying change. While running with their quarry in sight, each dog had given urgent yelps calling the attention of the humans to the scent. Now they gave loud voice continually, and Baldwin, as a hunter, knew what that meant: the quarry was held at bay. He slowed his speed and gave his Arab time to pick her way. If the harriers had the men, there was no point in risking her life.

The bank of the hill was quite steep, and all the horses were forced to tread carefully. Still in front, the berner egged his mount on, his face filled with anxiety for his hounds, and Baldwin knew what his thoughts would be. Would the men, now they were held by the pack, try to kill his hounds? It had happened before while trying to capture felons, when they had access to pikes or lances. It was easy enough to goad dogs into attacking, and spit them on a sword or long dagger like meat to be cooked over a fire. Like any good berner and master of harriers, the Abbot's man was fearful only for his precious hounds. They were more to him than his own life, and Baldwin thought, Woe betide you if you have hurt this berner's creatures!

At the top of the hill was a kind of rounded plain, and it was here they found the men in a small dead-end of rock. With high walls at each side and in front of them, the two had dismounted, and stood before their horses while the hounds circled, panting, eyeing the men with cautious expectancy.

Simon paused, resting his elbow on his mount's withers,

panting as if he had run the whole way himself. He cocked an eyebrow at Baldwin. 'Looks like they'll come along easy enough, doesn't it?'

'Oh, I think so,' Baldwin agreed as the other members of the posse joined them.

The knight wasn't sure the two Venetians had noticed they had company. Their eyes were firmly fixed on the hounds which barked and growled and howled all round. Antonio's horse was bucking while he cursed angrily, gripping its reins and flailing about him with his whip. Pietro's looked close to death with its head hanging almost to the ground. As Baldwin watched, he patted its head. That simple act of solace made the knight feel some compassion. Any man who could honour his horse, even when it had failed in its race, must have some principles, although he had to admit that any thief or outlaw was likely to regard his mount as more important to him than a wife, companion, or man-at-arms – the horse would always be the method of escape and safety, and deserved the best food and water even when that meant the rider going thirsty or hungry.

The berner dropped from his horse, calling to his hounds and throwing them scraps from his satchel. Gradually the milling beasts withdrew, and Simon could study the two Venetians.

Antonio stood, panting with exertion, his whip still in his hand as he glowered at the men. Recognising Baldwin and Simon, his features displayed shock. 'Sir Baldwin, you as well?'

His son let himself fall to sit at his horse's head. He patted its neck and refused to meet Simon's eye.

The bailiff sprang down from his horse and motioned to the men to rest. 'Who did you expect? The Abbot himself?'

'I won't surrender!' Antonio declared, and drew his sword.

'Antonio,' Baldwin said resignedly, 'what good will that do? It won't help your son's case.'

'What case?' Antonio asked reservedly, eyes narrowed.

'He's under arrest. He's been accused of murdering Torre and the monk Peter.'

'What? I thought you were with the rabble roused by that damned friar!'

'*Me*? Who accuses me of this!' Pietro demanded.

Baldwin and Simon exchanged a glance. His surprise seemed unfeigned. The bailiff said, 'You accused yourself when you decided to depart from the town in such haste.'

Antonio shook his head. 'That was because of the mob. Didn't you hear? They were incited to attack me by the friar. We didn't want to remain where our lives might be in danger.'

'It had nothing to do with fear of being discovered to be the murderer?' Simon asked sarcastically.

'I know nothing of any murder,' Pietro stated. 'I wanted to get away so that I could be with Avice, that's all.'

'And I joined him willingly!'

Baldwin turned to see the girl being led on her mare by a sweating, grumbling watchman muttering, 'She took us halfway to bloody Oakhampton.'

Kicking her feet free of the stirrups, Avice sprang down and ran to Pietro. 'I love him, and I won't marry the man my father has chosen. This is the man I will wed.'

Baldwin scratched his cheek and threw a glance at his friend. Simon was watching the couple doubtfully.

There was no denying the fact that the lad didn't look like a crazed murderer, the sort to kill a monk because he thought him a rival. And then another thought struck the knight. 'Avice, when did you agree to elope with this lad?'

And he knew her answer before she spoke.

Jordan and Elias Lybbe sat for the most part silently. The sun was creeping towards the horizon, and the stifling heat of midday in the cell was giving way to a damp chill. During the day the temperature had built steadily. The stone walls should have kept the little gaol cool, but the wide, barred window allowed the hot air to smother the interior, and in the absence of any wind the two men sweltered, sweating profusely. The little water they had been given when they entered was long since finished, and both felt its lack.

'You should never have come back.'

Jordan's tongue felt as if it was covered in rabbit fur, and swallowing was difficult. 'It seemed right to come back and see you. I'd been away for so long, I just wanted to see the town where I was born one more time.' He knew his brother couldn't understand the homesick aching in his bones. It had been unwise to return, as Elias said, but it was an urge which couldn't be refused.

'There was no point,' Elias persisted miserably.

'It seems not.'

'I wonder what will happen to me?'

'You should be all right. They'll soon catch the Venetians, and then you'll be safe enough. Not like me: I'll go to the gibbet.'

Elias brought his legs up and rested his head on his knees. He knew his brother was right. There could be no defence for a man once he was declared outlaw. 'You shouldn't have come back,' he repeated dully.

'At least I've seen my town again,' Jordan said softly. 'I've lived too long abroad. The land is good, rich and fertile, and the people live well, but it's not my home. I couldn't die happy there. Here I can die content.'

'Did you never marry?'

'Yes. She caught a fever and died. We had no children.'

'That boy – he's not your own?'

'No.' Jordan chewed his lip. He hoped Hankin was unharmed. 'I took him on when he was newly orphaned. He was a comfort to me, and I was able to keep him alive, so we were well suited.'

Elias grew too hot, huddled as he was, and stretched his legs out before him, groaning with the aching in his joints.

He needed water, but it wasn't that which gave his voice its sharpness. 'Was that to atone for what you did?'

'I've done nothing to be ashamed of, Elias, believe me,' Jordan said tiredly. It was hard to talk about the matter, it was so long ago. The bloody axe sprang once more to his mind, the woman's mouth wide as if screaming as she lay by the side of her husband's body, the girl sheltered behind her skirts. The memory made him close his eyes with a shudder. Although he hadn't known it at the time, that event marked the end of his old life. And now it had returned to haunt him and end his whole existence.

'The gang killed them all, didn't they?' Elias asked remorselessly.

'What could I have done against so many?' Jordan rested his head against the wall. He had always known his brother didn't believe his protestations of innocence.

Elias looked away. A member of the gang had approved, confessed in exchange for his life, swearing he told the truth. There was no reason for him to accuse Jordan if he had nothing to do with it. 'The bastards left an orphan, though, just like the one you picked up.'

'I remember.' Jordan gazed at the clear sky through the window. It was not something he could forget. The girl had been struck down, and with all the blood in the room, the men had assumed she was dead. It had been a huge relief to him when later he had seen her breast move, and he had taken her up and carried her away from that charnelhouse. It never occurred to him that he might be accused after saving her, but he had been, and he had to run for his life before he could be arrested. 'I'm only glad that I was able to make sure she lived.'

Elias sighed and shifted. Stones on the ground dug into his thin buttocks. 'Yes, but what about the lad?'

'Which lad?'

'The one you rescued – the one at your stall.'

'Hankin? He'll have to make his own way, I suppose.'

Jordan stared up at the sky once more, and had to blink away the tears, not only of self-pity but also futility. There was nothing more he could do to help the lad, he told himself. Hankin might be able to fend for himself . . . if the Abbot didn't take everything that Jordan owned as an amercement, he could give it to the boy.

'With nothing, there's not much chance of him surviving.'

Jordan faced his brother. 'If you do get out of this, Elias, promise me you'll look after him.'

'Me!'

'Someone has to, and the poor lad has no one. He hardly even speaks English now, he's been away so long. Swear to me, Elias – it's the last thing I'll ever ask you to do for me.'

'And it's no small thing you want me to do – only to spend the rest of my life protecting a beardless boy!' Elias grumbled, but before long Jordan had the promise he needed, and he could relax and slump back against the wall once more.

It was little enough for him to leave behind, but at least he had the satisfaction that Hankin would be provided for. Elias was scruffy and lazy, and he had a capacity for whining which disgusted his older brother, but he was sound enough, and Jordan was sure he would be secretly delighted to have the company of the boy. Hankin had been a good friend. It would have been an intolerable weight on Jordan's mind, going to the gallows knowing Hankin was deserted.

He looked out at the fresh, free world again, wondering what had happened to that other orphan, the little girl – whether she had survived the pain and terror of losing her parents so needlessly. It would ease his death if she had not suffered too much torment.

At the sound of harnesses and shouting, the Abbot left the refectory and hurried down to the Great Court. The men were all climbing from their horses with the steady and deliberate movements of the enormously tired.

'Sir Baldwin, you are all well? No one was hurt?'

'No, no one was harmed. And you need not fear for your harriers or berner. They are fine.'

'Sir Baldwin, they were far from my mind,' the Abbot chided him, but the knight saw his gaze moving past him to the wagging tails of the pack. 'The girl?'

'She is well, tired but fine – and her father will be delighted to know that she is not harmed in any way at all.'

'That will be a relief to him,' the Abbot agreed. 'Now, do you want to question the men immediately?'

Baldwin eyed the bedraggled figures on their horses. The shadows were lengthening, and dark was not far off. 'No, my lord Abbot. I am exhausted, and so are they – we have ridden almost to Lydford and back. It would be better to wait until the morning. Let my bones rest a little before I confront them, so I can think more clearly about what I am saying.'

'I will have them chained up in the cellar.'

'I wouldn't bother. And I am not so sure you need fear their escaping. Just leave a man at their door.' He nodded to the girl. 'Avice should be escorted back to her father's house.'

'I don't want to go! Let me stay here with Pietro!'

'You are your father's responsibility, not the Abbot's,' Baldwin said exasperatedly. 'And it would hardly be fitting that you should be kept in a room with two men – especially a dungeon. Come – let us take you home; I shall accompany you.'

'I'll join you,' Simon volunteered. His legs were stiff after their long ride, and he was keen to stretch them. Baldwin, he saw, seemed preoccupied, and while they proceeded up the road, the knight kept silent, his brow furrowed.

It took little time to get to the merchant's house. Arthur was waiting, and Simon explained for Avice how she had been brought back to the Abbey. 'She is perfectly well, sir. Have no fears for her, er . . .' He trailed off, with no idea how to finish the sentence. He wanted to say, 'She hasn't been touched, there wasn't time for them to spoil her,' but somehow the words were trite and irrelevant.

Avice stood beside him, her eyes downcast, and Arthur was caught between anger and sheer delight: anger that she had run away with the boy and not considered her parents; and fierce joy that she was back. As Simon watched, his expression softened, and he put his arms out. Avice seemed to be pulled forward as if by an invisible magnet until she was within the circle of his arms. There was a cry from within, and Simon recognised the strident voice of Avice's mother; the man and his daughter didn't appear to notice, but simply stood quietly in their firm embrace. After a moment, Arthur caught Simon's eye, and there was suddenly a tear falling down the merchant's cheek.

The bailiff nodded, smiling, and turned to go, but before he could leave, Arthur grasped his arm. 'Thank you,' he said hoarsely.

Then he had gone, and the door closed quietly behind father and daughter.

Simon gave a long, slow sigh. It was hard to imagine how he would have reacted had it been his daughter who had disappeared and then been recovered. It was nothing to do with Pietro: Simon was sure that whoever the boy might be, the fears and anxiety would be the same. Their potency could not be diminished by legal status or class. If his daughter was to go away, leaving her parents without a word, Simon knew he would be distraught. Arthur's gentle acceptance of her return made the bailiff hope he would continue to be as calm and understanding, swallowing his anger with his gratitude at seeing her safe home once more.

The memory of that silent grip at his arm made him fully aware of the merchant's pleasure. He had not been able to express his feelings in words, but that solid grasp had said as much as any sermon, and the bailiff joined his friend to walk back to the Abbey with a sense of pride at a job well-performed.

Baldwin had other thoughts on his mind. He had hardly noticed that they had given the girl back to her family. His attention was focused firmly on the murders, and he had no interest in Avice any more: she was an irrelevance now that she was found and her attempted ravisher – whether she might have been a willing or unwilling victim – was under lock and key.

The murders of Peter and of Torre remained unsolved. Baldwin did not like loose ends, yet there appeared to be many. 'Simon, do you think we are any nearer an answer to these killings?'

Simon shook his head. 'The more I think about it, the more confusing I find it. Elias had all the evidence pointing to him, but when we found his brother, everything which had indicated Elias pointed to him instead – especially since he admitted taking Torre's head. And his background as an outlaw shows he's capable of murder. But the Venetians are themselves felons – they were prepared to steal from an Abbot, for Christ's sake! If they could steal from a man of God, they must be capable of anything. And Pietro was seen in a monk's habit, which could mean he was the thief as well.'

'Jordan Lybbe is most likely – as you say, he was an outlaw.'

'Yes. But why should he kill Torre?'

'Similarly, what was Pietro's or Antonio's motive?'

'You don't like Lybbe's explanation: whichever of them killed Torre thought he was preventing his own discovery?'

'Oh, I don't know. Something is wrong about all this, Simon. My whole soul is shouting to me that I have missed something. There is only one thing I am sure of, and that is that Pietro didn't kill Peter.'

'Why?'

'Because Peter was killed *after* Pietro saw Avice. Avice

had promised herself to him when they met last night, so his motive disappears. There was no point in his killing the monk.'

'I see no reason for Antonio to have killed the monk.'

'Neither do I.'

'So we are back to Lybbe.'

'Yes,' said Baldwin, but when Simon glanced at him, his friend looked no better pleased than before.

Chapter Twenty-Three

The next morning Baldwin rose from his bed feeling unrefreshed after a sleepless night. He had hoped that some inspiration might strike him while he slept, but as he stared out over the court he felt no nearer a solution.

Seeing a figure hurrying across the court his mood lightened as he recognised Jeanne. She at least was fresh and wholesome. Her face would be a welcome sight after his dislocated sleep. Even as he was aware of the thought, she made her way across the court and through the door that led towards the Abbot's lodging.

Baldwin dressed and walked down to the court, sitting at a bench, Edgar at his side.

His servant had seen him in similar moods before. The knight sat with his chin resting in the palm of his hand, elbow on his knee, in an attitude of absolute concentration. His glowering eye was fixed on a monk sweeping the court, and he didn't glance at the servant by his shoulder. This was Edgar's accustomed place, a point from which he could protect his master. It was the station he had accepted when Baldwin had saved his life in the hell-hole of Acre, when they were both much younger and before they had joined the Knights Templar together. Edgar and he had been among the last to leave the city as the Saracens took the place, and it was due to the heroic bravery of the Templars that the two of them had managed to escape, so when they had recovered, both felt the same urge to join the Order which had saved their lives.

Later, when the Order they both revered had been destroyed to fuel the greed of a King and a Pope, Baldwin had been prone to darkly introspective moods, and today Edgar was at first anxious that his master had succumbed again. But then he caught sight of the knight's eye and saw the gleam. This was no black despair. Baldwin was simply focusing his entire being on the problem of the murders.

'Master?' he enquired quietly.

'What is it?' Baldwin snapped.

'Do you want breakfast?'

'I cannot be troubled with food now!'

'Master, you should eat something.'

'There's some detail we've missed, something crucial. But *what*?'

Edgar shrugged. 'Those who are innocent will surely be able to prove it.'

His master grunted dismissively. 'Like our Order did, you mean? Since when has innocence been a matter of justice? If you look right for the part a jury will assume you were responsible – you know that as well as I do.'

'You mean Pietro?' asked his servant with a frown.

'I don't know who I mean – I haven't seen proof of anybody's guilt,' Baldwin muttered irascibly. He was about to continue when the bell sounded for Mass. 'How can they think clearly here when the damn bells toll every few minutes?'

Edgar smiled to himself, and was about to speak when he caught sight of the startled expression passing over his master's face. 'Sir, what is it?'

'Gracious God, I thank You!' Baldwin cried, and rising quickly, he turned to Edgar. 'Find Simon and bring him here immediately. Go!'

Edgar set off at a smart pace to the Abbot's lodging where Simon and his wife had their chamber. Before long he was back. 'He's just dressing.'

To his surprise, Baldwin chuckled to himself and rubbed

his hands together. 'Excellent! And soon this whole matter will be behind us.'

True to his word, Simon appeared within a few minutes, his hair tousled, and his expression one of comical annoyance at the early summons. Simon liked to stay in his bed later than Baldwin. 'What's the matter?' he yawned.

'I have a clue, no more than that, but from that clue I think I can form a new solution to our problem.'

'And what exactly is that clue?' Simon demanded eagerly as they toiled up the hill towards the gaol.

'It will wait, my friend. For now we must get to the truth of another matter.'

They had arrived at the Abbot's clink, and Baldwin spoke quickly to the watchman at the door. The man glanced behind him. 'He's with the friar right now, Sir Baldwin – do you want me to interrupt them?'

Baldwin considered, and shook his head. 'No. It would be offensive if he is making his confession. We shall wait.'

It was not long before the friar came out, and Simon was struck by his thoughtful attitude. He scarcely glanced at the two waiting men. The guard leaned through the doorway. 'Lybbe? Come out here, mate – someone wants to talk.'

The merchant appeared in the doorway, blinking and scratching in the cool of the early morning, and gratefully left the gaol to stand in the sun.

Baldwin eyed him with sympathy. 'Jordan, I know you have no desire to assist us in finding the killer, for it can hardly help you, but I would ask for your help to stop someone dying unnecessarily.'

Jordan Lybbe cared not a fig for the fate of anyone else. His own life was soon to end, and that was a hard enough fact to come to terms with. 'Why should I help you?' he asked listlessly.

The knight could see his resentment. It was there in his eyes, glittering with jealous malice as he stared at a man who was not under sentence of instant death as soon as he was denounced. 'Lybbe, I cannot save you, but another man might be wrongly convicted unless I have your help.'

'*Another* man? What about me?'

'Do you deny your crimes with the trail-bastons?' Simon asked, and Lybbe looked at him coldly.

'I was never with that band.'

'Then why did you flee the country?'

'What would you do if you were accused like that? I heard that an approver had accused me – what else could I do but run? Who would take my word when a man had sworn on his oath that I was guilty?'

Baldwin's eyes narrowed. 'Do you swear that you are innocent?'

'Of course I do. Do I look like a murderer?'

The knight eyed him dubiously. Anyone, he knew, was capable of murder, given the motive. If he had to pick a suspicious-looking man, someone like Lybbe, with his strong build, thick beard and intense features, would rate highly.

Lybbe gave a bitter grin. 'So even you doubt me. I have no hope of a fair trial or justice – why should I help you?'

'For information I would gladly perform any service you asked of me.'

'Make sure my brother is freed and that my boy is protected by him, and I'll think about helping you.'

'You have my word on it as a knight. I will speak to the Abbot and demand the freedom of Elias from the gaol today, and I swear that I will personally take Elias to your boy and see the lad is safe.'

Lybbe raised an eyebrow at the conviction in Baldwin's voice. There was a degree of integrity there that surprised the merchant. He considered a moment. 'Very well: ask.'

'You told us when we questioned you that you left the inn after some time. Can you recall anything that would tell us precisely *when*?'

Simon glanced at his friend, and was about to open his

mouth to speak, but he was silenced by the Keeper's raised hand.

'It was a little after the bell for compline was rung.'

'I thought that was what you had said. You also mentioned robberies in Bayonne. Do you remember much about them?'

Lybbe shrugged. 'There were several. Men were knocked out and had their purses stolen. The last man to be robbed died; he was stabbed when he tried to defend himself, or at least, that's what everyone thought.'

'Did you not hear any hints as to who might have been responsible?'

'Well, after the Venetians rode off, it was plain enough.'

'Yes, but do you recall hearing anything before that? Was there no suspicion about who might have been committing these crimes before the Camminos disappeared?'

'There was one man . . . he swore he'd been struck by a monk. But no one believed him. I mean, it was rubbish – and anyway, when the Venetians disappeared, that showed he was wrong.'

Baldwin shot a glance at Simon. 'See?'

'No,' Simon admitted frankly. 'I don't know what you're getting at.'

'Simon, we've already heard that a man was hit on the head and robbed by a monk. The same happened in Bayonne, and the Venetians were there as well.'

'So we're right back where we started, then. It *was* Antonio and his son who robbed, both there and here.'

'A monk,' Lybbe said, staring at Baldwin. 'I saw a monk as we left the tavern, walking down to the Abbey.'

'Away from the alley?' Baldwin pressed urgently.

'Yes. And I saw him again when you had arrested Elias. I saw him pass the gaol, going up towards the fair.'

'Did you see his face?'

'No, he was going away from me both times I saw him.'

'You're sure about that? It was the same man?'

'Yes. It was dark both times, but he was quite distinctive. And he carried a cudgel.'

When Lybbe had been returned to the cell, Baldwin turned to Simon and punched his fist into his palm with a chuckle of glee. 'Oh, Simon, Simon. This is wonderful, really wonderful. We have here a known and convicted outlaw, a killer, and at the Abbey, awaiting their trial, are two more men, both of whom are assumed guilty. And one thing links them all: the fact that they ran away. If it wasn't for that, they might be given a fair trial, and then their innocence might be established, but no! They tried to escape justice as the people know it, so they must be guilty.'

'So who *is* guilty?' Simon asked as they began to walk towards the Abbey. 'Did Lybbe kill Torre, and Pietro by coincidence decide to rob some fair-goers?'

'Simon, I dislike coincidences.'

'What is that supposed to mean?'

'Only that I believe one man was responsible for the robberies and for the murders. Perhaps all these incidents are interconnected.'

'I don't see how they could be. Pietro has been seen in the monk's garb, so he must be the robber, surely. Do you mean he was the murderer as well?'

'Simon, we know nothing of the kind! All we really know is that *a* man dressed as a monk has attacked people, and that Pietro himself at one point used the same disguise to woo his girl.'

'And that someone did the same in Bayonne.'

'Yes, it would point to the Camminos being responsible,' Baldwin said, but there was suppressed excitement in his voice.

'Baldwin, what are you up to?'

'Nothing, but I think you and I will have to make use of a little subterfuge to complete this case.'

'Sir Baldwin. May I speak to you?'

'Of course, friar. How may I serve you?'

Hugo was silent a moment. His doubts had disappeared since talking to Lybbe again. Now he knew only a consuming anger that a man could so blatantly forswear himself. Hugo felt betrayed. He had saved a life, and yet his example had been ignored – worse, his example had been immediately perverted by a lie.

'There is something I must tell you about Jordan Lybbe.'

The Abbot was alone in his study when they arrived. 'Sir Baldwin, Simon, you are welcome. May I offer you a little wine?'

'Thank you, Abbot. Do you mind if we interview the two men now?' Baldwin asked. 'And could we have young Peter's notes with us here as well?' The Abbot nodded and rang a small bell. While they waited, Baldwin murmured something to Edgar. The servant nodded and left the room. In a few minutes Antonio and Pietro were with them. A monk brought Baldwin the novice's file of papers.

Hugh waited by the door with Holcroft to prevent escape. The Camminos stood, their hands manacled, while the Abbot studied them. He had not spoken to them or seen them since their return the day before.

Pietro looked as if he had hardly slept. His pale face contrasted strongly with his black hair to make him appear almost feverish. His father looked thoroughly broken, a dirt-streaked tatterdemalion. The suave merchant had been replaced by a man who might have been a peasant.

The Abbot sat on his great chair, Simon on his left, and Baldwin sat squinting at Peter's notes on his right. Champeaux surveyed the two regretfully. 'So, gentlemen, you have been accused of astonishing crimes while making use of my hospitality. What do you have to say in defence?'

'Trying to help my son marry the woman he chose is hardly an astonishing crime,' Antonio protested.

'Taking a maiden without her parents' consent *is* a serious

crime,' Simon said. 'Trying to make her your son's wife
through deceit hardly improves matters.'

'What deceit, bailiff? This was a matter of love, not—'

'You and your son have tried to make out you are a prosperous merchant. You used that status to gain the Abbot's
trust, and your son to win over the heart of a merchant's
daughter – but where is this fabulous wealth? Where are
your ships? Where is the money and the estates you said
you owned in Venice? It was all a sham.'

'I am from an ancient family in Venice and—'

'And you have nothing to show for it now. You could be
no more than wandering thieves as far as we know – no
better than common outlaws. Your claims to fortune, to
nobility, to power – where is the proof of them?'

Antonio stared. 'Why do you say this? Abbot, I don't know
what you've been told, but I am innocent! Who dares to
suggest I am a liar?'

'We have been told of your escapade in Bayonne,' said
Simon, running a hand through hair still awry and needing
combing. 'How you left so suddenly, how you took to your
heels when the townspeople tried to arrest you. In fact,' he
turned to the Abbot, and he and Baldwin exchanged a
glance, 'could we send Holcroft to go through their
belongings and make sure that there are no stolen goods in
their bags?'

Champeaux nodded. 'Holcroft, go and check.'

'Get their servant to help you, port-reeve,' Baldwin added.
'He will know what should be there, and what shouldn't.'

Simon carried on sternly as the door thumped shut.
'You've been using the Abbot's hospitality to weasel your
way into his trust, and I daresay you've used your position
with him to gain credit with traders in the fair as well.'

'That is a mad suggestion! To think that I and my son
could be so slandered, especially after being hunted with
hounds like a deer for no reason! I am staggered!'

'We accuse your son of nothing – yet,' Baldwin observed.

Antonio seemed to notice him for the first time and now gave him a pleading look. 'What is all this about? What is our crime? Is it wrong to run away from a mob baying for your blood? We have stolen nothing, harmed no one, done . . .'

'Do you deny inventing money and lands in order to con the Abbot out of his fleece?' Simon shot back, and the Venetian blinked.

'Of course I do! It's rubbish!'

Baldwin looked up from the papers, interested by the tone of outrage. 'Then why do you travel on broken-down nags? Where are your palfreys, if you are so rich? No banker or merchant would ride on such demeaning stock.'

'Perhaps not by choice, Sir Baldwin, but we don't always have much choice. When one is waylaid and robbed, one has to buy the best horse-flesh one can. Is it a crime to be a victim?'

'And what of your friendship with Bishop Stapledon of Exeter?' asked Champeaux.

'What of it?'

'I wrote to him, and I have heard that he hardly knows you.'

'The Bishop denies knowing us?'

Antonio's eyes grew round, as if he couldn't believe his ears. The expression was so convincing that the Abbot had to glance at Baldwin to gauge his feelings.

The knight was nodding as if it were no surprise.

'Abbot,' Antonio pleaded. 'Tell me what I am supposed to have done. Of what am I accused? Of trying to arrange a business deal with you? Of running from a mob determined to lynch me? What am I guilty of?'

Simon scratched his cheek. 'There were many robberies while you were in Bayonne. You were in the tavern on the night Torre was murdered. Some have said you saw Lybbe and recognised him from Bayonne. They say you knew that if he spoke of what you had been up to there . . .'

'I wasn't up to anything!'

'. . . you could be uncovered as a fraud and a thief, dressed up in expensive clothes. So you left before he could see you, and waited in an alley until he passed, then stabbed him. Thinking it was a job well done, you hurried back to be with the Abbot.'

'*Me!* I never killed Torre – why should I?'

'He looked the same as Lybbe, didn't he, from behind? Especially in the dark. Their figures were very similar.'

'Why should I kill him? And why cut off his head?' he demanded disbelievingly.

'Oh, we know all about that,' Simon said dismissively. 'Lybbe saw the body and realised you had done it thinking it was him. He took the head. But he only damaged a dead body; it was *you* who actually killed the man.'

'No! I had nothing to do with it – *nothing*! We saw him in the tavern, yes, but that was all. I'm no murderer.'

'And all so that you could rob the Abbey,' Simon continued.

'No, I swear . . .'

Baldwin turned from his ashen face to that of the son. 'What of you, boy? Did you know about all this?'

'Me? All I know is that I wanted to marry Avice. I still do, I love her.'

'You were seen the night before Peter died, wearing a monk's habit.'

The young man took a deep breath. 'It is true, and I apologise, Abbot. I will undertake any penance, but I never . . .'

'What? Carried out robberies as you had done in Bayonne?' Baldwin said sharply.

'No. I have never robbed or stolen.'

'Then why the monkish garb? asked Simon.

'How was I to meet Avice? Her father sent servants with her to prevent me from seeing her. I only used a habit as a disguise so that I could meet her. I returned it when I got back.'

'It was a serious crime, nonetheless,' said the Abbot sternly.

'You have my apology, my lord Abbot, but I did no harm.'

'Have you heard about the robberies?' Baldwin probed.

'What robberies?'

'When you were in Bayonne, there were rumours of a man in monk's habit who was attacking people. His last victim died. We know a man in monk's habit has been knocking men down here as well and stealing their purses.'

'It wasn't me! That evening when I went to see Avice was the first time I ever wore a habit.'

Baldwin saw the door open, and Holcroft's face as he hurried in, Luke behind him. The port-reeve held a bundle in his hands. 'My lord, this was found in Pietro's bags.'

Champeaux stared as he shook out the Benedictine habit. The black cloth rippled as the Abbot met Luke's eyes. 'Where was it?'

'In the boy's saddlebags.'

Pietro's mouth fell open. 'No! It's a lie! It isn't mine!' He moved forward convulsively, the chains of his manacles rattling as he reached towards the Abbot. 'Believe me, I know nothing about this.'

'Silence, Pietro!' Simon said quietly.

Baldwin's gaze was fixed on the servant. Luke was obviously terrified. It must be a novel experience to bear witness against his master, the knight thought. But not as novel as some of his other experiences. 'Edgar?'

Champeaux heard the door to his chapel open, and turned to see Baldwin's servant walk in with Jordan Lybbe. Baldwin glanced at the outlaw. 'Well?'

'It's him,' Lybbe confirmed, and pointed to Luke.

The servant was transfixed. 'What is this? Who is this?'

Baldwin relaxed in his chair. 'Abbot, you told us that on the night Torre was murdered, Antonio and Pietro were here with you as the bell for compline rang.' He passed over the novice's papers. 'Peter's notes confirm Lizzie's words:

she recalled the bell tolling as Torre left her. He was alive at compline, but then Antonio and Pietro were already here.'

'Yes, I remember.'

'But their servant wasn't with you.'

'No, we had our food in my study. The servants were in the hall.'

'This man went out of the Abbey and clothed himself in his habit. No wonder Torre didn't try to protect himself. If he saw his attacker, he would never have associated a monk with danger.'

'No, sir, it was Pietro,' Luke said, his face white. 'Why would I have killed the man? Pietro knew that he and his father were in danger if Lybbe recognised them. You would hear that your business with them was false, that they were trying to steal from you.'

'They were with me when he was killed,' Champeaux said steadily.

'You don't know that! How can you know exactly when he died? And why should I kill the boy, the novice? Pietro killed him because they were rivals for the girl.'

'That was what made me realise he could have had nothing to do with the murders. He knew he had no rival in love,' Baldwin said. 'Pietro *already* knew she had refused the novice. She told him when he saw her up at the fair – when he had borrowed your robe.' That was a guess, but when he shot a look at Pietro, he saw the lad nod with slow, appalled understanding.

'Why should I kill the novice?' Luke cried beseechingly, holding his hands out to the Abbot like a supplicant. 'I had no reason to, lord Abbot.'

Simon clapped a hand to his brow. 'He saw you, didn't he? He saw you in the street.'

'That's it, Simon,' said Baldwin encouragingly.

Champeaux looked from one to the other. 'So what if he did? Surely there were hundreds who would have seen this man if he was impersonating a monk?'

'Hundreds or maybe thousands,' Baldwin agreed. 'But none of them would have seen more than a habit. A portman would look at the cloth and see a monk. Another monk wouldn't. A monk would see a man, and a man he should recognise. You have what – fifty men in the convent who wear the habit? Peter saw a man he assumed must be a friend, but when he saw the face he realised it was an imposter.'

'Abbot, it's untrue!'

'Torre was killed because you thought it was Lybbe, and he could have guessed what you'd been doing, couldn't he?' Baldwin mused. 'And you had to murder poor Peter because he saw you in your robes.'

'No, this is all nonsense,' Luke declared, holding out his hands.

'You thought Lybbe might recognise you,' Simon said dispassionately. 'You weren't with Antonio when he came back here to dine with the Abbot. You saw your chance. Instead of going to eat with the other servants, you hurried to your room, took up your habit, and left the Abbey.'

'It was easy enough, for visitors are not to be kept imprisoned,' said Baldwin to the Abbot. 'He went off to the tavern, found a suitable alley, and lay in wait. When he saw his man, or someone who looked like his man, he struck. In the dark he did not realise it was the wrong man. Later, he was merely surprised when he heard about the mutilation of the corpse. It was a horrible thing to have happened to a corpse, but what would Luke care? As far as he knew, it was still the correct man who had died, so what did someone removing the head matter? The threat to his life was gone, that was all that counted.'

'Abbot, please! This is all rubbish, complete gibberish. I've not harmed anyone; it's a lie to say I killed these men.'

Baldwin ignored his cry. 'But it was truly foolish to try to pull the same method of escape as he had used in Bayonne.'

'What do you mean?' Champeaux asked.

'That little mob at your gate? It was a stunt to scare Antonio into running away from here, so that all guilt could be deflected from Luke again, and he could quietly vanish in a different direction with the money he robbed from your townspeople.'

'It was the friar's fault! He preached against usury!'

'It is easy to stand at the back of a crowd which has been drinking, and by dropping the odd word rouse them to anger – and who easier for a target than a usurer? Usury is a sin, yet usurers are rich. Jealousy as well as righteous indignation will make men want to attack them. You incited the people to anger against the bankers.'

'But why did he think he had to kill Lybbe?' the Abbott persisted. 'So what if Lybbe was in Bayonne? It was unlikely he would recognise Luke again – why should he murder on the off-chance?'

'Because I knew him from before then,' Lybbe interrupted firmly. 'This man was the approver who accused me of being with his gang. It was this man's word that declared me an outlaw.'

'Is this true?' the Abbot asked. He felt as if nothing new could surprise him today.

'No, my lord. He's just—'

'Listen to me, my son. If it is true, I can at least pray and intercede for you, but if you continue to lie there is nothing I can do. You will go to your death in ignominious falsehood. It will not save you in this life, and God Himself, from Whom no secrets are hidden, will judge you in the next. Can you not see that there is no reason, no justification, no security, in lying to me now? Please, *please*, as you love your everlasting soul, confess your guilt to me now if you can, for otherwise you will be damned!'

Simon knew how much the Abbot had liked the novice that this wretch had murdered, and if the bailiff had been in the Abbot's shoes, he would have wanted only to damn the servant. Yet the Abbot spoke with a strained, desperate sincerity. He was begging the man to confess so that he could do all in his power to protect his immortal soul. It was not a task Simon could have undertaken. He realised with a jolt just how awesome were the responsibilities of an Abbot.

Baldwin, he saw, felt a disgust similar to his own for the creature. His demeanour surprised the bailiff, for he knew of Baldwin's past as a Knight Templar, and half-expected his friend to desire the same protection of Luke's soul as the Abbot, yet he could see the knight loathed the sight of the servant, and with a flash of intuition he realised why: the Knights Templar had been destroyed, Baldwin had once told him, by lying spies who dressed as Templars in order to denounce them. In his own small and mean way, Luke had done the same. If his petty thefts had become widely known, he might have ruined the faith of the portmen in their monks, and that was something Baldwin would never be able to forgive.

Simon kept his face blank. He was not prepared to give the man any sympathy. Luke didn't deserve it.

It was then that Luke moved. He must have planned it for some moments, for the action was so smooth and executed so flawlessly that it could only have been considered well in advance.

As Simon and Baldwin watched, and the Abbot leaned forward with sympathy in his eyes, Luke sprang forward, shoving Lybbe from his path. Baldwin and Simon were transfixed in astonishment as Luke spun to a halt beside the Abbot and whipped out a small knife from under his shirt. He held it to the Abbot's neck.

'Keep back!' he snarled as Baldwin made to move forward.

Simon was rooted to the spot. The burst of energy had been so sudden, he had been incapable of action, and now it was over he was too shocked to move. The threat of the small blade was too obvious to risk.

Baldwin was speaking. 'You will never leave this

room alive if you so much as scratch his flesh.'

'I'll kill him if you come closer.'

'You will die first!'

'You think so? Maybe I'm better able to defend myself against you than you against me, knight! If you draw your sword, Abbot Robert will die.'

'I don't need a sword against you. A sword is an honourable weapon. *You* only merit a dagger.'

'You hear that, Abbot? I only merit a mean weapon, not a true and honourable sword,' Luke hissed in the Abbot's ear. 'I feel so sad. Perhaps with my little knife at your neck you feel the same, eh?'

Behind him was the door to the chapel, still open from Edgar and Lybbe's entrance, and while Baldwin sidled forward, Luke made his way towards it, still gripping the Abbot by the neck. He reached the door and entered, his captive glancing down with his eyes three times in rapid succession as he passed through.

Simon was still gazing uncomprehendingly at the closed door when the knight made a stabbing gesture with his finger. 'Edgar, wait here. If he comes out again, don't let him pass.' The Keeper darted from the room as his servant drew his short sword with a slither of steel.

'Oh, God's blood!' Simon realised the Abbot had been signalling with his eyes: there must be another door from the chapel. Beneath was an undercroft, and there must be a stair going down to it. He barged the dumbfounded Holcroft from his path and rushed after his friend.

The tiny, narrow spiralling staircase took them down to the gate beneath the Abbot's private chamber, and Baldwin saw in a flash that the door to the stew-ponds and orchards was firmly closed and bolted. Without looking for Simon he ran out into the prayle. He paused a moment to stare all round. There was no sign of the man. The Abbey church rose solemn and proud on his left, the dorter and reredorter were before him, the infirmary a broad block on the right, beyond which lay the small garden where the infirmarer kept his herbs.

The door to the undercroft was partly open. He made a quick decision and stepped to it, kicking it wide, peering in to pierce the darkness. There was no sign of Luke, but with the barrels and bundles lying all round that was no surprise. He muttered an angry curse. Motioning to Simon to run and check the infirmarer's herbary, he entered the undercroft.

A thin light lanced in through the narrow, high windows, and in it he could see the dust whirling and dancing. It lighted the stores, reflecting dully from the metal hoops and rivets on the barrels, glowing gently as it touched the yellow-grey sacks of meal and grain. He heard a skittering in a corner, and spun towards it, but the small shape that scuttled away so quickly was only a rat.

Breathing noiselessly, his mouth open, ears alert to catch the faintest sound, he cautiously stepped round the wall, keeping the light over his head so that he remained in the gloom beneath. The dust would protect him, shining in the light while he passed behind, but soon he realised that while it protected him, it also helped his prey remain hidden. It was impossible to penetrate the column of sunlight as he walked behind it; it was too bright, the rest of the chamber too sombre.

He heard a cautious footstep crunch on a loose pebble. Holding his breath, his scalp tingling with anticipation, Baldwin drew his dagger and edged silently into the room.

Chapter Twenty-Four

Simon pelted along past the infirmary, glancing at the door. If Luke had dashed in there, the bailiff reasoned, they must have heard the door slam as they came out of the lodging. Ignoring it, he rushed on to the herbary. Here he found an elderly monk raking a patch of neatly tended soil. The old man looked up, startled to see a breathless man rush past, and as Simon skidded to a halt, staring round the dog-leg towards the well, he leaned on his rake and watched silently.

'Has someone passed by here? He might have had your Abbot with him.'

The old monk shook his head, still mute, and Simon paused only to mutter an imprecation against the servant, whirled, and ran back the way he had come. Looking down, the monk sighed, shrugged, and began raking again to cover up the bailiff's footprints.

Baldwin took step after tentative step until he was at the entrance to an aisle between immense vats which stood one on top of the other, rising high over his head. He was aware of a tension, as if he was a machine moving forward, impelled by a great spring that took every ounce of his energy to simply move his legs on. It exhibited itself as a hollowness in his throat, and a certain lightheadedness. He was less aware of his arms, his legs, and how to use them. They were useless appendages now. His every fibre was focused on his eyes and ears. All his faculties were concentrated to ensure that in this infernal darkness he might see and hear the servant.

As he entered among the false pillars of wood, he was tempted to withdraw and seek Simon. It was less a reflection of his fear than of a natural anxiety to prevent the escape of the man he sought. While he bumbled around in the dark, for all he knew Luke might have sidled round to the door-way, and be preparing to escape.

The thought made the knight want to turn and watch the doorway, but he must not, he knew. His only protection from the servant's little knife was to keep his eyes constantly fixed forward. Only that way could he anticipate an attack. If he was to spin round, the man could be on him in an instant if he was nearby, and somehow Baldwin was sure he was close.

Taking another silent step, he thought he heard a noise, and he stopped, one foot half off the ground. It sounded like a quiet hiss, and he reflected that the noise seemed familiar. Then he heard it again, and leaped forward: it was the choking sigh of a man being throttled.

The huge barrels ended in an alley along the wall, and Baldwin ran into the stonework at full tilt. Momentarily winded, he turned this way and that seeking the source, then rushed off to his left. The sound came from there.

He heard it again, and skidded a little on the flags. Ahead, a short way down another narrow pathway he could see the two men. The Abbot appeared to be on his knees, his captor behind him, the two locked together in a hideous embrace. Baldwin shouted, gripped his dagger tighter in his fist, and charged. He saw the servant look up, the Abbot, released, tumbled forward to lie choking on all fours, and the knight felt a sudden loathing for the little man. He drew back his hand threateningly, but as he did so, his boot caught a lifted slab stone, and he lost his balance. With a horrified gasp, he threw himself sideways to avoid the servant's upward-thrusting blade, and struck his shoulder on a barrel. It winded him, and he bounced forwards, landing on his chest and striking his head on the stone of the floor. His dagger caught in a barrel as he dropped, and the blade snapped, leaving only the hilt in his hand.

In an instant Luke was on him, the knife under his ear, and he heard the man whispering viciously, 'Silence, or you'll die.'

Baldwin was still. With the man resting a knee on his back, he had no option but to remain there with Luke's breath rasping in his ear. He heard footsteps, slow, quiet and stealthy pacing, that approached along the next lane among the stores, then silence.

'Baldwin? Are you here?'

The sound of his friend's voice gave a renewed vigour to his strained nerves and muscles, but the knight hoarded his energy, willing his wounded body to remain still. There was no honour in winning a coffin, and he wanted Luke captured. While the servant crouched over him, he lay as one dead.

Hearing the steps retreat, Luke eased his grip on his prisoner's throat and risked a careful glance all round. He could not escape through the windows, they were too high. This man, this strong, self-sufficient knight would make an admirable captive to guarantee his safety. They would surely not threaten Sir Baldwin's life by trying to catch Luke while he could hold his hostage under the threat of instant death.

The feet hurried towards the door, and passed outside. Baldwin was suddenly aware of the weight on his back disappearing, and then he was hauled up by a hand on the neck of his tunic. All the time the point of the blade remained unwavering at his jugular.

'You will not make a sound, or your vein will be opened. You understand me? One move, and you die.'

He felt a fumbling hand tugging at his buckle, and there was a lightening at his waist as his sword fell to the floor with a dull clatter. Outside running feet passing by the door, then Simon's voice came from a distance, calling his name.

Suddenly he felt a kind of appalled despair. The shame of being snared in this way and held hostage by such a mean-spirited man was galling, but as he was pushed along, a hand clutching his tunic, the other at his throat, he knew he could do nothing. He, a strong and honourable knight, was entirely at the mercy of a mere servant. The thought made him give a bitter little smile.

As he came towards the end of the alley, he formed his resolution. He would not step into the daylight as a prisoner. It would be better to fight, even if he was doomed to failure. He would try to strike the knife from his neck at the end of the lane and attempt to turn the tables on Luke.

Even as he formed this resolve, as he squared his shoulders and lifted his chin, he heard a quick gasp. For a moment the knife was less painfully sharp against his skin, and he took his chance. He stopped and thrust back with his shoulder, whirling, and grabbing at the knife-hand. Luke was off-balance, and his hand was knocked away easily as Baldwin tried to grab at a barrel. It moved, and he fell back, and instantly the blade was back at is neck. Luke ducked as a dark shape loomed overhead.

There was a creaking, and a familiar voice called, 'God's teeth!' and then Baldwin saw the whole wall beside him moving. From the corner of his eye he saw the barrels slowly, but with a horrid inevitability, start to topple. Luke recognised the danger, and Baldwin felt the knife at his throat release its pressure a little. The knight grabbed Luke's knife-hand and shoved it away, and as he did so a figure dropped to the ground beside him, catching Luke's arm and hauling him back from Baldwin. The servant gave a short shriek, and even over the rumble of falling barrels Baldwin heard the sharp snap of breaking bone. Then his shoulder was taken in a firm hold and he was pulled to a safe distance from the collapsing wall.

The Abbot was carried gently upstairs to his chamber, and

the infirmarer was called to examine his master. Simon
stood by his side as the monk inspected the man's throat,
and finally declared him to be all right, providing he rested
for a couple of days. The Abbot gave him a look of gratitude.
'I never expected to hear you speak again, brother. Your
words are exceedingly welcome.'

Hugh and Holcroft had bundled Lybbe and the Venetians
back to their cells, and the room seemed oddly quiet after
the sudden violence. When Baldwin entered, Simon led him
to a chair. The knight was pale, but collected, and he cocked
an eyebrow at his friend. 'I'm fine, but no thanks to you!'

His bantering tone took the sting out of his words. Simon
shook his head in mock disgust. 'You think I failed?'

'I heard you shouting and yelling for me in the yard.'

'That,' Edgar said, 'was what we agreed.'

Baldwin looked from him to the bailiff. 'You agreed?'

'I knew you were in there,' said Simon. 'I heard
something falling to the ground.'

'It was my sword – he took it from me.'

'We thought either you had your victim or he had already
captured *you*. You didn't call for help, so I pretended to be
looking for you outside while Edgar slipped in.'

'I thought it would be best to climb higher to see where
Luke was hiding,' Edgar explained. 'When I saw you, you
were in the next alley, so I jumped over. Luke heard me, and
glanced up, just as you turned to free yourself, and that was
why he stopped dead like that. But my weight loosened the
barrels, I could feel them going, so I hopped down and
pulled you away.'

Baldwin nodded, his eyes fixed on his servant. It was all
said in a matter-of-fact voice, but Baldwin knew what risks
Edgar had taken. He gripped Edgar's arm. 'Thank you.'

'You saved my life once. It was nothing.'

The Abbot cleared his throat. 'Where is Luke?'

Simon answered, 'He's having his shoulder bound in the
cellar. Edgar broke his upper arm in several places, and it's

a mess. Right now Luke's learning the meaning of the word pain, though it hardly seems worthwhile taking such care over him and getting his arm set when he's going to end up on your gibbet.'

'I almost regret he didn't get crushed by a falling barrel and die in the storeroom, after all he's done. But perhaps it's best that he should stand trial for his crimes so that the townspeople can all see that Jordan Lybbe is innocent. Otherwise some might look at him askance for the rest of his life. This way Luke's guilt can be demonstrated in my court.' Champeaux closed his eyes, resting his head on the pillow. He desperately wanted a sip of wine, for his throat was on fire, and his skull felt as if a sharp dagger was slowly being inserted into each temple. The infirmarer had said it was the effect of being strangled, but all the Abbot knew was that it hurt. 'I must thank you both. You have saved the reputation of the Abbey and our fair.'

Baldwin reflected that it was typical of the man that he should thank them for saving the Abbey and its income from the fair as if they were more important than his life. But the Abbot knew the Abbey *was* more important, he corrected himself. The Abbey was there to save humanity: the Abbot was only a short-term tenant. For hundreds of years after Abbot Robert's death, his Abbey would stand and flourish.

The Abbot was speaking again, quieter, and with a contemplative sadness in his voice. 'So many deaths, and all because this man Luke was trying to conceal past crimes. Yet even if he had been denounced as the robber and killer of Bayonne, it would hardly have endangered his life here. Gascony and England have their own laws. It was sheer folly to cover up his crimes there by killing a man here.'

Baldwin gave a faint smile as he took a seat near the Abbot. 'Not, perhaps, so foolish.'

'But a crime committed in the King's territories abroad wouldn't be punished here.'

'No, Abbot, but a man's crime committed here would be.'

'Ah, but I meant there was no need for him to try to kill Lybbe here just to hide what he had done in Bayonne,' the Abbot explained.

'I know, but Luke was guilty of crimes here already. Do you feel well enough to listen to what happened? May I bring in witnesses? I would not ask while you are recovering, but a man lies in prison unjustly.'

'If it is a matter of justice, I have a duty to listen to whatever evidence you have.'

Baldwin nodded to his servant and Edgar left the room. A few minutes later he returned with the friar and Lybbe. Hugo walked to stand before the Abbot, but Lybbe stayed near the door, his eyes downcast, hands bound before him. Baldwin spoke to the friar. 'Brother, the Abbot is keen to hear your tale. Could you tell us about the trail-bastons of Tiverton?'

'My lord Abbot, I would have raised this before, had I known how important it was,' Hugo said apologetically. 'I kept silent because I thought the man had already paid for his crimes and to tell the watch or others about offences so many years ago could help no one, and would only result in his death. That seemed too heavy a price for him to pay when he had already suffered so much. I wish I could reverse that decision, for then I might at least have saved Peter's life, if not Torre's as well.'

'I am sure you acted through the best of motives,' the Abbot said soothingly.

'But the result was so devastating. Yet I must tell all I know now to prevent another unnecessary and unjust death.

'My lord Abbot, when I was new to my calling, I lived in the Franciscan house at Bridgewater. From there I used to travel far afield, preaching and hearing the confessions of the poor people. They were good days, when all over the country you could see hamlets being established, the forests being cleared as new assarts were thrust in among the trees, and the roads filled with merchants and travellers. Now, since the famine, many of those same places have been deserted. The survivors fled after burying the last of their kin.

'But twenty years ago the land was fertile, the people prosperous – and the idea of a famine inconceivable. Still, some were unprepared to work and earn their living as a man should, and these became gangs of trail-bastons – outlaws. They were like wolves feeding on helpless lambs; they would ride up to outlying farmsteads and bartons and attack, ravishing the women, murdering the men, stealing what they could from peasants and landowners alike.

'I saw little of the violence myself. Every so often I would come across a farm which had been devastated, or meet people flying from the trail-bastons, but that was all until I was myself taken.'

'You were caught by them?' the Abbot asked with surprise. 'They dared capture a friar?'

'Oh, I don't think all of them were in favour of it. Some wanted to let me go immediately, others wanted to ransom me. There was quite a debate. But after three days they did release me – once I had given them absolution. They refused to let me go until I had done that much.'

'It was meaningless if it was forced,' the Abbot muttered.

'True, my lord, but I hope that some of the men will have performed the little penances I gave them. It would be a terrible thing to see so many souls destroyed,' Hugo said piously. 'I was set free not far from Tiverton, a little to the north of the town, and the trail-bastons continued on their way. It was there I first met Jordan Lybbe.'

'First met him?' the Abbot interrupted. 'He was not with the outlaws?'

'No, my lord. I never saw him with them. When I was left by the men, I was lucky enough to meet a priest, and he took me to stay with him at his house. Lybbe was there. He was apprenticed to a merchant, and was travelling back from a fair, but his horse had become lame, and the priest had agreed to let him stable his animal to rest.

'I will say this. Lybbe was a well-spoken, kindly man. He was not so religious as I would have liked, but he gave me to believe that he understood justice and morality. He was no felon.

'We were both there some days later when we saw smoke from a nearby farm. Lybbe offered to go and see if he could help. He left me alone in the house – the priest had gone to visit the town – and hurried off. When he came back, it was with a young girl in his arms.' The friar stopped and motioned to the bearded merchant. 'Come, you tell your own story.'

Lybbe shrugged. 'There's little enough to tell. As friar Hugo says, I thought there had been an accident, maybe a barn had caught light; I went to help put out the flames. Instead, when I got there I found men capering about with pots of ale and wine. The trail-bastons had attacked the place and fired the stores while they drank themselves stupid. I could do nothing against so many, but gradually the men settled as the drink fuddled their brains. Maybe I should have fetched help to capture them, but I didn't know the area and couldn't tell which direction to go to find enough men, so I waited and watched.

'When the men were well into their cups, I went in. Inside the house there was . . .'

Lybbe's face was suddenly blank, and Baldwin was struck by his demeanour. If Lybbe had broken down and wept, Baldwin would have disbelieved it as an act, for this was a strong-willed man. His quick stillness was infinitely more convincing. That the scene had horrified him was clear from his careful words and unemotional speech.

'There was a family. The man lay on his back. His head had been cloven almost in two. Beside him was his wife. She had not died instantly – the men had put her to their own use before cutting her throat.' Lybbe could see the

scene in his mind's eye as he spoke. The woman with her
face turned to her husband in death, mouth wide in a silent
scream as if pleading with him to end her torment. 'At her
side was a girl, only a youngster, and all over blood. She had
been struck, but when I looked, I thought I saw her breathe.
It seemed impossible that she should have survived, but
when I felt her, she was warm. I picked her up, but not
before I saw Luke. He was there, drinking, a bloody axe in
his hand. He saw me, but I think he was so fuddled with ale
he didn't realise I was not of his band. There were too many
others around for me to risk fighting him, so I walked out
and took the girl back to the friar.

'That is almost all my story. While I treated the child as
best I could, the friar roused the men of the place, and soon
a goodly number was gathered. They chased after, and
captured quite a large number of the trail-bastons. Then,
the next morning, I went to pray in the church, and I found
one of them. It was Luke.'

'I was with him,' Hugo explained. 'I knew Luke from
when the band had caught me, and seeing him there
astonished me. He claimed sanctuary.'

'I wanted to take him outside and give him to the locals,'
Lybbe growled. 'I grabbed him, and hauled him from the
altar, and would have taken Luke outside, but friar Hugo
wouldn't let me. He insisted that the sanctuary must be
honoured. It was all I could do not to kill him there and
then.'

'It would have been an evil act,' the Abbot said. 'Brother
Hugo was quite right.'

'You and brother Hugo didn't see the family butchered
like oxen in their own house.'

Hugo continued, 'Lybbe gave his evidence in front of
witnesses, and soon after we both carried on with our
journeys. There was a guard set on the church to stop Luke
escaping, and the coroner had been called, so there seemed
little for us to do. I heard later that Luke had approved in

exchange for his life, and I must confess I was pleased to think that one man would have an opportunity of saving his soul. I thought he would be able to create a new life for himself abroad.'

'Yes, only he lied,' Lybbe said gruffly. 'He said *I* was one of his band; said I had killed the woman; said only his intervention had saved the girl's life. I stopped in Tiverton for a night, and while I was there I heard that I was being hunted. When I learned what he had said, I realised my danger. The friar knew I had not been with the trail-bastons, but I had no idea where he had gone. I could have gone back and told the truth, but what would have been my chances against a man who swore on his life? I was no local man, I was a foreigner to Tiverton. The priest was no use, he had been away. The only man who could vouch for my innocence was the friar, and he had gone. I thought I must escape home.

'I headed south as quickly as I could, but pursuit was only a few hours behind. I had never hidden the fact that I came from Tavistock. It was lucky that instead of going directly to my own place, I went to my brother's. Elias gave me a meal and went out to fetch ale, and it was while he was out that he was told I was sought. He returned, and we made a plan to escape. My only hope was to abjure the realm, so I went to the coast. I found a ship, and within days I was in Gascony. I've lived there ever since.'

Baldwin glanced at Hugo. 'Friar, was there any chance that Lybbe could have fooled you and been associated with the trail-bastons? Could he not have been sent on ahead to spy out the land before they attacked?'

'No, Sir Baldwin. I was with the band for several days, and met all their men. They were not trained soldiers, they didn't have men to scout ahead, they were just uneducated peasants. Lybbe was not with them. Then again, when I met him at the priest's house, he had opportunities to rob the place when he was there alone, yet he didn't. I have absolutely no doubt he is innocent.'

'Then why do you think Luke accused him?' the Abbot asked.

'Because Lybbe wanted to attack him at the altar; I have no doubt that Luke accused Lybbe in revenge. Perhaps Luke had been planning on escaping from the church and was only forced to remain when Lybbe arrived. That would mean Lybbe was the cause of his having to approve and abjure the realm. Some men would consider that sufficient cause to exact a vicious revenge.'

'And it would explain why Luke would be scared once he recognised Lybbe in the tavern,' Baldwin observed. 'It must have been a terrible shock to him to see Lybbe there after so many years.'

'But I didn't recognise him, sir,' Lybbe asserted.

'No, but you were distracted by seeing the others, weren't you? Tell me, though, did you see Luke while you were in Bayonne?'

'I never noticed him – the Camminos didn't have him with them when they went around the town. Certainly when they were out buying goods he wasn't with them. I would have recognised him for sure.'

'I wonder whether he recognised you there, or whether it was only when he came here, and saw you on your home territory that he realised who you were. Abroad he might hardly have given you a second glance, but here, hearing you speak English, he must have realised that you had escaped his vengeance.'

'It's clear enough what happened, though,' Simon said. 'Luke saw Lybbe in the tavern, recognised him, and immediately persuaded the Camminos to leave.'

'He pointed at me, sir,' said the friar. 'I had preached at them earlier that day, and Antonio had no wish to be accosted for a second time.'

'And then he left the tavern with his master and son. I expect his mind was spinning with the risk he was running, but back at the Abbey he had a thought. He still had his habit from Bayonne. He could throw it on, hurry back to the tavern, and wait for Lybbe. It was pure misfortune that he happened to come across Torre instead.

'He had not meant to kill Peter, but the monk saw him in town. I have no doubt that Peter accosted him, and rather than be exposed as the murderer of Torre and the robber of Ruby and others, he was willing to kill again.'

Baldwin agreed. 'But he had to escape from the town before he could be discovered. That was when he had the idea of duplicating the scene of Bayonne. He came across the friar giving a sermon against usury, and saw his opportunity. He mentioned to some of the men that there was a usurer staying with the Abbot. A few were already drunk, and it only took his subtle murmurings to rouse them. Luke was content that his master would be only too eager to escape from the town once he heard there was another mob baying for his blood.'

'But he didn't go with them,' the Abbot pointed out.

'No,' said Simon, 'and that shows a certain shrewdness on his part. How would it be if we had chased after the Camminos and then discovered a black Benedictine habit in Pietro's bags? We would have brought them all back to Tavistock, and Luke might have been uncovered. But this way, he could try to run off while the two were being interrogated, and then he would have to be unlucky to be caught. That was what he planned: to get away while we were trying to persuade Antonio and Pietro to confess their guilt.'

'Yet Antonio and Pietro were ...' The Abbot paused thoughtfully.

'We don't know they were guilty of anything,' Baldwin said pointedly. 'I think we all accept that the thief in Bayonne was Luke, and if that is so, we also have to assume that Antonio and Pietro only fled from Bayonne because of the mob. Likewise they left Tavistock in such a hurry because of the angry crowd here, in front of the Abbey gates.'

'I shall have to speak to them,' the Abbot said. 'Now we know of Luke, as you say, it all becomes clearer. There is one last thing, though, Lybbe: Torre's head. Why did you cut it off?'

Lybbe met his gaze steadfastly. 'My lord Abbot, I guessed as soon as I saw the body, as soon as Elias said it looked like me, that someone had planned to kill me. In the tavern I had recognised the Camminos, but I couldn't see why they should want to hurt me. Bayonne was a long way away. But the man with them had been familiar, and seeing Torre's body, wondering who could want me dead, I suddenly realised who it was.

'But I couldn't go to the watch. How could I, when I knew I might immediately be arrested for the crimes he had accused me of? I could say nothing. And if it was spread around the town that it was Torre who lay there dead, Luke might try to hunt me again. I thought that cutting his head off might leave Luke surprised, for he would have no idea who could want to do that.'

'*Surprised!* I should think he would be more than merely surprised to hear someone had stolen a corpse's head,' the Abbot said heavily.

'I know, my lord. It was a horrible thing to do, but I had to try to prevent Luke from realising he had got the wrong man. All the time he thought he had killed me, I was safe and had time to plan how to bring him to justice.'

'And there was another aspect which struck you, wasn't there,' Baldwin said quietly. 'I had wondered why the head was buried in Elias' yard. At first I thought you just didn't know where else to conceal it, but that wasn't it, was it? You thought the best way to show Luke was guilty was to somehow plant the head on him, didn't you? That was why you left it where you could get to it easily.'

Lybbe shot him a glance, but his eyes dropped. 'It was bad enough cutting his head off, let alone burying it. I just did it on the spur of the moment, I hardly thought about the consequences. Yes, I had intended to make sure it was left on Luke somehow. I wondered whether I could waylay him, and leave it on him where he and it would be discovered, or maybe plant it among his goods so that it could be found. Anything, so that people would realise he was the killer. But then it was found, before I could do anything at all.'

'It is hard to know whether you behaved well or badly. The intention was to show who was the murderer, which was justifiable, even if the method was deplorable,' Champeaux said. 'I would hesitate to condemn your act, when you had been so intolerably treated, but to desecrate a dead body that way was appalling.'

Simon was interested by another factor. 'Why didn't you simply tell us the truth once you were arrested? I can't see what you had to lose when you were already in gaol.'

'I hadn't any need to at first, because you hadn't discovered I was suspected of being an outlaw, so I held my tongue,' Lybbe said. 'And afterwards, what was the point? Would you have believed a felon?'

'It's true,' the friar said. 'I had first thought Luke was familiar when I saw him in the tavern, but at the time I didn't realise where I knew him from – I have no memory for faces. When Torre was killed, I had no inkling that Luke might be involved. And again, even when I knew who he was, I was disinclined to assume his guilt. Why should I? A man had been killed, but I had no idea the target was Lybbe. Then I saw Lybbe, and he explained about the similarity between him and Torre – that made me wonder – and when Lybbe was arrested, I knew I must tell you all, Sir Baldwin, but you had ridden off to hunt down the Camminos. I told you this morning as soon as I could.'

'I think that explains everything, my lord Abbot,' Baldwin said, and motioned towards Lybbe, who stood watching and listening. 'I think this man should be freed, and so should his brother. Do you want the Camminos to be brought to you?'

'Yes, of course, Sir Baldwin. Holcroft, please go and
release Elias from the gaol and bring the Camminos to me.
I think I owe father and son a sincere apology.'

'With your permission, Abbot,' Baldwin said, rising, 'I will
go with Lybbe here. I swore to him that I would see to Elias'
freedom, and to bringing Lybbe's boy to safety. At the time
I had not anticipated that Jordan would find himself in such
a happy situation, but that is no reason not to carry out my
oath.'

Chapter Twenty-Five

Holcroft soon had the Venetians freed, and arranged for them to be escorted to their old room to clean themselves before being taken before the Abbot. When he rejoined Baldwin and Simon, they left with the fretting Lybbe to fetch his brother; Edgar walked at Baldwin's shoulder as always.

'Your boy, Lybbe – will he be with your stall?'

'I hope so, Sir Baldwin.'

The knight eyed the merchant sympathetically. Lybbe was eager to see his brother released, and as keen to make sure Hankin was all right. Only a short time ago he had thought he would never be freed, and that after a brief trial he would be taken out to the Abbot's gibbet. Yet now he was safe; his life could begin again.

'Will you stay here, or go back to Bayonne?'

Lybbe didn't meet the knight's glance. 'I don't know, sir. After twenty years, it'd be hard to come back for good. Especially knowing what people wanted to do to me. All the folk here wanted to see me swing, and none of them would believe I might be innocent. I don't know if I could ever be happy here again.'

Baldwin nodded understandingly. 'It would be difficult to look someone in the face when you know he had expected to watch your final moment on the end of a rope. All I would suggest is that you don't make a quick decision. Wait awhile, and rest here. You may be surprised by how understanding people are, and I know the Abbot will want to help you to try to compensate you for the loss of everything you had.'

Lybbe said nothing, and Baldwin let him be. It would indeed be hard for a man to accept the justice and kindness of another who had once already condemned him wrongly.

Simon, seeing Lybbe's mood, was about to ask the portreeve to confirm the good will of the Abbot, when he noticed how cheerful the official was. While the watchman at the door went inside to fetch out Elias, Simon nudged him. 'Holcroft? I know it's good that we've solved the murders as well as the robberies, but you look as if you've lost a penny and found a bar of gold.'

Holcroft nodded. 'Soon I will be able to retire as portreeve, and some other poor bugger can do it. It'll be such a relief to be plain "Master" Holcroft again, burgess of Tavistock, without all the aggravation of the port's business.'

'My congratulations,' Simon said, but as he spoke, Elias walked, blinking, into the sunlight. 'Welcome, Elias.'

Jordan stood by his brother, who stared from one to the other. It was as if the cook couldn't come to terms with his sudden change in fortune. He was nervous before the portreeve, knight and bailiff, as though fearful that a wrong word could lead to him being incarcerated once more.

'Come on, Elias, It's all sorted out now,' his brother said gruffly.

'You have my apology, and the Abbot's, for being arrested,' Baldwin said encouragingly. 'It was largely for your own protection, in case your neighbours thought you might be the killer, but I know it must have been hard.'

Elias nodded dumbly, but when he spoke his voice was petulant. 'So you had me stuck in there even though you knew I was innocent? I reckon I ought to be given money to pay me back for the damage done to my business, let alone to my good name.'

'That's fine,' Holcroft said. 'But while we're looking at that, we need to see to the garbage outside your shop. Oh, and there's the matter of knowingly talking to an outlaw, your brother here, without telling the watch or the port-reeve.'

'But he was innocent! The Abbot's said so!'

'Yes, but you didn't know that, did you? As far as you were aware, he was still guilty. I think that lot should add up to more than twenty shillings' worth of amercements.'

'You can't do that!'

'Oh, I could. But maybe if you were to forget about trying to fleece the Abbot, he'd be prepared to forget your offences,' Holcroft grinned, and the cook subsided, grumbling to himself.

As they entered the fairground, Elias left them, hurrying off to his stall. Holcroft went off to check on the larger transactions. It was down to Baldwin and Simon to accompany the older Lybbe to find his lad.

Their path took them past the glovers' stalls, and the spicers', and they were soon taking a shortcut through the butchers'. It was here that suddenly a small figure burst from between two stalls and cannoned into Lybbe. 'Hankin? What are you doing here?'

Will Ruby leaned against his awning pole, arms crossed over his chest. 'Looks like you're his master, right enough.'

'Aye, and he should have been looking after my stall,' Lybbe said gruffly, but without real rancour, his relief was so great to see his lad again.

'Your goods are all right. I sent my own apprentice to look after it all. He's there now, and if he's lost anything, tell me and I'll see he pays for it.'

'I'm grateful to you.'

'It's nothing. If a man comes to a fair to trade, his goods must be protected. And his boy too,' Ruby added, explaining how he had found Hankin. 'After the thrashing they got, the watchmen won't have touched anything near your stall. They wouldn't dare return.'

The butcher was right. When they checked on Jordan Lybbe's goods, all were there, bar some items the boy had sold, the money for which he had wrapped up in a square of cloth in his purse.

'It would seem that everyone is happy with the result, then,' Simon said as they left Jordan and Hankin and began to make their way back to the Abbey.

'So far,' Baldwin said. 'I will be interested to see what happens to Pietro and young Avice.'

His wish was to be granted sooner than he realised. At the Abbey, they went straight to the Abbot's room, where they found the Camminos, freshly scrubbed and clothed in clean tunics and hose, sitting with Arthur.

'Sir Baldwin, Antonio has been explaining about his problems. It seems that it was not only the Lybbe brothers who deserve my apologies,' Champeaux said.

'With the murders, and especially with Luke changing into a monk's habit, I suppose I shouldn't blame you for suspecting us,' Antonio said. 'But we were completely innocent.'

'Why the poor horses, then? And the warning from Bishop Stapledon?'

'It is as we said: we were robbed on our way from London some days ago. The thieves broke into the inn where we were staying and stole our horses, but they didn't try to steal from the people sleeping there, and our money and valuables were safe – even the horses' tack, which was kept separate.'

The Abbot broke in, seeing Simon's dubious expression. 'Bailiff, there is another thing. My letter to Walter Stapledon was replied to by his steward, but fortunately he sent it on to the good Bishop. Today I have received a message from the Bishop himself, and in it he says that although he does not know the Camminos well, his good friend John Sandale, Bishop of Winchester, recommended Antonio to him. Sandale has used Antonio before to assist the Exchequer.'

Walter Sandale was the King's Treasurer, and Simon

knew as well as all in the room that if Sandale himself vouched for Antonio, there could be no doubt of his honour. Not where money was concerned, anyway, the bailiff amended. He nodded.

Baldwin was gazing at the Venetian with candid interest. 'You must be rich, Antonio, and you are known to the most important people in the country, yet you travelled to Bayonne for the fair, and then came here to Tavistock.'

Antonio smiled at the note of enquiry. 'Sir Baldwin, every now and again a merchant finds himself in an embarrassing position. It is easy to make great profits from importing spices – for one shipload can be enough to guarantee a man's prosperity for life, but the risks are huge. Pirates, other cities which are no friends to Venice, or even a crew which decides to steal the whole cargo and disappear, can all ruin a man. I have been unlucky. The French King has defaulted on a loan I made him, a ship of mine foundered off Crete, and to cap it all, a second was stolen by the mercenaries who have taken over Athens when it put into harbour for water. They demanded a massive toll, and when my captain refused, his ship was wrested from him. My son and I have travelled to many fairs to try to recover a little of our fortune so that we can furnish a new vessel to trade with the Byzantines, and that was why we went to Bayonne, but you know the ill turn our servant served us there.

'We had no idea what Luke had been up to. Our decision to leave was forced on us because of the violence of the mob that demanded our heads. It is always easy to stir a crowd against bankers, for no one understands the risks we run, but I think a part of it might have been Luke stirring people against us even then, so that he could make off with his thefts. When the posse set off after us, I and my son thought it was a section of the populace trying to attack us. It never occurred to us that Luke might have stolen from the Abbot, and when he let the packhorse go, we never had a chance of discovering what was on it.'

'So then you made your way here,' Baldwin said.

'Yes. We have gone all over the realm, to Westminster and Winchester, up to Northampton and Bury, let alone the Gascon possessions. And we have mostly been successful. The good Abbot's fleece would have been enough to make the whole venture a success. That was why I was unwilling to go, even though my son and servant seemed in such a hurry to depart. I only agreed when the Abbot rejected my offer – and then, of course, I was made aware of Avice Pole's elopement with us!'

Arthur rumbled, 'But you didn't stop to bring her back, did you?'

'Sir, put yourself in my position. I had just been told that all my plans had collapsed because the Abbot had rejected my offer for his fleece, I had been warned that there was a mob baying for my blood outside the Abbey, just as they had in Bayonne, and now I was presented with a *fait accompli* in the person of your daughter. My son and servant went to fetch her while I was waiting at the Abbey. Would you have tarried while you thought the mob might appear at any moment? I remonstrated with my son, I threatened Luke, which was why he refused to leave town with us, I told your daughter that she should immediately go home, for what would running away with us do to her honour? But when they all refused to listen, was I supposed to call attention to myself in a town where I believed my life was in danger?'

Arthur appeared to muse a moment. When he spoke again, his manner was off-hand, as if uninterested. 'So what additional investment do you need to make the venture to trade for spices a success?'

Simon left to find his wife, and shortly after Baldwin made his own excuses. The two merchants looked happier to discuss their business without others standing by and listening, and Baldwin was sure that they would appreciate the freedom to negotiate in peace. To his surprise, the Abbot motioned to him, and the knight followed him into his private rooms.

'Sir Baldwin, I hope you can spare me a few minutes?'

'But of course, my lord Abbot. How can I help you?'

Champeaux stood irresolutely for a minute or two, fiddling with the loose thread of a tapestry. When Baldwin looked about him, he was impressed to see how well-appointed the chamber was, with a pair of comfortable chairs, a table, and a fire burning in the grate. Tapestries of hunting scenes hung on all the walls. The Abbot made no move towards a seat, and Baldwin stood surveying him doubtfully, wondering what the cause of the meeting might be.

'Sir Baldwin, I will not ask you what your intention is towards the Lady Jeanne, for I am sure you are honourable. I probably have little right to ask, in any case, yet I feel I have a duty to take an interest in her since her husband was one of my knights, and a baron should protect the widows of his servants.

'But there is more to my concern than you may be aware of. With all this discussion of the trail-bastons, and how Jordan was so badly betrayed and dishonoured by Luke, one should not forget the little girl he saved.'

Baldwin felt his eyebrows rise. 'What of her?'

'Sir Baldwin, that little girl was the daughter of one of my tenants. I own land up beyond Tiverton, and in other parts of the country. I have a duty to the girl, do I not?'

'Are you saying that the girl was Jeanne?'

'Yes. When I heard of her parents' murder, I went immediately to her. When Jordan said that the hue was right behind him, I wonder whether it was in truth his pursuit or just the messengers sent to tell me of the killings. Either way, it doesn't signify, for the result would have been the same, because the men told me that Jordan Lybbe was responsible for the murders, and when I sent to have him taken, he had already flown, which was enough at the time to convince many of his guilt.'

'Was it you who arranged for her to be sent to Gascony?'

The Abbot looked up. 'What else could be done? There was nowhere in the Abbey here for a girl. Though I daresay I might have found a place for her in the town, it seemed better to me that she should be among her own family. Her uncle had bought his freedom some time before, and I knew where he lived, so I sent a message to him. He had become quite a wealthy man, and agreed to look after and raise her. She was only a youngster. When a few years ago I heard that Ralph de Liddinstone was to wed her, I was pleased to hear that she would return to Devon, but I must confess to a qualm that she should marry him. Sir Baldwin, Sir Ralph was no gentle husband.'

Baldwin wondered what was the point of this discourse. The Abbot stood meditatively staring out of the window as he continued: 'I am sure that he beat his wife regularly, and without good reason. When he drank, he could be abusive even to me, and if he felt his wife had slighted him, I am sure he would be quite brutal to her. It was no happy thought that she had bound herself to him.'

'I am grateful that you feel you can confide this in me, my lord Abbot, but what has it to do with me?' Baldwin asked gently.

'Sir Baldwin, if you have any hopes of wooing Lady Jeanne, I would want you to know that she has not enjoyed an easy life. Her childhood was ruined by Luke and his men, her youth was spent in a strange land, and her marriage was not successful.' His eyes met Baldwin's as he continued quietly, 'She deserves better, Sir Baldwin. You are a kindly, gentle knight, a man of integrity. If you could win her, I would thank God for at last giving her someone who would love her and treat her as she truly deserves.'

'I would be honoured to win her affection,' Baldwin said hesitantly. 'But I hardly know what her feelings might be.'

The Abbot peered through his window. 'Perhaps you should try to find out, then. The orchard looks a pleasant place to walk in peace, does it not?'

Following the direction of the Abbot's glance, Baldwin saw Jeanne's figure. 'I think it looks a splendid place, my lord Abbot.'

In the bright sunlight the orchard seemed to glow with health. Underfoot the grass was thick and springy, there was a constant chuckling from the river to his left, while in the trees doves from the Abbey's cote murmured and cooed. The apple trees themselves appeared so laden with fruit that Baldwin was vaguely surprised the thinner branches could support the weight.

Ahead he saw her, and he stopped and watched her for a while.

Surely, he thought, she deserved a more gentle life now? He was not rich, but he was comfortable, and he could give her a degree of security while he lived. And she had shown him that she was receptive, once they had both overcome their embarrassment at being watched closely by all around. Almost without realising, he found he was walking towards her, and when he was a mere few yards from her, she turned sharply, hearing his steps.

'Lady, my apologies if I alarmed you.'

'No, no, Sir Baldwin. I simply wasn't expecting anyone,' she said.

'May I walk with you?'

'Of course.'

'You were deep in thought.'

She glanced at him. 'Even widows can think, Sir Baldwin.'

'Of course. I didn't mean to infer—'

'I know. I'm sorry, I'm just rather on edge today.'

They were silent a while as they meandered among the trees, but soon their aimless wandering brought them to the great stews where the Abbey's fish were kept. Here they followed its banks.

The sunlight reflected from the water onto her face, and

her features became dappled with the golden light as they walked, always changing as they passed from reeds to places where lilies floated. All had their own effect on her face, and to Baldwin she was almost painfully beautiful.

'My lady, I . . .'

'Sir Baldwin . . .'

Both paused, then their expressions lightened, and after a few moments' polite invitations on either side to continue, Baldwin yielded to Jeanne's repeated pleas.

It was not easy. He avoided her gaze, staring at the river in search of inspiration. 'My lady, I have enjoyed your company over the last few days, the more so since you appear not to have been averse to mine.'

'Have I been so forward?'

'No, Jeanne, not at all!' he declared hotly, then grimaced as he saw her face. 'And now you make me look a fool. Perhaps I am wrong, and should not . . .'

'Sir Baldwin,' she said, and touched his arm lightly. 'Forgive me. I am sometimes too frivolous. Please, carry on.'

He gave her a doubtful look, then took a deep breath. 'Jeanne, I have only a small estate, but it is good and provides well. My lands extend from Cadbury down to Crediton, with farms and mills spread all over. My house is a large place, with good rooms, and is warm in winter and cool in summer. My lady, I think the whole is empty. The land is to me a desert, the mills are broken, and the house a ruin, because when I look at you, I see what is missing. There!' He sighed heavily. 'I have said it, and can say no more. Do you look on me as an utter idiot, or could I hope that you feel even remotely the same?'

Jeanne stood and stared away from him towards the trees at the opposite bank. 'Baldwin, you do me a great honour. No,' as he began to interrupt, 'let me finish. You do me as great an honour as any man could do a lady, and the fact that I know you to be an honest and decent knight means much to me. I feel more . . . privileged that you should offer me this than I would if an earl did.'

'But you must refuse me,' he said.

'For now, yes. Baldwin, don't look at me like that. I am a widow, with a life just ended. Oh, I know the Abbot would like me to be wed again, not because he begrudges me the manor or the living, but because he is fearful for my safety, a poor woman on her own up at Liddinstone.' She gave a little laugh. 'But I can manage Liddinstone as well as my husband ever did.'

'So why do you refuse me?'

'I do not refuse you, Sir Baldwin, but consider: how long have you been alone? All your life, and now, over the space of a couple of days you have decided that I am a suitable wife for you. That is most generous, and I feel the honour of it, but I am new to being alone, and in truth, I am enjoying it. Why should I immediately seal a new contract? At the least I think I deserve time to consider your proposal.'

He gazed at the ground testily. This was a new situation for him; he was unsure how to continue. An outright rejection he could have coped with; a straightforward acceptance would have been preferable – although he candidly admitted to himself that it would have been almost as daunting – but this nebulous 'maybe' was confusing.

'So, lady, if you do not refuse me, but do not say "yes", what must I do to persuade you to agree to my offer?'

'Sir Baldwin, you asked me whether I should like to see Furnshill. Perhaps you could invite me to visit you with the bailiff and his wife when they next stay with you. And then – who knows? Perhaps I will say yes.'

It was with a light heart that David Holcroft walked into the room over the gatehouse to the Abbey. His duties as a port-reeve were almost at an end, his wife's moodiness was explained at last, the murders had been solved, and the weather was excellent. Life felt good.

His clerk was there already, and Holcroft seated himself in the chair with his small sack jingling merrily, bellowing, 'Come on, then!' Soon the men were sidling in. He had already seen to the mounted ones, they had all been paid at the stables where they were resting before making their way home. Now there were only the watchmen on foot.

He dropped the leather bag on the table-top, and as the clerk read out the amounts, he carefully counted out the pennies and slid them across the table. A man would walk up on hearing his name, and David would have the coins ready as soon as the hand was held out. It took no time at all, but today there was a long and pregnant pause.

It was when the men from Denbury appeared.

Holcroft sat back and stared, dumbfounded. There was not one who did not have a bad bruise, a broken nose, or a bandage round his head. All stood in glowering discomfort as the other watchmen tried to restrain their amusement. Holcroft was not so reserved. He sat back on his seat, his hands behind his head as he took in the immensely pleasing sight. The chagrin on the face of Long Jack was emphasised by the large black eye that had almost closed it, giving the man the appearance of a furious one-eyed owl. 'We want our money.'

'Not made as much as usual? I didn't think you'd need these few miserable pennies,' Holcroft said happily.

The watchman snarled incoherently, and Holcroft felt his smile broaden. All of a sudden his day was looking better and better.

'Where's our money, then?'

Holcroft came upright and slowly counted out each coin, but before he slid them over, he gave the men a speculative look. 'Tell me, before I give you this lot – when did this happen to you?'

'On St Rumon's Day. The crowd went mad, beating us with our own belts and such.'

'You deserved it, I daresay,' Holcroft said dismissively.

'That's not fair! We did our job for you, kept things quiet, all orderly, like you wanted.'

'But you are all in a mess.' Holcroft looked Long Jack up and down, then nodded at the clerk. 'They're each amerced two pennies per day since the attack. We can't have watchmen in our town looking like this.'

'You can't do that!' Long Jack growled.

'Can't I? You can demand justice from the Abbot, if you want, but if you do, I'll bring out three men who'll swear that you have all been forcing honest traders to pay you for not damaging their businesses. You want that?' Long Jack eyed him with something of the expression of a horse watching a frenzied terrier – there was contempt for so small a creature, but also nervousness in the face of such suicidal recklessness.

'You wouldn't dare.'

'Take your money and be grateful. And next year, don't return: you won't be wanted. I will inform the Abbot that you have all been getting into fights this fair. He won't want you back.'

He dealt with the rest of the men with the smile never leaving his lips. Afterwards, he took a quart of ale with the clerk, before bidding him a cheery farewell and setting off for his home. All was well with his world. The pressure of the fair was waning, and he could feel the load of his work lightening, and there was a new child to look forward to. It was a contented Holcroft who stepped out through the wicketgate into the street.

Simon sat on his horse with his leg crooked over the beast's withers as he read the paper.

'What is it, Simon?' the Abbot asked.

Simon passed him the paper. 'Only another farmer complaining that a tinner has infringed his lands and refused to pay compensation after letting his sheep run free.

He claims three have been eaten by wolves.'

'Is it true, do you think?'

'No! I've no doubt that when I get there to find out the details, there'll be several lamb pelts hanging up to dry as evidence, but this is just one of the normal complaints one receives every month. The moors are constant only in the amount of paperwork and litigation they produce.'

'I defer to your greater knowledge,' said Champeaux thankfully. It was good to know that his bailiff understood the land so well. He would be able to save the Abbot much work with his position of Warden.

It was two days since the death of Luke and the resolution of the murders, and Simon and his wife were preparing to leave for Lydford. Their packhorse was loaded, Margaret was waiting to mount – she knew she would be sore from the saddle over the miles to their home and had no wish to begin the pain earlier than was necessary. Hugh scowled from his pony, Edgar sat at ease on his palfrey, and the only one missing was Baldwin. Simon glanced round the court as he waited. 'Where is he?'

The Abbot said, 'I saw him walking with Jeanne a short time ago. He will be here soon.'

'Don't fret, Simon,' Margaret said. 'There's plenty of time.'

'But what is he talking to her about, eh? What could be so urgent when he's had all the time here to talk to her?' he grumbled.

At the gate he suddenly caught sight of a pair of figures, a man and a woman. The bailiff swung his leg down and found the stirrup. 'Is that him?'

'No, it's Avice and Pietro,' the Abbot said. 'They look happy, don't they?'

Margaret nodded. 'It is good to see two youngsters so wrapped up in themselves.'

'It's better to see their fathers so easy in each other's company,' Simon said, pointing with his chin to the two men trailing along behind the couple, heads close together.

'Yes,' Champeaux said. 'It is less a marriage of two families, more one of two businesses.' But beneath his light words, he was secretly delighted to see that the girl and her swain were so happy. After the elopement he had thought that their chances of persuading Arthur to allow them to wed were reduced to nothing, yet the two merchants had discovered ventures which could offer advantages to both, and the prospect of marrying her daughter to an old Venetian family had finally swayed even Arthur's ambitious wife. Antonio's uncle was an Italian noble, and he was reassuringly bereft of children, so there was the likelihood that on his death the title would fall to Antonio.

Hearing steps, Champeaux saw Baldwin and Jeanne approaching. The Abbot's eyes slitted keenly. He wanted to see the widow happy, and he wasn't sure she was. She looked a little stiff to him, and Baldwin appeared reserved, as if uncomfortable. The Abbot felt his spirits fall a little. 'Have you had a pleasant walk, Sir Baldwin?'

'Yes, very pleasant. And now, I think I recognise Simon's expression. He is eager to be off, as usual. My lord Abbot, my thanks again. It has been a very enjoyable break for me.'

'My thanks go to you, Sir Baldwin. You and Simon have saved Jordan Lybbe from the rope, and if you never achieve anything else in your life, that act will ever be to your credit. And I personally owe to you the fact that my port has enjoyed a successful fair, and not one which has been over-shadowed by either unsolved murders or unjust hangings.'

Baldwin showed his teeth in a grin. 'In which case we are both well pleased with each other's company, Abbot. And now, seeing Margaret is mounted, we should be off.'

Simon bowed in his saddle to the Abbot and Jeanne. 'Abbot; my lady.'

Margaret watched as Baldwin bade them farewell and rode through the great gate and set off up the road towards the Abbot's gibbet and Lydford. Jeanne, she saw, kept her eyes downcast as Baldwin spoke, but stared after him as he made his way up the road. Then, as Margaret passed, Jeanne glanced up, and Margaret saw a curious, measuring expression in her eyes. It was only there for a fleeting moment, and then Jeanne was smiling again.

The bailiff's wife urged her pony up the hill after her husband and the knight.

The town was quieter now, most of the traders having left as soon as St Rumon's fair was over, and the streets were getting back to normal. Margaret saw Elias outside his shop haggling with Will Ruby over a basket of meat, Jordan and Hankin watching on. Elias' elder brother wore a broad grin which froze on his face when he caught sight of the knight. Jordan seemed to have to remind himself he was free now and no more thought of as a felon. He gave a curt nod, which Margaret saw Baldwin return absentmindedly.

Margaret was eaten up with curiosity. Baldwin had told her and her husband nothing of his talks with Jeanne, yet Margaret was sure that she and the knight had reached an understanding. They had spent a great deal of time alone together since Luke's capture, strolling in the fair or walking in the Abbot's orchard and private gardens, but both Baldwin and Jeanne had been silent on the subject of their talks.

'I will miss Jeanne,' Margaret said after a few minutes.

Baldwin cocked an eyebrow at her. 'Oh?'

She pursed her lips with frustration. 'Yes, Baldwin. I will miss her, and I would like to see her again soon. Especially since I would like to know whether you and she intend to meet again. Some might think you were enjoying keeping us in suspense.'

'Oh, I hardly think so,' Baldwin said, urging his horse on once more.

'Baldwin, tell me!'

'There is little *to* tell,' he said, but then he cast a glance at Simon before giving Margaret a quick grin. 'But if you truly feel you will miss her, perhaps you should arrange to see her again – and soon. Oh, and it's surely time you came to visit me at Furnshill – maybe you could bring her with you? Jeanne said she would like to see the place.'

They carried on past the last of the houses. The road began to climb, and near the top of the hill Margaret saw Baldwin frown and stiffen. Following his gaze she saw the dismal clearing where the gibbet stood. Here there was a steady breeze, and the leaves rustled on the trees as the little cavalcade approached.

To Margaret's surprise, Baldwin stopped his horse and pointed at it. 'When we first came to this town, I was almost jealous of that gallows. It is so much newer and more solid than the scaffold at Crediton, and I thought it was a symbol of the Abbot's power and wealth. Now I don't know.'

'It's only a gibbet,' Margaret protested.

'Yes, and as such it is a potent reminder of justice. But if we had not understood the meaning of the clues at the last minute, if Hugo had not been here, or if we had simply been lazy, the wrong man might have been hanged. Then it would have ceased to be a mark of justice and would have become the representation of evil. I loathe the sight of it.'

Simon gazed at the simple wooden frame. 'I don't understand you. There must be thousands of identical ones all over the kingdom. Do you mean you hate this one because Lybbe was nearly hanged here by mistake?'

'Mistake? It would not have been a mistake but a simple travesty of justice. If Lybbe had died here, it would have been because Luke had perjured himself. Fearing retribution from neither God nor any man, Luke swore that Lybbe had been a trail-baston purely for his own revenge. Luke would have made a mockery of justice to see an old enemy hang, and that act would have polluted the whole town.'

'But God let you see the truth, Baldwin,' Margaret pointed out gently.

'God? Perhaps,' he muttered, his attention still fixed on

the gibbet. After a few moments he spurred his horse and they passed by the wooden frame. As he rode, Margaret's words rang in his ears. They carried a serene confidence, proof of her religious faith.

But Baldwin could recall the faces of friends who were dead, Knights Templar like himself, men who had died during torture, or been hanged or burned alive. They had been betrayed by politicians who coveted their wealth. The loyal knights had all been unjustly slaughtered, and God had not helped *them*, even though they were dedicated to His glory.

Suddenly he felt sick. All those good men were gone now, yet Lybbe had *not* been hanged: why should *he* live when the Templars had suffered so much? Baldwin did not have the comfort of belief. He could never again trust in God's justice. As he passed the gallows, he made himself a vow: he would not rest if he thought that his own efforts could save an innocent man.

The gibbet squeaked in the wind. It almost sounded like laughter, and Baldwin shuddered. No matter what his intentions, the Abbot's gibbet seemed to be reminding him that long after he was buried, it would still be there, ending other lives, whether justly or not. Its very permanence mocked him, and made his resolution futile.

But it did not change his decision.

The Merchant's Partner

Michael Jecks

Fourteenth-century Devon . . .

Midwife and healer Agatha Kyteler is regarded as a witch by superstitious villagers of Wefford, yet she has no shortage of callers, from the humblest villein to the most elegant and wealthy in the area. But when Agatha's body is found frozen and mutilated in a hedge one wintry morning, there seem to be no clues as to who could be responsible. Not until a local youth runs away and a hue and cry is raised.

Sir Baldwin Furnshill, Keeper of the King's Peace, is not convinced of the youth's guilt and soon manages to persuade a close friend, Simon Puttock, bailiff of Lydford Castle, to help him continue with the investigation. As they endeavour to find the true culprit, the darker side of the village, with its undercurrents of suspicion, jealousy and disloyalty, emerges. And what is driving the young foreigner, son of a nobleman, who has visited the normally sleepy area only to disappear down towards the moors?

0 7472 5070 7

HEADLINE

The Rose Demon

P.C. Doherty

In Paradise, in the glades of Eden, Eve was tempted twice: first by Lucifer. Then by Rosifer, who offered her a rose plucked from Heaven.

Matthias Fitzosbert is the illegitimate son of the parish priest of the village of Sutton Courteny in Gloucestershire. His struggle with Rosifer, the fallen angel, the spirit he loves yet hates, strives to placate but ultimately flees from, is played out against the vivid panorama of medieval life: the fall of Constantinople; the last throes of the Wars of the Roses; the terror of witchcraft; the loneliness of the Scottish marches; the battlefields of Spain; and finally the lush jungles of the Caribbean, where the Rose Demon and Matthias meet for a final, dramatic confrontation.

'A master storyteller' *Time Out*

0 7472 5441 9

HEADLINE